HE WHO IS A LOVER

SADIK
BOOK 2

LOVE BELVIN

MKT Publishing, LLC

HE WHO IS A Lover

THE Sadik SERIES 2

∞|∞

Day Four...

"Hurry," I moaned, turning from my side onto my back in the massive bed. "Missing you like crazy down here."

His five-dimensioned eyes: that dark brown perimeter enclosing the hue of green then yellow, and an unreal orange before a spec of black at the axis of the iris. They mesmerized me, as they always had. Those dark brown, unruly brows were stark over his honeyed eyes as usual. The man was a wonder. As I held my phone in the air, admiring his beauty, I could only imagine what torture his admirers before me, who'd never experienced his attention or touch, felt.

His face wrinkled, but lips curled with wicked perception. "What are you staring at, girl?"

A flutter glanced my belly and I averted my eyes to the right, where the patio doors were open. Squalling into the master suite was the fierce sun. The boisterous oceanic waves below wouldn't be outdone in creating the perfect ambiance to wake up to. First, a call from my gorgeous fiancé from his private jet, then the unbelievable vista of the beach. A panorama he'd purchased for us. For my happiness.

"You know I'm not going to let you ignore that question. When I get there, I'll have my ways of prying it out of you," his silky alto warned.

A smile almost ripped my face into two. "Bring it," I challenged, sex clenching in heavy anticipation.

My attention went to the chanting seagulls outside of the bedroom. Their squawks may have annoyed some, but the sound was music to this city girl's ears.

Heaven...

God, I loved this place.

"How much longer do you have?" The only missing ingredient was him.

I needed his touch to inspire me today. Needed his keen attention to make me feel beautiful and adorned. It was the only way I now knew. His attention was the only I craved, and that nurtured me beyond physical manifestation.

"Thirty-seven minutes till landing," he answered, reclining into the plush leather seat as we *FaceTime*'d. "Let me see my baby."

Another face splitting grin opened on my face. Why I was so embarrassed by carrying his child was beyond me. We'd spent weeks performing the act with reckless abandon that brought along my condition.

With little hesitance, I lowered the phone to my bare belly. Because he wasn't here with me, I could sleep with clothes on and chose a camisole and panty set.

Feeling silly, I giggled. "There's not much there. For the most part, my usual little pouch."

"Nah," he breathed, voice inspired. "I'm familiar with your cute little paunch. I see a small bump there." A guttural groan pushed through his nostrils. "I need to be there with you two, Nalib."

My lip was pinched between my teeth before I uttered emotionally, "Then hurry up." My eyes swung to the roiling water. "I'm so lonely." A cry gripped my throat.

A phone ringing in the background caught my attention. At the same time, concern washed over his face when I braved another look at my screen. "You mean alone. You don't get lonely. Remember?" he recalled from our conversation at the park while listening to jazz months ago, when I explained the distinction.

Unexpected tears spilled from their ducts, down my face. I shook my head. "I'm lonely. I've got no one anymore. I had a brother. He was incarcerated, but still a living being...my family. We were dysfunctional—he loathed my existence—but he was here. Now, he's dead."

His jaw flexed with anger beneath the tangerine five o'clock shadow. "Who killed him, honey?"

I shrugged, trying to manage my breathing. "I don't know. They tried killing me, too. Just like you killed Damien. But they used a gun on Abshir. You used a rope on Damien. And I don't trust you to me, or my baby."

Those kaleidoscopes darkened. "You will not keep me from my baby, Bilan!"

I nodded. "You're a murderer—your family members are murderers. I don't want to die. I don't want my child to be a murderer, too."

My sobs competed with the thunders of the ocean.

"Bilan, I'm on my way to you and our child."

"No!" I screamed.

No!

No!

No!

"Nooooooooo!" I rolled over, eyes opening to the morning sun and the sounds of angry waves shooting to the shore. My heart pounded, pulse rang in my ears, and body soaked from sweat. Unremitting ringing had me turn to the floor, where my phone lay.

Sadik.

It was his usual time to call. He was consistent with his morning calls, if nothing else. As I reached for it, I had an idea of the time. We didn't keep the same hours. For the past four days, I'd finally drift off to sleep after four in the morning and didn't wake until his call. The call I wouldn't take. Just like all the ones before it. I pressed the two buttons on either side to power off the phone, swiped to confirm the command then tossed it to the other side of the bed.

Panting, my eyes shifted out to the ocean, my therapy. My mental quiet. I kept my attention fixed on the water until my pulse muted and body temperature regulated. Then I foolishly glanced up toward the ceiling to the manila ropes, stretched horizontally across the roof of the canopy. My heart pounded again at the sight of the missing three.

And so did my clitoris.

My eyes blurred with tears. "This is sick..."

A spate of chatter rang all around me as the call went to voicemail in my wireless earbud. It always went to voicemail, but a soupçon of hope always prevailed in my determined head. My compromised heart.

I cleared my throat, pushing my phone up the conference table. My eyes brushed past all eleven members at the table.

"So, we're in agreement to change the company that makes the port employees' uniforms?" I asked with indifferent interest.

The word "*yes*" echoed across the table as I crossed that line item off the list.

"I can't believe we're just deciding on that," Shirley groused. "They been getting over like a fat rat for years. People *been* complaining about loose threading and the logo tag peeling from their shirts after one wash."

A few agreed with her. *I* wanted to move on with this meeting. "What's next on the agenda, Kim?" I asked the secretary.

It was the quarterly *Port of Paterson* meeting. Seaports in the area were run exclusively and wholly by *The Port Authority of New York and New Jersey*. That was an interstate compact governed by Congress. The *Port Authority* managed a wealth of infrastructure such as bridges, tunnels, and airports along with the seaports in the two states. That was all except the *Port of Paterson*, which was established only thirty years ago, well after the venture between New York, New Jersey, and the United States government was made.

In an unusual turn of events, Paterson opened its own port with limited capacity, but an added option for the customs business. The *Port of Paterson* was operated by the city, but governed by *Port Authority*. *Port Authority* yielded very few resources to the *Port of Paterson*, but monitored it regularly. The *Port of Paterson* was extremely small compared to the *Port Authority*, and so unique and independent that it established its own *Board of Commissioners*. The board regulated the port, addressed employee issues and concerns, and monitored safety measures. We basically ran our own shit with the governor of New Jersey and the *Port Authority* over each shoulder. They didn't bother us much, other than requesting egregious amounts of paperwork each month to be sure we kept in compliance with their regulations.

At the head of the *Board of Commissioners* was me. I'd been the chairman for the past four years. Had been on the board for over fifteen years, since beginning my customs business. It was arid work, listening to the complaints of people I didn't exactly interface with— but my staff at *Ellis International* did. There were lots of gripes about cleaned facilities on the grounds and traffic control, which were all the usual seaport operations. As lackluster the task, it was a sacrifice for power, my position on the board, but one I knew would come in handy a time or two. Like today.

My third-party logistics firm, *Ellis International*, had business out of both ports—clearly more out of *Port Authority* as it was the larger port. However, because of my tenure in customs, I was nominated, then voted into the chairman seat, where I oversaw meetings and weighed heavy decisions. Today was one of them. Salvatore Rizzo was the chief of operations at the *Port of Paterson*. He managed the hiring, terminations, traffic control, storage, and security. He was basically the superintendent of the port. And he'd still been acting out the vendetta on my father's empire.

The DEA still had the laundromats shut down, and the health departments paid visits to each respective district where his grocery stores were. And two days ago, at their commission's meeting, Rizzo moved to drop my father as a member of *The Commission* because Damien's murder happened without its permission. There was one primary rule of *The Commission* that all had to adhere to, which was no member could be killed without a majority vote. Rizzo and every other man in that room may not have known my father's plan to kill Damien, but knew the details of Damien's murder. They understood the urgency of my actions. Salvatore Rizzo seemed to forget how Damien tried to kill him recently without permission. However, with Rizzo being the most vocal one as the founding father of *The Commission*, his opinion was most aggressive. While the vote had not been made to remove my father, this vote today would be key in my decimation of Salvatore Rizzo.

"Salvatore Rizzo's position as chief of operations," Kim answered. "Do we move to replace him, or do we invite him to recycle the seat?"

There were low rumblings around the table. Rizzo had held the powerful position for over twenty years; longer than I'd been in business.

"There have been lots of complaints of nepotism," Marsha Jackson, a government affairs liaison, provided. Her role was to be sure the entities communicated fully. Her neck rolled and lips balled with implication. "And we know how well that works in a city like Paterson."

"And I heard there was a break-in back in the spring. There's someone on duty twenty-four hours a day out there," Jim Bell protested. "How in the hell could it be robbed? What are we paying this guy for?"

"Is there a police report?" Shantee Brown, the head of accounting, asked.

"I asked security a week later, when I found out," Marsha griped. "But they said no official report was made to the city police. That sounds shady. I say we vote to get him out of here."

"Yup," Shantee agreed. "He's been here for too long, and I've never liked the vibe of the place. It's been too old world around here. Time to get someone with better vibes."

"Like who?" Jim asked as people around the table were still muttering and mumbling their agreeance to Shantee's point. "The problem has always been competence. Rizzo has been the chief of operations for so long, he knows each inch of the seaport in his sleep."

"That's true," Lee Lewis seconded. "Who else around can say they know each facet of that place?"

The table quieted.

"Abram Murphy," I uttered.

All eyes shot to me.

"The longshoreman supervisor?" Shantee asked, placidity in her face, doubt in her voice.

I nodded. "He's been employed at the port for close to twenty years...started right out of community college. He's come up in the ranks and has been denied opportunities to grow here. He's been the longshoreman supervisor for over ten years and even fills in as a forklift operator, and works with the engineer techs and equipment team when needed. He knows the seaport, knows the system. I believe he'd be a great fit for chief of operations."

The table began its low chatter again. Abram had seriously been overlooked. Too many *ahh*'s for me to believe he'd been in their minds as a viable candidate. Attaining the position of chief of operations at the *Port of Paterson* was no easy feat. But Murphy had the qualifications and time in to pursue the prestigious role.

"Then it's settled," Marsha asserted. "He's been nominated."

"Please get that on record, Kim." Shantee pointed to Kim's laptop as she took notes.

While the table continued with their talks of Murphy, Jim whispered to me, "I thought Rizzo was a friend of yours."

As I adjusted my tie while sitting, I returned, "There are no friends in business, Bell. My business is customs. What matters is what's best for the port."

And that Rizzo is annihilated...

I took a deep breath, regard going out to the table at large. "If there are no objections, we'll move on to the next item."

Back at *Ellis International*, I stalked heavily toward my office, bypassing my assistant while she took a call at her desk. My attention was fastened to the phone in my hand. The emails for my customs, real estate, dispensary, and investments businesses demanded my time and leadership. But first, I had a staff meeting here with all of my warehouse and trucking staff. *Ellis International* employed a fluctuating seventy employees, and there was constantly a need to meet. I had an established rule here. No traffic in my office before a meeting of any kind. Today, more than any other, I needed a moment to prepare my resolve.

But when I stepped into my office, I realized it would not happen. Across the room stood wide hips in yellow cropped pants and a white tank tucked inside, displaying her tapered waistline. The tall heels of her *red bottoms* accentuated the shape of her broad ass. An ass I'd been well versed with. Tiffany faced the sculpture of Christ on the cross, studying it as most did when visiting. I ambled over to my desk, placing both phones down before taking to my seat.

"Didn't know you remembered this place," I murmured, knowing she heard me come in.

From my peripheral, I could see her turn around, almost surprised by my presence. I tapped to wake up my computer, needing to fire back emails of instruction to several people. With ease, I ignored her seductive strut toward my desk.

"Oh!" There was a smile in her voice, on her way to me. "That Tonya knows your schedule to the T, I see. You think she has colleagues just as efficient?" I didn't answer. She knew I couldn't stomach small talk and was even worse with it at my place of business. I heard Tiffany take in a fortifying breath, happy for her to get on with it. "You didn't come to dinner last night at *Elliswoods Palace*."

I issued her a hard gaze. She needed to speak, and right away. I had shit to do.

Tiffany, understanding my disposition, poked her lips as her eyes fell away. "I told the family me and Larry broke up."

"That happens in relationships." I continued typing into my keyboard. "Ebbs and flows in each one."

"He proposed."

My fingers froze. "You broke up with him because he proposed?"

Tiffany shook her head. "He broke up with me when I told him I couldn't."

For a stretch, no words were spoken over my desk.

"Look, Tiff..." I blew out a deep breath. "I don't think I qualify as a confidant for your relationship. I have no advice—"

"I'm not asking for any," she made clear.

"Then why are you here?"

"Because we discussed it as a family...and..." Her lashes fanned her cheeks. "Poppa Earl told me about Bilan. He said he thinks you two may be done and thought we should talk."

"About what?"

Tiffany took a deep breath, pushing up from my desk and turning away. "Sadik, I've been trying to talk about this all damn year, but you get all funny and shit about it." She paused, and I didn't offer a lifeline by asking her for details. She was right; she had been hinting around, each time her agenda becoming more clearer, but Tiffany never asked. Had she asked, I would have made my position clear. "You're not getting no younger, and shit." She scoffed. "My ass needs to push out a baby before my insides rot and fuckin' mold. Why can't we do us? Why haven't you ever considered that about me?" She finally turned to face me.

"Why do you speak of us as if it's some obvious solution?" My head shook softly. "Why do you think we're compatible for parenting?"

"Why don't you?" Her voice rose. "Why can't you see the woman you settle down with needs to be built for you. Built to join the Ellis family."

"Aren't you already in the family?"

"But not like that." She shook her head. "Not like I want to be, and you know it." As I sat back in my chair, visibly frustrated, Tiffany's volume increased. "Your father knows it, your mother knows—hell, everybody fuckin' knows except you, it seems."

I did know, and Tiffany knew I did. She likely got ahead of herself with her overly dramatic plea.

"Tiffany, you've had a man for how many years, and now you're in my office, theatrically telling me you've wanted to be with me for some time?" I shook my head with a tightened forehead. "Sweetheart, do you understand how silly that sounds?"

"You ain't been with other women these past few years we've been fuckin', Sadik?" she challenged me.

"I haven't been in a committed and exclusive relationship these three years we've been fuckin'," I qualified.

"Okay, and I'm ready for one now. What's the problem?"

I shook my head, unbelieving of the timing of this. Being totally honest with women no matter how difficult the truth was something my father taught my brother and me since we found the first strand of hair around our dicks. He explained the most complex relationships wasn't in business or family; it was between a man and a woman, and especially those who invariably wanted more out of the relationship than you. Tiffany may not have been family, but she was as close to it as my conscience would allow my dick to swell over.

"Tiffany." I licked my lips, giving a pause to focus on my delivery. "That isn't possible."

"Why?" she demanded, leaping back, propping her hand on her hip, and rolled her neck.

"Because I'm engaged."

I watched the blood drain from her face. The lapse in time was surreal, but I gave Tiffany enough of it to process my words. She was owed that.

"You're not serious."

"Was my mother present when my father suggested you 'talk' to me?"

She nodded, tears pooling in her eyes.

"Do you remember what she said?"

Tiffany swallowed, eyes cast into the distance stubbornly. "She didn't say anything. She like..." She swallowed again, rolling her eyes. "It was like she was mad, but I know how she can get about you."

"Yeah, but it's also because my parents both know I asked Bilan to marry me two months ago. He knows it, she knows it." I scoffed, mocking her to drive home the point. "Hell, the whole family knows it. But your godfather failed to clue you in on it." I stood, realizing I'd killed all the time I had to return those emails. I needed to get to the meeting in my conference room. I'd try to attack them there. "I need to go, Tiff."

She wouldn't look at me or acknowledge my apologetic tone, so I grabbed my things and left from behind my desk. On my way to the door, I backed up and sauntered over to her, placing a gentle kiss on her forehead. I wanted the best for Tiffany, always had. I may not have been able to give her all she wanted over the years, but I never misled her and wouldn't start now. My father's indifference for my relationship with Bilan had caused him to do exactly that to her, but I wouldn't. My plate was full now, shoulders weighed with more bullshit than most could handle. The last thing I needed was the guilt of mishandling a loved one's expectations.

"Never lie. Never mislead. It's always been my promise to you," I whispered before taking off.

I was sure to close the door behind myself, knowing she needed a few minutes to gather herself. My assistant was off the phone when I strode past her desk.

"Tonya."

"Yes, sir?" her pitch expectant and bright.

"Only my family is allowed to wait for me in my office."

"Yes, sir," she replied downcast as I walked off.

There were always people bustling in a fury at Penn Station in the City. The warm August night seemed to have even more out. If given a moment to observe the droves of people scurrying around, creating a humming energy, you'd wonder if they were traveling away or returning home, using one of Penn Station's vehicles as their mode of transportation. Were they being waited on at the other end of their destination? Was there an emergency where they were headed?

Were they running away like me?

"Bilan?" a feminine New York accent called out.

I turned to my right and between hurried figures, the sea parted and there was a mushroom of voluminous hair bouncing against the shoulders of a chocolate goddess. Lex's tall and thick figure was stark tonight. When I met her back in March, I didn't realize how Amazon'ish she was in stature. On approach, I noticed she was alone and unsmiling. Her coffee eyes swung all around cautiously.

"Are you safe here?"

I nodded, feeling embarrassed once again over this, though I really didn't know how safe I was in the moment. I had no clue what type of people I was dealing with anymore. Could I have been followed on the bus ride from downtown Paterson to Penn Station in New York City? I wasn't sure about much of anything anymore.

My shoulders collapsed and eyes fell toward the ground. "I feel horrible about this. I would have had access to my money if I'd remembered to put my debit card in this crossbody when I did my ID and the little cash I had." I lifted the Saint Laurent wallet on a chain that felt silly carrying now. It was one of Sadik's many spoils. "I was rushing out of the apartment to an event I wasn't even going to attend, and—"

Those words reminded me of Abshir's betrayal, causing the faucets to run again. I'd told myself when ditching the truck I wouldn't cry until I made it out of the Tri-State area.

"Can I hug you?" Lex's leggy frame was inches away, her arms were midair, eyes beseeching.

I nodded and she wrapped herself around me, pulling me into her bosom. Her touch and fragrance reminded me of the first time I experienced it back in the spring. I pulled away, memories of our strange encounter coming back in spades. My frame tensed.

"Do you know?"

Lex withdrew, her face expressing confusion. "Know what?"

"About the baby—the pregnancy." Her husband called this. He said a time would come where I'd need to flee. And here his wife stood, ready to assist. "Do you know?"

Her eyes narrowed, lips pouted. Lex's hands reached for her abdomen. "You know I'm pregnant?"

"No—" I rolled my eyes. She wasn't understanding, but a new revelation came to light. "Not you. Me. You're pregnant?"

A forlorn smile lifted on her face. "Yeah. Tasche didn't tell you?" I shook my head. "I'm still adjusting to the news. It was unexpected." Her eyes cast out to the sea of busy people dashing all around us. "I have two babies under three years old. I swear, I was just demanding a tummy tuck a few months ago. Seems like my poor uterus can't catch a break!"

"You said it was unexpected."

"Yeah. All my pregnancies were unexpected."

My face tightened. "I was going to ask if your husband knew exactly what brought me here this very night with you." I was desperate.

Lex's head shook softly, coarse fleece of dark hair shifting around her shoulders, down her back. "It's like I tell everyone who asks: he may or may have not known. But all he's going to tell you is what he's told to share, so we will never know. Is there anything I can help you with? What's going on?"

A cry ripped from my lungs and my hand flew to my mouth. "It's too much. Too much drama that ended up with a baby, and I don't know what to do."

"Are you in danger?"

"Yes."

"From the baby's father?"

This line of questioning was unreal. This couldn't be happening to me!

"Possibly, yes."

Her hand landed on my shoulder, attempting to comfort me. "Let me help you. I can get you a safe place to stay."

I shook my head, drying my face. "I have an idea of where I'm going to go. It should be safe. I need to leave this region now. I just don't have the money to get there, and don't know how long I'll be there."

Things got quiet between us. I could sense Lex's cautious gape on me.

"I'd really love to know what your husband was told." It could help me figure out what was next for me. "But now, I don't know if I should believe it. Am I just as crazy as he is? You just told me your pregnancy was unexpected, too. Does that mean he didn't see it coming?"

A soft, yet loaded smile broke out on her face. Lex took a deep, calming breath. "My husband has a gift. A gift I can no longer deny. The Holy Spirit talks to him, supernatural events occur around him, because of him. Because of his faith. And it's more than he reveals to me because it's beyond me. It's not my gift. But when it comes to the matters of my husband's household, his family—what's directly in front of him—he's as dumb as a doorknob. He doesn't see in his front yard. It's his blind spot. I have to be the one who sees us. I have to help him see us." She rolled her eyes away, chuckling to herself.

"But you just told me you didn't know about the baby either."

She snorted. "No. That's not what I mean. And it's kind of hard to explain. But as it relates to this matter, we know when I'm expecting because my husband develops a mean ass craving for DiFillippo's." Just the mention of that restaurant brought fond memories. I hated it. It made me feel like the naïve fool Damien proved I was earlier. I shouldn't have fond memories of Sadik. "It's really been a rough time since finding out."

I scoffed. "Rough time. Tell me about it," I murmured to myself.

"Well, it couldn't have been too rough of a time for you if you were able to make a baby," Lex suggested. "I don't know anything about you other than what Tasche mentioned, but I would hope you wouldn't give your body to someone who didn't treat you right."

"Oh, he treated me well!" I asserted, angry. "That's the problem. He's of another world. We're completely different people. His life is so grand—and complicated—I don't fit in."

"*Then join the club.*" *Lex's voice was of a maternal disciplinarian. "I married a man with a lifestyle I don't fit into, either. I don't know if Tasche told you, but I just finished yanking a bitch for trying to come for my husband on a fuckin' prayer line.*" *My neck jolted at the complete change in her delivery. She'd turned into my Tasche in a split second.* "*I'm a first lady, getting pregnant every damn year while I'm trying to find myself in this world that's smothered by an evangelistic, prophetic fuckin' pastor. So, I get it.*"

Silent energy bounced between us again. Lex had said a mouthful. Enough to have me questioning my threshold for a relationship with a complicated man. She seemed tough and resolved to fight for her place alongside her strange husband, and not just in her grand stature. It was her warrior spirit. She may have admitted to her stressors, but she wasn't out here crying like I'd been.

Finally, she moved to open her purse. Lex pulled out a sealed envelope, handing it to me. Quickly, I received it, understanding we were out in the open among thousands in the busiest metropolitan city in the country. There were crooks and criminals all around. Someone was watching. They always were around these parts.

"*Inside is my card. You obviously have it, but we always include it. If I can be of any help, you have all of my numbers on there, including my home.*" *Lex's clean, professional presentation had been restored.* "*I rarely give that out. But I'm here. If, for some reason, you can't reach me, have Tasche do it. Anything I can do for you, I'm here.*" *Lex took a deep breath, straightening her spine.* "*I'm not going to ask where you're going. But when you get there, please send up a smoke signal or something so I know you're alive.*"

I nodded with firm resolve and a broken spirit as I backed away, sauntering off to blend into the blustering crowd. I slipped into the building to use one of Penn Station's vehicles as my mode of transportation to escape.

My eyes flickered open, a deep abdominal pain striking and sprouting to my chest and the back of my skull, fully awakening me. Recognizing the sensation, my lids burst open. I was weak, entire frame weighed down like sandbags. My system...my body had changed. I couldn't go long periods without stuffing something into my mouth. My body demanded food, and often. That necessity overpowered my indifference to eating. And even more than breathing, all I wanted to do was sleep. I found comfort in the numbness of sleep during the day—because it wouldn't happen at night. At night, I sat up and cogitated, fretting.

But waking up like this—and from another dream—reminded me of how alone I was, and how much was at risk. My head tilted against the pillow and I peered over to the old, half-eaten pizza I'd bought from the boardwalk the afternoon before. Most of it was still there. My arm slowly reached out, muscles vibrating from weakness. And while holding my breath, straining, my fingers successfully reached the crust. As expected, it was cold and hard, but I pulled my arm back to the bed. It took even more effort to sit up enough to eat. My head swirled as much as my belly toiled.

Panting, I bit and chewed the tasteless crust, unable to care from which side of the pizza I ate. My eyes closed and body tensed as I chewed. The food churned slowly in my dry mouth. My brain couldn't decide whether to continue with what was good for my body or allow my stomach to upend what was being put into it. My body was just as confused as my heart, and my poor mind overworked to keep it all together.

I was pregnant and while I didn't look it, I felt it...every day.

Four small bites in, I had the energy to reach over to the nightstand again for the half empty bottle of *Gatorade* from yesterday, too. It took less effort for me to get a good amount of that down. Now, I felt full. And sleepy. God, I was so sleepy. Managing the rest of the pizza that would likely be dinner and the empty bottle back to the nightstand, I was prepared to ignore my raging bladder to return to the bliss of sleep. I'd get up. In a couple of hours, I'd be up, and with enough energy to go out to the water and possibly stroll to the boardwalk for more tasteless food. Because invariably, I'd get hungry again. And if I didn't eat, I'd get sick. When I got sick, my body weakened.

Just as my eyes closed, happily ready to succumb to numbing

sleep, the phone rang at its usual morning time. My eyes flew open and I reached for my cell on the floor. His name lit on my screen, bringing with it the usual awareness of my grim predicament. Swiftly, I powered off the phone, tossing it to the other side of the bed. Then on a slow lift, I pulled my body from the mattress and swayed to the bathroom.

My nieces' chatter always lightened the room. It was comforting, even if playing the background of my swelling thoughts. Movements in my peripheral had me laying my fork down. Candy, one of my mother's kitchen assistants, reached over me for my plate.

"Can I have a plate made to go for you, Sadik?" My regard swung up to the head of the table, to my left. My mother lowered her chin gently, voice controlled. "You may get hungry later."

That's when I peered down at the plate in Candy's hand before me. I'd barely eaten half my food.

"No thanks, queen," I murmured, brushing my palm over my face. "I'll be fine."

She nodded with a kind smile, alerting me of the tension at the dinner table tonight.

"Uncle Deek," Iesha cried. "Don't forget we're playing checkers after dinner."

"Ooh!" Ivana's eyes widened. "I wanna play!"

"You'll have to wait. I already got him to say yes," Iesha made clear.

Then an argument ensued over the topic. My face stretched into a needed grin. Their fighting brought back memories of Iban and me when we were kids, only there was a bigger gap in our ages. My eyes swung over to him, sitting across the dinner table from me. Iban was heavily engaged in his phone while his wife, next to him, closely observed the girls. My father, at the other end, sat pensive. Brows punched together, lids narrowed as he stared at nothing in particular. His right elbow on the armrest with his hand lifted in the air, fingers twisting about.

"We done. Right?" Iban grumbled, pushing back from the table with his phone in the air.

"I guess so," my mother muttered.

Everyone began scooting their high wingback chairs back from the table to go.

"Sadik," my father called over to me. "I need to rap to you. Meet me outside by the fountain for a smoke." He hardly peered my way while making the command.

Somehow, my eyes caught my mother's, whose batted away, clearly concerned.

"Ah!" Iesha appeared at my leg, pouting. "We're supposed to play now!"

I squatted down next to her. "Baby, I'll meet you in the game room as soon as I'm done with PaPa."

Ivana broke in between us. "And I'm playing after you, Iesha!"

I stood, grinning with my face and smiling with my heart. Ivy's was the first forehead I planted a kiss on, and Iesha was next.

"Come on, girls," Monica called out for them with an extended arm. "Let's have dessert in the kitchen."

As they took off, so did I, but in the opposite direction. By the time I made it outside and to the fountain in the back, clouds of smoke could be seen over my father's head. The sun was setting, and the breeze gained aggression. Summer nights on the *Elliswoods* compound had always taken on a magical aura, almost as much as Christmastime. He sat on the wooden and black iron bench with his back to me. On my way to him, I could feel my phones vibrate. With anxiousness, I checked both, but none were pertinent calls. None were her.

"Care to indulge?" He offered a stogie.

It was a perfect night for one, but not one ideal for comfort. At least for me, it was not.

"I'm good," I muttered before taking a seat.

"You got my Irene worried," he began at his point, which I preferred.

I had shit to do.

With my elbows resting on my knees, I fixed my gaze out to the fountain, admiring its festive colors and varying faucet pressures. "About?"

He blew out an irritated breath. "You know what about, man. You know if you ain't straight, she trippin'."

I drew my regard to him. "I'm the only one preoccupied at the table?" I tossed my head back toward the house.

"You're the one she's sensitive to the most." His neck slowly turned so he could face me with righteous indignation. "You know that."

"What I know is I have a lot of shit on my mind."

"Apparently, it's been since the shit with *Low*." Damien. "How long?"

I turned to him. "What are you asking me?"

I waited for him to take a deep pull from the cigar, his eyes on the fountain. "I need my money washed, son. This shit we doing through the liquor stores ain't enough. It's causing a bubble in the tube of my income. Soon, we're gonna be over three milli in dirty money 'cause we can't clean it fast enough."

"I'm working on it."

"Is that what has you stressed?" An authoritative maternal tenor rang out from behind me. My mother was rounding the bench, holding a tray of tumblers in her hands. "Work?"

There was a hint of desperation in her voice, no matter how calm she tried to deliver her words. She served my father brandy first, then me.

I mumbled my appreciation before answering, "Amongst other things."

Quietness settled over us as my mother perched on the arm of the bench next to my father. She was cautiously waiting. He was brooding. I was drained. Frustrated. Stressed the fuck out. Pops and Iban plotted behind my back. It wasn't about the kid, Ab. I couldn't give a fuck about him. It was his sister that caused me pause. And even if they *were* right about me mixing business with personal matters, I still felt a sting of betrayal from their private agreement. My father pulled a stunt I couldn't respect. Never had he bet against me with Iban. Ever. Typically, he relied on me to balance, regulate, and/or compensate for my brother's ineptness. Sending Iban behind me to execute Ab was an action in reverse.

And this whole shit with me being involved in the first place. He knew I wanted no parts of this. Of his world. We'd been over this since I was a kid. Other than the power he commanded, there was nothing compelling about my father's vocation. The price that particular power came with wasn't a recurring penance I could carry to bed each night. His underworld required deception, creating unrest, and murder.

"Gone 'head on and ask him," my father barked, his free arm flailing in the air.

My gaze reached my mother, who bit her lips together.

Her brows lifted. "Is it Bilan, too?" When I didn't reply, she got more specific. "Was it the *B-Way Burger* incident? Was that too much for her?"

With my eyes cast out to the fountain, I answered, "That would be too much for the strongest of eyes. She's never seen anything like that before."

"Well, it's out of the way," my father stated unapologetically. "I've always taught you boys, a woman who doesn't understand our line of work is one who has no business in our world—our family. She ain't built for this shit." He tossed his head in a shrug. "Move on."

I took a deep breath to cool my temper.

"Did she break up with you, Sadik?" my mother asked.

"No." *Never!* "It's understood she needs space to process what it all means. She's away."

"Where?" she asked. My father's eyes were now on me. "Is she with family? I can reach out to her."

I wouldn't tell them where Bilan was. My father didn't need to know after the bullshit he and Iban pulled. And my mother would innocently tell my father in a subsequent conversation. I didn't want to ask her to hold my secret.

I shook my head. "She'll be fine. She requested time, and I'm going to grant her that."

"So, the engagement is still on?"

My family knew I'd proposed to Bilan back in June, but they didn't know I moved her in with me right after. Bilan felt it was too much too soon, and asked that I kept that new development between the two of us. I suspected she didn't want to broadcast it because of the mediocre reception into the family from my father and Iban. If space was what she needed, I had no problem giving it to her.

"Of course," I answered.

And if time is what she needs now, I'll give her that, too...

"Mr. Ellis..." Both my father and my heads went up. It was his assistant, Palmer. "We need to talk. Looks like Lopez got some smoke."

"With me?" my father asked with incredulity. Palmer nodded, affirmative. "Shiiiit," he swore daringly. "For what?"

"Said we clipped one of his low levels. Kid supposed to be his great-nephew, or some shit."

"We did it?" my father questioned for clarification. "As in *my* camp?"

Palmer nodded again. "Said he was with Ab when we got him."

My father asked, "What's the kid's name?"

"Manny, or some shit like that." Palmer shrugged.

My father's eyes met mine. It dawned on me the kid in question was the one I had Rory pop because of his disrespect to Bilan.

I stood and sauntered past my father to kiss my mother. "See you later, queen."

"Where you going?" my father demanded, but softly.

"To honor my commitment to my nieces before I head home." I began down the glossy cobblestone walkway to the house. "Tell Lopez to teach his underlings not to disrespect women."

My back was to him as he shouted, "This was his family!"

"And Bilan is your family." Fuck him. "I call it even. And I'll have Jamil hit your men to tell them where his corpse is buried."

"And the dumb fuck was 'posed to know the girl belonged to you?"

"He knew," I assured him, turning to face them. My heart was heavy, sacs even heavier, thanks to Double E Bags' business. He'd have to eat this one, and it felt damn good. Fuck the Lopezes. "I can bet a few stacks every nigga from Passaic to West fuckin' Paterson know that girl's marked with Ellis stains."

"Shit, man," my father droned, understanding he'd have to answer for the kid's death.

Not that it was an impossible or difficult feat addressing the Lopezes for Double E Bags. But I was sure it was a task he could do without, considering the swelling bubble of his income. It was a duty he'd have to take on alone. I was busy cleaning other shit for him.

I reached the door and strolled inside, reminded that I was the one with the true quandary. I was going home again to an empty, cold fucking bed.

Day eight...

As I amble down the narrow hall toward the kitchen, the scent warms me all over. I'm back here again. The sounds of the floor creaking beneath my feet, the clanking of pots and pans as I near the back of the restaurant instinctively revs my pulse.

And as expected, they're here. My dad and mom are busy with cooking and food prep. Dad's sautéing the roux for his recipes, and Mom's cutting vegetables on the workstation in the center of the small room. There, near the back door, is old Vernon, peeling potatoes. He doesn't even look up when I enter. No one does. This small restaurant in Newark is what's considered a "hole in the wall," which means high traffic from open till close on most days.

"Hooya." I try controlling my excitement.

"Hmm?" my mother replies in that warm tone.

And as much as I want to express my jubilation for being in the same room as them again, there's a force keeping me from tripping over my feet to smother him in my arms, or falling into her protective bosom. It's as though time hasn't traveled...but I have.

My hand goes to my belly that still hasn't changed much in size, but feels completely occupied.

"You remember that talk we had the other day?" It wasn't the other day, but it was.

"What're you talking about, Lani?" Her eyes don't come up from the table right away.

I sidle up next to her so aabo can't hear me. "About making babies before getting married," I whisper.

Her busy hands freeze and seconds later, she peers up at me. Her regard brushes against my hand, holding over my nonexistent belly before meeting my eyes. After breathless, soundless and heart-racing seconds, her face opens with wide eyes and an even broader mouth.

"Asad!" she shouts for my aabo's attention. "Asad! Oh, Allah," she murmurs, her fingertips going toward her mouth. My father uncharacteristically leaves the stove, face tight with anger for having to do it. "He did it!"

"What?"

My frame trembles with fear. What am I doing? They're going to kill me.

"The young man—the one with the colored eyes," hooya tries to explain to my aabo. "The one who came to talk to us. He did it!" A merriment I'd never heard from her shoots from her belly. "They're having a baby, Asad! A baby."

Tears well in her eyes and throat, preventing her from speaking. "He married Lani, Asad!" She's cheerful and wrong. "Our baby girl is married. You hear that?"

My father's eyes are fastened to me, oscillating between my face and belly that reveals nothing at this point. "You did right, BiBi." His voice was taut.

With pride?

I, too, am overcome by emotions. My head shakes, eyes close.

I swallow hard before I confess. "No. I'm not married. We—" My regard falls to my left ring finger, where his promise sits. Its radiance glistening, reminding me of the attachment.

Sadik.

My eyes blink hard and in quick succession. "We never got married."

"But you will," hooya assures with confidence. "He's crazy about my Lani." Her shy smile can't be missed. "Am I right, Asad?"

Aabo nods with a soft smile. He looks good, unlike he will in a few short years. And hooya is unusually happy, glowing from my news.

I shake my head again. "I don't think so. So much has happened."

"It's okay, BiBi," aabo ensures. "He talked to us. It's what he wants." His head nods softly.

"What?" I'm confused.

"Both—everything...you," aabo quantifies.

"He wants it all with you, Lani." Hooya can't fight her smile, eyes still wet. "He told us before giving you that big ring. He wanted our approval."

"He's a good man, BiBi." Aabo nods again. He's never been a man of many words. This is all too much for me. "He'll be good to you and the kids."

"You gotta eat to feed that baby, Lani," hooya warmly rebukes me. "You have to let it all go to be a strong hooya and proper wife. You know how to. You just have to be strong. Let it all go, and be what you're meant to be for him...and his family."

My eyes grow wide. "No, hooya. They're different. They're not what you think."

"Are they together?" Aabo asks about Sadik's parents.

"Yes."

"His father provide for the whole family?"

"Yes."

"Does his mother keep the house and feed the family?"

"Yeah, but—"

"No family's perfect, BiBi," aabo states the obvious.

"And the worst kind of family is the one that's not together," hooya gripes. "He told us you'll be welcomed into their family."

Aabo's calloused hand brushes over my belly. "He's going to give you a family."

Hooya giggles. "Looks like he started already. That young man seems to be a force to be reckoned with."

"You don't know the half," I grumble, regard to the floor.

A phone rings and my eyes squeeze closed. We have a lot of ground to cover here.

"I bet that's him, Lani." She giggles as my father turns back for the stove.

I know it's him. He calls each day, several times, and around the same times.

I raise an index finger in the air as I reach for my phone. "Aabo, hang on. I'm not taking it. We still need to talk."

My mother turns back toward her vegetables, too. Panic strikes my chest. I need to speak to my parents. But the stupid phone doesn't stop ringing. No matter how many times I push to quiet it, the thing continues to ring.

What in the world? My heart's racing and I feel tears pooling at my eyes as I fight with the phone. My parents resume their usual scuttle of food prep. I'm sure there's a line out at the counter collecting now.

"No..." I demand to the phone.

It needs to stop ringing.

My eyes bulged open. Across from the bed, the door to the en suite bathroom is open. The room is motionless. I reached off the side of the bed, patting blindly until my hand hit the ringing phone. I lifted it to my face.

Sadik...

Before tossing the phone to the other side of the bed, I powered it off. Then, inescapable nausea settled over me, bringing me back to the here and now. After only a couple of hours of sleep, it was time to get up.

My lids were swollen, face puffy, heart numb, belly empty, and eyes dilated on the waves lapping over each other. My heartbeat synced with the tempo of the cries of the ocean. It was only when I gazed out to the water that I didn't cry. Mental rest was a joke. As I scrutinized my favorite vista, tormented emotion rolled over me like the billows of the sea.

I was alone, lonely, down to my last twenty dollars, and plagued with morning sickness and the blues. It had been eight days since I'd arrived at my "dream" home. My plans never included staying this long. I was only supposed to be here a couple of days to collect my thoughts. But pregnancy symptoms attacked my vulnerable frame just days after my arrival. Now, I felt stuck.

I'd been able to get around a little, making trips down to the boardwalk for food. My first trip there, I purchased cheap flip flops, two overpriced beach dresses, deodorant, toothpaste, a toothbrush, and a comb. The house had a few toiletries like lotion, mouthwash, and laundry supplies from our trip down here in June. There was a washing machine, dryer, stove, fridge, a case of bottled water, packs of toilet tissue and paper towels...a few basics, some we never used. That first trip here seemed so long ago now.

And, today, Sadik was a green-eyed murderer, and Abshir was dead. Dead. He was sprawled out on the floor and I ran, leaving him there...alone. Alone. That's all I knew now, was to be alone. Well, now, I was really alone. My father—my *aabo*—was gone. Mommy was gone. And now Abshir. My brother and I had more than our share of battles; some typical sibling rivalry, and some more severe. As the water receded from the shore, I recalled tearful moments from my mother, and speechless ones from my father after a fight between my brother and me. I didn't appreciate their reactions then, but understood now. Siblings are parents' gifts to their children. At some point, the bonding should begin.

But not with my big brother. He enjoyed taunting me. We lived in the same house, but preferred avoiding each other. The bickering got so bad, we were all relieved when he set up his bedroom in the basement. Abshir began showing signs of violence by breaking my things and shoving me. Nothing I did was right—even my silence. He'd provoke me for simply cleaning the kitchen. Or maybe that was his manner of paying a compliment. He'd say I looked "good and at home" when cleaning: the only thing I was missing was a swollen belly filled with a bastard spawn.

Even now, as I sat on a beautiful, quiet beach, I could hear his taunts.

You're sitting here crying like a fuckin' baby. Grow the fuck up, Bilan! You so fuckin' weak. This nigga bought you this lit ass crib, and you out here crying like he slapped you or some shit. How long you gon' cry? Till you make your own fuckin' ocean? You need to man the fuck up, and think about how to get outta this shit instead of crying over it!

I leaped on the sanded floor, hitting my chin with my knee. His voice sounded so crisp and near! I was panting, frame trembling. He was wrong about me. I was hungry, down to my last few dollars, and alone. I was not weak. Maybe my line of vision narrowed, peripherals blinded, but I wasn't weak. I'd just been a mere survivor, living months and years in a fog of pain and grief from losing my parents. I didn't date seriously or vacation, but I was smart and capable. There may not have been much I knew about what was going on around me, but I knew Bilan.

He knew that Bilan...

My hand lifted, and eyes strained from the diamond on my finger. Its reflection practically exploded against sunlight. Not only was it radiant, it was generous in size. The ring was a statement maker. A conversation starter. I instantly wondered if that was his intent. Sadik was so forceful, so tornadic with his entry into my life. My world no longer felt like mine. Look at where I was. My physical condition! A tear slipped when I subconsciously admitted I couldn't look at a single part of my body and not think of him. In five short months, Sadik infiltrated my life, my body.

Even my dreams...

"*That young man seems to be a force to be reckoned with.*"

My mother shared that so vividly...so believably, it made me wonder about lots of things.

The house...

My spine whipped as I turned back to face it. When we'd spent the first couple of nights here, it had never dawned on me rentals didn't come sparsely furnished. The place only had a bed in it. In all that time, I was so swept away by the romantic gesture of being at the beach again, I never thought past the generous notion. But now...the house...the bed he'd had here waiting on us...the furniture we purchased together...the security system he had installed days after we'd left—it was all strategic. Sadik planned it all out.

As I continued to gaze suspiciously at the house, it appeared smaller now. The deck off the second-floor master suite revealed a bit of the room from my vantage point. The back porch appeared empty. The beach grass danced, the seagulls crowed.

And my mind sharpened as did my vision.

Rory...

A clear memory of leaving this place that last day bloomed. As I plodded down the stairs, Rory handed Sadik a package.

"It's an Ellis tradition that when we purchase a new home, we leave money inside before we settle in. It's good faith in our absence."

With strength I didn't know I could summon, I pushed to my feet with just one arm. My body turned so fast and moved so swiftly, up the beach and to the house, it snatched my breath. I raced into the kitchen, tracking sand into the pantry as I searched for something to stand on, eyes whipping wildly around. A chair. Back out into the kitchen, I made a dash for one of the chairs at the table. I pulled it into the closet behind me and positioned it next to one of the shelves. Hastily, I climbed up and used the bottom of my palm to bang the white plank of wood up. It took several tries, even a few with the side of my closed fist, but eventually, it popped open. Blindly, I reached up into the dark area, patting for it. Sadik wasn't too much taller than me and I hoped his arm length didn't extend beyond mine too much.

I climbed onto a shelf, hoping not to break it and my neck as I discovered his reach *was* longer than mine. Holding a tight breath with the edge of a plank biting into the back of my arm, I felt a piece of the plastic. My body trembled with unbridled excitement as I was able to pull it back with small results. Then I eventually grasped the body of the package into my sweaty palm and brought it out of the ceiling. With a tense frame, I climbed down onto the chair, then the floor. I vibrated with fear and desperation as I tossed it to the floor and sat on the chair gaping at it.

It took a few seconds, but soon, I was able to gather the strength to get the kitchen scissors and cut the gray plastic. When I was able to see the corner of twenty dollar bills, I thought wise enough to get up and lock the doors. Grabbing the money into my chest, I took to the stairs and trekked to the master suite to close and lock those doors, too. Then I settled into the walk-in closet, on the floor to pull all the money out. After close to thirty minutes and seven recounts, I dropped the wad of bills to the floor. Fifteen thousand dollars. This man left fifteen thousand dollars in an empty home! Who did senseless things like that?

Sadik…

My heart galloped in my chest, mouth went pasty and, for the first time in days, I couldn't sense my morning sickness. Blown. My mind totally crashed at this discovery. Here I was, glad to have a few dollars to crawl down to the boardwalk for another couple of slices of pizza it would take two days to get through. Instead, I found a small treasure.

In that moment, several things clicked for me. Several very powerful revelations. One was if I didn't go now, I'd be too sick to move soon. However, the boardwalk wouldn't be my destination now. I needed more substance than it could offer.

∞3∞

He slipped inside the car, closing the door behind him. Paolo gave Rory in the driver's seat a nod through the rearview mirror before he began.

"It's set. Amato is willing to meet with you. He did his homework on you...your family. Sees you're legit and connected. *È stato approvato*." He wiped down his mouth with his thumb and index while gazing out into the dark lot of the parking building. "*Una condizione*." His dark eyes swung my way.

I asked, "*Che cosa?*"

"It happens on Amato's playground. You must go to him. *Casa sua*." He shrugged. "That's the only way."

After a long pause, I shrugged my acceptance with my mouth. Then I opened my suit jacket, reached into the pocket, and pulled out an envelope stuffed with cash.

"*Grazie, Paolo*." I smiled. "*Molto apprezzamento*. Be well."

After a firm nod, Paolo accepted the cash and left the car as smoothly as he glided inside. Rory fired up the engine.

"So now you gotta go over to Sicily to get the shit with Rizzo put to bed?" She petitioned me with her eyes through the rearview mirror. I nodded as my mind spun with details. "You just gon' fly out there?"

I considered that without words first. "Ultimately, but I need a plan first."

She blew out air, readjusting herself in her chair to drive. "Whatever the fuck it is need to hurry the fuck on. The war in the streets between ya pops' men and the Rizzos is getting wetter every damn day."

"Let's get to this next thing so I can get on with my day, Bean." I picked up one of my phones as she pulled out of the parking space.

Rory was right. The war between my father and Rizzo was mounting each day. The police departments spread across several counties in Northern and Central Jersey were working overtime to keep up with the shootings and deaths of both parties. It was mostly Rizzo's stubborn ass losing men weekly. Because my father employed distributors throughout the entire state, Rizzo didn't have the army needed to endure a long war. But his stubborn ass remained in the race, fighting dirty. He hit my father with the government and in the streets. And in return, my father put pressure on me to decimate his new arch-nemesis.

A few minutes later, we pulled up to the backdoor of *Pulse*, Tiffany's second club. Rory and I walked in together. At the door was security, calling her assistant to the floor. He invited us inside. My eyes swept the place, looking colossal while empty. It was dark and sexy inside, just like with *Energy*, but the clubs had two different vibes.

My admiration and steps halted when I caught Tiffany at the

other end, near the bar, chatting with Ricky. His crew surrounding him spotted us first, I could tell. They communicated with each other about our presence. That had my one brow raising and hands going to my waist. Tiffany, wearing all white, jean shorts and an *Ase Garb* tank with gold heels, caught my attention. Her ass sat right, causing me to blink.

My head fell and I rubbed my eyes. Tiffany was no longer an option for me.

"The fuck he doin' here?" Rory grumbled my sentiments.

"Oh! Hey, Sadik!" Tiffany's assistant, Monique, greeted as she walked up on us. "She should be closing up on that meeting and will be with you right away." Her smile was cheery, shoulders lifting. "Can I offer you two a drink?"

I took a deep breath. "Ummmm... Maybe now isn't a good time for her." She asked to speak with me and I told her to name the place and time today, and I'd make it happen. This was no popup visit for me. I had shit to do. "I can reschedule."

"No!" Monique yelped too expressively. "She's really looking forward to seeing you." Her cheery smile returned. "Please. Let me get you two something to drink. Try our new signature cocktail." Monique began backing toward the bar.

We followed her and as we neared, Ricky glanced over his shoulder. He was much taller than everyone in the group with a clear vantage point. Tiffany kept her head below as she wrote on a clipboard. I took a seat at the bar while Rory stood behind me.

"Oh, Deek, man," Ricky's voice was subterranean deep and with Haitian Creole intonation. "Whaddup?"

He turned completely to face me.

I offered him a nod before murmuring to Monique, "Just water for me, sweetheart."

I was sure he felt the slight in my lack of reciprocity. Fuck him. *The Commission* Rizzo put together was all turning against my father. No one was defending him, even if their feelings were indifferent. Ricky and his two *Commission* cohorts knew Rizzo declared war over some bullshit.

I accepted a bottled water from Monique and took a sip. Before

I was done, Tiff was on her way to me with Ricky and his crew around her.

"One sec, Deek," she offered. "I'm going to walk Ricky out."

Ricky stopped near me before I could respond. "Yo, Deek..." He was awfully loquacious today. "I'm throwing a party here. You should come through, my nig."

I found my brows raising again. "You? Having a party?" Ricky was a known recluse, on the run from the law. It was a wonder to see him out in the daylight. I was sure his warrants were nearing the double digits. One thing that could be respected about him, he successfully evaded the law. "Shit," I spat. "It's about to blizzard in August out this bitch."

"Nothing too big. I hear you in with Randi's friend." I hated the glimmer in his eye. Fucking hated it. "Maybe y'all two'll come through."

I turned fully to face him. "Perhaps. I'll see what the lady decides and'll move accordingly." I was sure to lift one side of my face in a smile for pleasantry sake.

With a full-on grin, Ricky stepped off in his *Timbs* and green camouflage cargo shorts. His upper torso was covered in a white tank and bulletproof vest.

His country ass...

"It was good seeing you, Rory," one of his guys taunted.

"I swear, feeling my heat on ya tongue's a lot better." A few of us snickered at her wit. "And seeing me bust down ya throat'll put ya bum ass out ya misery."

As they traveled toward the back door, the group cracked the fuck up.

"I'm just fuckin' witchu, Rory," dude clarified. "No disrespect."

"I 'on't see no kids around this bitch," Rory countered. "I'm unfuckawitable, my G. Fuck outta here."

His laughter turned nervous. But everyone heard her threat and the joke was on him. Rory was the only one unsmiling. I didn't get why motherfuckers tried rattling her cage. Her reputation was solid. She was tried and true.

Less than two minutes later, Tiff was back, sliding onto a barstool near me, leaving one between us. Rory took off to give us privacy.

"Thanks for coming." She handed the clipboard to Monique with words of instructions. Then she turned back to me. "And to make it so convenient."

"I was in the area. No biggie." I turned to face her. "Everything okay?"

"Yeah." She scraped her top red lip with her bottom teeth. Tiffany couldn't look me in the eyes. "I need a favor."

"Of course. Name it."

"It's pretty big," she warned.

My head shook softly as I stretched my palms out over my lap. She needed to get on with it.

"I got an invitation to the governor's ball." She cracked a smile, rolling her eyes. "I'm sure you did, too."

I grabbed the bottle of water and twisted the cap off. "Yeah."

"I have a designer I want to try out. He's offering me a custom piece." She flashed her teeth nervously. "He's in Rome."

My brows lifted. "Okay."

"I asked your father, but he's flying out to Antigua to oversee the development over there. You think I could use your jet to go? It'll be just a couple of days; he swears it." Her teeth flashed nervously again. As I turned for the bar to readjust myself, pondering it, she blurted, "And I know I ain't ballin', but I could give you five stacks for the trouble. That should cover gas and something, right?"

I mentally did the flight calculations for Rome to Sicily. This was the plan I was looking for. This was the break.

"I can understand if—"

"How soon are you trying to go?"

She took a deep breath, clearly relieved from my answer. "Shit," she breathed out, eyes to the floor as she thought. "I got a lot of shit poppin' off between both the clubs this weekend, but I can break out...Monday or Tuesday, if that's not too soon for you."

I was already off the stool and ambling away before she was done.

"I'll be ready to fly you out, shawtie."

Day ten...

After stirring the big spoon in the *Maraq Fahfah* for the last time, observing it was done, I turned off the eye of the stove. It smelled like home now. I felt less distant from my mother with the aroma of coriander, lamb, and cabbage filling the air. I felt less alone. Quickly, I decided to let the pot cool while I trekked upstairs to my new tool. I had lots of work to do. Loads of considerations to undergo.

On my way up, I could feel the beginning stages of nausea. Today was a better day than yesterday. I had a hearty breakfast consisting of a plain, untoasted and undecorated bagel at the kitchen table. I needed to for my commute.

Yesterday, after uncovering the money, I walked into town and asked a few people where could I catch a taxi service. My phone had died at that time, but even if it hadn't, I wouldn't have used it, trying to stay beneath the radar. The people in *Macen Beach* were unlike any I'd ever met. They were kind and generous. Several offered to take me where I needed to go without charge. However, I declined, explaining to them I needed to learn the ropes of the town. The restaurant owner, where Sadik and I had lunch the day we went shopping, allowed me to use his phone to call a cab.

The cab took me to a neighboring town, where there was a grocery store. I was able to buy a few things to store and cook for a few days. I needed my strength. Between the dream about my parents and the money discovery, I knew I had to do better. For my baby. There was an electronics store in the same lot as the grocer. It was there that I was able to purchase a charger for my phone. *Not that I would answer it*. After finally coming back to the house, I put the food away and scarfed down half of a homemade turkey and cheese sandwich. I was wiped out. So, I showered and crawled into the bed.

Today, I was on a new mission when I woke up. I walked down to the boardwalk to a convenience store I'd come across when going to get pizza. There were two things I needed from my army box when I snuck inside my childhood home for it that night. One was the keys to the *Macen Beach* property, and the other was my mother's old cell phone. When she was hospitalized months before she passed, I'd broken down and gotten her one, though she'd always refused to own a cell. My father was gone and brother was in prison. I needed her to call me in the event of an emergency. It was a pre-smart, flip phone. I knew I'd need it to call a couple of people like Tasche and Randi to let them know I was okay.

I could also use my mother's old phone to call a taxi to return to the electronics store today to purchase a laptop and a wireless hotspot device. I didn't spend lavishly, just purchased what I needed to connect to the outside world in a manner untraceable to me.

Now, up in the master suite, I was anxious to get started. I sat in the middle of the bed and propped the laptop on my crossed legs. Dramatically, but unbelievably nervously, I took a deep breath. My fingers tingled as they approached the keyboard. I needed to know what was being said about the mayhem ten days ago. My first stop was at *Paterson Chronicles*.

I closed the laptop and scooted back on the bed. Glancing to the right, I noticed the sun had gone down; I'd been on the damn thing that long. Sometimes, when you go looking for things, you find more than you bargained for. That was my case today. One search about the killings over a week ago led to morbid curiosity of the Ellises. I'd *Google*'d them before as an outsider who'd only met one of them. Now, I'd interfaced with the entire clan—and managed to have the one, who seemed as the most influential of them all "fall in love with me"—I could view what had been reported on them with new lenses.

My search began at *Paterson Chronicles* and journeyed from there. The police were framing the murders in the abandoned *B-Way Burger* building as an amateur vengeance murder turned arson with accidental deaths. When I was done with the account at that newspaper, I went to others. According to several media sources, the police believed Damien Brown, who they were aware was a drug dealer, had been looking for Derrick Little to kill him.

Derrick...

Derrick's face in the articles was an old high school picture. He looked young, healthy, and promising, as most kids that age do. It dredged memories of me losing my virginity to a guy I found cute and nice, a trusted friend of many years to my older brother. The sight of him was bittersweet, bringing back tender emotions of betrayal and deceit. I had no recollection of him being in that building. And now, he was dead. In fact, according to police, Damien was responsible for killing Derrick, Jamal, and Lenny. They wouldn't release specific details, but the finger was being pointed at Damien. And oddly enough, Damien died that evening because of a fire started by one of his associates, Jayshon Wright. He was the kid driving the van when Damien took me from the diner that afternoon. The police had Jayshon's prints from several gas canisters outside the building.

The police believed it was Damien's intention to cover up Derrick's murder by burning his body after hacksawing it. That reminded me of the chainsaw I'd seen Damien's guys carry into the building. The police didn't give too many details, but believed after killing Derrick and butchering his remains, Damien and his guys set the building on fire, a fire that grew wild in no time at all. The amateur, Jayshon, who poured the gasoline, poured it near the exits of the building too, trapping them inside. Their bodies were charred so bad, authorities had been unable to identify several of Damien's collaborators.

But this isn't true. Any of it. I was there, and Derrick was not...

Damien had been right: the Ellises wanted them all dead. Jamal,

Lenny, Derrick, and my brother, Abshir; they were all dead. Even Damien was dead, but specifically because of me. The Ellis family was that ruthless. That murderous.

That truth led me to *Google* again for the Ellis family. If Sadik was able to take another man's life so effortlessly—artfully— without blinking, what were they putting in the Ellis kids' formula? While I had not gotten much from Irene and Taaliba's searches other than what I'd known about *Ellis Academy* and its accomplishments over the past few decades, I did see images of them at the courthouse during Iban's trial. There were more of Earl, Irene, and Monica than Taaliba. And conspicuously, there were almost none capturing Sadik.

Odd...

And the details of Iban's crime was chilling. It could have possibly been because I'd been a target of his disdain recently. He tortured a man named Hubert Jackson before killing him. Iban carved out the man's lips and pushed the flesh around the man's penis. It was heinous. And Iban still got off. What started as a charge of first degree murder ended up being reduced to passion as a result of reasonable provocation manslaughter—whatever the hell that meant. Not many details were available about how Iban's crime had him facing thirty years to life, but ultimately was reduced to less significant charges, resulting in just a four-year sentence. The Jackson man had welts around his neck resembling strangulation, but had bled to death from hours of torture.

Two other odd things I learned in my search jarred me. There was a war going on, mostly in Northern and Central Jersey between alleged members of an Italian group against Blacks. Fourteen people had been killed in six days. The second peculiar thing was there was no mention of Abshir's death. The possibilities as to why sickened me. Was he still there? Alone? Had the Ellises burned down my family home to destroy the evidence? I had no way of knowing. I checked the gazillion of texts and voice messages collecting since I'd been down here, and no one mentioned my home being destroyed. But he was alone.

Or maybe not!

Maybe he was lying in a morgue unaccounted for because he had no next of kin available to contact.

My eyes slowly closed as nausea rolled over me. The first thought was because of all the information I consumed over the course of a few hours. Then reality hit me: I hadn't eaten on time. The *Maraq Fahfah* soup. I swallowed a gulp of thick, metallic saliva. My head spun and belly toiled viciously. With unbelievable determination, I swayed downstairs to eat, hoping it would stay down.

"I can have Candy make you a plate to go," my mother offered from the other end of the table. I glanced back down to my plate and realized I'd done it again. *Shit...* Most of my mother's swordfish, in some type of coconut sauce I usually loved, took a backseat to my ruminating. "I mean..." She hesitated. "I made that with you in mind, my love. It won't be too much to do."

Of course, everyone at the table except for my nieces, who were preoccupied with their iPods, gazed my way curiously.

"You good, man?" Iban asked, hand rubbing over his injured arm.

"Just take the shit to go," my father mumbled.

I took a deep breath, sitting back in my seat. I hated disrespecting my queen's efforts at her table. Her offer to send me home with food had been unusual because I was a plate cleaner when it came to her culinary skills.

"I.... Uhh..." I scratched my chin, catching the concerned regard of Taaliba. "I have a flight to catch tonight."

Oh, damn...

My thoughts went to the time, and I reached for my phone lying on the table.

"Oh, right!" Iban's voice hiked. "You and Tiff flying out."

"Huhn?" Monica's voice, that hadn't been audible at the dinner table for weeks now, was sharp. "Where?"

"Rome. Where niggas go to get that dome!" Iban rhymed. His laughter was menacing and humor unshared.

"You okay going out there like that?" my mother asked with measured speed.

"I could have flown out with Tiff for you," Taaliba offered.

Both women questioned my actions with Bilan in mind. And as though predicted, I turned to Monica, whose eyes were animated with the same concern.

My father's salty ass scowl remained from the opposite head of the table. He was throwing dark energy my way and I knew why, but wouldn't address it.

I took another deep breath, my hand going to the end of Iesha's braids as she sat next to me. "Tiff and I can use the time to talk about what my life with Bilan will mean for the family as it concerns her. Because of how unconventional our relationship and connection is, it's important I handle her feelings and expectations delicately." When I saw the women hadn't let up on their expressions, I explained further. "We'll be away for just three days, and coming right back. The designer swears that's all the time he needs. I'm also going to spend time with a fellow-*Blakewood* alum, who just moved his family out there when he took a role at a technology firm."

I felt the need to explain because I knew their expectation of me was to be an upstanding man, unlike the older Ellis men. Their hope was in my fidelity. Though unspoken, it was expected of me to be better in that department.

"Can we get some desert?" Iban broke the awkward silence in my mother's dining room. "Ma, you said you made some ambrosia?"

"Ooh, Nana!" Ivana breathed out, hella excited. "You made ambrosia?"

My mother smiled brightly. "I've been meaning to make your dad some all summer." Her brows hiked.

If I didn't head out, I'd be late for the flight. The drive to Teterboro was considerable from *Elliswoods Palace*. I was stern with my advice of Tiff being there on time. I stood from the table. It was time to go. My mother rose to her feet from the other end.

"Already?" She was almost alarmed.

I tried cracking a grin, the type that usually disarmed her. She met me halfway, then we embraced.

"I'll call you in the morning, baby," I assured her on a whisper while everyone else spoke amongst themselves behind us.

"You better, boy," she murmured back. "I'm so worried about you. You're thinning in the face."

A pang lanced my fucking stomach. Rarely did I worry her legitimately. It had been so long. In many ways, my mother was my best friend and trusted confidant. Over the years, she identified the limitations I set for our relationship and adhered to them. Right now, between us were two barriers. One was the truth about Bilan and me. The other was my obligations to fulfil for my father. His business was never an open book to her.

"I love you, queen," I shared before kissing her forehead. It was the only peace of mind I could attempt to provide her.

"Not half as much as I do you, boy." There was a bite in her tone. A warning.

After another hug, I released her and turned to leave. In my peripheral, I could see Taaliba stand, too, but didn't pay it too much mind as I gave my goodbyes to the room.

"Got a call today. The police in East Orange are naming me as the leader of the attacks in this street war," my father quickly muttered as I neared him. He was standing as though waiting on me to pass his way. I stopped. "Me. He named me." His nostrils widened.

"I'm working on it, Pops. You have to trust me."

"Oh, I hope you are," he murmured in a similar fashion to my mother moments ago. "You on this 'no blood on our hands no more' tip. Meanwhile, this fat muthafucka fuckin' with my bread while cuppin' my goddamn balls. And I ain't the type of man to sit around while another man's getting *off* or over on me. Ya hear?" He was out of breath.

The table was loud and self-entertained. I doubted if many of our exchanged words could be heard.

"You tasked me with this. Trust me to take care of it."

"By you flyin' to fuckin' Europe, man?"

"Sir, I have a flight to catch."

"And I gotta—" He gained control of his volume. "goddamn business to run. I'm depending on you to get shit done. Big John took one to the chest walking out of the barbershop today. Big John!" he repeated for emphasis. "That nigga been with me for sixteen solid ones, and I had to tell his old lady he might not make it." He backed away dramatically, hands drawn behind him, and chin in the air expectantly.

I took yet another leveling breath, my eyes darting over the room behind him. "Respectfully, Dad, once this shit with Rizzo is complete, how about you don't task me with shit I have no business involving myself in the first place? Hmm?"

His face fell flat and before he could utter a response, I walked off.

As I was in the hall, on my way to the front of the house, Taaliba called for me. I stopped, turning to her.

She was damn near out of breath when she reached me. "You know what I hate more than you two beefing?" I lifted my chin in response. "You stressed the hell out."

I shook my head, eyes closing. "I'm good, baby girl."

"No, you're not. Don't fucking placate me with that patriarchal tone. I know *you*." She pushed her palm into my chest. "You're hurting and stressed. And I know Bilan's got something to do with it." Her eyes widened and nose rose in the air daringly. "Lie and say I'm wrong."

A chuckle escaped my lungs. My baby girl was a full-fledged woman now. She demanded recognition of it. "Isn't that what you gorgeous women were created to do to bull-headed men like us?"

"She's done more than stress you out." Taaliba cracked a knowing grin. "I've seen you two together. You fed her. Worshipped her soul wrapped in her pussy. It's sweet, Deek. I for real, for real didn't think your smooth ass was capable of being that affectionate with any woman without the Ellis surname."

I chuckled at that, too. "She will have the Ellis surname."

Taaliba's beam waned. In fact, her face fell. "I hope so, for your sake." She shook her head, melancholy filling her eyes. "I've heard whispers of what happened with her. If she can't deal with our kind—"

"Hey..." I pulled her into my arms and silenced her point with a kiss to her temple. "Bilan's a grown ass, bad ass woman. She's stronger than most perceive. Has more of a sturdy resolve than she's had to use. We'll be fine."

Her fretful regard climbed to meet mine. "You sure?"

"Do I lie about what I'm going to do?"

Taaliba shook her head to answer. I nodded softly in response. That caused her to smile, though faintly. This girl was able to discern my moods so keenly. She was a marvel.

"Yeah," she snorted. "Because the poor woman won't have a choice in the matter, leave it to you."

With my lips drawn up, I shook my head, agreeing with her.

"But you're tired, bullet head. You're no good to anybody if you're not rested."

Taking a step back, I inhaled deeply, scratching the skin of my head. "Yeah. I'll rest. Should have only a few more weeks before I can finally get it in."

"No." She went into her pocket and pulled out a teal green plastic bag. Taaliba opened it and sniffed. "This should help."

"Whoa!" I laughed as I extended my arm, rejecting her offering. "I don't smoke, young lady. I'll leave that to you millennials. I just manufacture the herbs."

"First of all, people of all ages enjoy your product. As you know, it's a more widely accepted pastime than it was in your hay, old man." She rolled her eyes. "Secondly, this isn't dro. It's an herb mixture, though. It's tea." She held the bag open.

"Tea?"

"Yeah."

"Why are you giving me tea?"

"Because it's my new business." Her smile was luminous. "I'm an herbalist!"

"Herbalist? What the hell happened to photography...acrylic painting?"

Her shoulders lifted blushingly. "I still dabble. You know I go wherever my creative flow takes me. I've been studying under an herbal savant for eighteen months now. And she's *gooooood*, Deek. I've been able to put something together to help Mommy with her nighttime bloating. She hasn't had it for a month now." When my head rolled over my shoulders in exhaustion, her volume increased for the purpose of convincing me. "That was something *I* created! What I'm giving you is an ancient recipe that even commercial companies have, just with a higher dose of lavender to encourage sleep."

I chuckled. "Baby girl, I don't need sleep. I need more hours in the day and a boost of energy." That mention caused a yawn to squeeze my damn lungs.

Taaliba was pulling out another bag. "I came prepared." She shrugged. "Let's just say, after twenty-six years of knowing you, I knew what to expect. This is an energy enhancer. It's a mixture of adaptogenic herbs that aren't habit-forming or over-stimulating. It doesn't inhibit normal body function either. That's the magic of my skill. There's some rhodiola rosea, panax ginseng roots, and maca—" She sucked in a breath as her brows lifted. Then she winked. "That heightens libido and improves semen quality." She winked deeply again while making a clucking sound with her mouth.

I rolled my eyes at her. My semen quality was just fine, at least I thought so.

"Those herbs and a few more mixed together in tea form will give you an extra dose of élan to help tackle a demanding day. But first, you have to take this..." She raised the original teal green bag. "to rest. A combination of nervine herbs to help with the nervous system: valerian root, organic catnip and skullcap...a few others to ease you into a good resting state. You know that flight to Rome is long as hell. Have your flight attendant prepare this for you. If you like it, I'll have more for you. If you hate it..." She hesitated, rolling her eyes desolately. "Well, just forget about it."

The air was out of her sails that quickly. I hated that shit. Without further reluctance, I took the bags from her hands and tossed them into the pocket of my suit jacket.

I grabbed the back of her head, pulling her in for a final kiss on the forehead.

"I have to go. Of course, I'll give it a try. I'll buy my next supply if it works. But if I die from it, I'll kill you."

I turned to take off. Taaliba giggled. "Be careful," she called behind me. "You're an Ellis: that threat takes on a different meaning leaving your tongue."

While I knew she was mostly joking, that, in fact, was a truth of our family I detested.

I was the last to board the jet, signing paperwork for the captain.

"Thanks, Mr. Ellis. Let's get in the air and off to Fiumicino," the pilot, Captain Willie, assured, tipping his hat.

My security was already on the jet, settling in. I was delayed, handling last minute business with one of three of my regular pilots. Captain William Baker, the grandson of sharecroppers, had been flying aircrafts for close to thirty-five years. He'd had my confidence each time I scheduled a flight and he was available.

"And get you back in time for your thirtieth wedding anniversary," I teased, taking the stairs up to the aircraft. "I don't want her upset with me because you're working on her thirtieth big day with you."

His high-pitched laughter behind me was infectious. "She's had more than twenty-nine of them with me. Hell, I hope she has! She done had birthdays, Valentine's Days, Christmases—shoot, she makes up dates!" he carped behind me in good-humor. "She gotta first date day, a first kiss day. Oh, the missus got days!"

We both chortled at that statement, stepping into the jet. Oddly, images of my first kiss and date with Bilan flashed through my mind with lightning speed. A ghosted scent of her sweet breath and her perfume had me fucking stumbling over my feet.

"You okay there?" Captain Willie inquired behind me.

With wild eyes, I turned to face him as he was positioned to go the opposite direction, into the cockpit.

"Ye—" I swallowed and blinked hard. "Yeah." I felt dazed all of a sudden.

"Go in the back room and get you some rest. Lords knows you got plenty of time on this flight. Mel is working this one. Lynn wasn't available. I can have her turn down your bed."

Still feeling off, I shook my head, swallowing again. "I'll have her make me some tea. That should help."

I started toward the inner cabin.

This shit Taaliba gave me had better work...

God knew I needed something.

My mother discovered Mel, a young Black flight attendant with her own stewardess company. She was a regular vendor my father and I often elected to do business with. Mel was professional, accommodating, and tactful about her presence on flights.

"Mr. Ellis." Her brown eyes beamed, but platonically. "Welcome aboard *The Ellis II*. Our estimated flight time from Teterboro to Leonardo da Vinci International Airport is eight hours and fifty-five minutes. I understand you've had dinner already. I did prepare several snacks for you and your guests this evening. Can I get you a drink to ready you for the flight?"

I hesitated a moment before reaching into my suit jacket pocket and pulling out the teal green plastic bag.

Handing it over to her, I murmured without confidence, "I'll take two mugs of this, back to back."

After paying several seconds of inspection to the bag, Mel nodded. "Right away, sir. I'll take your suit jacket now."

After removing and handing over my jacket, I grabbed my tote I'd carried on and began toward the first lounge area of the cabin, where my security was seated. Rory flipped through the television channels. My new security, Johnson, was laying out his guns to clean. The other men were busy with their devices. And as I moved toward the middle section of the cabin, Tiff was toeing toward me from the back. She wore a flannel *Blakewood* pajama shirt and white ankle socks. Her hair was pulled up over her head, earlobes glistening from the *Chanel* diamond studs plugged into them.

She stopped at one of the seats, resting a hand on the top of it while crossing one ankle over the other. "Told you I could be on time!" Then her regard moved over to my security. "What we watching?"

Rory mumbled, "*Pretty in Pink.*"

"*Pretty in Pink*? Ain't that, that old ass movie about that awkward, red-headed high school girl?"

Without looking at her, Rory answered, "Molly Ringwald, yeah."

"The fuck you watchin' that for? You feel some kinda connection to her plight, Rory?"

Johnson and the guys snickered as Rory's little ass head rolled around to look at Tiff. Tiff deflected by turning her attention to me.

I spoke first, considering her attire. This could only mean one thing. "You took the bedroom?"

Tiff's hand went to her belly and her face contorted. "I'm PMS'ing really bad. That's why I showered before coming to the airport and got comfortable right away." She was acting like a damn baby. "You okay with that. Right?"

Taking a deep breath, I powered around her to the middle of the cabin. I had shit to do and began unpacking my things right away. Rachel, my former employee, was moving forward with her wrongful termination lawsuit. And because of that, my legal team was preparing to drop the hammer on her ass. This shit didn't feel good. I cared about those employees I saw on a regular basis. I contributed to their celebrations throughout the year and supported their families' endeavors when I could. This lawsuit shit was twofold. One issue was she was trying to rob me because she decided to put my company at risk with her irresponsibility. That was fucked up. The second blow of it all was discovering she had a drug problem. I wasn't unsympathetic to that fact, even as the son of a tenured drug lord. She had underage children who likely felt the effects of her addiction.

I pulled out my laptop and phones, preparing to get a few things done. While bent over, digging through my tote, I heard from behind me, "I could sure use a back rub." Tiff's hand reached to her lower back, kneading her muscles. "We can share the room if you want."

She made a facial expression of torture as she massaged herself. Another act of deflection.

"I'm good out here, Tiff," I murmured, going back to my tote.

Eventually I stood, placing everything I needed near my chair. I felt a kink in my neck, and my damn feet throbbed. But my mind wouldn't slow. New federal regulations for my dispensaries I needed to go over and initiate rollout plans for—there were always new fucking regulations in the industry! I loved my life and was grateful for it, but I hated the idea of going back to all work and no recreation. No one to share the bullshit with. No one to connect with.

Shaking my head, a thought hit me. I moved to one of the overhead compartments and grabbed a small *Ase Garb* shopping bag. Inside were a few odds and ends I'd tossed inside during flights over sometime. Like panties. The first I'd seen of hers. The first I confiscated. I pulled them to my face and inhaled deeply. *Yes.* That fragrance I could never forget was still there. The scent of undeniable, yet restrained desire. The fragrance of purity I'd sensed from her, and later learned I was right. Bilan had only been with one other person before me: a boy which, by many measures, made me her first lover.

My eyes were closed when I heard movement behind me.

"Here's your tea, Mr. Ellis," Mel informed as I tucked my secret into my pant pocket. "I have cheese, crackers, and fruits for you, too. I'll be back with the second serving of tea in about twenty minutes."

She smiled and gave a neck bow.

I returned the gesture. "Thanks, Mel. You can close the curtains on your way out."

As she closed my section of the cabin off, I dumped myself in a seat. Captain Willie announced for us to buckle in as we were headed for the runway. I took a deep breath before complying, then reached for the tea. Minutes later, as we ascended into the night air, I sniffed confiscated panties before taking a sip of Taaliba's tea.

Thirty minutes into the flight, I was dozing off with a half empty mug of my second serving.

$\infty 4 \infty$

Day sixteen...

The sun glimmered over the water. The moving waves were mild in volume today, as was the wind. It was perfect to be out back, on the deck, folding laundry while watching a streaming ceremony from the laptop. Having to do laundry was laughable, but necessary seeing as I only had six sundresses I alternated between. I had just as many panties and fewer bras. Laundry was a mandatory action every five to six days.

As I folded the wrap gowns, I watched a Christian—*Pentecostal*—installation ritual. The church was *Redeeming Souls for Abundant Living in Christ Family Worship Church*, also known as *RSfALC*. A few days ago, I *Google*'d Lex's husband, Pastor Ezra Carmichael, and learned he presided over one of the largest churches on the East Coast. There were loads of information on the bearded codger, who predicted my world would be flipped upside down—twice—and was accurate about much of it so far. I learned a great deal about him. Ezra Carmichael obtained dual undergrad degrees in seminary studies and sociology from *Pepperdine University*. When I decided I was impressed, I further learned he had a master's degree in engineering from *"the" Oxford University*. The guy also earned a master's in counseling therapy. Interestingly enough, he actually had a job running *Kaiser Laboratories* in Kearny, New Jersey.

And with all of that, he had the time to play psychic and loosely predict my cinematic-like life since meeting a Sadik Q. Ellis. I didn't stop there with my *Google* tendency. Somewhere in my reading of one of his many biographies on the organization's governing *RSfALC* website, I discovered that among Carmichael's many spiritual gifts was the one of prophecy. I knew what the word meant, but wanted to know what it meant to this religion. That's when I grew even more intrigued. Carmichael was known to be used as a mouthpiece for their God, serving as an intermediary. He supposedly delivered messages from the Supernatural Source to other people.

That's when it all clicked for me, and I began to stalk him on social media and his church's website. I learned they streamed their services on Sundays and Thursdays—archived ones, too. It had been announced how today would be Pastor Carmichael's elevation service. He was being installed as the bishop of the church. I had no idea what this type of service entailed until today. I didn't let my perpetual sleepiness or morning sickness allow me to miss this event.

As I folded another panty, placing it onto a stack of them, I was overwhelmed with the amount of detail put into this ceremony. It had been going on for over an hour, beginning with top apostles, bishops, and such from their organization. In a processional, they marched down the long aisle of *RSfALC* as cameras snapped and dramatic music played. Several gave words on the stage, affirming Carmichael's impending appointment by way of pleasant and powerful memories of his ministry. Pastor Carmichael's grandfather, Bishop Travois Daniels, was mentioned with the highest regards.

Interesting...

It was all interesting because I was a softy for family and culture. Belonging. Familial connection. So, hearing about his relationship with a noble man resonated with me. *It also reminded me of the father-son relationship I'd still been trying to wrap my head around.* One of the last speakers was a man several described as Carmichael's mentor and best friend, Bishop Jones. His vocal delivery was raspier than Carmichael's, just not as deep. He orated with luxuriant articulation, even exuded charm with his stories. It was amazing! Positive and better than reality television!

Then came the portion of the ceremony where Carmichael entered the immaculate and packed sanctuary. He, too, strode inside in a processional manner. He wore a white robe trimmed in gold with a matching miter in the crook of his arm. His beard was stark: dark and full. His eyes beneath thick brows were expressionless, mouth hidden.

Behind him was his chocolate Amazonian goddess. Lex's wild, wooly hair was drawn behind her shoulders, her long lashes fanned her cheeks as she marched in a humble posture. Her palm cupped the other at her pelvis line. She appeared modest in a gold embroidered A-line dress that began at her neck and ended at her toes. Yet she had a worldly flair with a tastefully made up face, long untamed hair, and a gloriously feminine cut dress. All of that and not an ounce of flesh showing from her neck, down to the floor. Lex also didn't appear pregnant at all.

Like me...

Behind her was an older man, round, with glasses. He wore his red and black miter on his head. It corresponded with his robe. It was the current bishop, Pastor Carmichael's father. Next in the processional was a woman escorting a toddler and infant I knew to be the children of the Carmichaels. The ceremony was detailed and strategic. I held onto everyone, tried to follow each ritual. When Ezra took his oath, right hand on a Bible and left palm in the air, my belly fluttered. It wasn't the baby, but since there had been a baby in there, it was where I felt my deepest emotions.

The crammed temple shouted their riotous jubilance once the oath was taken. Then a fierce prayer of declaration was done by the Bishop Jones guy. And I watched with bated breath as Carmichael gathered Lex into his thick arms, swallowing her with the strength of his passion. The first tear slipped when he began to cry into her woolen hair. Lex held his miter upright on his head with one hand and roped her arm around his broad back with the other, clasping onto him as she, too, cried and spoke unclear words to him.

I began to bawl out of control. The panties bunched in my palm were now used as a tissue. My sobs rivaled the sounds of the waves to the right of me. The music was compelling and moving. The specific details of each portion of the ceremony created an absorbing ambiance. I was sure this was more powerful to those affiliated with them. To me, it was a lost promise. An unattainable fantasy sprinkled in with envy.

As I cried into the cheap cloth of my underwear, I pondered. Why couldn't I have encountered a safe, promising man? When Ezra was able to release her from his bear-grip, he kissed Lex unapologetically with a tear-stained face. She received him with ease in that act, too. Then they turned for their children. In an instant, a great crowd of admirers flocked to the stage all around them. Some praising their God, others cheering for the Carmichaels and, I was sure, all caught up in the meaning of unity. Unity with their God, and that between a man and his wife. This was their moment. It was shared with Ezra Carmichael's community—*Lex said she had been thrust into his world.* The moving scene had me hugging my belly.

God, if you know me like Carmichael said, why did the first man who claimed he loved me have to have a sordid, avaricious community?

I didn't know what I expected from a reputed arms dealer and prostitution ring master in Sicily, but a full city on a big ass mountain with countryside views wasn't it. We drove winding roads to the broad apex of a mammoth ass rock. The highpoint was crowded with Spanish colonial-style structures. Buildings, homes, and churches filled the streets.

It was the second day of our visit to Italy. Tiffany was busy with fittings and photoshoots with the designer and his affiliates while my team and I slipped out of Rome by way of a small *Cessna 208 Caravan* Jamil was able to arrange out here. I'd been to Europe several times; Italy twice, and never had I seen such a landscape as I'd seen today.

We drove into an alley between two tall, brick buildings. Three cars deep, half my team remained outside while I traveled inside a metal gate guarded by an olive-skinned man with stark black hair and a *Chauchat* machine gun resting on his shoulder, pointed toward the heavens. Sans a smile, he invited us in by a nod of his chin. Johnson was in front of me while Rory and Myers, an ex-military op, were behind.

My view opened to a backyard, modest in size but with full view of the peaks and valleys of the hinterland below. Several men stood, gaping our way. Most of them flexing in place with not-so-concealed guns. Pleasant animation could be seen in one of their eyes. He had to be Marcu Amato. He was about my height, graying, and modestly built. He stepped out with wide arms before clapping his hands.

"Ah! He's arrived. The bright apprentice of the Black American marvel!" he announced in Italian.

Then he used a phrase I didn't understand while sniffing and pulling up his pants at the buckle.

Another younger and short man stepped out almost shoulder to shoulder with him. "Mr. Ellis, my name is Paulie Amato. I'm Marcu's nephew. I'll be interpreting for the two of you today."

As he placed a gentle hand on his uncle's shoulder, he confirmed my instinct. Marcu nodded as though he knew what his nephew had conveyed.

"I understood what he said," I shared in Italian. Then I quantified in English, "At least, most of it."

I learned Italian, Spanish, and French in high school. My mother hired tutors, but Iban refused to learn, preferring the streets instead.

That left me alone to absorb as much as my flighty mind would allow.

"Ah," Marcu reacted again. "Welcome to my country. Welcome to my home, Ellis." His arms stretched wide in demonstration.

I offered a firm nod in reply. "I appreciate the invitation," returned in his language. "*Abbiamo bisogno di una pacca giù?*" I mimicked, searching my body with a smile.

Marcu shook his head with a solemn face. "There's no need to search you and your men for weapons. Salvatore doesn't possess the balls to send anyone into my land under the guise of seeking revenge on him. The motherfucker thinks I've forgotten all about him. Doesn't even know he's been living in his last days. *Per favore.*" He extended his arm. "Have a seat."

Quietly, I gaited over to one of the few chairs in the yard and sat.

When Marcu sat across from me, I asked, "*Perdonami?*" I sniffled with mirth, swiping my nose with my index finger. "But why trust my men and I are earnest in our reasons for being here, but make this trip to your home necessary for me?" His nephew interpreted it for him.

"Ah!" Marcu's face fell toward his lap as he grinned. Then he demanded one of his men to have one of the girls to make him a drink. "What's your poison?"

His nephew's eyes jumped from his uncle to me in case I needed assistance.

"I'm a *Mauve* man, myself, but forgive me." I patted my stomach. "The ride over in an old ass aircraft has my stomach upset."

"Ah! I understand!" Marcu answered in English. His eyes were large and animated. He sat back in his seat and crossed one leg over the other, face relaxing. "Your question." He cocked his index finger in the air. "You want a man dead. If I'm going to make this happen, at least let me look the man who wants me to play contractor in the face."

I made the tsk sound with smiling, yet narrowed eyes. "You have to come better than that," I advised in English.

His nephew, Paulie, interpreted. Marcu sputtered a sheepish laugh.

"How could you be so sure?" Marcu asked, still humored.

"You said it a moment ago. I am a student to the great Earl Ellis. You've done your research on him. There's no way he'd run the state of New Jersey as he has with no understanding of the human mind," I explained in English and observed each body in my line of sight.

Most of Marcu Amato's men stiffened in stance. One's hand went to his waist as a precautionary measure. There were several long moments of unpredictable stalling before anyone spoke.

Finally, Marcu began clapping his hands. Measured laughter accompanied it. "You win. I have not been honest. You're right. I have read up on your father. And pardon me for being so..." He paused to word search. "...small-minded, but I have never heard of a Black man doing as much as your father, and for so long. I've heard of crimes in America—I even know what Salvatore Rizzo does on the side to bring in cash. I have Mexican...Russian associates. They all do great and fail in the U.S. Many have had a long run, but eventually unfortunate times fell upon them, their families, and..." He made the swiping X gesture with his arms and hands, communicating their various demises. "*Comunque tuo padre*, he's been very successful, and for so long. Salvatore was wise asking him to be a member of *la sua Commissione*."

A long standing, powerful, and rich nigger. But still a nigger...

"*The Commission* doesn't belong to Salvatore, Marcu. It doesn't belong to my father, either. *The Commission* exists for the safety of New Jersey's residents. Salvatore used wisdom in proposing the agreement, but he doesn't own it. He does not get to choose who eats, who has peace or—"

"Who your brother fucks?"

Surprised, but not rattled, I lowered my chin, now measuring *my* words. "That's an example of totalitarianism, yes."

"Yes." He leaned over in his chair, elbows going to his knees as he ignored the woman clad in panties only, placing his drink on a small table next to him. "I've learned lots about the Ellis family. It is the only reason you've been invited into my home. I needed to be sure we shared the same level of grievances."

"I've not retained any information you might need to know. At least, not deliberately. I didn't know a man with your type of disdain for Rizzo would need petty American, soap-operatic details. I thought I'd simply provide the ground-level intel you need on his location. I was told you wanted to avoid U.S. law enforcement as much as you can...as well as local attention." My brows shot up at the same speed of his revelation. "*Ho fatto anche i miei compiti*, Amato." I had to let him know how I, too, did my homework. "And I know the only reason you've been so patient with executing your revenge on Rizzo for fucking your ex-wife is because of the godfather you two share. You know if you kill him the way you've been wanting to, you will not get the legacy he can offer you."

I wasn't exactly sure about how it worked in their culture, but here in Sicily, Marcu Amato had a bigger boss, who so happened to be connected to his family. He was equally close to the Rizzo family. From what I gathered, Salvatore Rizzo could never come back home and be as revered as Marcu Amato here. However, Marcu Amato murdering him would bring disgrace upon their community. The godfather was old as hell and sickly. Amato had likely been trying to wait the old man's life out.

I leaned over my knees toward him to create a posture of intimacy and spoke in his language. "Men like you, me...my father don't do well with sharing a woman we once marked as ours. She can give up on us for the bullshit we've committed and move clear across the land, declaring she's done—we're over—and mean it." My nostrils swelled from the passion of my words. My mother in mind when she tried leaving my father years ago. My Nalib in *Macen Beach* in that very moment. "We may even let her. But until we say she's fair game, she belongs to us. Her pussy, passion, and heart included." When I saw Marcu's face hardening, I offered, "I get it. Not many understand men of our convictions. But I do." I sat back. "*E anche mio padre.*"

And so does my father, for real...

It wasn't but seconds more before Marcu's arm extended toward me and our palms met. *Good!* I was ready to get this shit over with. I had to get my lady back. It couldn't happen until this war with the Rizzos was done and the man himself paid for disrespecting her.

"You're a good man, Ellis." For the first time, there wasn't an ounce of humor on Marcu's face or in his voice.

The man was teeming with murderous energy from all the talk of a woman who once belonged to him, and his revenge. I understood that, too.

"Sadik," I corrected. While I was a proud Ellis, my identity continued to draw too close to my father and brother's. "Please call me Sadik." I needed the distinction.

On my way to the gate with my staff around me, Marcu called out to me.

When I tossed a glance over my shoulder, I dipped my chin to let him know he had my attention.

"*Due settimane.*" His tone was firm. "Give me just two weeks to gather my men for the trip. You're going to assist with the discretion. Correct?"

My face opened brightly as I turned my entire body to face him. "Oh, of course. Some place only those closest to him knows he is. On Thursdays, hidden between containers inside a trailer he's made into a lounge spot. I'll make sure it's quiet on the seaport."

Marcu began to nod, swag still missing from the aura he presented with when I arrived. "*Grazie*, Sadik," his pronunciation of my name foreign. "*Grazie.*"

I turned to take off again, feeling the weight of his shoulders. I may not have known much at all about his former marriage, but I knew enough to understand the complex nature of letting a woman walk away when she still carried your heart. As I slid into the back-seat of the car, I struggled to cognize how my feelings for a woman could multiply and deepen as fast as they did with Bilan. How could I feel, without a doubt, she was the woman I wanted to join lives with? The woman I wanted to have my children and build a legacy with?

We took the winding roads back down the mountain with the gorgeous view. I closed my eyes, wondering what she was doing.

Day twenty-three...

Sick. Literally and physically, I felt ill. I didn't feel well, struggling with nausea as I left the house. But I forced myself out for fresh air. I'd been doing good at getting out of the house and around people on most days. I told myself to come to the restaurant and order a salad to nibble on for help. But just as I'd been doing in the house, I brought my laptop, copped a booth in the back, and pored over the pictures more.

Ice water now room temperature, salad untouched, *but* I'd been able to pick up several imperfections in the voluptuous diva's ensemble at the governor's ball in New Jersey last night. They weren't obvious for the first few hours. It was after careful scrutiny that I began to pick up on the smudged eyeliner, the faint deodorant track just above her armpit as she lifted an arm into the air. The expired pink lipstick I had to beg myself to believe wasn't courtesy of the man next to her.

Sadik...

He looked damned regal in a simple black tuxedo. I'd seen him quite a few times in formalwear, but no new experience was less alluring than the previous. He stood in the picture with her sporting the dimmest smile while people danced and mingled around them. His golden eyes were mesmerizing, and those full lips with a compelling cupid's bow seized my lungs each time I got caught up in them. I hated myself for still being helplessly attracted to him. The spellbinding draw to Sadik was still so potent in my blood. And I despised each weak cell of my body because of it.

Enough!

I closed the laptop and buried my face in my palms. My stomach felt so queasy, but I had no desire to eat. Seeing Tiffany unleashed an unfamiliar emotion of jealousy I should have been ashamed of. Were they together now? Had I been rescued, then forgotten about?

"Excuse me," I called out to my passing waitress.

She came to my booth right away. I gauged her to be in her mid-twenties, considering her small, yet untoned build. Her eyes were bright and caramel skin unblemished.

"Are you done?" she asked with a friendly smile, no southern accent detected.

"No." I snorted, realizing I'd been here for way too long. "I was wondering if you had a few sheets of printer paper and a pen."

She considered the request for a few seconds. "I think he has an old fax machine in the back. I'll check."

"Thanks." I tried forming a smile before going for my mother's old phone and dialing Randi.

She picked up after four long rings.

"Who the fuck is this?" She could be nasty when she wanted.

I rolled my eyes, feeling guilty on so many levels.

Clearing my throat, I muttered, "It's me. Bila—"

"Bitch!"

My eyes slammed shut and face fell. "I know."

"You know what? Because seem like everybody know shit except for me."

"I told Tasche to tell—"

"Why the fuck Tasche telling me my girl from day one is good after I don't hear from her for over a fuckin' week?"

I sucked in a heavy breath and let it go slowly. Sometimes, it helped with the nausea. Two weeks ago, I bit the bullet and called Tasche. After a string of questions and threats for making her worry, I told Tasche I decided to get away for a few weeks. It was clear to me her friend, Lex, hadn't whispered a word to her about my quandary, for which I was grateful.

Just as she asked, a few days after I arrived here at the beach house, I sent Lex a text telling her I was fine. She requested I call just so she could know it was actually me *and* that I send a picture of myself so she could see my physical condition. I acquiesced to all of her requests and made one of my own: I had to be the one to tell Tasche at my pace. Lex agreed to it before we ended our ninety-second call.

Back to Tasche... When I spoke to her and assured I was okay, I asked her if she could reach out to Randi to let her know, too. It was cowardice and irresponsible, but back then I didn't have the courage to endure Randi's questions or the stomach for her "I told you so's." So, I figured I'd let Tasche convince her, and that would be the temporary solution.

"I feel like crap," I admitted to Randi.

And for more reasons than one. I was sick—in the head! How could a manipulative, ultra-alpha murderer be the subject of my jealousy?

"Your ass should!" she continued firing off. "You back yet?"

"No."

"Where the hell you at now? When you coming home?"

I licked my lips, forehead wrinkling. "I don't know. I'm still... enjoying my...spontaneity." Those words weren't exactly planned, but sounded plausible rolling off my tongue.

"Spontan-fuckin'-what? You wanted some spice to ya life? I thought you had that with Sadik. He done moved you in and shit."

I rolled my eyes again. *This* was the energy I didn't want from her. Why did I let my emotions get ahead of me and call her against my better judgment?

"How's everything there?" One of my eyes opened and scanned the area suspiciously.

I was nervous about what she could say. I still hadn't heard about Abshir.

"Boring as fuck. It's been the boringest summer of life, yo. Ain't shit to do but stay in the house. Can't go to certain parts of town because of this stupid ass war they say your boyfriend's father is behind. Can't go to the fuckin' club or skating rink. You heard how them Italians shot up the fuckin' rink filled with Black kids? This how the fuck I know Black lives don't mean shit to people! And especially in Paterson. I hope that Julius Richards guy win. We need more Black people in power. Fuck that."

I swallowed hard. She mentioned Earl Ellis, then Italians. I'd been reading about shootouts, robberies, and murders, but never considered it to be anything unusual. Hearing this from someone at my level set off alarms in my brain. Italians as in the Rizzo man, Lia's father?

"You said Italians?"

"Yeah. Them racist muthafuckas think it's open season out here. I keep telling Ricky to lay low. They wildin' like they don't care."

My fingers began moving over the keyboard of the laptop.

"Any fuckin' way...I thought you been away with him all this time until Ricky told me he ran into him at the club."

My fingers froze and body steeled. "What club?"

"One of the clubs that chick, Tiffany, got. I ain't ask which one. Plus, you know Ricky 'on't like gossiping with me."

"Sadik was at a party?"

"No. It was during the day, I think. Ricky call hisself planning a party. Cracking me the fuck up. You know his ass don't like being out there."

"Bilan?" A masculine voice sounded. "Is that you?"

My eyes shot above my head. The last person I thought I'd see anytime soon, if ever again, was beaming down over me.

With a collapsed jaw, I murmured into the phone, "Randi, I'm going to call you back."

"Huhn? You wait three fuckin' weeks to call me, and then you got the nerve to—"

"What are you doing here?"

"Are you by yourself?" Without waiting for the answer, he sat on the bench across the table. The excitement on his face couldn't be denied. "I told you and Professor Langston I had a few small gigs down here."

I hardly recalled that mention. Seeing him felt like a lifetime ago, much less a conversation with him and Professor Langston.

Stunned, my forehead stretched and eyes blinked deeply. "You'll have to forgive me. I can't believe you're here, in this small *Macen Beach* restaurant. How long have you been down here, Jason?"

His head swung back, faux dramatically. "I told you in that same conversation I'd be leaving a week after graduation. I was on a plane a couple of days after your party."

The mention of that made my belly flutter, and I swallowed hard.

My face fell. "I'm so sorry about that thing at my party—"

"Not a thing," Jason corrected with gleam in his eyes. "Your boyfriend. He made that quite clear. It's fine, Bilan. Really." His chuckling wouldn't stop, convincing me it had really been put behind Jason.

It *had* been a while. No need to hold on to some insanely handsome and rich older man, laying his claims to a girl you'd been crushing on for years.

It didn't matter that said older man embellished on his title in my life...

But that was Sadik: brazenly possessive. *Dangerous!* For seconds long, all I could do was stare at Jason. He'd been growing his tight coils out, looked tanned. Healthy. *Safe.* I found myself questioning, similar to how I'd been with Ezra Carmichael. Why couldn't I settle for a nice, regular guy like Jason? His younger age didn't matter to me much. Why couldn't ordinary be enough?

Why was I drawn to sordid, precarious darkness instead?

My shoulders dropped and I exhaled. "You look good, Jason. The sun has colored you."

We laughed together at that.

"Really? Because I was just crying to my parents about being stuck in an office day and night. From seven in the morning until around one in the afternoon, I'm in a stale ass nursing home. Then from around two until sometimes eight, I'm in a stinking ass veterinarian office. It's insane."

His gaze jumped over my food. "How long have you been in town?"

"A little while now. Are you staying close to here?"

"Not really. I'm kind of house-sitting my uncle's friend's property down at the lower end of the beach, near the pier. I'll be down there for a few more days until this guy comes back. Then my uncle leaves for New York to see his kids off for their first few weeks of school, and I'll be at his place."

"And after?" His eventless life seemed so interesting to me in the moment.

"I don't know. That depends on if I'm done setting up the two offices or—"

The waitress returned. "Hey! I had to actually swipe these from the printer in his office." She laid a small stack of white printer paper near my laptop. "Sorry it took so long. I had to get an order out."

"Oh, thanks!" I offered her, totally forgetting about the paper.

"Or maybe my crush'll agree to letting me bunk at her place until I figure shit out." Jason sounded to be charming as I placed the paper on top of the laptop as to not soil it.

Jason's arm snaked around the waitress's waist, pulling her into him as he sat. His eyes and smile were on me. This whole scene made me anxious. Jason was groping a stranger.

I shook my head, eyes blinking heavily. "Come again?"

The waitress laughed. "Would you stop it?" She giggled. "You're weirding her out."

"You two know each other?" It finally dawned on me.

"This is Linda," Jason finally explained. "Linda, this is a good friend of mine from back home, Bilan."

She extended her palm my way. Slowly, I obliged, stunned by all that had happened over the span of four minutes.

"Hi, Linda," I murmured.

"Nice to meet you," she returned. "Man, it is a small world! You from Jersey, too?"

With a collapsed jaw, I nodded.

"We just graduated in May," Jason explained. "So now you have proof I'm no fallacy. Someone, other than my uncle, can vouch for me."

She laughed, eyes shrinking, gums bulging. "You're so crazy, man!"

"I'm serious," he continued.

"I have to check on this table. I'll be right back." Linda took off.

Jason turned fully into the booth now and exhaled. "She's a piece of work." He shook his head. "Obviously, not like you, but...I haven't exactly met a woman like you yet, Bilan."

My face folded as a warmth of familiarity blanketed me. While I was in no position of entertaining the possibility of an affair or relationship with Jason, it felt good experiencing something close to normalcy for the first time in months.

"So..." He sat back, taking a breath. "Where are you staying? You never told me what you're doing down here."

That feeling of warmth I mentioned had just turned cold in no time.

$$\infty\,5\,\infty$$

Day twenty-nine...

"This boardwalk wasn't here just a few years ago—certainly not when we were kids," Linda shared.

"No?" My brows lifted.

She shook her head. "I've only been down here for close to four years, but between what my dad has told me and what I've heard from the beach community, much of this was developed a few years ago. It's still coming along. Businesses are dying for real estate here, even if just rentals."

Jason asked, "Why don't they just put their bid in?"

I twisted around in the low beach chair, giving Linda my full attention. It was well after eight at night on the beach, yards away from the festively lit boardwalk. I was invited to hang out with Linda and Jason's friends again. They'd come out here with chairs, blankets, wine, and beer to just chill. Grateful to be out and around people instead of at the house sick or obsessing on *Google*, I was more than happy to hear stories about a beach town I'd never heard of until a few short months ago.

"Because much of the commercial property is owned by one family: a Black one. They say a couple moved down from my home state, New York. I heard from some project housing in Brooklyn. The husband won a substantial lawsuit from his employer at the time."

"And they invested it down here?" Jason summarized. "That's what's up."

"Not exactly," Linda qualified. "It wasn't enough for what they were able to do here. The wife has a brother who was heavy in the drug game. She went to him and he flipped the money. The husband and wife eventually moved down here and opened two businesses: a restaurant and strip club."

"Wow..." I breathed.

"Yup. When they came down here, there wasn't much of a board-walk. A few Blacks, but mostly whites. At the time, most people were into Myrtle Beach. But this couple got in good with the mayor and then the governor. They said that wife was something else." She chuckled.

"She has to be, to snag a man with an entrepreneurial mind like the husband," Wandra, Linda's friend, noted.

"No. That's not what I mean at all," Linda corrected as she shifted between Jason's long legs on a beach towel. "That bitch was a bad Black broker!"

A croak of laughter hurled from the back of my throat. I couldn't twist much, but when I calmed myself, I pulled the glass of beer behind me and poured a bit more out on the sand. It was something I came up with the first time I was invited out with them and didn't want to keep turning down drinks.

She continued when I turned back around, humming out a breath as to act casual.

"She was at every table her husband cut a deal. In fact, she brought the table, from what I heard. They were equal partners, and she was damn aggressive. She's the one behind the pitch to the mayor's office to commercialize the boardwalk and create events like *MB Day*."

"You going?" Jason posed the question to me.

"Oh, you have to come!" Wandra whined. "It'll be so cool."

I shrugged stupidly. "What is it?"

Wandra answered, "It's a banquet for the town. People come to network, eat, drink, and look good in their fashions." She rolled her eyes, pulling a Styrofoam cup to her lips as her regard went to the purple water.

"I've never been. Should be cool." Jason tried pushing me for an answer.

"When is it?" I yawned.

"On Sunday," Wandra answered. "I'm still debating if I'll go with Brian or Leon," she mused out loud.

My face wrinkled. "Is it like a couples' event?"

"No." Linda laughed. "A community event. From what I hear, it's been a *Macen Beach* tradition for some years now. Even after the wife died, they continued it."

"The wife died?" My eyes ballooned.

"Did the husband find a new bad ass bossy Black wife?"

"No." Linda shook her head. "They both died. Together."

I swallowed hard, not expecting that.

"Some plane crash. Right?" Wandra asked.

Linda shrugged. "Something like that."

"Damn..." Jason breathed out.

"Yup." Linda swiveled around between his legs, sporting a charming smirk. "That's us New York bitches: ride till we die."

He captured her mouth with his own for a quick kiss. By the way he sucked in her lips, though just momentarily, I could tell they'd been intimate. What tickled me was Linda was from the burbs. Huntington, a quaint, affluent section of Long Island, on the water. She moved down here after graduating from *Brown University* and having a meltdown about being a "real" adult after undergrad. She was adopted as a newborn by a Japanese father, who owned several upscale furniture stores, and a Swedish mother who was an executive at *Essence Magazine*. What did she know about being like a ride or die from a Brooklyn project? She didn't even speak like one. I didn't hold it against her. I actually liked Linda. She'd been cool to get to know these past few days.

"At least think about it," Linda advised with a smile and wink of an eye. "It's kind of a big deal around here. That's, at least, if you're going to be around for a while."

"Do you work in town?" Wandra blinked my way with a stretched forehead. "I never asked you that."

As she finished the question, an unexpected yawn pushed from my lungs. "Sorry about that. I didn't sleep too well last night," I explained honestly. "No, I don't work in town." I moved to get up.

I was ready to go. The gods of morning sickness had taken pity on me. Not only had my days of morning sickness lessened, but it consistently let up during the evenings, which was great. That was usually the time when Jason, Linda, and their friends were off of work and we'd hang out. Being with them again, tonight was no less fun. However, I was bushed.

"Awwwww!" The back of Linda's head dropped on Jason's chest. "Is it that time already? I'm not ready to be an adult," she whined.

I stood from the low bench chair, reminded by my wobbly legs how I must get back to fitness. I could use a thorough workout and good stretching in the worst way. For close to a month now, I'd been laying in a curl, enduring nausea.

"Sorry to be the first to leave the party, folks." I pointed behind me. "My bed is calling."

Jason lifted from behind Linda. "I'll drive you."

"What about me?" Linda meowed.

"I'll give you time to prepare for me. The backdoor to my uncle's place is unlocked," he shared. "Unless you want to meet at your place?"

Linda shrugged, eyes pink and glossy. "Doesn't matter. Your uncle's place, it is."

"I can walk. It's not that far." I was fine.

"Don't be silly. No way I'll let you walk again. You've done it too much already." Jason stood, shooting me a stubborn regard.

I believed he was serious. And I was tired. Bumming a ride didn't sound like a bad idea at all. I said my goodnights to the group then trekked over to the garbage can to toss my bottle of beer. As we stomped toward the boardwalk, Wandra shouted behind us.

"Hope to see you at *MB Day!*"

I laughed and waved at her.

"Shit, Bilan!" Jason breathed with his hands dramatically cupping his head. "This is some fucking bed!"

I was busy gazing over the balcony for any movements or people out. On our way to the house, I could have sworn we were followed. I didn't utter a word to Jason and didn't believe he knew. But I was almost sure. Since I'd been hanging out with them in the evenings, I'd had the sneaking suspicion of being followed.

The roaring waves dominated my senses. The moon glistened over the water. I didn't see anything out of the usual.

"Wait!" he croaked. "Why are there ropes missing from the canopy?"

My head whipped inside the master suite. Jason stood there, eyes scouring each inch of the bed. Maybe it wasn't such a good idea giving him a tour of the house. There were some things I wasn't prepared to answer, like how I came to stay in this secluded beach house and what my former fiancé did to those three missing ropes.

I moved into the suite. "Defect, I guess." I rubbed my face. "Listen, I just wanted to give you a look at the place since you've been accusing me of being reticent."

Jason's head swung toward me animatedly. "You are!"

"I'm tired and hungry. Dying to turn down."

"You? Hungry?" He scoffed. "You don't eat around me. You never eat. Even with food in front of you, you don't eat."

"I do!" I snapped. "Follow me." I ambled out of the room, knowing he'd follow.

I needed him out of the master suite. Having a man other than Sadik in there, gazing at the bed felt like an aberrant occurrence.

I led him to the kitchen and opened the refrigerator. "See! I have food. Food that needs to be cooked, too."

"You cook?" His eyes lit anew. "Wow!"

I pointed to the stove, where a pot of spaghetti I hardly touched was. Okay, so maybe I didn't eat...much. But I'd been trying since I learned the correlation between eating and nausea for me. It was a hope that my time with morning sickness was coming to an end. I read the term varied by woman.

"Maybe I can come stay with you if I'm not done with programming by the time my uncle comes back."

My eyes bulged. "I don't think so."

"Why?"

"Because I don't know how long I'll be here. The owner of this place isn't that generous."

"Are you still not going to tell me what brought you to little *Macen Beach*, Bilan?"

I took a deep breath and allowed the lie I'd been using to roll off my tongue. "After putting in years of school and working two jobs—one of which, I wasn't paid for—I decided to get off the grid. Explore a little." I swung my arm to the back of the house, where a clear view of the ocean could be seen. "What better place than the beach during the summer?"

I dropped my chin, emphasizing my impatience.

Jason chuckled dryly. "Okay. I'm going. But you're hosting our next kick back. This place is awesome!" He whistled, heading out.

As I watched him drop down the porch, concern grew in my belly.

"Jason..."

He turned to face me.

"Text me when you get in—before you get into your girlfriend." I rolled my eyes playfully.

I wanted to be sure he was okay. What if I was right about being followed? The Ellis family was conversant with violence. I didn't want Jason harmed in the event Iban Ellis had found me and wanted to finish the extinction of my immediate family.

"She's not my girlfriend, Bilan!" He laughed, continuing to his car parked out front.

Once Jason pulled off, I closed and locked the door, feeling a chill coursing my spine. Oddly, I didn't feel fear or sense danger. Couldn't be in danger if protective eyes were on you. The concoction of emotions and reasoning warring in my mind and heart was sick and exhausting. I needed to sleep.

I tighten my jacket at the chest, hiking toward the back door of the diner. With only seconds to spare, I have to move it or see that look of reprimand in Nicky's eyes for being late. I can't have him thinking I've been taking liberties now that I have my degree.

My feet stop their hike before the rest of my body catches on at the sight of the ruby black-colored Mercedes-Maybach. A small boyish body steps out of the driver's seat. Her eyes are glued to me, face expressionless.

No...

Seconds later, he stands from the car. His eyes are an uncanny orange as he gazes upon me. With those fixed irises, he's upon me in nanoseconds.

"It's not what you think."

My eyes grow wide. "No! You let me go. For over a month, you didn't come for me. Didn't worry about me!"

Slowly, his radiant eyes mirror mine in size. His jaw drops, too. "Is that what you think? That I 'let' you run? That I didn't care?"

"It's what I know. You knew my struggles with loneliness. You drop a bomb in my world and let me go!"

Sadik's head shakes, eyes remain dancing in mine. "I know it was only a few months we'd been together, but you should know me better than that, Nalib."

I charge back, "I thought I did! I knew you were dark, could sense knavery in your aura. But I didn't think an ultra-alpha would let me disappear and never care where I was."

"You should know, I knew where you were from the moment you landed in Macen Beach. There's no way I'd let you out of my reach for a moment."

I move past him toward the door. "Well, it's too bad you didn't make your presence known."

"What did you expect?" he barks, snatching my attention. My head whips to face him. "Would you have rather that you had your autonomy and chose your reaction to my ugliness, or should I have held you captive in Elliswoods Palace until you came to your senses and accepted me for all of what I am?"

That question stumps me. Have I accepted him? My brother was dead. Damien was dead. Everyone was dead, thanks to the Ellis family. How can I accept murder?

I can't help the heavy blinking of my eyes as I turn away from him murmuring, "I have to go. I have work."

"It's time for you to come back, Nalib." His soft voice is melodic, pleading.

"Back? Back where?"

"Back to me. There's nothing else for us. We're our destiny, you and me. It's time to live it out." He pushes his palm my way for offering.

The pleading in those kaleidoscopic-hued orbs pulls at something so deep within. There's a promise there, a belonging. It's something I need and have been wanting so badly. My resistance level grows low each second I'm caught in his deep gaze. The next thing I know, my palm is meeting Sadik's. I can't say no, although I know it's what I should be shouting.

As we stand, hand in hand, I hear the sound of a car door. Crawling out of the Maybach is Earl Ellis, next Iban stands, holding onto the open door. The Cheshire smile on Iban's face makes the hairs on my neck stand.

No...

Both father and son gape our way. My attention goes back to Sadik's and my joining hands, and I try snatching mine from his fierce grip. Only I can't. Sadik has a tight hold on me. I yank away at my shoulder. It causes a sharp pain in my back.

"No!" I scream. Rory's nearing us, her big, button eyes locked on me. She's coming to do Sadik's dirty work. "Please! No!" I cry, tugging my body from him. "I swear. I won't say a word. Just let me go."

Sadik smile's incongruent to my end-of-life panic. "I can't do that, Nalib.

When I gave you autonomy, you viewed it as a lack of attachment to me. You belong to me, baby." His free arm swings back toward his father and brother. *"With us. You're permanently connected to us now, sweetheart."*

"Noooooooo!" A smart pull in my abdomen had me curling over in agony.

I gazed all around in the dark room. The roaring of the ocean marked my reality and signaled safety. Out of breath and cringing, I waited out the pain. It was a nightmare. Just an illusion created by my subconscious fears. It wasn't real. Though the vividness of it all had me leap unwisely into the air.

My baby...

I rubbed my belly and unpremeditatedly began fumbling out words of prayer. At first, the words were foreign until my brain caught up and I recalled many of the words being learned from the streaming services—archived and live—I'd been hearing of Ezra Carmichael. I declared survival, health, and favor for my baby.

Oh God, please...

"In *my* house?" I asked, staggered by the information.

Rory didn't respond. Her big ass eyes fell away. My regard rolled into the night air, anger boiling in my fucking belly. This shit hadn't been easy, that was for damn sure. I couldn't be happier it was coming to an end tonight.

"Here they come," Jamil informed from the front seat.

I glanced out to the unsecured gate, where two black *Suburban*s were being allowed through. No stopping, no questions by the security at the main entrance; exactly as I arranged it. The trucks pulled around to park near my team. I left my car and we met Marcu Amato and his men off behind the utilities building, where there were small utility trucks. A few of us jumped on them; several jogged after the vehicles in the dark of the port. I murmured directions to Rory, who drove the one I was in, being careful of keeping quiet. I didn't want to alarm our target.

We drove into a yard of unused cargo containers. Some of them were damaged, many old beyond repair but hadn't been discarded due to poor yard management; others with goods that were still in limbo because of clearance issues, and all abandoned. As we traveled deeper into the lot, I could see why Salvatore Rizzo chose this to be his place of escape. When Marco, Salvatore's son, told his crew about this trailer, describing it being between three *Hanjin* containers, I had my staff pull up an old aerial surveillance map. The program was passed on to me by a former chairman of the *Board of Commissioners*. I was sure very few knew it existed. With it, I was able to locate Rizzo's trailer of leisure.

When I felt we'd driven long enough, I asked Rory and the others to stop so we could continue the rest of the way on foot. Guns were drawn, and Amato's men surrounded him as my crew did me while we journeyed. After a few turns, we'd made it to the trailer. It was rather small and unguarded. Since the port was robbed last spring, Rizzo wasn't smart enough to have security on while he retreated back here. I signaled my guys to approach the door. Amato's men fell in place to support them. But as agreed, it was my introduction to make.

Jamil opened the door, and Johnson moved in with a drawn gun. I heard a scream, then a bark from a man. Rory entered immediately after Johnson to cover him. It was my turn to stroll inside. My eyes swept over Rizzo wearing a white wife beater and socks. The woman he was with was down to her bra and jeans as she began to sob.

"Are you fucking serious, Ellis?" Rizzo began, red faced. "Who the hell do you think you are, busting up in here like this?"

"Well, well, well," I hummed, moving farther inside, though there was very little room: a seven by twenty trailer that had been decorated for minimal comfort. "Smells like mendacious pussy in here.

This is a luxury the taxpayers reward the chief of operations at *The Paterson Port?*

"Fuck you!" he shouted. "You're a dead man. This goes against all the fucking rules of *The Commission*, motherfucker." Rory leaped to grab the walkie-talkie before Rizzo's fat fingers could reach for it.

I shook my head. "You have transgressions to answer for."

"This fucking war with your father? Is it worth opening the can of worms you just did by coming into my private space? That goes against the rules."

"Nah." I shook my head, quietly chuckling. "Making them up along the way does. You owe my father an apology for fuckin' with his money, and the men of his who were lost and injured in your stupid ass war." He began to speak, but I spoke over him. "*But* before I ask for that, you owe my lady an apology for your irrevocable disrespect." I browsed around, pretending to be in search. "Obviously, she isn't here to collect, but I'll serve as her proxy." My chin dropped and fingers interlocked at my pelvis, waiting.

"The fuck for?" His expression was flabbergasted. "I don't even know the bitch you speak of. Fuck you, Sadik. Your family disgraced mine. Your brother knocking up my sweet Lia—"

"Fuckin'," I corrected.

"What?"

"My brother has been and will continue to fuck your sweet Lia until he's done with her." I cocked my head to the side. "See... In order for pregnancy to happen, fuckin' must take place. You know... Him putting his big black dick in her 'sweet' little pink cunt."

"Fuck you!" He charged off the futon, forgetting his balls were bare. "I'll kill you, motherfu—" Rizzo fell over his lover, who screamed.

"Last chance," I offered, brows hiked.

"Fuck you!"

"You're the one with your ass in the air," I jeered. "Okay." I began backing up toward the door. "Since you don't want to claim culpability in any of your wrongdoings, I'm afraid there's no need for further discussion. Let me reacquaint you with a mutual friend of ours."

One of Marcu's men stepped in first, and the blood drained from Rizzo's face. He shot from his knees and fell over backward, on his ass. The woman screamed again.

"Oh, no!" Marcu stepped inside, his eyes scraping the walls before landing on the couple. "Oh, no! Oh, no! Oh, no!" She couldn't stop screaming.

She was now trembling, teeth exposed as she did the ugly cry.

The smile spreading on Marcu's face as he examined the woman was something for the books. A scent I couldn't initially identify emanated from him. "*La mia bellissima, Vero*," he breathed.

Vero?

Why did that name ring familiar?

"No, Marcu! No!" Her head shook vehemently! "Not Salvatore! Stop it!"

"*Ti avevo avvertito che avrei finite*," he reminded her he'd warned her he'd end their affair. "*Non io?*"

"*Per favore*, Marcu!" she begged.

Marcu demanded of his men, "*Silenzio lei!*"

Two of them went for Vero and, within seconds, her mouth was duct taped, silencing much of her wails. She was placed in a chair in the corner, sounding to be hyperventilating.

"And you..." Marcu addressed Rizzo in Italian. "You thought because I've been keeping quiet, biding the time, you were untouchable. Hmmm?" He gritted his teeth. "You fat, Americanized fuck. You're worthless...spineless. And now, you will pay. And don't worry about who will learn of this." Marcu pretended to tend to his nails. "This will never reach back to Sicilia. Neither of you will live to share a word."

Salvatore's muted regard hit me with a mix of anger and fear.

But I didn't regret an ounce of what were the last minutes of his life. With a smile, my face wrinkled and I murmured, "I warned you back in May: I'm not *that* Ellis. Did I not?"

This was the moment my life, for over a month, had been on hold for. It was for the vision of *this* very position Rizzo was in that I held strong to my vision. My desire to have him addressed, and not at the hands of my father's gun. When he caused the fear in my Nalib, *this* was the moment I prepared for him. But I didn't want an Ellis pulling the trigger. We had to stop with the murders, at the very least. Damien was my first attempt, but he couldn't be spared the moment he decided to involve my Bilan. There had been a trail of bodies we removed life from that could stretch the entire damn state. It was enough of that. Our enemies had their own. With patience, we could connect them and allow them to off each other.

With a nod, I dismissed my crew. Our job here was done. As they began to file out, my eyes were on Salvatore Rizzo.

"Please! I beg of you, Sadik. Don't do this!" Rizzo pleaded. "He's not one of us. Your father would explain; he's not *Commission-*minded."

"And neither have you been, as of late." My face folded.

With a hard face and trembling lips, he choked out, "Maybe from your brother, but never you. I never thought you'd be so cruel."

I scoffed quietly before qualifying in terms I'd come to know he understood. "Better it be the educated nigger than the crazy one." My brows lifted, then I turned to Marcu.

Our palms met, sealing the deal. Quietly, I sauntered out of the door of the trailer, happy as fuck this deed had finally been completed.

Three days later, I was in my father's warehouse. At least thirty of his men were present with a drink in their hands, boisterous and lighthearted. Music played, adding to the festive air. I stood against a brick wall with a cup of something potent, staring at nothing at all.

"Fuck you standing on the wall for?" Iban laughed as he strolled my way. "We won, nigga. Another street war: we won, and that fuck, Rizzo, is dead!" His exuberance for death was unleashed.

I couldn't muster the reciprocity to reply. Was I glad the shit was over? Hell, yeah. But there was always that other piece...the not so black and white detail that didn't quite resolve the problem—at least, not all of mine.

Vero Amato was missing, and Rizzo was certainly dead. The detectives had just closed up shop of their crime scene at the *Port of Paterson*. Because the murder took place in the yard and not exactly on the docks, the investigation didn't interrupt business. However, there was a dark omen looming. The head man died on the grounds. Salvatore Rizzo employed many of his family and friends, so the morale, I'd been told, was glum. This morning, I called for and presided over a *Paterson Port Board of Commissioners* meeting, naming Abram Murphy chief of operations.

Salvatore Rizzo's second in command forfeited in the war against my father's men. Ironically, my father's lawyers conferenced him three days ago saying the audit of *Ellis Soaps* had been lifted and he could resume business two days from now. They found nothing, which wasn't surprising to me. My father had been many things, but foolish when it came to his freedom wasn't one of them.

"Come talk to this nigga," Iban encouraged my father as he approached us.

Iban took off, swaying just slightly as he did. My father stood next to me, cupless and damn near stoic compared to his underlings celebrating.

"You look like shit," he observed with his regard fixed ahead.

My mood was dreary. I was comatose. Beyond exhausted. I'd slept all of six hours in the past two and a half days. The energy tea Taaliba formulated for me had helped keep me afloat for a couple of weeks now. The problem was, I hadn't taken the one encouraging sleep in half that time. It was self-torture. I didn't want to sleep. Refused the benefits of repose, believing avoiding it would prevent me from missing the perfect idea of putting the last piece of the puzzle in place.

Bilan.

The shit with Rizzo was over. I'd once again fulfilled my father's relentless expectation of me, even at the expense of my own peace of mind. Now, I needed to get back to me. I had to put the pieces of my life back together. I needed to continue building what I had been with Bilan.

If she'll have me…

The murders at the old *B-Way Burger* were considerable. She'd never seen anything like that before. Bilan's periphery to crime around her, growing up in West Paterson, was nonexistent. She didn't see shit—although her brother stayed in it. After the planning I'd done for the demise of Salvatore Rizzo, using getting Bilan back as the end of the carrot stick, I wasn't prepared for *this* moment. The one when revelation hit: she may not be willing to resume. Spending four and a half weeks apart may not have been the wisest decision on my part.

"We have another problem."

Halfway paying attention, I murmured, "What's that?"

"I need the Lopezes handled." I turned to him, unalarmed, but undeniably astounded. He couldn't even look at me, training his eyes and expression. "Luis Lopez is about to move on two of my biggest properties in Newark and Passaic." I let out a distressed breath. "I'm ending one war to start another." He finally turned to me. "I need you, brother."

I tilted my head. "For what?"

"To take that muthafucka down. Any nigga that steal from Double E Bags is a dead man. Lopez done fucked up now."

I shook my head, unbelieving of this. My father, the man I honored, respected beyond compare had been seeing past me all this time. For years—since I was fifteen—I'd been telling him I had no interest in the drug game. When I graduated with my first degree, I explained I didn't have the appetite for a life of crime. I understood I couldn't pursue my passion in politics, but I couldn't have a relationship with law and order either.

I began my businesses, traveled, and invested in them. He'd been right there watching. But in this moment, I realized he had never respected my position. He didn't care about my decision or preferences for my personal life. He only tolerated my efforts in a legitimate industry. And I'd aided his disbelief. I'd never put my foot down. Never drew the line. I had never said no. For countless crimes of my father, I was guilty by association if not deed.

No more...

I placed the cup on an empty table next to me, then turned to him.

"This will be my last time in this warehouse."

"What?" His head jolted back.

"This is my last time coming to your place of business. Any dealings you have with me moving forward must be conducted outside of here. I can no longer be your personal assassin, highbrow, or ringmaster. I am my own man—"

"You sayin' I 'on't know that shit?"

"I'm saying I've been stretched." I measured my tone. "I've had to run three enterprises and be your think tank so you and Iban can stop killing people. I can't tell you the last time I enjoyed a meal. I'm fuckin' beyond fatigued, sir. Haven't had a taste of pussy in over a month." My eyes narrowed. "Respectfully... You hustle like that for your own empire?"

"Hustle?" he scoffed. "Brother, I been at this since before you were a result of my nut sac. I hustle every damn day for the next day. I been fighting for your fuckin' future since I was a kid myself! All I ask is that you respect my sacrifices over the years. I'm getting old. The future is damn near here. And guess what? I'm still fighting! For you, son."

After a hard glare down, I offered, "Enjoy the festivities, sir. I'll be off the grid for a couple of weeks." I turned and sauntered off.

Fuck that. I had to fight for my own damn future.

∞ **6** ∞

"I don't know... I just don't know." Linda shook her head, clearly overwhelmed with emotions. She swallowed hard, eyes plastered to the cloth table top.

"You should just be frank with him," Wandra advised frankly. "He owes you that," she murmured.

There were four of us at the cocktail table. As I pretended to enjoy the glass of white wine in my hand, I turned smoothly to peer behind me. The conversation was one I hadn't been prepared to have. At least, not at this "popular" town event they practically begged me to attend tonight. The *MB Day* banquet wasn't so bad. The room was nicely lit and entertained by a live band. The event was at a restaurant on the water. Blue suede walls, wooden floors, and velvet and leather furniture gave the party a mellow vibe.

The place was almost packed. I could tell this wasn't an event open to the general public. There was a culture to the atmosphere.

The guests knew each other. Business owners were informed about their peers' enterprises. There was minimal pretentiousness, but this was definitely a closed affair.

I arrived over an hour ago with Jason. He picked me up. Linda, Wandra, Brian, Rocita, and Rico were waiting. This was their usual crew; the people I'd been hanging out with for almost a week now, even planned on spending Labor Day with them. Wandra and Brian dated. Rocita and Rico messed around. And now, Linda was confirming she wanted to upgrade from bed buddies to official couple with Jason.

And Jason?

Well... He was being Jason, flirting with me and every other girl not nailed down to a visible guy. As I listened to Linda's whispers of woes behind me, I considered her plight. She had apparently fallen for a guy who hadn't shared the same feelings for her. I couldn't understand how she didn't know. I'd been around them this short time and I knew. Oh, I knew!

It was clear to me a few days ago when the "party" was at "my" place. The usual crew came through, drank, ate, and laughed their asses off to sleep at three in the morning. I crept upstairs to my bed. Just as I'd gotten comfortable in the sheets, I had an uninvited guest. Jason. The sight of him had me jumping out of bed. I thought he'd crashed with everyone else. Linda had fallen asleep on top of him. I was wrong. He tried to shoot his shot, but I declined, making it clear there was no way I'd betray Linda that way. He didn't fight with me much, but did ask to use my bathroom, claiming to have a full bladder from all the beer he drank.

That...

That was a disaster. *That* was when he learned about my pregnancy. I'd stupidly left out the four tests I'd taken the morning of the nightmare I'd had about Sadik confronting me at a job I no longer had. My paranoia about the stretch I felt in my abdomen had me flying to the store for proof of my baby still being alive. It was ridiculous, I knew. Jason asked for answers, to which I declined. I asked him to leave my bedroom, and he did. When he was gone, I tossed out each test—*and each one I'd taken since that day.*

Things had been awkward between us since then. Even on the ride here, he'd been quiet, until we turned into the parking lot and he blurted he'd help me raise the baby if I'd just give him a chance. The poor guy had no idea of my circumstances. He begged for details of my life I couldn't give. And the less he knew, the better off he'd be.

Now, combing the room for him, I hoped he was okay. The last I saw Jason, he was on his fourth drink. Hearing Linda bemoan him made this event not so festive.

"You've known him longer than anyone," Wandra spoke loud enough to have me returning to the conversation. Everyone's regard was on me expectantly. "What do you think? Is he a playa-playa?"

I smiled, caught off guard. "I really don't know. Jason's a nice guy. He's still young, you know? Maybe he's still figuring things out."

"Like you've been doing down here?" Linda asked with suddenly alert eyes. "That's what he told me, at least."

"Ummmm..." I rubbed my lips together. The lipglass must have dulled on them. "I guess." My face folded. "I'm a few years older than him—"

"And me," Linda provided. "You're older than all of us."

"Are you?" Rocita asked. "I'd been wondering all this time. Linda told me not to ask."

Linda's eyes ballooned. "Because Jason told me she was private," she replied defensively.

"See! So, you two *do* know each other well," Wandra argued. "Told you, Lin!"

My face dropped. "You guys talk about me behind my back? Wow..."

"It's just that you popped up out of nowhere," Linda grumbled. "You're the only person who knows my boyfriend, outside of his uncle."

"I think you were establishing he wasn't your boyfriend," I annunciated slowly.

"Well..." Linda swiped her hand in the air. "You know what I mean."

"I don't."

"You never said how you ended up here, and Jason couldn't give me anything about you that made sense. It's no big deal."

"It's no big deal?" I chuckled.

"Not really. *Macen Beach* is pretty exclusive at this point. No one just blows into town. Look at Jason: he has a relative down here while he's working two jobs. He still can't afford a rental."

"Okay?" I swung my neck, wanting her to finally make sense.

This was high school'ish.

"Okay!" she whispered harshly, as though not wanting to draw attention to our table. "So, I followed you home a few nights after meeting you. When I saw you were staying at the offset beach house on the south end, I searched the owners and saw you were listed."

"And?" I was now angry.

"And that's it." She rolled her eyes, but not in a rude manner; in an embarrassed one.

I caught the sheepish, salacious hybrid expressions on her friends' faces and felt somewhat betrayed. Not in the sense of them owing me loyalty, but in that of there was more to this story. There was no way she looked up the house and saw I was the *only* name on the deed. I'd seen the paperwork. I knew who was listed there. One *Google* click of the Ellis name revealed more grist to the rumor mill than the average girl—like me—could handle. I knew because I'd been obsessively doing just that since purchasing the cheap laptop a few weeks ago. Linda told her friends more than what she'd just admitted to me. This was messed up. I thought hanging out with them was a great distraction while I got my mind together. But between this and Jason's unrelenting crush on me, clearly I was wrong.

Pushing my lips out, I took a deep breath, making a split-second decision. The girls' gapes bounced between Linda and me. She couldn't look me in the face. I left the table without a destination in mind. As I moved away from them, I figured the bathroom was a good place to think. Once I made it to the door, my bladder made demands. Annoyed even more, I went on ahead to relieve myself. After washing my hands, I decided to leave. I'd call a cab.

"Excuse me..." I motioned for the bartender stocking glasses behind the bar. "Can I use the phone to call a cab?"

I realized on the way here I'd left both phones on the bed when Jason blew the horn announcing his arrival.

"Yes, ma'am," the bartender replied. "I can actually call for you."

I nodded, agreeing and thanking him at the same time.

My thoughts immediately drifted to me sitting out on the beach when I got back to the house. I'd map out my plan to leave town. It was time for me to go home. It was something I'd been thinking about while the morning sickness had been subsiding. I'd get access to my bank account, where I had a few dollars to get an apartment. Grad school was set to begin in just a few days. I couldn't keep stowed away down here. I had a life to live.

I bowed my head, taking a deep breath with my elbows resting on the bar top. So much had happened in my life in the past six months. Things I submitted to and made adjustments for. I needed to respond to my circumstances. Mold them for my suiting; reject them if necessary. I needed my life back.

The infinitesimal hairs on the back of my neck stood straight; a stroke to the nerves in my spine had me shiver. My lungs shuddered, eyelids collapsed, head swayed over my neck. Breathlessly, I counted to five before turning to peer over my shoulder. I should have been frightened by what I saw. I should have run. Shouted for my life. But instead, I welcomed the allure of the kaleidoscope-hued irises beaming onto me with fixed intent.

He stood against a wall, an arm resting on the ledge, and one leg propped in front of the other as his foot sat on its toes, crossed over the other. The air between us motionless. I couldn't feel, couldn't breathe, couldn't sense the energy around me. Everyone mingled around us, between us as my murderous, fine as sin fiancé devoured me with his eyes.

He pushed against the wall and began a purposeful gait my way. That's when I tried to move my tongue, but it was too heavy to lift. My neck was too stiff to turn away.

When he arrived next to me, Sadik casually leaned against the bar. His irises ran across my head and shoulders. He didn't speak right away. His hand lifted to my head, where I felt him pull strands of my hair. Immediately, I felt self-conscious. I'd gone to a barber a couple of times, but the maintenance of my pixie cut was on me. I wasn't skilled at doing hair, but did my best to not look crazy while holed up in a southern beach house, afraid for my life.

I sucked in my bottom lip as my pulse banged in my neck.

"It's been a while," he murmured so softly, wafting a gentle scent of peppermint and jasmine. An innocuous beam opened on his face, as though these past four weeks hadn't happened. As though the reset button had just been applied to our lives. "Is this something new?" He referred to my dress.

It was a clearance item on a rack at a *Marshalls* in the next town over. I thought it was the perfect steal. Did he not approve? Of course, Sadik didn't approve. He was extremely particular about my clothes.

The musk of his cologne had my eyelids collapsing. The audacity of his aura had my resolve strengthening. I peered into his eyes that were closer, I could see the stormy orange hue of them.

I grated through clenched teeth, "What are you doing here?"

His smile widened. "Coming to pick up my fiancée and take her home."

"You have no idea where my home is." Neither did I. "I'm not your responsibility." His index finger stroked my cheek as his gaze locked onto me, adoring. I hated the confusion it stirred in my heart. "You've got some nerve coming here."

"Why, Bilan?"

"Because I'm not going anywhere with you," I hissed.

A few knocks on the wooden surface captured both our attentions. It was the bartender.

"Someone should be here in five minutes," he advised quickly and continued with his work.

"Where were you going?" Sadik asked.

"It's none of your business." I twisted to leave the bar.

As I swept through the room, I could see the girls at the table. Wandra peered up first; her eyes widened and shifted behind me. She tapped Linda next to her. That's when I knew Sadik was on my heels. I kept my pace all the way to the lobby.

"Bilan, please don't run," I heard him call after me.

I ignored him, continuing to the entrance. He couldn't do this. What was he thinking?

"Bilan?" I heard barked.

It stopped me in my tracks. Jason was nearing me from the far end of the lobby. As he approached, his steps grew noticeably shorter. Even inebriated, I registered concern on his face.

"Ask him to leave," Sadik commanded softly in my ear, the deceiving jasmine and peppermint aroma deluding me momentarily.

I leaped around to him, suddenly reminded of his dangerous pedigree. Seeing Jason all the way down in South Carolina could be equivocal to a distrusting mind.

"Don't you dare!"

Sadik's unruly brows met. "Dare what?"

"Don't you threaten or harm him." I kept my tone as low, as he did.

Thankfully, Sadik was being discreet. My heart galloped at the possibilities.

"You okay, Bilan?"

I turned to Jason. "Yes. I'm fine. Go ahead back up to the party. Linda's looking for you."

"And where do you think you're going?" he asked, I knew encouraged by the alcohol raging in his blood.

"With her fiancé," Sadik answered *unequivocally*.

"Fiancé?" Jason spat, as though confused.

In that very moment, a small ephebic body approached behind Jason. Her big eyes were narrowed and locked onto him, her hands in the pants of her boyish suit.

Visions of Rory with the gun behind Damien's collapsed body flashed in my mind.

"No!" I yelped. My body turned fully to face Sadik behind me. "No! Don't you dare!"

"The only reason I won't address him is because he left my

bedroom a few nights ago when you turned him down for ass." His words poured slow and emphatically. "Now, ask him to leave."

Our eyes bounced against each other, the energy now static. His expression was marked by a quiet threat. Sadik wasn't compromising. The threat loomed over me. His brows lifted, and a heap of air flushed from my lungs.

My body rolled back toward Jason. "I'll stop by your job before lunch time. I think you should go check in on Linda."

Jason was seething, face tight. And I couldn't come up with words to help paint this picture for him. He could possibly lose his life if he made the wrong decision. *I* could lose my life if I didn't play this thing right.

Sadik took me at the small of my back. "It's time to go."

I shifted with apologetic eyes to go.

"I know who you are," Jason informed Sadik. "I know all about your father and brother. I know it all!"

Sadik shifted me ahead of him, toward the revolving doors. He then leaned into Jason and calmly murmured, "Good. Then you understand the grace I'm offering you here."

With a wink, Sadik stepped off, hand now possessively at my hip. We sauntered out of the restaurant without another word from Jason. My sights were immediately met with a black *Mercedes* sprinter. The presence of any automobile resembling a van brought on revolting anxiety. There was a small *Volkswagen Beetle* waiting aside the sprinter, likely my taxi.

I leaped around to him. "I'm not going anywhere with you." I was sure to control my volume.

"You don't have much of a choice."

"How do you figure?" I glanced back at a skulking Rory, who couldn't look at me. "Are you going to abduct me in full daylight while in public?"

His head shook softly as he peered so deeply into me. "No, Bilan. I won't abduct you."

"Then what are we doing here?"

"I'm here to present your options."

"What options, Sadik?" I yelled, losing my patience.

"If you'll just get into the sprinter, I'll tell you."

"Tell me now."

"You're trying my patience, Bilan. I won't discuss anything with you out here." He gave me a pointed stare. "If you decide you want to go back to the beach house after I share some information with you, I'll take you there. No questions asked."

Tapping my foot with crossed arms, I angrily considered his offering for a moment. Then I took off for the sprinter. Rory opened the door and I stepped inside with ginger movements. Sadik followed right behind me. Before he could get settled in, the sprinter took off.

"I'm not going with you. You're a murderer! Your whole family is." I swung my arm to the front seat. "She is, too! All of you are murderers! You, your family...you've killed everyone. Damien told me everything. He said your father would kill them all because of the robbery." My voice cracked. "Your father killed my brother." Depleted that quickly, my lungs gave out on me.

When I thought he'd respond with verbal threats, Sadik pulled out a phone. He dialed a number to *FaceTime*.

Within seconds, someone answered. "Mr. Ellis?"

"Yes, Nurse Gladney," he replied. "Mr. Asad-Yasin, please."

My heart thundered, belly leaped at the sound of that name. Strangely, it brought my father to mind. He pushed his phone into my peripheral. Before I could expound on it further, I watched the screen travel toward a bed. Before I knew it, a body came into view. A man. Abshir's beard is what I noticed first. His face was covered in hair, but I recognized his eyebrows. They were our mother's. His skin tone, then his resting facial features were clear to me.

He had a tube running from his mouth and beeping machines around him as he slept. My gaze shot over to Sadik glowering my way, golden eyes blazing.

"Is he..." I croaked.

He pulled the phone back and straightened in his seat. "Thanks, Nurse Gladney. Please remember his sister will be there tonight for a brief visit. Thanks for allowing her that."

"You're welcome, Mr. Ellis. I'll let the staff know."

The call ended. All I could do was gape motionlessly at Sadik, who kept his regard forward as he adjusted his jacket in his seat.

"Your things have been packed. The thirteen thousand, sixty dollars of unused money has been returned to the hiding space in our home. The house has been locked up for the season. A cleaning service has been scheduled to scrub the place clean of every finger-print that muthafucka has left in there since the first time you okayed their bum ass party." My spine trembled at the palpable disdain of the words he spoke.

"We didn't do anything," I tried, voice quaking.

"You let a kid who wants to fuck you into my home. That shit was out of line."

"With his girlfriend."

He finally turned to me. "Who ain't his girlfriend if he's trying his hand with you while she's in the same fuckin' space!"

Abshir's alive...

I turned away, focusing on that miracle instead of fighting with him.

"How is he alive?" I asked. I'd seen him shot and lying in a pool of his blood.

"Because I acted quickly."

My head whipped to face him. "How did you know?" Sadik's eyes darkened as he gaped my way. He wouldn't answer a question that would incriminate him, clearly. I sniffled. "He's been alive all this time."

"They're not so sure about his outlook," Sadik murmured. "This is why I didn't have the patience to fight with you."

It was why he came when he did. I wondered if Abshir had died at the house, would I be seeing Sadik now? I didn't care to ask. Neither did I care to thank him.

I decided to ride in silence, so many running thoughts to resolve. As I gazed blindly out of the window, I eventually realized we were pulling into the same small, private airport I recalled from my first trip down here with him. This was it. It was really happening. I was returning home—

I turned to him again, swiping an errant tear from my cheek. "Where am I staying when I get back to Jersey?"

I could bunk with Tasche for a few days until I got myself together.

"The same place you stayed before this shit storm unraveled. No negotiations."

With a gaping mouth, my eyes rolled behind closed lids. The guy driving, who didn't look familiar to me at all, stopped on the tarmac. Everyone filed out. Sadik stood outside the door to assist me. I ignored his hand, wrapping my arms around my belly once out of the sprinter.

Rory and the driver stood, waiting for their boss to move. Feeling an uncanny surge of anger from having no option in the matter, I turned to the man I once adored, my index finger pointed toward his face.

"I'm not in love with you. I know you told me you fell in love with me, but I haven't with you. The only reason I'm coming is because I don't have an option." I pointed in his face again. "You're just as unstable as your brother. You bulldozed your way into my life without my permission. And *maybe* for some God-unknown reason I've claimed your heart, but you've not claimed mine. You may be in charge moving forward, but my heart belongs to me. And I give it away at my will. It's not for you to take, trample over, or hijack."

Sadik turned and walked away. His vicious team of killers followed suit.

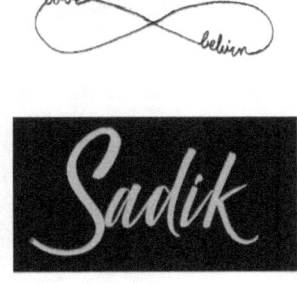

I had to walk away. My dick grew rock hard at her bold rejection. I believed every word of what she said about our feelings for each other being lopsided. More than that, I was turned on by her assertiveness. It demonstrated her maturity and accentuated her brazenness. She also expressed her true feelings without some type of juvenile action like she did when admitting I was the first to provide her an orgasm.

We all eventually boarded the plane. Bilan moved briskly past me as I spoke to the pilot. When I was done, I paid a few words to Jamil about his time off, starting tonight. It had been a long few months, and he deserved a break. *I* needed it.

"Mr. Ellis, can I get you something before we taxi?" Mel asked.

I scratched the back of my head, feeling the miniscule growth of my scalp. That's how stressful this reunion with my fiancée had been.

Letting out a deep breath, I answered. "Tea. Call my sister and have her drop off more nighttime tea to the lobby of my apartment building. My housekeeper will retrieve it from there."

The flight would be short, but the night would be long. I needed the aid.

"Sure thing. *Mauve* in the meantime?"

I nodded and Mel turned on her heel for the back of the plane. It was the direction I was headed to. When I got to the middle section, Bilan was typing into one of her phones awaiting her on the jet. She wouldn't look up, and I decided not to further rattle her. Continuing down the walkway, I settled into the bedroom.

The moment the jet landed, we headed straight to the hospital. It was a small, private hybrid care facility with acute readiness and chronic capacity. Nurse Gladney was his primary caregiver, a trauma nurse. Waiting on us in the lobby, she instructed Bilan and me to follow her. The place was virtually empty, quiet at the late hour.

"You only have thirty minutes with Mr. Asad-Yasin," she reiterated. "because it's well after visiting hours. Of course, we're making an exception because of Mr. Ellis' request."

I trailed behind Bilan, who appeared tense from head to toe. *Tense and desperate*. She was markedly quiet the entire ride up to the second floor and down the sterile hall, until we stopped at the end unit. As we approached, Ab's resting body could be seen from the window next to the door.

Nurse Gladney opened the door, and Bilan timidly promenaded inside first. I remained behind her. For long seconds, she didn't utter a word. Bilan gaped his way, unblinking. Her hands below her belly, fingers attacking one another. Eventually, my regard reached back for the nurse. She motioned she would step out. I quickly decided I should do the same. Bilan deserved time with her brother alone.

Just outside of the room was a large observation window. Beneath were seats where I sat, taking a deep breath. There was a strange concoction of emotions competing in my mind and chest. I focused on the plan. Bilan was home. I could finally breathe.

A phone vibrated in my suit jacket pocket. It was Iban. My gut told me not to answer. I'd put myself on a vacation from all drama, at least that was my plan. But pausing my family had never been an option.

"Yeah."

"What it do?" his voice conspicuously low. "Where you at?"

I glanced behind me, seeing Bilan was now at the foot of her brother's bed, clutching his feet. There was no way I'd share where I was, because sharing that would require revealing the Ab kid was still alive—even if he was in poor shape. My father asked about Abshir a few days ago, wondering why he hadn't heard about a funeral. How that would play out depended largely on the kid's survival. Either way, I had big shit to sort: his sister.

"With my lady and her family. What's going on?"

"You think you could break away, bruh?" there was a slight croak in his voice.

"What's going on?" I asked again.

"I'm..." He took a deep breath. "I'm starting to feel the shits again."

My lids stretched.

Anxiety…

"What's got you stressed?"

"Man," he whined. "Shit with Lia and the baby…"

"What shit?"

"She tripping, tryna keep me from coming to see the baby, and shit."

I rubbed the top of my head. "Why?"

"She think she ain't getting no support on her pops' passing, and shit. She said I ain't over there enough. She 'on't think Mommy doing enough, even though her and Taaliba was over there last week, bringing a whole bunch of toys, clothes, and shit. But that don't count now?"

Rizzo's death…

Lia was asking for the support of a boyfriend or husband, forgetting the rules of infidelity. Iban was neither to her, though he provided her with the benefits of one.

"She want me at her side for the funeral, and shit. Yo, you know how wild that'd be? How fuckin' disrespectful? I ain't going nowhere near there. No goddamn way! I told her to let me come by her place, but she swear she and the baby been at her mom's crib since the murder. I ain't going over there. And now she saying she won't make a special accommodation for me. Fuck outta here!"

There was no way I could explain how Iban had made this shit complicated by fucking with Lia in the first place. What was fucked up was I believed he was really in love with her. That wasn't a question I could ask my brother. The answer would vary depending on his mood, and either one could be a lie. Judging by their interaction over this year alone, I could deduce Iban had strong feelings for the girl. Those feelings, however, didn't supersede his commitment to his wife.

"And Monica trippin' the fuck out, too, bruh-bruh. She been actin' so fuckin' cold lately. It's like it's been just about her and the girls. She said she don't wanna see the baby! The fuck? Even Mommy done seen the baby a few times!"

My lids closed again; strain from behind my eyes was ascending to my scalp.

I murmured into the phone, "Are you taking your medication?"

"I hate the way them shits make me feel."

"It'll give your mind a break."

"I don't need a fuckin' break, bruh! I need for this shit to work out."

"Monica's pregnant." I swung my hand out, shrugging, though he couldn't see me. "She needs consideration, Ib."

"I know! Shit. Don't you think I know? But the baby is innocent."

"Your ongoing relationship with her mother isn't. You're asking for a lot."

"I just need Monica, Lia, and Mommy to work together so I can deal with this Dominicana thing."

That drew my antenna. Dominicana was the Lopezes.

"Gotta throw them thangs with them," Iban shared.

War...

I dropped my face into my hands. Another street war.

Fuck...

"Big bruh, you don't have the capacity to take that on," I tried.

"The what?"

Shaking my head, more at myself, I went a different route. "You have too much on your plate, on the home front. You just had a baby girl. Monica should be into her third trimester now. You've got too much shit going on."

"It's what I do, Deek."

There was a long pause. I hated his truth. Hated he perpetuated something so unnecessary. Iban was a fucking terror on the surface, but deep inside, he was a human being suffering. One who wanted to be loved and understood. But what he was being used as, unwittingly by our father, was a hood legend, monster.

"Look...." he pulled in a breath. "If you ain't 'bout to come out with a nigga, I'll holla at you later. I need to get into something before I lose my fuckin' mind."

When I thought to ask what that meant so I could talk him off the ledge, I peeked over my shoulder again, seeing Bilan in the same position over her brother, and thought twice.

"Hit me in the morning. I'll be in all day."

"Yeah." He sounded defeated.

"Love you, bruh."

"Luh you."

The call was disconnected and I went to check my email. I worked hard to stay on top of them. I had a conference call with a new public relations candidate. My lawyers advised me to seek out services before this lawsuit with Rachel grew any messier. I had my assistant to set it so it could happen from my home. In fact, lots of my schedule had to be modified now.

At some point, the muscles around my eyes felt too strained. It had been close to thirty minutes since getting lost in work. I put the phones away and sat back, my fingers pinching between the eyes until I heard the door open. My torso swung up, head whipped toward the door of the hospital room.

Bilan stepped out appearing comatose. Spooked. Categorically jolted. I stood right away, unreasonably furious at her state. She was hurting, and there wasn't a damn thing I could do about it. For over a month, I tried preparing myself for this, too. And in the moment, I felt powerless. Smaller than the occasion. I was afraid to approach her because doing that would have involved me touching her. Holding her.

I braced myself, taking a deep breath.

"How long has he been here?" her voice was but a whisper as she gazed ahead.

I swallowed hard before answering. "When you took off from the warehouse, the first place I thought to look for you was at your parents' house. That's when I found him and made a few calls."

She still couldn't look at me when she asked, "Why isn't he in St. Joe's?" Her voice so stoic.

"Because they would have asked more questions and notified the police sooner than we knew his condition."

"He's hooked up to a lot in there. This place is small, but advanced." Her puffy eyes were on me, turning my mood violent for her pain. But who would I take it out on? "Why did you keep him alive?"

"Because I knew losing him while running from me would destroy you." I scraped my bottom lip against my teeth, uncharacteristically shrinking in confidence. "I thought trying to keep him alive would be best for you."

Her eyes rolled to the back of her head before closing. "I don't feel so good."

In two lunges, I was on her. Bilan didn't reject my aid.

I unlocked the apartment door, pushing it open. Before I could step aside to let her enter first, Bilan shot past me, dry heaving into her hand. She ran all the way to the powder room. On my way there, I heard her forceful hurl. When I made it to her, she was over the toilet, spitting up rounds of liquid. On my approach, she held out a palm to create a distance between us.

I froze fucking helplessly.

"Can I get you something?"

Bilan didn't answer. She upchucked another round, then another before wiping her mouth down with toilet tissue. When she struggled to her feet, I leaped for her again.

"No!" she made clear.

I stilled again. Slowly, she made it to her feet, eyes half opened, mouth slack. She took two steps before falling into the wall.

"Listen, I know I was coarse earlier. I know I'm the last person you want to see right now." I took a cautious step toward her, wondering if this was how vulnerably emotional my brother felt between his wife and mistress. "But please, baby, let me help you. Anything. Just tell me what to do."

Bilan's eyes were closed and she was panting when she whispered, "I just need a shower and the bed."

When I turned the knob to quiet the jets and opened the shower door, never in a billion years did I think I'd accept an open towel from Sadik. I had no idea he was even in the bathroom. Yet, there he was, standing in trouser socks, suit pants, and a dress shirt with the first few buttons undone, the sleeves rolled up his hairy arms.

Hesitantly, I stepped out. That's all I had to do. Sadik walked into me, wrapping a massive towel around my frame. He wiped my body down as much as he could without making the act sensual, his movements too fast for that. But the act itself was intimate. As much as I wanted to scream for him to stay away from me, my brain felt cut off in so many ways. There were the simple functions I could conceive and act on, but my emotions wasn't one.

I moved to the sink to wash the taste of vomit from my mouth. While brushing my teeth in a zombie-like fashion, he appeared behind me with a smaller towel, rubbing my wet hair strands, then wrapping them. Sadik left the bathroom right after. When I was done, I couldn't feel my feet as I moved to the two-level, walk-in closet. My assigned drawers were still filled with clothing purchased for me, some I'd brought over from my parents' home.

Oh, God. The house…

I didn't have the faculty to think about that right now. I found an old pajama shirt my mother bought me in high school and slipped it on. The towel remained tied around my head. I didn't have the strength to address my hair either.

When I made it out into the master suite, Sadik was just laying a tray of tea and something smelling sweet next to the bed. I stopped. He stood straight, wiping his hands down his thighs. He gaped at me for a moment, feline eyes an animated green.

He pointed toward the tray. "I had Kimmy bake some bread for tonight. She made tea, too." There was an abbreviated pause before he murmured, "I'm going to take my tea in my office. Let me know if you need anything."

I didn't respond to him, my face impassive, feelings so numb in the moment. This didn't feel real. I wasn't back in Jersey. This wasn't Sadik's stately posture before me. There were no ocean cries beyond the walls of this great bedroom. No. Only a congested Route 22 beyond a small field of trees. *But...* My brother was alive. How much longer? I didn't know. But for now, I needed to sleep.

Sadik drew in a deep breath, then ambled around the bed and out of the room. He closed the French doors behind him, messaging privacy. Slowly, I walked over to the side of the bed I used to claim. I sat behind the tray table, wafting in the baked goods. Sadik didn't mention it was banana bread. There were several slices nicely arranged on a plate. A small cup of soft butter and a knife were there, too. The tea smelled amazing. Fragrant.

Of course, my stomach rumbled. Of course, I was reminded of the life inside me. I couldn't deny myself food now. Couldn't ignore the obvious. I was depleted. So with heavy arms, I reached onto the tray and began to eat. I poured tea, squeezing lemon slices in the cup. After three slices and nearly two cups of warm, flowery tea, I lay back on the bed. The last thing I recalled was thinking I needed to call my friends to tell them I was back.

His scent hit me before I could open my eyes, and the distinctive sounds of snoring were what had me turning over to find Sadik lying next to me on his stomach, lost to slumber. His lips were slightly parted, and curled lashes met. He was sleeping hard. Although he'd done it once or twice before, it was a strange concept for me, seeing the sun was up.

And me...

I rubbed my eyes, realizing how hard I'd slept last night. It was the first full night's rest I'd gotten since... Perhaps since leaving for *Macen Beach*. I wasn't groggy, but did feel as though I'd just come out of a blackened hole for inducing sleep. Though still tired, I felt rested.

I groaned internally. My bladder felt about to explode. I turned for my side of the bed and paused. It was visceral. Just four weeks ago, I wasn't allowed to leave this bed without his permission. Was I trained, even after all this time? Deciding not to dwell on it, I toed out of the bed and into the bathroom. I had things to do today.

The most important is to see about Abshir...

After a quick shower, washing my face, and brushing my teeth, I toed out into the closet. Sadik still appeared deeply asleep, which was good. I threw on a sweat suit and one of his *Balenciaga* hats. Then I packed a pocket book, making sure to have my keys and cell phone with me. When I crept out of the suite, Sadik had still been resting like a giant captor. Quietly, I moved down the hall until I reached the cabinet above the console table where he hung his keys. The space he earmarked as mine was empty. That made me think.

My eyes fell to the purse hanging from my shoulder. I'd had my keys to the *Range Rover* all this time since abandoning it in downtown Paterson. I wondered if it was downstairs. There was only one way to find out. I peered behind myself before taking off to the door.

Down in the garage, Sadik had several parking spaces assigned to him. In fact, he had his own section. The truck shouldn't have been hard to find. As soon as I walked into his section, I smelled cigarette smoke. It was strange, slowing my pace. I could see the roof of the truck almost right away, soaring my mood. But as I ambled around to the driver's side, a small adolescent frame rounded the hood of the vehicle, eyes shrunken as she took a long pull of a cigarette.

My heart exploded before I recognized Rory.

With my palm to my chest, I panted, "You scared the living daylights out of me!"

She pulled the stick from her mouth and delayed her smoke exhalation, swaying in her boots. "I been down here for a couple'a hours, waiting on you. I see both y'all asses slept in. Must be nice."

I hardly registered much of what she said when I leaned over slightly. "Were you waiting for me?"

"Yeah. You got somewhere to go. Don't you?"

"Yeah, but—"

The truck chirped, headlights and interior lit up.

"Let's do this then."

"You don't have to chauffeur me around, Rory. I'm capable of taking myself."

She switched weight on her hips, dropping her head to the side. "We saw how that worked out for the big homie last month." She shook her head. "Ain't no way I'mma be at the other end of the gun for that shit this time."

My eyes ballooned and suddenly, I felt sick at that reference.

"Oh, shit," she breathed. "Bilan, you gotta loosen up. I ain't mean it that way. He only fired the nigga. He still working; just not with Deek."

Swallowing a billion times, trying to recover from that thought, I pleaded, "Can you just tell him I declined your help for the day?"

Rory croaked a laugh, then mocked me. "Can you just tell him I *declined* your help *for* the day?" She took another pull from her cigarette and chuckled while blowing out the smoke. "It don't work that way, sweetheart. My checks get signed by one man. That pain in the ass nigga is upstairs resting, and already gave me my marching orders for the day. He told me he don't wanna be bothered, too. You know what being bothered to S.Q.E. mean?" I didn't answer because I knew she would. "It mean Bilan gotta be perfectly safe and not high tailing it the fuck outta Jersey. So let's fuckin' go."

She moved for the driver's seat.

"The last time I saw you, you were prepared to kill a man!"

She turned around, then made a show of discarding her cigarette on the ground and smashing it with her boot.

"You saw some killed, if you didn't do the deeds yourself," I continued.

"Bilan, you scared of me?" She swung her head. "You feel in danger...threatened by me right now?"

My forehead wrinkled, chin lifted into the air defiantly. "No."

"Then get ya ass in the fuckin' truck, and let's go where you need to go!" She turned for the truck again.

My mouth moved wordlessly at first. Between her boyish frame —not a single curve in sight—and her palpable respect for Sadik, I was baffled. She *had* been complicit in murder in some way. But she was right; I didn't feel threatened by Rory. This morning, she was the same irascible, eccentric-looking bodyguard/personal assistant she'd been when I met her earlier this year.

"I don't need a chauffeur to get back to the hospital. I'm going to see my brother. What escape will be happening with him in this condition?"

She'd disappeared behind the truck at this point. "I 'on't know and ain't gone stress it..." Then she appeared in the doorway of the driver's seat, standing on the step. "because I'm taking you."

Rory slid into the truck, adjusted the seat, and kindled the engine. I sucked in a heap of air as it dawned on me I was back in "*Ellisland,*" where there was a set of rules no one broke. I needed a way to assert my own agenda and will. A way to put my foot down *and* survive their tyranny. But for now, I had a brother fighting for his life. I didn't have it in me to ask questions last night; I was so over-whelmed at the fact of his existence. When I last saw him, I ran when I thought he was dead. That decision would haunt me for the rest of my life. Today, I would get answers. Today, I would saturate his sleeping body with my hopeful energy.

I ambled to the back door and stepped inside the truck.

The first thing I did when we pulled out of the garage was send out texts to Randi, Tasche, and Jason. I told the girls I was back in town, and Jason how I'd decided last night I would end my vacation and return home. Jason's text came through first, which made sense given he was a 9-5 man.

Jason: *just please tell me everything's okay. tell me that fucker didn't try to hurt you! i'll call the police!*

I rolled my eyes, gaze randomly going to the front seat where Rory's little arm mimicked a large man's, spread over the center console. Her head bobbed softly to *"There'll Never Be"* by the group *Switch*. I knew this because I watched their *Unsung* episode. If I wasn't in the middle of calming Jason, I'd laugh.

Me: I'm fine. I swear it. I'll call you later. Please tell me you made good with Linda.

As much as she annoyed me last night, Linda was cool. She had been a good distraction the past couple of weeks or so.

Texts from Tasche and Randi buzzed on my phone concurrently.

Tasche: *Bitch you wildin! Where you at? I'm cumin thru.*

Randi: *Meet me at the diner at like 12. I'm goin bck 2 sleep.*

I shot a text back to both, explaining I had errands to run and would make plans to see them later on in the week. Just as I hit send on the last one, the music halted and a phone rang through the system. After groaning, Rory answered.

"Yo..."

"Rory..."

"Yeah."

"Where's Deek?"

My belly leaped at the sound of a woman asking for him.

"Why?"

"Why?" the woman sucked her teeth. "Because I need to ask him something and he ain't answering his phone. I called his office and they said he ain't in today."

"Whatchu' need, Tiff?"

Tiffany?

Had to be. She did carry a bit of slang to her delivery when she wasn't putting on for Earl and Irene Ellis.

"I haven't gotten a RSVP for Ricky's party yet. Tomorrow's the deadline."

"Shoot 'im a text. He'll get back to you," Rory advised.

"Damn! What happened to the days of him just picking up the damn phone when a bitch calls?"

Rory fell silent. Her saucer-sized eyes brushed against me in the rearview mirror. Then she scratched the back of her head, uneasy.

"Shit, Rory!" Tiffany seemed to have grown impatient. "Did he say if he took the invitation seriously or not? I need to properly lay out these VIPs."

"He just said what he said that day at the club."

"That he'll see what his 'lady' gotta say to that Randi bitch?"

Ricky was throwing a party? That was impossible. He was a legend...in the way you didn't know if he really existed or was still alive. I'd only heard about his movements through Randi.

"Yup."

"Well, when she gon' speak to her friend?"

Rory's eyes moved past me again. "I 'on't know, Tiff."

"Poppa Earl told me she been outta town. I gotta wait till she get back or till he answer the damn phone?"

"She back, and he gon' answer your text. That's the best way to get him. He shutting down for a few days."

"Because she back?"

That's when I swallowed the lump in my throat.

"Yo, Tiff, you need to talk to him." Rory's tone was of impatience.

"Alright. Love you, Rory." Her voice turned tender.

"Yeah." Rory disconnected the phone, but she wasn't being cold.

The music resumed and I was annoyed past ten on a scale. Rory broke asshole code with a former lover of her boss, but could never with me. What was up with this weird group of people? I tapped the back of her headrest. Rory muted the music.

"You have a lot of affection for her," I observed aloud, my regard going to the streets outside. "What does it take to qualify for that? Can't just be sex with your boss, because I've done that." I scoffed, hand brushing past my belly. "Lots. And it can't be the promise of marriage because he proposed to me. So what is it, glorified assistant?"

Rory turned up the volume of the stereo, effectively blowing me off.

The machines beeped; one sloughed oxygen into his lungs. There was even a feeding tube. A wide bandage was wrapped around his forehead. Abshir's only chance at life was being aided by technology.

Three bullet entries.

In the thigh.

In the shoulder, traveling diagonally, inches away from the heart.

In the head.

The past few hours, as I sat at his bedside, I couldn't ignore the palpable awkwardness. His limbs were chilled. Last night, I kept touching his feet, somehow thinking it would warm him. That was comical, considering my older brother had been cold to me for so many years. Also, when in his presence, Abshir was rarely quiet. He was either with a friend, yapping about one thing or another, or finding a reason to gripe at me or our parents. The hospital room, though, had a peaceful quiet to it.

For the past three hours, as I sat with him, I felt like an interloper. I was sure Abshir would prefer any given friend over my presence. He may have even preferred being alone to me. But I couldn't care. He was my only family. Yes, I had aunts and their families, but they'd given up on us when my father's addiction spiraled out of control. We were no longer accepted in whole. Even the day of my mother's funeral, I was the last to leave the graveyard. My aunts, her sisters-in-law, and their family left the moment her cold body lowered into the ground. There was hardly a repast. The totality of the repast were my mother's friends. Our family drew a wedge years before her passing.

Abshir's street habits didn't help. He'd already earned the reputation of a street thug or wanna-be, depending on who in the family you asked. His temperament vacillated between brusque and standoffish. Those qualities weren't exclusive to me. He'd given that energy to them as well. When they would provide Abshir and me with the occasional invites, he would decline or ignore them. He was a callous man.

But he was my brother. We'd shared a womb, even if not at the same time. We'd grown up with the same set of parents, had been taught the same values. We were held to the same set of morals. We shared the same features, went to the same schools. Endured the same ups and downs of our childhood. That meant something to me. It was what had me here, leaning over his cold bed, emotionally drained...feeling unwelcome, even as his body fought for his life.

My head reared at the sound of the door opening. Rory was rolling in a tray of food. I swiped my eyes, then wondered how was she able to bring in food on a tray in a hospital. It was in bags. *DiFilippo's* bags. My eyes went to the clock above the door at the same time my belly growled. I'd forgotten to eat. I told myself I'd go look for some place to grab a bagel. It must have slipped my mind.

"What's this?"

"Lunch," Rory grumbled. "The S.Q.E. said to check ya phone."

She turned to head back out of the room. My eyes shot over to the corner, where my phone had been buried in my bag. With a few long steps, I was there, surfing through. I had several missed texts from everyone: Tasche, Jason, Randi, and Sadik.

Before I could tap to return any, the face lit with an incoming call.

I took a deep breath as I answered. "Hello."

There was a pause before he replied, "How are you?"

My brows shot up. "I don't know how to answer that question."

"It isn't a trick one. I'm sure it's difficult seeing him that way."

My regard swung back to a motionless Abshir, rage coursing my belly. "You have some nerve!" I whispered hard, away from Abshir.

I could hear his deep breath. "I'm only showing empathy."

"I guess that's the least you could do, seeing it was your family who put him here."

"I'm sorry, Bilan. I'm trying to do all I can to make sure you have the support you need right now."

"How? By taunting me at my brother's bedside with a faux call of care, or by feeding me while I'm paying vigil at said brother's bullet-ridden body?"

He didn't speak right away, and that didn't surprise me. Sadik's actions and words often seemed thought out. He'd had four weeks to plan his stance to me at my brother's side.

"I know you've spoken to Nurse Gladney about his prognosis." Yes. It was grim. She said at this point, considering his injuries, there should have been signs of improvement in some form. His level of consciousness—something about a Glascow scale—was a six when he arrived here. Anything below eight or seven was considered a coma. A significant portion of the skull had been removed temporarily during a craniectomy procedure to decrease pressure inside the skull. His bullet tract was extensive, which affected his prognosis. For weeks, it had been a waiting game, one of the doctors feared for the worst. "I think this would be a good time for you to contact your aunts. They can be a support to you and sources of positive energy for your brother."

A tear slipped down my face. I quickly swiped at it, turning back for another glance at Abshir. Of course, Sadik would know the appropriate thing to do in this case. He had a formidable bond with his family. It's what they would have expected of each other.

"I have to go," I whispered, overcome with sadness.

Without a moment to spare, Sadik returned, "Please eat, Bilan. You're of no help to Ab if you're not whole. You need sustenance."

My eyes narrowed as I faced the corner again. "You don't know me." I resented him so much in the moment.

"You didn't eat breakfast before leaving. You haven't eaten this afternoon. I know you need to eat. I know you already have a problem with eating regularly, so I can imagine your distraction now."

"Well, let me tell you what I know. I know your family did this to him. To me. You and your family live in this alternate universe where time and other people's feelings and plans don't matter."

"Bilan—"

"Oh, it's true!" I scoffed. "Even now, I'm here, under guard because you, for some insane reason, believe there could be something between us after this. Let me tell you something, Sadik Ellis. Here is where you'll learn you don't get to choose someone else's destiny," I whispered into the phone, curling over into the corner. "If he makes it out of this mess alive, I'm leaving. If he doesn't, I'm leaving. So have your fun hanging the expenses of his care over my head. But I swear to everything blue in the sky, I'll get the last laugh!"

"I'm not extorting—"

I hung up on him, unable to hear another note of his voice. Taking a deep breath, I swallowed back tears of anger, frustration... loneliness. Then my stomach growled again, inconveniently. I peered over my shoulder to the cart of *DiFillippo's*. No matter how defiant I wanted to be, I had to use my noodle. My baby needed nourishment and, foolishly, I failed at it again. As I sauntered over to the food, I was reminded of the appointment I needed to make to be sure I hadn't screwed up this one piece of fortune.

The apartment was quiet when I strolled in close to ten at night. I kicked off my shoes by the console table and disrespectfully rested against the rusted copper wall. Once again, I found myself drained. I stayed at my brother's side until visiting hours were over. I prayed over him—the way I'd learned watching Bishop Ezra Carmichael pray during one of his sermons about the strength in prayer. His nurse, Nurse Gladney, was clear about Abshir's condition not being in his favor. She also explained how I must make him feel his recovery was expected.

As I tried rubbing the tension from my neck, thoughts of my call to our aunts, Franzel and Astur came to mind. I told them about Abshir's condition, leaving out the details of street involvement. But they knew. I could feel it from their responses when they asked questions I told them I had no answers to. That was difficult and embarrassing. Having to share news of that sort with family of their type. It was hard. Less than thirty minutes after getting off the line with my Aunt Franzel, my cousin, Joslyn, called, circumventing the questions with details of her "wonderful" life as a wife and mother. It was annoying.

And now, when all I needed was a bath and a bed to help break up this nightmare, I was here, at my captor's home.

"Oh!" My eyes flew open to find Kimmy, Sadik's housekeeper and cook. She was startled. "Bilan!" she breathed, palm to her chest. "I'm sorry. I must have been lost inside my head." She giggled.

"I was, too."

Her beam widened. "He told me you'd return this week. Did you like the banana bread? It was my grandmother's recipe. I don't eat bananas, so I don't make it often. Mr. Ellis asked if I could do it."

My brain had to travel to the subject at hand.

Last night...

Oh! "Yes. It was good. I inhaled like three pieces."

Her shoulders lifted and chin dipped from the flattery. "Mr. Ellis has eaten already, but I left aside prawn risotto for you. I even made a bowl of seafood macaroni salad for you. I remembered you liking that earlier this summer."

A lazy grin crested on my face. "Thanks, Kimmy."

"No problem." There was a pause as she gaped at me, even swiping my full frame up and down. "If I may say so, you have a glow about you."

My hand went to my face. "Do I?"

"Yeah. You look thinner, too."

That doused a bucket of ice over my head. It was a blameless shot at my lack of eating.

"Mmmmmm..."

She reached to grab my lower arm, a smile in her eyes and face. "I'm so glad you're back. It'll be great to have more girl power around here. You were a pleasure to service. I'm looking forward to many more moons of it."

Oh, no...

Kimmy was sweet, nothing short of warm, professional, and efficient. But how much did she know about her employer's murderous family? Did she know I'd run from Sadik? How my brother was almost killed?

On a shaky breath, I returned, "Thank you, Kimmy." It was all I could say to keep this exchange pleasant.

She nodded with a gleam in her eyes, then continued to the front door. "He's in the television room. Been in there practically all evening. Let me know what you think about the risotto and the salad."

When the door closed, I took another deep breath and proceeded to the back of the apartment, avoiding the television room.

She said I had a glow to me...

That complicated everything.

"So, what do you propose? Let's get right to it," I urged the gorgeous mocha public relations professional.

On my wall monitor, I had two conference screens. Dawn Taylor of *DT-PR* was to the right while one of my attorneys, Rashib, was to the left. We'd been on the call for over ten minutes now, doing the introductions and briefing her on my brand. Taylor was one of three public relation firms we'd been vetting.

"Well," She giggled. "Provided the information I've been given, I'd begin a rigorous push for new programs coming out of your Human Resources department, possibly even develop a new role to man them. One should focus on holistic care and wellness. There's been this huge push for mental health awareness that's even reached celebrity realms. Gaining a good presence in the form of an HR rep would add substance to your staff offerings."

"And what about exterior posturing?" I asked. "How can we deflect what others are seeing as a result of this lawsuit?"

Rashib's head angled as he focused into his screen at her, eager for her answer.

Dawn's lips pressed tightly together as her eyes widened. "My diagnosis is to do nothing. Lawsuits come a dime a dozen in this climate. I'm sure this will blow over and be forgotten about in no time at all." Then she paused, sucking in a fortifying breath. Her thick, wavy tresses meeting her right shoulder. "Can I ask you a question?"

Movement in the corner of my eye had me glancing toward the left, where Bilan was ambling down the hall. She'd been predictably distant, and I wouldn't push her. The difficult position I'd put her in made me deserving of her remoteness. But I hated each moment of our disconnect. Yesterday, she spent the whole day at the hospital. When she got in, she showered, thankfully had dinner, then went straight to bed. The fact of her eating on her own, without having to be told, bothered me. I missed feeding her. As perverse the pleasure, I enjoyed it.

This morning, she left for the hospital first thing again. When Rory texted me earlier, she said Ab had to be taken for a round of testing for brain activity and other functions, so Bilan would be back here for a bit before heading back to see him. Rory mentioned Bilan saying something about purchasing books for her fall classes today.

"Sure," I finally answered Dawn, then my regard shifted back to her.

"Do you wear contact lenses?" She bit her bottom lip coyly.

"No."

Her brows hiked and grin spread. "The hair on your face—"

"Ah... Ms. Taylor," Rashib interjected, knowing where this was going. "Is there anything more you have for Mr. Ellis. I assure you, he's a busy man."

"I'm sorry." She chuckled casually, boldly, and in no rush. "It's just that I have a specialty in branding the business of the man outside of his enterprises. I can arrange a photoshoot and have you marketed as the next *Mauve* man, or *Essence*'s top eligible bachelors. There's a lot I can do to commercialize your image."

A quiet scoff left my nostrils and my eyes narrowed as my head bounced softly. "I think it's best we focus on my business at hand. Thanks for your time today, Ms. Taylor."

"Okay," she singsonged unabashedly. Then she pursed her full lips again. "The offer stands if you're interested. I hope I've screened favorably for this role. I have so many aggressive ideas I feel your 3PL would thrive from. Thanks for this opportunity, Mr. Ellis."

I nodded, ready to be done with this call. Rashib recited the closing remarks and Dawn Taylor's image disappeared from the screen.

"What do you think?" he asked.

"I don't, really. She seems charismatic, but offered shit for services. That generic HR addition recommendation has already been rolled out this summer, since this shit hit the fan."

"Yeah," he sighed, rubbing his forehead. "And for her to say public relations during a lawsuit isn't necessary. Who the fuck says that on an interview?"

I shrugged with my forehead. "A sexy ass, narcissist vixen." And one I didn't have time for.

My phone vibrated on my desk. "Rah, I have to take this. I'll hit you in the morning with my final thoughts."

"You got it, man."

He ended our video conference as I answered the call.

"Palmer..." I rubbed my eyes.

"Hey, Sadik." There was a slight pause, concerning me. "I... Uh... Dominicana. I know your position on it."

"Then what's the point of this call, Palmer?" I knew the reason for this call. It was Double E Bags making another attempt at his will.

For my life...

"Sadik, he turning seventy soon. He can't keep going hard like this. Running with these young boys is a stallion game."

Palmer had been my father's assistant for forty years or more. Anything Double E Bags did, including fucking and paying taxes, Palmer knew. He'd been to almost all of our family celebrations: graduations, weddings, trials, and sentencings. He was a reserved man in personality. Extremely polite and trustworthy. And right now, his role was mediator between father and son.

"They threatening islands, man." *Turf...* "And strategy is needed."

"Didn't I just do a sweep? Where's the respect? That's not what I do. You know it, and he knows, too. Right now is my time."

"Islands add up—"

"How's Livia, Palm?"

He groaned slightly before answering about his daughter. "She good, man. In North Africa now... Morocco, Africa. She making her way to some place in Spain. Been out there since like May."

I nodded, proud of Palmer for knowing. He should have: he sponsored his thirty-plus year old daughter. Even at her advanced age, Palmer wrote checks for her leisure and at her every whim. He'd been doing it all her life, to replace his presence in it. Why? Because as the assistant to Earl Double E Bags Ellis, your life belonged to him. It was a surprise Palmer had the time to fuck when working in my father's demanding organization. He never knew her mother past an encounter at a local bar in Hillside.

"When's the last time she's been home?"

There was a pause because I'd hit a nerve. Palmer didn't exactly celebrate his paternal absenteeism. In fact, I was confident he wished he could be more present for her. Livia was weird as fuck, and this was coming from a privileged Black man with a father possessing endless resources. I'd traveled and gotten educated with the crème de la crème, but I had a sense of self. Loads of cultural pride and a consciousness of belonging. My family believed Livia was airy and unrooted. Palmer knew it, too, but had no influence in her upbringing. Their relationship was estranged, but she was comfortable calling back home for money, which was all the time. She traveled all over the globe at least ten months out of the year for well over ten years now.

"Deek, man," he groaned, understanding the rabbit hole he'd entered.

"Palmer, I have a very legit, very demanding conglomerate I've been successfully growing for over sixteen years. I've worked hard. I've straddled the fence to accommodate. I've gone days, underfed, under-rested, and lonely as fuck. I now have a dynamic in my world I'm not trying to sacrifice for the team. I want a child...a family to come home to at night. I want to blow raspberries into a fat belly, whoop some juvenile ass before the pigs find a reason to, threaten a muthafucka checking for my baby girl, teach my son how to beat the shit out of a bully, pay tuition, and secretly cry in the back of the church after giving my daughter away to a fuckin' kid while my wife comforts me." I blinked as my neck twitched. "Oh. I would need a fuckin' woman to get a wife, to have kids to do all the aforementioned shit with."

"Deek—"

"I can't do that and take over my father's business, Palmer. You're his right hand: convey this to him."

There was another long break before I heard him grunt uncomfortably.

"Okay, man. I'll talk to him." Though buried, I could hear the dejection in his voice.

"Enjoy your evening, Palm."

The call was disconnected and I pushed the phone toward the top of my desk, my fingers tenting as I tried to organize my thoughts. This wasn't easy. It went against my nature to deny my father.

A glimpse of Bilan passing my office door again reminded me how complicated life was. It was why I had to be firm.

My phone vibrated again.

"Hey, queen," I droned, exhausted that quickly.

"Hey, you, handsome." I could hear the smile in her heart. "I was hoping you could bring that bottle of the vintage *Sterling* cabernet you've been sitting on for some time."

My fingers reached to my scalp for a scratch as I leaned over my desk. "Queen, I won't be there tonight for dinner."

"Oh?" was the short for *'boy, you better explain!'*

"Yeah..." I stalled. "Bilan's back home, and..."

"Oh, right! Your father mentioned that last night—or this morning." she stumbled on her words. "It was late, so I can't quite remember the hour."

That led me to believe they'd shared a bed recently. There's no way she could confuse night and morning with my father, unless they spent the night together. The kid in me was thrilled at that slip. But it also guided another thought.

"*He* told you she's returned?"

I hadn't mentioned it to him.

"Yes, handsome. He said Tiffany had brought it to his attention recently."

Ahhhhh...

Rory told me about Tiff's call while she was in Bilan's truck.

"I see."

After a spell, she offered, "You know, instead of being a retired golden-ager, he's too often stressed about the business."

"When you're the architect of your own wealth, you often are, is what he taught me."

"Yes, he did. And that's quite true, but in spite of what pressures he placed on you, you have to remember how special you are to him. You're the son he prayed for."

"And that means he cherry-picks my path?"

"Absolutely not!" She was firm. "You know I've never agreed to that destiny for any of my children. It doesn't matter that I fell in love with and gave my heart to a man in his line of work; I never wanted my kids to know a day of his business. However, what I do want is for you to know what you mean to us. And you, Sadik, are his pride and joy, unlike anything he's ever created."

Hers, too, but respectfully, she wouldn't say it. The liability of being the favorite of a parent—or in my case, both—is the expectation they lay on your back to carry through. I didn't want the expectation, just the respect.

A conceding sigh left my lungs. "What's the plan for his birthday?"

"Oh. I have several tricks up my sleeve!" she chirped. "So..."

And like that, I'd successfully re-navigated the conversation.

Bilan

"Do she gotta be here?" Tasche groaned, rolling her eyes at Rory patrolling from fifteen yards away.

I closed my eyes while shaking my head. It was enough to have to catch them up on what's been going on with me. I didn't need the stress of Rory's presence. I'd been home three days and had somehow gotten used to her hovering.

Just as Sadik advised I would in the jazz park...

"Chill with that," Randi snorted, warning Tasche. "Rory's grade school-patrol looking ass pretty solid. I'm surprised to see her with you instead of attached at Sadik's hip."

"I 'on't give a single fuck, yo. This my backyard. I can speak freely if I fuckin' want," Tasche made clear. "Fuckin' Harlem pride, for real over here." She raised a closed fist.

My regard darted over to Rory smirking while bringing a lit cigarette to her mouth. It was an antagonizing move, clearly.

I placed my hands over Tasche's shoulders and turned her away from Rory.

"Focus here." I locked eyes with her. "Please."

"So, Ab's in the hospital?" Randi asked, inviting me to continue.

"Yes. And he's not responding at all."

"That's fucked up, yo," Tasche remarked. "And this been for a whole month?"

I nodded.

Randi deduced, "You left a month ago."

I nodded again, this time my eyes were blinking guiltily. "Ironically, yes."

"I thought that nigga snatched you." Randi's grin was grimy.

"Yeah! And had my Black ass believing it," Tasche charged. "I was ready to call my Harlem World niggas."

My eyes shot over to Rory at that threat. Thankfully, she'd just taken a call and had turned her back to us to tend to it.

I lowered my tone, "Look, guys. No, Sadik didn't snatch me. Yes, I was perfectly safe. I just needed time away. Life was happening too fast for me. You two remember the break-in from the house. And yes, Sadik's wining and dining and moving me in was a lot for me. It was a good time to get away alone."

"But why the fuck you was acting all secretive and shit? Calling from another phone?"

"My phone broke the day I left. It dropped out of my hand." The lies fell so effortlessly from my lips. This was so wrong. "Do you know how hard it is to get a phone while traveling? My line now belongs to Sadik. He took over the payments when the iPhone he bought me was activated."

"Sounds like I was right." Randi smiled as she smacked on gum.

"About what?"

"Sadik fuckin' your head up so bad, got you lookin' for ya' wig."

My face fell. When I opened my mouth to respond, Tasche did instead.

"You also said he was gonna fuckin' leave her ass. But that nigga proposed to her and moved her in. He obviously still in love with the pussy 'cause he snatched her ass back up in his crib."

With a measured smile, Randi rolled her eyes away. That exasperated my already irritated state of mind.

"What is up with you and Sadik, huhn?" I asked Randi.

Tasche's forehead lifted.

"The hell you talking about?"

"Since day one with him, you've been negative. The same friend who's told me at least on a half a dozen occasions to sleep with a guy just for money. Then a guy comes along with loads of it, and you've been foreboding from the jump." I crossed my arms, awaiting an answer.

"First of all, chill with those big ass fuckin' words. You ain't in class, bitch. We in the backyard of a Paterson four-family. Why you spazzin' the fuck out on me about lookin' out for my girl? You know I been at this for a minute. You know I'm actually *in* the streets, not around the corner from them like you was in West Paterson." The stiletto head of her index finger went to her chest. "I been fuckin' with niggas like Sadik. I'm fuckin' one now—living with the nigga. I just know you and don't think you deserve the bullshit that come with it 'cause you ain't built for it."

I was stunned, face screwed. "You don't know Sadik at all. The man you described hasn't reared his wig-snatching head in five months."

"Give it time, sweetheart," Randi argued, keeping her voice down. "Them niggas always do."

"He doesn't need time, Randi. A man of his caliber—the one you actually know—doesn't need to waste his time on women. They come a dime a dozen to them."

"That's true, yo," Tasche agreed.

"I have nothing more to give him, Randi." My arms flogged in the air. "He's slept with me more times than I can count. Contrary to popular belief, pussy isn't made of gold. The most talented isn't. And mine didn't have much before him. Could you just keep the negativity out of this and be my friend? I could sure use one right now!"

Tasche took to my side, wrapping an arm around me, and *God,* that simple act of humanity felt like everything. I'd been running on autopilot these past three days since being back in town, and without a soul I could tell the absolute truth about what had been going on, I'd once again found myself feeling lonely.

"You love suckin' her ass," Randi hissed, rolling her eyes.

"Fuck you. I love being a friend." Tasche didn't skip a beat. "You heard her. Ab been shot the fuck up. How would you feel if that happened to your peoples, yo?"

That was such an amazing perspective from her, considering Tasche had never met Abshir, unlike Randi. She released me and I gave her another one of my guilty smiles. My heart was so conflicted on this. I wished I could tell my friends everything, but I hadn't had time to sort my own thoughts and feelings on the current state of my world.

"This shit is getting mad touchy," Tasche stated after a muted period.

"And so unnecessarily," Randi returned swiftly. "Bitch, you know I got your back. You want me to come up to the hospital with you?"

Before I could process her offering, a blanket of guilt covered me. I'd been unusually snappy. Cranky and short of patience. This wasn't my norm. Randi was my girl. She found interest in me when I had a rather dull life. We'd had loads of laughs together.

"Sorry, Randi," I murmured.

"It's all good. I be on my bullshit, too." She slapped my shoulder playfully. "I can still come with you."

"You don't even like Abshir," I scoffed, my icy mood melting.

"Shit. He ain't never like you either, but you there with him," Randi quipped.

I rolled my eyes at that. She was right, but it still felt wrong.

"I'll be fine. I need to get out of here." My eyes brushed over to Rory, who was gazing in the opposite direction. She'd been distant these past two days since shadowing me, but patient. I didn't want to push it. "I need to run a few errands before going back to see Abshir."

"Yo, just make sure you taking care of yourself. You look a lil' smaller, ma," Tasche observed. "You naturally beautiful. I 'on't want that shit to change."

My face opened in a smile. "Thanks, Tasche. You should have seen me before I got my hair done this morning." My hand swept down the back of my tapered head.

That ShawnNicole worked a miracle, and quickly. I was in and out in less than two hours this morning.

"That shit look dope as hell, yo."

"Thanks, Tasch."

As I started toward the gate near where Rory stood, Randi called for me.

"You coming to Ricky's party. Right?"

That brought Tiff's call to mind. "When is it?"

"Less than two weeks. Sadik ain't say nothing to you?"

I flipped my palms in the air. "It's been so crazy lately. Maybe he did. I'll see."

"Don't see, bitch. My man's having a party!" She laughed. "You know his spooky ass never come out. You better be there. It's at *Pulse*." And there was that wicked gleam again.

Foolishly, it charged something childish in me. Suddenly, I actually wanted to go. It didn't matter that Sadik and I hadn't exchanged many words although we'd shared a bed these past few nights. I would go just to see him in the same room as that Tiffany.

Sick...

I was sick with an unreasonable lack of desire to run from this man who was capable of murder.

"I'll see and get back to you," I promised.

There was also that keen loyalty streak in me wanting to support Randi, as she did me with my graduation party.

By the time I made it to the other side of the yard, Rory held the gate open for me.

"You really wanna go to that shit?" she croaked.

"Why not? Maybe *Tiff* can provide tips on how to be revered in this world. Y'all's world."

"*Rever* what?"

I rolled my eyes, heading to the truck.

It was well after ten at night when I toed down the hall for the kitchen. I was freshly showered and hungry. Instead of the fancy, long silk robe hanging in my side of the closet courtesy of the landlord, I opted for a long, braless NBA jersey and short, cotton elastic waist shorts. It was slightly inappropriate, but a rather warm September night. I wanted to nibble on whatever Kimmy prepared and head to the patio to get school work done. The semester had begun and already, I was behind.

"Hey." I smiled, sauntering into the oversized contemporary kitchen. The dark panel floors glossed, chrome fixtures almost sparkled, the long and broad black wooden cabinetry gave the room a mature feel, and the appliances were the perfect touch. I loved the room. It also spoke to the exquisiteness of the owner. "You're still here?" I asked Kimmy as she packed up a bag.

"Yeah. I needed to reorganize the linen closet and pantries." She placed the last of a stack of magazines into a canvas tote. "I had to rotate his magazines and books, too."

My face wrinkled. "Books from the bathrooms?"

"Yeah. And the living room. Those are the two places my employer likes to read, in particular." She winked. "I have your food in the warmer. I can wash my hands and serve it if you want."

"Noooo." I playfully scolded. "I have it. Your work day is done. I can take it from here."

"It won't be a problem at all. In fact, I should slice you a few pieces of the French bread."

"I can do it, Kimmy. Really." I gaited over to the bread cabinet, though I would unlikely eat much of it. "He's been quiet lately, huhn?" My eyes skirted over to Kimmy behind me.

"Mr. Ellis?" I found it strange each time she referenced Sadik. Kimmy had to be somewhere around my age, but her approach to her job was consistently professional. "Well, he made it clear once you returned, he'd be around more."

My brows met. "Did he?"

"Yeah." She walked over to the sink to wash her hands. "He was even particular about the menu these next few weeks. He asked me to help him remember the dishes of mine you like most. It was cute." She chuckled. "I overheard him telling Rory, too, he'd be home more for the next few weeks."

"Interesting," I remarked, watching her put together a place setting for me at the massive island.

Kimmy paused, regard to the high framed ceiling. Then it was narrowed and on me. "He's tired."

"Tired?"

She nodded, going to the drawer for utensils. "He's the hardest working man I know. Only one man worked harder. My daddy, working construction from morning till evening, then fixing cars at night, six days a week. But he's now retired." She pulled out a wine glass.

Alarmed, I pushed my palm into the air. "None for me tonight." I tried smiling. "I have to endure school work."

Quickly, she exchanged the stemware for a traditional glass. "Cranberry juice?"

"Yes. Please..." I pulled the plate from the warmer and sauntered over to the island.

"Yeah. He's tired. I couldn't wait for you to come back from visiting your family. I know you were only here for about two months, but I enjoyed you. It made him happy. Brought him balance. When you left, he was out working, sometimes for days." She placed the glass next to my plate, then went back for the bread I pulled out. She quickly sliced two pieces, bringing only one to me. "Now, you're home. And now he rests." She walked over to the sink to wash her hands again. "Oh, happy day."

The smile she was able to evoke from my heart annoyed me feverishly. There was nothing remotely romantic about my relationship with Sadik at this point. It was psychotic and manipulative. His family tried to kill my brother, and he likely knew it would happen as he distracted me for months with gifts, trips, designer apparel, jewelry, and orgasms. Lots of orgasms.

And now, I'm stuck here while awaiting my brother's fate...

"It's good to be welcomed back, Kimmy. Thanks."

"You're very welcome."

"He has been quiet lately. That explains it, I guess."

"He's been resting, and I'm happy."

"Yeah. He's been sleeping in since I've been back. When I came in yesterday to do a few things online, he was in his office. Sounded like he was on a business call."

"Mmmhmmm..." She nodded. "Working from home more. I told you. When he's done, he's either napping in the television room, letting the system watch him, or in the living room knocked out. He's in the television room now. It's good to see him in casual clothes all day. He needs rest. And now with his woman home, it can happen."

Taking a deep breath, my brows shot up as I started in on my food.

"I'll see you in the morning, Bilan." Kimmy was at the entryway of the room. "Oh! I baked a peach pie. It's in the fridge."

"Yum!" I cheered playfully—and respectfully.

"Mr. Ellis likes his with vanilla bean ice cream. There's some in the freezer."

I flapped my fingers her way. "Thanks so much, Kimmy. Have a good evening."

She took off, leaving me to her delicious spaghetti. I wasn't alone too long before a figure entered the kitchen. The shine in his bald head was stark, and the orange hair growth on his face was down-right distracting. He wore a black t-shirt and blue jeans with nothing on his feet. When he bent over, into the fridge, his shirt lifted and the band of his jeans pulled, exposing the golden skin of his back.

"How are classes coming along?" he droned. My eyes popped wide. "Were you able to order all of your books?"

Sadik pulled out a bowl of strawberries, placing it on the counter. He popped one into his mouth before moving over to one of the pantries.

"It's moving fast." I thought the first two classes of each course wouldn't consist of much, seeing it was the start of the semester. But

I was wrong. These were all online courses. Work began on the first day. "I have more catching up to do tonight."

He strolled back around with a bag of microwavable popcorn. "Anything I can do to help?"

"Short of taking the classes for me and me owing you my ovaries and a lung? No, thanks." I cringed the moment those words left my mouth, particularly the ovaries one.

Sadik closed the door to the microwave with his honeyed eyes on me. They said so much, though his mouth spoke not a single word. What's crazy was I knew what he would say if the circumstances were favorable. He'd assure me my ovaries belonged to him already. The longing in his regard shouted his sincere feelings for me. No matter how awkward and cinematic our situation, he wanted me. Sadik yearned for my acceptance.

"How was Ab today?"

My eyes rolled and I began to rub my temples. "I momentarily forgot about that stressor." This exotic apartment could do that to you. It was a haven. "Not much improvement." I wasn't so sure Sadik really cared. "An added pressure is my family finally coming to visit tomorrow. I'm so not looking forward to it."

"I'm sorry."

My head whipped up. "Are you?"

Sadik would only stare at me for a few seconds, allowing the awkwardness from my blurt to fade out.

"There's a fundraiser happening this Friday." His words were delivered stoically as though his mind was split, performing two different processes. Sadik couldn't shake my jab, though he tried moving past it. "A friend of mine, Julius Richards, is raising money for his campaign. I'd like if you come with me."

Julius...

Sadik's completely heterosexual man crush. His good friend. It was nice to hear about him supporting Julius' efforts.

"I don't think so. I don't know the first thing about political fundraising. I wouldn't know what to wear or to expect."

Why was he even asking me?

That was the thing, though. Sadik was asking, not demanding.

"I can have the boutique send you over a few things to choose from," his tone so soft. His countenance so tortured.

Tears sprouted unexpectedly, the emotions tumbled through.

"What do you want from me?" I croaked through tears.

"To be friends again."

"We tried that. Friends don't leave friends in the dark about the safety of their only family."

His now green orbs fell away, forehead wrinkled. "I know. There's so much I have to explain to you—want to explain to you."

"Try again!" I demanded through gritted teeth. My pulse raced, limbs trembled, and nipples stung against the fabric of the jersey. There was a dangerous divide happening again with my mind and body. Some...parts of me were innately drawn to this man. This murderer. "What do you want from me?"

I saw as his eyes brushed against the pout of my lip, beating pulse in my neck, the heaving of my chest, the balling of my fists, and the pebbles beneath my jersey.

"To be your friend and lover," he rasped.

The microwave sounded its end with his darkened orbs stapled to my breasts. I couldn't take the heat shooting from them. Could no longer endure the throb from below.

With a heavy banging of the table with my fists, I leaped from my chair. "Fine. I'll go with you to your friend's event. But not because we're friends—and you know we're no longer lovers! But don't you ever look at me with those betraying eyes again."

I stormed out of the kitchen feeling weak. How could I say no to going with him? Would he continue to pay for Abshir's care? Likely not.

I sat in the corner of the hospital room. A textbook lay on my one inclined leg, a writing pad on the other. In between reading and jotting down notes, I reflected on my call earlier to the school. I called the bursar's office to discuss payment plan options, something that should have been done ahead of time. However, with so much going on, I'd forgotten to.

When the woman pulled up my account, she told me the tuition had been settled for the semester. I politely advised her of a mistake. She explained she had to move on to the next call unless I had another question for her that couldn't be answered online. It was rude, but I couldn't find anything about payment options on the school's site, hence my call. I swallowed my pride and didn't return the same energy she'd given me. After the call, I logged back into my account and was floored by the zero balance I saw. When I wanted to call back and ask for answers, the only possible one came to mind. Sadik.

After I was able to calm my mind from that discovery, I took my phone down to the lobby for a private call. Of course, Rory followed me there, but she did allow me privacy. I was able to call Dr. Clifford's office for an appointment. Why did I call there instead of a neutral place? Because I planned to keep my baby and, therefore, Sadik would learn about my pregnancy. And no matter how much I fantasized about disappearing from New Jersey for good with my child, I knew it was impossible. I was carrying an Ellis, and whether I liked it or not, Sadik would slay a dragon, police force, and the U.S. military to be in his child's life. And I now knew he didn't need his father and brother's arms to assist.

Dr. Clifford's office said the soonest they could see me was Monday, which wasn't too bad, I guessed. I'd been out of the morning sickness phase, thankfully, and had no other major issues. So, with that and school being settled, it only left one thing to see about: my parents' home. A shooting had taken place in there. I didn't have the stomach to call the bank about its foreclosure status. That was a battle I decided to put off for another day.

These were just a few of the thoughts running through my head as I sat several yards away from Abshir, studying to get caught up in school that began just days ago. To be honest, the sounds of the soft music I played while here calmed me.

"Business to Business Marketing: Analysis and Practice," I heard rasp

near me. I glanced up to find Rory bending over to read the front cover of my textbook.

I sat up in my seat, eyeing her warily. I may have shared a bed with her boss at night, but I trusted none of them.

"It's for school." My face wrinkled. "Duh."

"What class?" She stood straight, thumbs hooking into the belt loops of her suit pants. Her short legs spread apart and she bounced on her toes. "It sound serious."

My brows lifted, annoyed. "Business-to-Business Marketing."

"Def-netly serious." She confirmed, nodding.

This was not like Rory. Since when did she care about what I was reading or doing alone?

"What do you want?" I asked firmly.

She swiped her nose as she sniffled. "Ya peeps here." She pointed behind her.

I glanced in that direction and saw my aunts and cousins outside of the room, appearing as a herd of sheep, waiting to be guided.

"Shoot!" I scrambled to my feet, catching the textbook and writing pad before they met the floor. Rory leaped to assist, though unnecessarily. "How long have they been here?"

"Just a couple 'a minutes," she answered.

They were all peering through the window at us.

"Shoot! Shoot! Shoot! Shoot! Shoot!" was all I could manage without moving my mouth. My mouth! "How do I look?" I was sure to apply a bit of makeup today in anticipation of this.

"The fuck you want me to say?" Her one brow shot into the air as she scowled.

I made quick work of straightening my clothes. Taking a deep breath, I grimaced as I tried to remind myself how I'd prayed about this all night. It was going to go over well. It had to!

I glided past Rory and headed toward the door. On the way, I could see Aunt Astur peering through the glass, head swaying to be sure she caught every angle. Her daughter, Mimi, was next to her standing stoically. It was clear she was uncomfortable already. Aunt Franzel's attention was around the hallway, observing the facility. Her daughter, Joslyn, snapped a quick picture of Abshir through the glass, annoying me instantly. Two more of my cousins were present, too. They were younger. One, Angela, was on her phone. The other, Brenda, was the most dejected of the group. Her attention was on nothing in particular.

"I'm going to survive this," I murmured to myself just before grabbing the door handle and pushing down on it.

"Who is that?" Aunt Franzel was the first to speak.

My eyes darted around. "Who?"

"That young..." She hesitated. "...woman, I guess."

"Don't be silly, Franzel. That's a young boy," Aunt Astur corrected on a whisper.

Angela and Joslyn snickered, shifting the vibe in the air already. That's when I turned around. Rory came into view, short legs spread, the toes of her thick-soled boots facing outward like a duck. I mean, yeah, her presentation was gender ambiguous, but her ponytail gave her away.

I turned back to face my family, prepared for my first lie of the day. "She's my friend. She's been here with Abshir and me faithfully."

"Your friend?" Aunt Franzel's brows hiked and chin descended, questioningly. "Not your..."

"Boyfriend? Lover?" Brenda surprisingly grumbled, rolling her eyes away.

Whoa!

Brenda was twenty and...strange. She wore only oversized, grungy gear. Her hair was always in plaits: two French braids or cornrows. Her mother, Aunt Astur, stopped fighting her so much on her appearance just a few years ago. She dropped out of *Rutgers University* after just two semesters and now worked in sanitation. Needless to say, that had been a huge point of contention for their family.

"No!" Aunt Franzel gasped, offended. She threw her gaze to her sister for help. "Why would she say that? I didn't say that!"

Aunt Astur shook her head, dismissing all of it. "Can we now get in to see my nephew?" Her chin in the air. "I don't have long to be here. I'll have to go soon. A last minute call at work. You understand, don't you?"

Blinking, I reared my head. "*Su*—sure." I pushed the door open behind me.

They began piling into the room.

When it was Joslyn's turn, she was sure to ask, "So you were with your boyfriend when all this stuff happened?" I nodded, unable to look her in the eye. "I didn't know you had a boyfriend to go away with for a whole month. That's expensive." She was doubtful of the story I gave my aunts about Abshir's shooting.

I told them I'd been away with my boyfriend, celebrating my graduation when Abshir was shot. I was sure to include that because of mine and Abshir's estranged relationship, there was no next of kin information on him, which was why I didn't know until I returned and ran into a friend of his at the diner. *They didn't know I'd quit months ago either.* The benefit of being alienated from my family was the lie I could weave to make this story believable. While my story was, indeed a neat tale, little did Jos know, the plausibility of my "boyfriend" taking me away to celebrate was not.

I forged a smile. "We can talk later, Jos. Right now, Abshir needs to be the focus of our attention."

"Oh, I wasn't trying to be nosy!" She moved past to let Brenda and Angela inside the room.

I offered a smile as a response. Today was not the occasion to get into a competitive back and forth with my cousin. Joslyn was older than me by one year, but at least ten ahead of me as far as progress went. She was the cousin with the degree, husband, and child already. She had accomplished more than Mimi, who was older than the both of us at thirty-two, with two degrees and a husband.

While I watched them closely scrutinize Abshir's body as though he was a museum exhibit, I was reminded of the dynamics in this family—my father's sisters and their children. One was the numbers game in my generation. Abshir was the only male grandchild, which likely lent itself to the competitive game we female grands found ourselves contenders in. Education was a big deal as first gen Americans. Our grandparents were academic scholars. Our grandmother was an exceptional chemist with the *Food and Drug Administration*. Our grandfather was a mathematician, eventually earning his doctorate degree. There were four categories you marked the score-board with: a degree, marriage, children, and financial stability. At twenty-eight years old, I made my first score. That lowered the bar for Brenda at twenty. She had plenty of time to catch up with me.

That thought had me rolling my eyes. Rory, moving toward the door to leave the room, caught my attention. She murmured into her cellphone, answering a call. When my attention returned to my family, I saw them in various asanas, praying for Abshir. They were in yoga prayer positions, but all were on their feet. This reminded me of family. It was tradition. Unity. Though I knew my aunts would burst an artery if they learned I'd been studying Christianity. Okay... practicing it for weeks now.

Respectfully, I waited until they were done, finding myself pray-ing, too.

Our Father, who art in heaven...

∞9∞

...in Jesus' name, I pray.

Slowly, my eyes opened, finding several others on me. Did I miss something?

"Did you hear me, Bilan?" Aunt Astur posed.

I blinked. "Come again, please."

"What type of music is this? It's creating a mood in here." Her face was hard.

But my heart swelled. "A jazz piece I found the other day. Ragee and Take 6." I smiled.

"Take 6," Aunt Franzel remarked, gazing her sister's way. "I remember them. They're gospel. Right?"

"Yeah," Mimi interjected. "And Ragee can go either way. He's a church boy, I hear."

"So, this is gospel music?" Aunt Franzel summarized.

"You listen to gospel music?" Joslyn's tone was accusatory.

"This boyfriend of yours, what religion is he?" Aunt Franzel inquired.

My grin was tight when I answered, "Christian."

Then I cleared my throat, heat rising in my groin at the memory of the gold sculpture of Jesus Christ on the cross in Sadik's office. The things occurring after that discovery were likely heretical to his beliefs.

"Hmmmm," Aunt Astur grunted.

"Have the doctors said anything new?" Mimi asked.

"Not much." I swiped the back of my head. "He's still classified as comatose. His last MRI and CT scans showed minimal evidence of what's called brainstem function, and he no longer has evidence of an intracranial hematoma that might be causing the coma."

"He looks the same, though," Mimi noted. "Other than the head band..."

I cleared my throat again. "He's had two brain surgeries. The wounds from them and the bullet entry are still healing." My eyes watered.

"Do they know who did it?"

It took a while for me to answer that one. My hand fingered the dip in my collarbone. The hospital had to notify the police when I got back into town. They questioned me two days ago. That was scary.

"They haven't found them yet. The closest suspect they had is dead, too." I shrugged.

It was a joke. They suspected a guy he'd gotten into an altercation with over cigarettes in Paterson a week before the shooting. They discovered he, too, had been shot, but by a gang he'd had a beef with.

The room drew muted. My aunts' suspicious gazes were on me. Mimi and Joslyn were shooting each other messages via their regards. Angela couldn't keep her eyes off Abshir's body. And Brenda couldn't keep hers from Rory, pacing out in the hallway.

"This is a private hospital. Expensive."

My eyes skirted to an expecting Aunt Astur. She worked as an executive at a senior assisted living facility for decades. If she claimed to have an idea of the reputation of this place, I believed her. I stood motionless, heart pounding out of nowhere. How was I going to answer that?

"You know," Aunt Franzel thankfully cut in, her face collapsing into her hand. "I told your father—my brother—he should have never raised you kids that close to Paterson. It's brought such repercussion on your family." *My* family? "When Astur and I moved south, Asad should have come, too. He could have opened a restaurant there. And now..." Tears choked out her words. "It's just sad!" The waterfalls began.

She talked about my father as though I wasn't in the room. I was here, healthy, fighting every day to make the best decisions possible. I'd been a good kid, a productive adult. Yet there was still this omen over my father's wing of the family. And she had been right.

"Our father would be so ashamed," Aunt Astur added.

"Oh!" Aunt Franzel snorted. "Hooya would roll over in her grave. You know Asad was her favorite."

Untimely, my belly fluttered. It was so unrelated to what was taking place, but I was too preoccupied to figure it out in the moment.

"It's like the whole family's been wiped out." Joslyn was the author of that ridiculous statement.

I wanted to scream, *I'm still here, idiots!*

"Who the fuck is *that*?" Mimi broadcasted.

"What?" Aunt Astur chided while all of our gazes followed Mimi's out the window.

Ambling down the hallway with the speed of purpose was—

I choked on my spit. This explained my belly flutters from moments ago. Irene Ellis was headed to the room. Her graceful gait was captivating. What was she doing here? What did this mean? The moment her eyes found me, they lit with wonder. *Me?* It was surreal.

"Who is this?" Aunt Franzel parroted Mimi's inquisition.

Rory leaped for the door, opening it for Irene, and she swept through the room.

What hit me first was her enthralling floral scent. I nearly dropped to the floor when her arms widened. "Bilan," her chords billowed with emotion as she swept me into her chest. "He just told me," she whispered so covertly, I was sure no one could hear. "I'm so sorry, honey. My husband and son do not know, nor will they."

My eyes ballooned, body tense all over. However, I was still able to observe the fascinated gapes of my aunts and cousins out of the window, to the man accompanying Irene. At this point, you could hear a pin drop in the room, but for the machines aiding Abshir's life. I now knew the cause of Mimi's vulgar outburst moments ago.

Irene released me. "Is this your family, Bilan?"

Her regard turned to the group of women expectantly.

I took in a heap of air. "Yes..." Then my mind went on autopilot, thanks to a surge in anxiety. "This is my aunt, Franzel, and her daughter, Joslyn." I waited as Irene shook both their hands.

"Nice to meet the both of you." Irene smiled.

"And this is my aunt, Astur, and her daughters, Mimi, Angela, and Brenda." As I called out their names, Irene shook each woman's hand and greeted them.

They were all captivated by her aura. Irene had royalty-like presence about her. It was uncanny.

"I see so much of my Bilan in all of you," Irene gushed. "You're truly a good looking family."

"*Your* Bilan?" Aunt Astur questioned.

"I guess she failed to explain. I'm her future mother-in-law." Irene's hand swept to the window, where her son's kaleidoscope-hued eyes were glued to me even as he exchanged words with Rory.

Several gasped as Aunt Franzel pointed toward Sadik and asked, "That's your real hair color?"

She made the generic correlation. Irene's thick blonde tresses were in meticulous waves down her back and over her shoulders. And Sadik's orange beard was trimmed today, though still very much grown out.

"Yes. That's my handsome young king, Sadik." Irene beamed.

"What?" Aunt Astur questioned. "Future mother-in-law?"

Irene sucked in a breath, immediately understanding. "Oh, you didn't know?"

At that very moment, Aunt Franzel and Irene's regards went to my left ring finger. My world was crashing in on me.

I bit my lips together, then explained, "I rushed out this morning and forgot to put it on."

"Oh," Irene was the first to respond with forced understanding.

"How long have you been engaged?" Joslyn cried.

I combed the back of my head with my fingers. "Since June."

The choir sang, "June?"

"Yes," Irene answered. "She's been an answered prayer, if you know what I mean. Did she tell you their birthdays are a day apart?"

Aunt Frazel's eyes widened, and Aunt Astur gave Irene a catty once over from bottom to top. She was trying to figure her out...or size her up. Either way, it wasn't good energy.

As if on cue, Sadik entered the room. His gaze brushed over the women as he took to my side, hand protectively gliding over my hip. He whispered in my ear, "I hope I didn't just fuck this up."

His breath...

Oh, God! It smelled of jasmine and a hint of peppermint. This was entirely wrong and unfair to my fluctuating hormone levels. My days of nausea were officially gone. Here were the days of a resumed libido and a still incredibly alluring Sadik.

I gave a faux giggle. "Sadik." I was grateful for the distraction, even if only momentarily. "This is my family."

When I thought that general introduction would be fine, Angela, Joslyn, and Aunt Franzel shifted in our direction at the same time with their hands proffered. So, of course, I had to do the individual introductions all over again. They were absolutely mesmerized...all but Brenda, who left the room after shaking hands with Sadik. The other women's eyes never left him. I was sure no one noticed her leaving. And his cologne. My God, if I thought Irene's perfume was a lovely experience, Sadik's was entrancing. It was commanding and alluring enough to make me forget I was supposed to hate him.

"Oh, my..." Aunt Franzel giggled uncharacteristically. She aged in reverse about fifteen years. Sadik caught on right away, unleashing a killer, sleek grin. It was unfair. In mere seconds, the roles had reversed. My family were now the victims of my awful antics. "You're..." She couldn't speak.

"Bilan's husband," Sadik amended, "prayerfully in the near future." I didn't realize when he'd reached inside his suit jacket pocket and pulled out my ring. The thing almost blinded me, it sparkled as though recently cleaned. When I searched his eyes, I caught my answer in the orangey storm passing through them. "You forgot this today."

I didn't make a fuss and let him slide it on my finger. The last inch took a little force. Sadik's face folded in curiosity, but he didn't utter a word.

"How could you get engaged, then go away with your fiancé a whole month and still not contact your family to let us know?" Joslyn asked, sounding offended.

I shook my head, completely exhausted at this point. "It's been a breeze of a summer. So much going on," I droned. "I'm sorry to spring this on you guys now."

"Yes. In fact, I believe the nurses need to get in here," Sadik announced, bringing our attention to Nurse Gladney and her colleague waiting outside.

I asked her to come in for his bath after they'd been here for at least twenty minutes. This was after she gently informed me of the guest number limit and how I'd be exceeding it today. I was sure The Ellises' allowance was purely political. They had the spoils of the world at their fingertips.

"We need to give them the room, ladies," I agreed. "I'm sure this energy is more than Abshir needs." I pointed toward the door.

With little delay, the women began to file toward the door. Sadik was sure to beat them there and open it.

"I hope we don't have to leave the hospital," Aunt Astur cried. "I feel like we just got here. I have so many questions." The one who mentioned how short her visit had to be today. As she moved toward the door, she continued, regard exclusively to Sadik, "You don't mind if we have some for you? You're willing to answer. Right?"

"Anything you need answered, I'm willing to."

"Yeah?" Aunt Franzel asked as she passed through the door. "Like... Are you Black, Black?"

"One hundred percent, dear," Irene answered without skipping a beat.

And that's when I got it. While I knew Irene and Sadik's pop-up here was a part of an orchestration to drop in on my family, there was a bigger picture to it. Without giving me the heads up, Sadik's appearance today was to draw an illustration. He wanted my family to believe I was supported with Abshir. He could have shown alone, but Irene being the overly-doting mother she was had been the icing on the cake. She embraced me in front of my family, legitimizing me in a way I'd never been. By them being here declaring their close alliance to me, I was no longer bastardized. I'd belonged. It was the reason for the ring. He had to bring the ring to prove his commitment to me.

This was all so messed up because no matter how you diced it, the family claiming me was the cause of my brother being laid out helplessly in that bed to begin with.

I may have been temporarily grateful for Sadik's efforts today, but he was still no friend of mine.

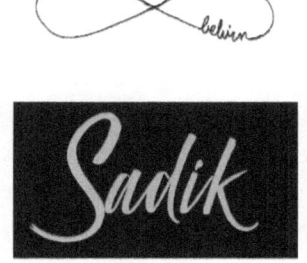

Lying stretched out in the bed while flipping through political talk shows felt like cheating, but so fucking good at ten o'clock at night. I'd eaten, had showered, and was now down for the night. This shit didn't even feel real. But it had been my new reality since getting Bilan on Sunday. This was something to get used to.

Flipping from *CNN* to *Fox*—because keeping an eye on the right-wing style of reporting was almost equally important—a frame approaching from the bathroom, in my peripheral, captured my attention. I caught her regard on my bare chest before her eyes met mine. She was done with her shower and had changed into a loose tee and shorts.

"Hey," she breathed.

"Hey."

I watched her rub her lips together, seemingly fortifying herself.

"Thanks...for what you did earlier...with my family." She pulled in a breath through her nostrils.

I met her family. It was something I knew would happen, but thought it would be under different circumstances. They were... everyday folks to me, but to Bilan, they were upper echelon, based on family history and politics.

"It was nothing," I murmured, using the remote to mute the television.

"What did you tell Irene?"

"The truth."

"Which is?" Bilan's gaze turned determined.

I tossed the remote on the bed, next to my thigh. "Are you ready to finally talk about all this shit? I'm more than prepared to explain it to you. I want to."

So fucking bad, Nalib...

"I just need to know what your mother knows. She's offered to come by the hospital often to be a support. But I don't want that type of generosity from Earl or Iban."

I shook my head and assured softly, "You don't have to worry about that. He wouldn't make it another day if they find out."

She broadened her shoulders and lifted her chin, likely not knowing I could see her fortifying herself again. A tear fell from her eye, but Bilan quickly wiped it away, heavily panting a full-blown cry away.

"Will she tell them?" I shook my head. "How do you know?"

"Because she's my confidant, too. I asked her for a favor, told her what she needed to know, and the terms of her assistance. That included confidentiality. She understands how sensitive and precarious this situation is."

Bilan nodded, eyes to the floor, blinking back the tears. She twisted her torso, looking about to leave, something I didn't want. I missed her terribly. I'd still been getting to know her before all the shit blew up in August.

"Why did you save him?" Her regard rolled up to me. "Why did you get him help, knowing it would cause this conflict in your family?"

This was the part I wasn't comfortable with: the opportunity to say something—express my feelings—at the risk of sounding insincere. Then she wouldn't trust me at all. Because Bilan still didn't reciprocate my feelings. She hadn't loved me. Yet.

"You know why, Bilan," I sighed those words. Then I sat up in the bed, bracing myself for her to fly out of here like a bat out of hell. But I wouldn't allow that dour possibility to keep me from being transparent with her. Bilan needed to know it all so she could decide. So she could choose me. "That day Damien kidnapped you —" Bilan sucked in a breath, reacting to my words. I can only imagine the trauma it caused her. "I'd met with my father and brother with a plan to finally address him. My father had two agendas: to kill Damien and...Ab."

I eyed her before continuing. "I asked them for the Ab job."

"Why?" she demanded.

I shook my head. "I don't know why, honey." It was something I couldn't explain with words.

"You're never short on articulation," her voice was unsteady. It amazed me how she could sense my thoughts. "You can explain."

"Because of you."

"You were going to kill my brother *for me?*"

"No!" I shook my head. "I didn't know what I was going to do. They doubted me because of the conflict of interest, and I don't take too kindly to challenges. As immoral as it sounds, I couldn't have my brother or his men take violence to your home. So, I went."

Bilan rocked on her toes. Her palm slapped her mouth. She gagged several times. I shifted in the bed to go for her until her other palm pushed into the air. I watched her swallow several times, eyes blinked hard until she got her body under control.

"You were—" She swallowed deeply again. "You were at my parents' home before he was shot?"

"Until I got the call about you being taken from *Michelle's*. I think Ab knew, but wouldn't tell me."

Then several tears fell, but Bilan fought for a stony resolve. "He set me up. He told me to meet him there," she squealed.

Shit...

My eyes swung to the floor. That was the most despicable act I've heard of a person who was not addicted to heroin. Ab led Bilan there that day. Memories began coming back in spades. Bilan wasn't feeling well. She'd told me she wasn't going to Nicky Ricci's party at the diner. We were supposed to talk that night when I got in. I promised to pick up a vintage port from *Elliswoods Palace's* cellar.

"So, were they right?"

Her question broke my thoughts. "Who?"

"Earl and Iban? Were they right about sending you to kill my brother?"

I didn't answer it directly. "When I got there and...experienced his disdain for you, I felt there was something missing. Some significant details to explain why you hadn't spoken much about him since I'd met you. Why would he threaten you with sucking his friend's dick?"

"He told you that?" Her eyes widened.

I swayed my head left to right. "In an around about way, yes. And as you can imagine, it didn't sit too well with me. It just didn't add up."

"What?" she asked with tight lips.

"You hardly speaking of him, not going to visit him. Him regarding you with such condescension. I don't believe I've ever seen it to that degree." I tossed my head to the side in a shrug. "So, I asked him about it." My eyes swung over to her, apologetically. I never wanted Bilan to think I didn't have her back. "He told me the story of the hustlers running up in your parents' restaurant for money your father owed."

A wrinkle dented between her brows. "What about it?"

"They threatened to kidnap you until he paid. And he begged them to take Ab instead."

Bilan's regard swept to the ceiling as she scoffed hard into the air. Her head shook indistinctly and her lips parted. I didn't want to overwhelm her with stories of her past, so I waited until she spoke next.

Her eyes met mine again. "Thanks for today." She looked as though she'd speak again, but strode off instead. That was awkward. And I didn't want her to go. I needed her to stay and talk. We couldn't move forward until our communication resumed. I lived to hold her attention. To have her interest in any manner.

I called behind her. "Did I say something wrong?"

Bilan stopped before pivoting slightly to catch my eyes. "No. But Abshir lied to you." I felt my face tighten in questioning. "Those guys didn't come in there about my father owing money. Abshir did. He robbed them." Tears pooled in her eyes as she fought to school her expression. "It was the fourth time someone, including the police, had come into the restaurant behind Abshir's miscreant behavior. My father had even been jumped by kids more than half his age over Abshir, three months earlier. *Aabo* had no money to repay the debt." She scoffed. "I think it was eight hundred dollars. They wanted to take me for eight hundred dollars. My father told them no." She turned toward the French doors. "Abshir wasn't the sacrificial lamb as he tried to describe. He lied to you." She sauntered away. "I have school work to get to." I caught the undeniable cry in her last words.

Fuck...

We'd driven past the playground, the tennis court, the pond, and the gates separating the state park from private property. Rory took to the unpaved dirt roads as though she'd driven them all her life.

Ironically, we'd been here just a handful of times. It was one of my most preferred, though because the undeveloped land was private. This desolate property was mine.

We drove over rocks, unleveled roadways, and broken branches for a few miles before Rory made a turn onto another manmade roadway for another mile. There, deep in the middle of nowhere, was the nondescript, black *Dodge Charger* I'd come to see. Rory pulled next to him, and I hopped out and into the *Charger*.

"Damn," Jefferson, my law enforcement plug, scoffed. "That's how we feeling today?" He remarked as I lowered into the passenger seat and closed the door.

I offered him my palm. "Come again..."

We greeted each other with a hand dab. "You, rocking a green sweat suit? I'm used to seeing you in suits," he jeered with mild seriousness. "What's that? *Gucci*?"

"Hell nah! *Ase Garb*," I answered, observing my clothing. "I just left the gym." Shrugging with my mouth, I explained, "This is my only appointment of the day."

"Rory had more questions when I requested to meet today. Did I hear correctly, you've been cutting back?" He chuckled, friendly.

"Yeah," I sighed, scratching my neck as I peered ahead, outside of the car. "It's been a busy season for me." Far more complicated than I cared to share. "But never too busy when you're requesting time. What's up?" I faced him again, expecting paperwork.

Jefferson's regard was now outside. "So, this is some sensitive shit." There was a slight, dramatic pause, and I waited it out. "A buddy of mine in the *Special Division Unit*—goddamn weak belly who ain't got no fucking business playing with big boys like that, but his father-in-law has high rank—mentioned some interesting shit to me the other night. We were out drinking after a colleague's funeral. All past wasted, all talking shit at this point. But my buddy and I find ourselves in a corner, alone now, and he mentions how the lieutenant heading up the *SDU* has them all focused on *The Commission*."

His eyes met mine. "*The Commission*'s existence has only been rumored. No one has been able to corroborate its factual existence. Until now." He gave a pause. "Apparently, one of its members is caught up in some shit with the *Bureau*. Heavy enough shit that has him cooperating. And to kick off the new relationship, his lawyer mentioned *The Commission*."

I considered that plenitude of intel he'd shared. *The Commission* was comprised of six parties. Damien and Rizzo were departed, and my father wasn't courting the *Federal Bureau of Investigation*. Either Jefferson's buddy hadn't named the person or Jefferson would not release the name. The fact of him meeting here eliminated the latter: why share this at all if he wouldn't give me a name?

"Has he given anything?"

"Not yet. The negotiation period isn't long, but the *Bureau* must be so confident in what they have on him to have given him their attention, period."

"Find out what you can. I'm not privy to such a group, though I'm categorically interested in who would turn against it."

Jefferson knew my father was a member of the organization. He also understood my need to separate myself from it.

"I thought you'd be. So much I invited his lightweight Irish ass over for my football night. The *Kings* are going to murder the *Patriots* next week."

I held my hand out to him, in the air. "For sure."

We met palms, then I dug into the kangaroo pocket of my hoodie and pulled out an envelope.

His face folded. "This isn't scheduled."

"This ain't for you," I made clear with hiked brows. "It's for your new addition...technically, her momma." I gave a slight bow. "Congrats to Mandy on delivering your legacy. Salute to you for expanding your loins, king." Jefferson lifted his arm, offering me dap. I pounded my chest before indulging him and continuing. "The Ellises are big on legacy, and I'm happy for you, man."

"I appreciate that, boss." He accepted the money.

"Now, let me take my green-eyed ass home so I can try and create my fuckin' legacy."

Jefferson laughed. "I hear that. Much respect, Ellis."

I left the *Charger* and deposited myself into the backseat of my ride. My attention immediately went to my vibrating phone. There was a text from *JAGMisha Boutique* advising my order had been delivered. Then my other phone vibrated.

"Queen," I answered. "Everything good?"

"Hey, handsome," my mother greeted with a thickness in her vocals in a way only a mother could. "I hope I'm not interrupting you."

"Not at all. What's going on?"

There was an abbreviated pause before she spoke again. "Is Bilan pregnant?"

My head jerked back. "No." I scoffed, forehead tightened. "Where'd that come from?"

She purred, hesitating. "I've only been here with her for two days, but she seems different."

"You hardly know her, queen." I chuckled.

"Yeah, but... These are distinct changes. She has a natural glow to her. She's got this perpetual exhaustion to her presentation." She paused again. "And when she's heavy in thought, she rubs and scratches her belly."

I'd seen her naked in the shower just the other day. The only noticeable difference to her appearance was Bilan had gotten a little smaller. And considering the shit storm she experienced last month, it was plausible.

My mind was preoccupied with more pressing matters, and I needed to end this conversation. "As inappropriate as this comment is to share with my mother, I'll do it anyway. Bilan's on birth control."

As soon as those words left my mouth, my attention went to Rory, catching her eyes in the rearview mirror. *Shit...* The conversation needed to end.

"Uh...oh. Okay." She sounded deflated. "Well, I thought I'd ask."

"It's all good, my love."

She giggled. "I'll let you go. Love you, honey."

"Love you, queen."

I dropped the phone, peering out of the window to the darkness of the night.

"Everything goodie?" Rory inquired.

We pulled off, engine purring over the dirt road.

"Yup." I sighed, beginning a text to Taaliba about a re-up on my tea order. "Just the *FED*s possibly about to shut down the crack, gun, car chop shop, and human trafficking rings of New Jersey."

Rory kicked the brake, jerking the car turbulently before realizing the action.

Taking a deep breath and blowing it out, I glanced across the bed at the three gowns. They'd been delivered this morning while I was at the hospital. One emerald green tulle, the other all black lace, and the last a blush sequin. They were all beautiful, regal even lying flat on the guest bedroom's queen bed. But which would fit? Then there were five pairs of sandals lining the wall ahead. Four clutches lay behind me on the bed. I had options for each evening gown. Decisions had to be made.

I was in no mood to figure it out now. Rory was waiting for me to text her when I was ready to go. I needed to meet my Aunt Astur back up at the hospital this afternoon to have a sit-down with the doctors. I was surprised she'd shown interest. She called last night asking to be there for the next update. I needed to be mentally prepared for that, too.

Lazily, I took to my feet and headed out of the room. I dragged my weighted body down the quiet hallway, feet pressing into the cool, marble white and gray, veiny flooring. I tapped my phone for an app to make an appointment with ShawnNicole for the fundraiser on Friday. When I stepped into the master suite, I could see the lights in the bathroom lit. Sadik was in there. Kimmy told me he'd just gotten in from the gym. It was bizarre how he had a loaded gym on the upper level he'd use in addition to one off the premises.

The closer I drew to the doors of the master suite, the louder I could hear blasting music. After a few seconds of lyrics, I recognized Xavier Omär's voice. Who knew Sadik was on to Xavier Omär? The man had the most varied palate.

I ambled into the closet to grab a pair of thick socks and indoor booties. The hospital room got cold, and I couldn't endure another evening of chilled toes from wearing my sandals. I pulled out the sock drawer and immediately peeped the two unopened boxes of condoms I'd taken to Costa Rica. My belly fluttered. What a joke. Suddenly, I wondered what my anxiety levels would be like had I insisted he used these. Had I continued to insist, at least, until my birth control began. That thought led me to another of my appointment on Monday. I'd been taking the pill daily, not knowing I was pregnant. Of course, I stopped right away when I knew, but in the recesses of my mind were concerns of harm to the baby.

Gosh...

I still couldn't believe I was pregnant—

My thoughts were interrupted by the sense of a movement from the corner of my eye. Sadik sauntered into the two-story closet naked, baring each inch of his golden skin. Each corner of his caramel body, each stitch of colored ink on his muscularly carved frame. His gait was with confidence and total virility. His profile powerful and captivating. Until he sensed my presence.

Sadik's eyes didn't balloon in surprise when they met me. His body paused and eyes narrowed. Posture nearly like a jaguar. Then he straightened, face impassive as he shared my gape. My greedy eyes bounced over every strapping inch of him again, helplessly. It felt like a lifetime ago that I'd seen *all of that*. Felt his skin roll over mine in passion, or explore me in adoration.

And like a panther, he stalked toward me, crossing the space. His thigh bulging each stride he made. His dick swelling until it bounced just above his belly button. I swallowed involuntarily as he walked into my personal space. Unaccustomed to this proximity to him anymore, my heart galloped in my chest, my lungs immobile.

"I'm sick, missing you."

My mouth fell open before I could find the words of rebuttal. "How can you miss someone you share a bed with at night?"

"You're not *here* with me. As selfish and territorial a muthafucka I am, I have to give you your space."

My eyes descended his chest, down to the standing beautiful, one-eyed veiny creature. Now, that. That was my friend, not its owner. The tip of his bulbous cock produced a weep of liquid. One bead was followed by another. When I lifted my head, Sadik's movements mimicked mine. A sleek grin widened on his golden face. He knew what I saw, intuitively understood exactly how my body was responding.

"*This* is space?"

He leaned into me, but I could still see the unruly spikes of his dirty blond eyebrows. They were drawn together, but his jaw was loose. Lips ajar and hungry.

"I'm ready to talk...about everything."

He was so close. God, he was so close. I could smell the jasmine and mint on his tongue. The woodsy fragrance of a recently shaven head, and the floral scent of his washed beard. And Sadik. His natural body odor that I'd never realized I was drawn to. It was sick. The innate animal attraction. The acute sexual draw. My chest heaved, breathing was audible and uncontrolled. Centimeters away now, I breathed in the air he exhaled. I tasted the jasmine and peppermint. So help me, I could ravish *him* the moment he hiccupped and pushed his luscious lips into mine. My knees went weak, trembling. Blood rushing in my ears. Mouth unbelievably salivating.

I'd never been so attracted...never had such a visceral connection to a human being as I had to Sadik Q. Ellis. And right now, with my resolve deliquescing, he knew. He knew I not only wanted him, but sickly needed him. All I had to do was move or verbally acquiesce.

"Nalib," he droned with hungry need, eyes molten with lust.

It was Sadik who conceded to begging. The heavy drums and seductive chords of Summer Walker's "*Prayed Up*" blasting in the entire suite deluded me. My body begged my brain to yield. Just lay

aside the stressors of your world for an hour for unparalleled pleasure. You deserve this.

He owes you—

"How was Derrick's body found in the burned down restaurant?"
I breathed into his parted lips.

He audibly sucked in a breath as he reared away from me. My
spine straightened and chest continued to heave.

"Bila—"

"I walked into this with my eyes wide open. I welcomed in your
seduction through frills of your lavish lifestyle. The private jets, the
designer clothing, exotic trips, affluent family, and generational
wealth." I nodded. "Yeah. I was there and conscious for it all, but
here is where I draw the line, Sadik! You're a murderer, a goddamn
gangster in a corporate CEO's chair! You're not that different from
your father or your brother."

I slid around the island. "But my name isn't Irene or Monica. I
don't choose this. There are just some things that green eyes, orange
hair, and a talented dick can't control or influence." My shaky hand
landed onto my chest. "My heart. The mind can be tricked sometimes. The heart discerns everything. You're not who you sold
me on."

I turned to leave.

"So where does that leave us?"

I shifted to his naked frame, cock still intimidating, resting
size now.

"Leave us?"

"Yeah. I'm not who you thought I was, but I know with every
fiber of my being we belong together."

I shook my head. "The DNA traits have been made clear to me."
I scoffed. "You belong to your family; a descendent of that dynasty."

"Yet, somehow, you own me."

My head reared, chest jolted. The wind had been knocked out
of me.

Sadik rounded the island, stretching his arms out. "This is me.
Everything you see." He gestured around. "All I have. You own me!"
his bark was full with a similar vulnerably resentful emotion he'd

expressed when announcing his love for me. After what I'd recently been through, I was no longer that Bilan. I would likely soon be without a member of the family I once knew. I had a baby on the way, barring no complications.

I could never be her again to survive him. His family that would inevitably be in my life forever because of the bundle incubating inside of me.

My head swung left to right as I peered him directly in his striking irises. "There's so much about me you don't know. So many components to my existence. But remember, my eyes stay open. This time, wisdom will be employed. And wisdom is telling me to be deliberate with my dealings with you and not yielding. You say I own your heart, Sadik?" I scoffed. "And wisdom tells me you're no good for mine. The next time I open any part of me to you, it'll be on my terms and not yours!"

I grabbed my things and left the closet.

"Hey," Kimmy, craning her head into the doorway, greeted.

"Hey." I peered over my shoulder. "What's up?"

I was wrapping up the gowns I decided against to have sent back to *JAGMIsha Boutique*. Oddly, one, the emerald green tulle, was too big.

"Ms. Taaliba's here and wants to see you."

My face fell. Taaliba? Here? No one ever came here, which was the only peace I had about returning to Sadik's place. It was enough that I'd accepted Irene's assistance with Abshir. She was even there now, giving me time to come to the apartment to sort through the gowns and shoes for tomorrow's fundraising dinner. But *another* Ellis?

"Everything okay?" Kimmy asked.

My forehead lifted, face opened to correct my expression. I took in a hefty breath. "Yeah. Yeah." I nodded. "I'll be right out."

"Okay. I'll tell her." Kimmy took off.

I took a moment to remind myself Taaliba had been sweet to me in all the encounters I'd had with her. After finishing up in the guest bedroom, I made my way to the front of the apartment. After searching the television and living rooms, I found Taaliba in the kitchen with Kimmy. She was there, wearing hunter green parachute pants, a thin heather gray t-shirt loosely draping over her breasts, and red and white checkered print slide-on sneakers. Her varied bracelets were in place: beads, strings, and a few metals, collectively four to five inches wide. There were no earrings, and the small chain necklace could barely be seen. But it was her.

"Hi, Taaliba," I greeted stiffly as soon as I entered.

She glanced behind as she sat at the island. Taaliba's smile was bright when she immediately slid off the stool and headed my way.

"There she is!" Taaliba cheered, sweeping me into her arms for a tight hug. "Mom told me you were back in town."

As my body tensed into almost a knot, I was able to see Kimmy across from us, smiling.

Taaliba released me, leaping back. "Are you okay?"

"Yes!" I tried for cheery. "Yeah," I stammered. "I'm okay. Just tired, I guess."

Taaliba's eyes expanded, as did her mouth. "I have something for you!" Her palms met. "Has he told you yet?"

Who?

My face fell.

"My new profession. Did Sadik tell you?"

I grinned, warming already to Taaliba's affectionate spirit. There was something about the way she regarded her brothers that appealed to me.

"No. I don't think so." I moved toward the island for a seat.

"I'm an herbalist." She swung her arms in the air, presenting herself. "I've been studying under a tenured, well-respected professional for some time now. He hasn't told you about my teas? That's why I'm here." She moved toward the counter and gestured to two jade green bags. "I'm re-upping him on my energy booster and sleep time teas. And can you believe he's actually paying me?" She laughed excitedly.

"Wow," was all I could say. Taaliba was clearly excited about this. Then something occurred to me and I asked Kimmy, who was writing out a list on her tablet. "Is this the stuff I've had?"

"Yes," Kimmy answered, half her attention to our conversation. "The first night you returned home, he asked that I make you the banana bread and this tea to help you rest after your travel. And a couple of nights ago, when you were out on the patio studying, I fixed that."

Suddenly concerned about my pregnancy, I blurted, "Please tell me these are all natural!"

Taaliba placed a comforting hand on my shoulder, so she thought. "*All* natural. Not an ingredient a baby couldn't take—not that I'd serve a baby tea."

I watched as Kimmy left us in the kitchen alone. "And the energy booster?"

"That's a hit with many. I made some for my mom, and she's been running the streets lately. I haven't been able to find her, which is weird." She frowned, eyes cast to the floor. She shook off that thought. "Anyway...it's the jasmine I love the most about it, other than the effect it gives for hours long."

That made me think, too. "Jasmine and peppermint?"

She nodded. "And a few other add-ins, yup." She resumed her stool at the island. "Enough of that. How are you? I can't believe you left that long. Sadik has been a wreck."

Grinning, I shook my head. "A wreck."

Yeah, right...

"He has, which is why I made that particular energy booster. He'd barely have enough energy to finish a damn meal. I mean, I swear." Her chin dipped. "I thought you two broke up and he didn't have the heart to tell the family that the one girl who managed to get his nose wide opened dumped his ass."

My eyes ballooned, lips spread in a tight smile. I didn't know what to say.

"Interesting." I placed my elbow on the countertop and rested my head on my hand.

"I'm just happy you're back. Spending a whole month away with your family after busting wide open on a dude was a boss ass move, if I may say so myself." She offered me a high-five, and I didn't have the heart to deny her. "Having a man is completely archaic. Relationships between a man and a woman are completely passé."

My forehead wrinkled. "Are you...gay, Taaliba?"

Her style was not boyish, but Taaliba's hair was cut into a pixie style similar to mine, spikier with no ironed curls. Honestly, her style fit her. However, I could never figure out who Sadik's sister was. Her career hops didn't help, either.

Taaliba stood from the island and promenaded over to the cabinet for a wine glass. My face folded again as she picked up an opened bottle of wine. She brought it back to the island, pouring herself a glass.

"You want some?"

"No." I shook my head. "I'll be out tomorrow...drinking...socially," I lied.

Taaliba shrugged, then lifted the glass into the air, saluting. "I'm free."

"Okay..."

"And of course, your next question will be *what's free*."

"It's not for me to pry. Not my business." I swiped my palms in the air and swung my neck.

"No. It's okay." Her words and body language turned eager. "I don't mind sharing it with you. You're going to be my sister-in-law." *I doubt that...* "I'm asexual."

I blinked hard. "Asexual, as in you don't have a desire to mate with either sex or can't relate to either?" I motioned, being stuck with my words, rolling my wrists in the air.

Taaliba turned away from me, going for her glass and taking a sip of the red wine. Her verve since I walked into the kitchen had certainly waned.

She shrugged. "Asexual as in I don't care to give my heart or pussy to either."

"Does your mom know about this?" Taaliba shook her head. "You don't feel comfortable talking to her?"

It felt like an eternity until she spoke again. "She's too busy doing what I have no desire being."

"And what's that?"

She tossed her regard my way. "Being what Monica is...and what Nena is...Diane is, and now Lia, and god knows the number of other women connected to the men in my family are. Negotiators."

I snorted, "Negotiators of what?"

Taaliba finally turned to me, opening her body language to engage again. "Of their affection, hearts, total beings, their souls. Do you know how many souls my father and brother, Iban, have claimed and gave a shit about?"

"No, but I trust your judgment." We caught eyes for seconds long before she went back to her wine. My lips poked and twisted as I considered my next words. "So you've never seen any positive examples of how a man commits to one woman?"

She sighed. "I'm sure you're going to say you have the perfect fiancé. And my brother's one of a kind...you've never met a man like him and such, but there's nothing new under the sun when it comes to the dynamic between men and women."

"Perfect?" I turned away, scratching my neck as I murmured, "You don't know your brother." I faced her again. "Howeveaaa!" I made a dramatic expression with my index finger in the air. "Never in my life have I come across a Sadik. An Ellis, no less." And I was sticking to that.

This family was murderously insane, even if it was only the men.

When Taaliba's expression was one of confusion, I decided to move on.

"Have you ever been with a woman?" For some reason, it felt like a possibility with Taaliba.

She downed the glass and stood to return to the bottle for more. Her movements toward the counter were uncomfortably rapid. Taaliba poured the wine in silence.

With her back to me, she began, "Once and a half." Then she finally turned to face me, this time resting against the counter across the room from me.

"Okay." I nodded emphatically. I wouldn't judge her. She needed to know this. I was curious about who Taaliba was, not what I thought she should be. "And were you in safe, trusting relationships with them?"

She shook her head while gulping down more wine. "The first was more interested in turning me out. We kissed, she groped and went down on me. It was disastrous. I told her to stop and left the house party right away. Alone. I couldn't scrub my skin hard enough. I felt dirty for days."

"And the other half of one experience?"

With one arm wrapped protectively beneath her breasts and the other holding her glass into the air, Taaliba gazed outside of the window.

"That one was more gentle. It was intimate. Sweet. She was my philosophy professor. It was my second year at *Howard*."

I nodded. "Did you love her?"

She shook her head. "I trusted her. She was in love." Her brows lifted. "With me. And I believed her. The prospect was too enormous for me. What the fuck do I know about pleasing a woman mentally, emotionally...spiritually." There was a pause before she shrugged. "I broke that shit off. It was too much pressure. And I didn't want to be the fuck up past the lack of reciprocity."

"You didn't want to be your father or brothers."

"Or my mother."

My eyes narrowed in confusion. "I don't understand."

"She gives her heart to only one man, but her body to him and others. If that's what commitment is like, I want no parts of that shit."

My eyes fell away. "I see."

"No, you don't. I've studied the art of love, marriage, and romance. I read the evolution of them over the years. The premise of marriage...the ancient Greek, where marriage was simply for the perception of happiness. Childbearing was a key factor in the union amongst Spartans. Or the Athenians who believed marriage to be significant for social and political purposes. The ancient Hebrews practiced polygamy, per the Bible. Look at Solomon's king ass with his whole fucking 700 wives and 300 goddamn concubines! Then when you recall arranged marriages and the rules of remarriages for widows. It's all bullshit."

"Okay. But what about your primal needs?" I asked. "You can help who you fall in love with, but not who you're attracted to. Whether we hate it or love it, most of us are sexual beings. Who do you find yourself drawn to gender-wise?"

"Me!" Her gaze on me was defiant.

I nodded again, not wanting her to believe this was a debate so much as it was an exploratory conversation. That quickly, I gathered this had been a huge issue for Taaliba, and for quite some time. Sexuality isn't discovered in your mid to late twenties.

"Bilan." Kimmy appeared in the doorway of the kitchen. "The courier's here from *JAGMisha Boutique*."

That snatched me out of this trance I'd that quickly slipped into with Sadik's sister. I couldn't believe the rabbit hole I'd found myself in, in such a short period of time.

I turned back to Taaliba, who now had wild eyes and tense shoulders as she sipped on her wine. "I'll be right back. It should only take a few minutes."

Taaliba nodded her acknowledgement, and I quietly left the room. As quickly as I could, I dashed into the guest bedroom, wondering how I'd carry two heavy, bagged gowns and four boxes of shoes to the door. Like an angel, Kimmy was rolling a bellman's cart into the room.

"Thank so much!" I chuckled nervously. "I didn't know how many trips this would take."

"No worries at all." She began for the gowns.

"I can take it from here, Kimmy. I'm sure you have more important things to do."

She froze. "You sure?"

"You spoil me. Are you kidding?" I smiled. "Go!"

She laughed. "Alright. Call me if you need me."

It took no time for me to load everything onto the cart and, minutes later, I was pushing it out of the room and down the hall. I recognized the guy from the boutique who helped me with putting the bags in my father's car months ago.

"How are you?" I asked as he began toward me for assistance.

"I'm fine. Thanks. Sorry these didn't fit. Mishka has a knack for sizing. She's going to be disappointed she missed this one."

"Oh! The blush sequin fits just fine. And to be honest—" my voice drew low. "—I've lost a few inches in the boob area recently. I'm sure they'll be back in full bloom soon." Believe me.

"I'll let her know."

"And I'll walk you down," I offered because the bellman's cart needed to come back up.

I followed him out and, without much further conversation, we were downstairs where security allowed him to double park. He placed the clothing in his car and took off. I was on my way back up to the apartment, feeling tired. My bladder was heavy, so once inside, I used the powder room to relieve myself. Once done, I padded into the kitchen, hoping I hadn't kept Taaliba waiting too long.

Vulgar expletives had me halting.

"The fuck, Leeb! I've been honest. Been fuckin' patient, too," a deep male's voice declared in only a way he would to someone he was sincerely trying to appeal to. "You asked me not to chill with her no more, so I backed out of the Ivory Coast trip. Now, I'm saying it's not a good time to take you on my family trip back to DR, and you say it's too fuckin' much?"

He was annoyed.

"Danny—"

"Don't fuckin' *Danny* me, Leeb! I'm too old—you're too old—for this teasing shit! You said you were gonna give it a try. I stopped all my shit this summer for you. Everything. Every fucking body! Haven't I been good to you? A man of my word?"

"Yes," she droned, dipping her head.

I craned my neck a few inches toward the right to see where she was, then darted back. Taaliba was talking via *FaceTime* to a very... beige man. I looked again and found him gazing away, appearing to try to calm himself. He was shirtless and had lots of hair pulled into a ponytail on top of his head.

"Did I give you my undivided time all summer, even following your chocolate ass to Canada for your art exhibit? Had me hiding like some fuckin' punk in your hotel suite. I did all that shit to prove to you I'm finally ready—"

"I know—" He interrupted her this time.

"All for your selfish ass to basically tell me to kiss ya ass because some shit came up and I can't take you with me. That's fucked up, but it's all good." There was a lazy, urban undertone to his speech.

His dialect switch from street to formal was even looser than Sadik's. But this guy didn't seem "streety," though. "I can't keep doing this, Leeb," he warned.

"Doing what?"

"This! This shit we been doing all summer. Chilling, going slow, you suckin' my dick, but I can't return the favor. You don't want to make love. Don't want to take this to the next level. You gave me all that bullshit about nobody catering to your unique needs, but you do for everybody else. Well, I dedicated my whole fuckin' summer to going at your pace. All for this shit to blow up in my fuckin' face."

"Danny—"

"Don't fuckin' *Danny* me, Leeb!" he groaned. "I gotta run. I'll hit you later."

The line went dead, and Taaliba's face dropped toward the countertop.

I stepped inside the kitchen, resting my back against the edge of the archway.

These damn Ellises!

My face wrinkled. "I don't think sucking dick all summer falls under the description of asexual." I wrapped my arms beneath my breasts. Who's the lucky guy?"

Taaliba didn't lift her head when she murmured, "I was hoping you wouldn't be back before that call was done."

"I can see why. He's crazy about you."

"Miguel Daniel Lopez is the only guy I've done anything remotely sexual with," she defended herself. "And I've known him since sixth grade, if that counts for anything."

My brows met. "Sounds to be something more to me...and Danny."

Her head pushed up, but Taaliba didn't look back at me. "Sucking dick isn't a big deal. I'm twenty-six years old and waited this long."

"I'm twenty-eight and sucked my first one this summer, too."

"And?" she grumbled.

My head bobbed up and down as I chose my words. "And it was pretty amazing; life changing, actually."

Her head swung to face me. "Ewwwww, Bilan!"

"Eww what?"

"Sadik's old. He'll be forty soon."

"And very much virile with the stamina of a steed."

She gagged. "I think I'm gonna be sick."

I pushed from the wall and ambled to her. "My point is, it wasn't something requested of or thrust upon me." I nodded. "It was something I wanted to do. Turned out to be quite a task. Enough of one for me to *have to* decide if I wanted to do again. And I did." Again and again and again. *God... First nausea, then an indescribable perpetual ache in my groin.* Then again, I'd been that way since the Pixie concert. "It was a desire...for sex. It was my sensuality at work. Asexuals don't have that function."

I kept my tone gentle, low. Taaliba was only two years younger than me, but the age gap felt wider for some reason. I also wondered why couldn't she discuss this with her mom...brothers. She, Iban and Sadik didn't have the contemptuous relationship I'd had with my older brother. Why couldn't they just talk about the basics?

Or had Taaliba explained that? She mentioned the rampant infidelity happening in their family. Clearly, it had far reaching implications. Poor Taaliba here seemed to have defined her sexuality because of it.

"You can't put a label on me," she claimed defensively.

I could see right through her fearful veneer.

"I'm not. I'm just trying to understand why you're clearly running away from someone who wants more of you. You've known him since eleven—twelve years old: his feelings for you didn't begin this summer. You two must have a history. My question is, why have you not shared with him your 'sexuality?'"

"He knows." Taaliba's regard went to the window. "He knows me better than anyone."

Whoa...

That was girlie; it was cheesy.

I stood to leave the kitchen. "Then you need to figure out your identity and what that means to your relationship with that Danny guy. He seems to be hurting." When I made it to the archway, I glanced back. "Did you know your brother wasn't home?"

Taaliba nodded.

"And you stop by to drop off tea anyway?"

She shook her head. "If I can be honest, I came to see you. I just flew in from Napa Valley a couple of days ago when Mommy told me you were back. She hasn't been around, so..." She shrugged. "I was hoping you'd be home."

The last thing I needed was Sadik's sister getting attached to me. I wouldn't be here long. But what was I supposed to do? She had no idea of what had been going on.

"Well, I need to go buy a bra for this fundraiser your brother's taking me to tomorrow," I tried ending this visit.

Taaliba stood from the island. "I'm free for the rest of the day."

Dear, God in heaven...

Just... Wow...

I'd never been in a room of mostly Black and brown professional people in my life. Yet they were all here, in suits, gowns, and hard bottom shoes. I was being introduced to so many of them between Sadik and I crossing the room, and them greeting us independently. He held me possessively at the hip, the groove in my lower back carved perfectly for his height, it seemed. We'd only been here for twenty minutes, and I felt like I'd shaken hands with three dozen people already. They seemed familiar with Sadik. To say the least, I was overwhelmed.

I thought I knew Paterson, having grown up next door to it and working there for so long. But I'd never seen this Paterson. Even those not from the city had some type of investment or interest there. Their titles and affiliations varied, from government to established businesses. Who knew so many people were into politics?

And of course, the event wasn't held in Paterson. We were at a lavish banquet hall in Totowa. It was large, plush with massive chandeliers and silk drapes hanging from tall windows. Wait staff in tuxedos, men and women. There was a deejay in a tux, playing instrumental jazz music, lending itself to the ambiance.

Sadik looked god-awfully amazing in his tux, per usual. His head glistened, lips sheened, and his scent had me leaning into him as we traveled the room. His facial hair was cut close to his face, and his eyes sparkled under the golden lightning of the room.

"A drink?" he offered close to my ear, voice low, yet he was detached.

It was how I preferred it. So far, all was well, but I knew this would be a rough night for me. All week, I'd only seen Sadik in passing and shared a quiet bed with him at night. He'd only pushed that one time in his closet. But here, I was underneath him, meeting his associates. And now I'd been offered a drink. I was prepared.

"Yes." I cleared my throat. "Please."

He motioned for a waitress, carrying a tray of wine and champagne. She came right away, threading through the stately crowd. Sadik handed me a red wine, and he selected bubbly for himself.

I pretended to take a sip like I did in *Macen Beach* with Jason and his friends. With my lips pressed to the rim of the glass, I pulled the bottom up to let the liquid touch the tip of my lip, then lowered it.

"So this is your crowd?" My eyes swept the extravagant room.

I could feel his regard land on me. Sadik didn't answer right away. "I don't think so, no."

"You seem pretty popular." Why couldn't I look at him?

Just stretch your eye muscles to the right...

"It's kind of hard not to be in New Jersey. I own businesses here. The state isn't that big on a political level." I was able to see his hand gesture the room.

"Sounds like they don't know you." My eyes danced over the lively room. "It makes me wonder who does."

When I felt his gaze on me, I robotically turned to him. "I guess we're two in the same."

"How so?"

"I don't think your small circle knows you completely. Your family doesn't, and neither do your two friends."

"They know me."

Sadik's head shook softly while his yellow eyes danced in mine. "Not in totality, they don't." His voice was soft, emotions not so controlled. "If they did, they wouldn't have bought that bullshit story about you up and taking a trip, needing a break from everything and everybody."

"How do you know I told them that?"

"Sweetheart, I had to know everything. You were down there, virtually alone. I needed to see all the moving parts on the board."

My face folded. "Virtually alone?"

Sadik took a sip of his champagne. He took his time swallowing it back as he gazed ahead. "You think I'd let you go alone and unprotected? You'd never been to *Macen Beach* before this summer. And even if you had, at this point, you can't go anywhere without security."

I finally turned my entire body into him. Coolly, Sadik did the same. "You had someone watching me?"

I knew I'd felt eyes on me. The suspicion grew after I'd run into Jason. It had possibly been there before, but I was shut in, sick, and depressed.

"Bilan, leaving you unprotected could potentially cost your life," his words fell regretfully.

"How?" I demanded, body tensing, hands fiercely gripping the stem of the glass. "I was 'unprotected' before you. I was fine."

"You were. But you've been seen with me. People—good and not so—learned of our engagement. That alone attaches you to my family. I explained this to you."

He had. The night I acquiesced to move in with him. He mentioned it at the jazz park months earlier, too.

"Who was it?" I asked. "Who was shadowing me?"

He pivoted, taking another sip. "It's inconsequential now. You're safe."

My eyes fell as I processed it all. "You knew I ran into Jason."

"It didn't make me happy, but yes."

How much did he see?

Does he know?

"You knew when I found the money?"

"I got a call when you were on your way to the grocery store. The next day, when you bought the laptop, I knew for sure."

My stomach fell to the floor. He'd been watching me. All those weeks of feeling like I was alone. Dreaming of my parents...him. Those dreams kept me sane, almost driving me crazy at the same time.

I gazed up, narrowing my eyes to him. "Did you get a report on how many times I cried?" I swallowed back tears.

Sadik turned to me again, crowding over me with dark amber eyes. "You finding that money was the first time I knew without a single fuckin' doubt, outside of making love, we had a connection. You remembered a personal, intimate, and non-sexual moment we shared. It was more than survival. It was a connection burned into the meninges of your brain, the ventricles of your heart. Something innate you were able to pull out while in your fight mode. I knew you'd use it resourcefully, if needed."

My jaw collapsed. "You knew I'd go there! You—" I caught the volume of my voice and lowered it. "—knew I'd go to the house?"

This night had quickly turned into an unexpected event. We'd waited all week to have this discussion in public?

With his eyes locked to me, his head shook softly. "I *prayed* you'd go there instead of your family. When I saw you didn't go back to your parents', I swear—" His eyes closed for several seconds. "—my heart stopped beating for a full thirty seconds. I prayed for more than the control of your destination. I thought I'd die the first day, until I got the alert of the security system being disarmed. You didn't catch a flight. I called in a favor to check. Bilan," he droned, eyes rolling to the back of his head. "I've never felt so fuckin'...lost in my entire life."

His eyes reddened in an instant. I was utterly speechless, gaze tossed to the bodies moving around us. "That makes two of us."

"And you worried me those first weeks. You wouldn't eat—"

"I ate!" That flew from my lungs defensively.

"Two slices of pizza every two days isn't eating, Bilan," he whined, turning into me.

My breath held in my chest, head spinning, and belly flipping over at his sheer vulnerability. He knew what I ate and when I ate it. What was this level of fixation?

"Excuse me," I breathed. "I have to go to the restroom."

I turned on my heel, leaving him there in his twisted truth alone. Stopping to ask a member of the wait staff, I found my way to the restroom. It was large with stalls around the sink area sitting in the middle of the room. I cut a right as soon as I entered and found an open door. Once in the stall, I paid a few moments to getting my breathing under control.

"Did you see who's here?" one woman asked with humor in her voice.

"Yup," another woman returned, her tone hushed as the other's. "You're not surprised, are you? I knew he'd be here."

"How did you know? You said you hadn't seen him all summer. By the way, he's looking delicious in that fucking tux. Damn!" she breathed.

"If you're done lusting over the man," the other woman playfully scoffed.

"My bad, girl." She giggled.

"No. I get it. His appeal is undeniable. He's empirically superior on many fronts; however, in politics, he is not."

"Yeah. Yeah. I knew you'd say that. But what you haven't said is how you knew he'd be here."

"That's an easy one. Look whose event this is, for one."

"True."

"And secondly, I had lunch with him a few weeks ago."

There was a gasp. "I thought you said he officially ended things back in the spring."

"What I said was..." her voice lowered even more. "He explained he'd gotten into something he wanted to give a fair shot. I'm not the one to play games or hedge around reality. So, I took his words for religion and stopped contacting him."

I didn't know how long I'd stay inside the stall, but now felt like an awkward time to go.

"But you knew he'd be here?" she reminded her.

"Yes. He's at our table. I believe next to your library head guy. I had dinner with him last week."

"Really?" the woman's voice had hiked, excited.

"Nothing happened," she droned. "Other than the light once there in his eyes when I'd see him didn't appear not one time."

Heels click-clacked against the floor, and her voice grew faint.

"Really?" the woman's gasp sounded distant.

They were leaving.

Yes...

I was ready to go. I didn't use the bathroom; didn't have to. I was now calm, thanks to eavesdropping. So, I left the stall and washed my hands. I headed out and back to the ballroom when I heard my name.

It was a male's voice, so I turned, looking for Sadik. I never expected to see Tom Banks. I stood stunned as he sauntered my way.

"I thought that was you." His expression matched how I felt. "What are you doing here?"

"What are *you* doing here?" I smiled to soften the blow.

"My boss bought a few plates and invited me," he explained.

"Oh. That's a good boss."

He pushed his hands into his pockets. "Your turn."

I shrugged, crossing my arms beneath my breasts. "My boss bought my plate, too."

The last time I saw Tom was at *Elliswoods Palace* for Iesha's birthday barbeque. Tom remained in one area of the garden, similar to how Nena and Diane primarily stayed in another.

"Unless you've picked up a job since July, you don't have a boss, unless you mean your fiancé."

I laughed. Like genuinely guffawed. Tom pinched the bridge of his nose and shook his head dramatically.

"How did two kids from West Paterson end up mixing in the Ellis family?"

"Oh, I can tell you how I did." He scoffed, brows hiked for emphasis.

I pretended to cover my ears. "No gross stories before dinner."

Tom laughed, and I couldn't help but to as well.

∞||∞

Tom's humor was cut, thanks to his phone. It must have been vibrating in his pocket. As he pulled it out, my eyes swept the lobby for familiar faces I foolishly thought I'd see.

"Shit," Tom swore beneath his breath.

I smiled his way. "That bad?"

"Just spoke her up."

"Who?"

"Irene. She's been calling since I got here, which is funny as shit. I haven't been able to get her when I wanted her all week. She's been on some weird shit. Nobody's been able to get her until she wants to be available. Now, she's calling like crazy." My brows met. Irene had been with me this week, at the hospital with Abshir. "Got that nigga calling me," he mumbled, rolling his eyes.

"Who?" I thought fast. "Earl calls you?" I whispered hard.

"Hell, no," he snorted. "But he damn sure know how to reach me. Palmer hit me up."

Palmer was Earl's personal assistant. He did all of Earl's civilized work for him.

"Oh."

"Yeah. It must be bad if that old man's looking to me for answers."

"Hey, Banks," someone greeting from behind me.

I turned to find two young women. One was black, jet black bob with her bangs meeting her lashes. She wore a burnt orange tube top gown, A-line cut with her pouch of a stomach evident. Next to her was a brown beauty. Unless she was mixed, she couldn't have been Black based on her undertones and hair texture. She sported a smoky green and black lace gown. Makeup mild, lips a neutral *MAC C-Thru* shade. Her tortilla shoulders were exposed. They were narrowed and cut, making it clear she worked out. Her arms were bronzed, adorning a single black threaded bracelet. Her ebony eyes bounced between Tom and me as her friend approached.

"Brittany," Tom greeted. "Hey, girl."

She gaited straight into his arms. "I knew I'd see you. Guess who'll be tablemates?"

Her nasally utterance rang familiar to me.

"Really?" Tom replied, chin tossing in gesture to the woman with Brittany. "Sofia, too?"

Brittany giggled again, head bouncing up and down. "Yeah."

Sofia forged the faintest smile before going to her phone. She gave off a frigid vibe.

"That means I'm at the cool kids' table," Tom joked, towering over Brittany.

"Your plantation owner spared no expense for this one, chief," Brittany jeered.

That laughter cemented the possibility of her being one of the women chatting in the restroom earlier.

"This should be fun," Tom replied as Brittany moved away to rejoin Sofia.

"See you in there." Brittany waved cheerily.

I turned to Tom. "She sooo wants you, Banks! Oh, my god!"

"Lots of them do, girl."

"But you prefer seasoned women," I teased as his attention went to his phone again.

"No," he spoke while observing it. "I particularly like one seasoned woman, whose needs for me are limited." His eyes narrowed as he read something on the screen. "One who won't let up on me right now," he murmured. "I have to take this, Bilan. I'm sorry."

"No. Go." I waved my hand. "It's okay."

"I should see you inside," were his parting words. "Besides, looks like your 'boss' is summonsing you right now anyway." He pointed over my shoulder before breaking in the opposite direction.

Sadik stood in the doorway of one of the ballroom's entrances, a drink in one hand and the other in his pocket. He was summonsing me, all right. Words weren't necessary when his eyes were fixed onto me. My nipples stung, belly fluttered in excitement. I groaned inwardly, hating this visceral reaction to him. For chrissakes, I shared a bed with him at night and still didn't know who he was. Or did I? Sadik had been the same alpha male he was when I met him, only now with patience.

He seemed at peace, even with the distance between us this week. I'd been hearing about his decision to be home more now. He'd been sleeping a lot in between working out and conducting business from his home office. Sadik's presence was heavy. It didn't matter that he didn't make demands on me to take a vacation, to quit my job, or which type of degree to pursue for my master's. His aura could still be felt, whether I was at his place or in the hospital with my brother. I'd actually come to appreciate it...*as sick as that sounds*.

Ugh!

Although my brother fought for his life every second of the day at the hands of the Ellis family, I felt more alone before meeting Sadik, and in *Macen Beach* last month than I did dealing with this. I was never alone. Didn't have to worry about bills, food, or safety—as long as those other two Ellis men stayed away from me—while enduring this.

And he remained, quietly lurking in the shadows of the safety net he'd been providing me.

Without further delay, I began his way. Sadik offered his arm when I arrived.

"There are a couple of people I'd like you to meet," I shared when she curled onto my arm. "You okay?"

Her bolting out of here the way she did earlier concerned me. On the one hand, I was happy to cut through the wall she'd put between us, but on the other, I didn't want to upset her. I'd been going crazy each day I couldn't touch her...talk to her casually.

"What does Tom do for a living?" She totally re-navigated the topic of conversation as I retrieved a flute of champagne from a passing waiter for her.

"Who?"

"Tom Banks. What does he do?"

I straightened before answering. Who the fuck gave a shit about Tom Banks? "Director of the Paterson libraries."

After a few steps, Bilan's broke. She stumbled slightly.

"You okay?"

"Ye—yeah." She smiled up at me. "I'm fine."

I was just about to speak again when I heard, "Shit! Now, I have to pay up."

It was Julius headed our way with Keisha.

"Shut up," Keisha rolled her eyes, then she offered her hand. "But I am surprised to finally meet you!" She and Bilan shook hands as Julius snickered. He was going to be a dick about this, I could tell. "She's beautiful, Deek. And those freckles!" She gushed.

Yes. Those goddamn freckles kept the front of my boxers wet

every morning when getting out of bed this week. A few times, I found myself staring at them before she woke up. Bilan's beauty needed no fucking foundation covering God's ornaments.

I gave a slight bow in response. "Bilan, this is Keisha Richards. And this is Mr. Keisha Richards, also known as my friend, Julius," I joked.

"Oh." Bilan chirped, I guessed putting faces to names. "You're Julius Richards!" She shook Keisha's hand again, this time with more verve. Then she went for Julius'. "It's a pleasure to finally meet you. Sadik has had wonderful things to say." Her eyes flickered my way.

"And don't believe a word of it, unless it includes me being the flyer kid in *Blakewood*," Julius joked. "It was the accent the ladies all fawned over with me. Those cat eyes and that corn-colored hair of his totally went unnoticed when I stepped into the room."

"Shut up, Julius!" Keisha faked cried. She couldn't keep her eyes off Bilan long. "This is what he does every time Sadik comes around. This is the dynamic of best friends."

"Best friends?" Julius frowned. "That dude ain't my best friend. He's a former pussy magnet." He pulled Keisha into him. "Once I got the one for me, I dismissed his ass."

The three of them laughed as I took a final sip of my champagne. A passing waiter caught my attention and I waved him over.

"Yes!" Julius approved as he grabbed a flute. "This is a momentous occasion. Yes, we're going to hopefully make a few dollars for my campaign, but I'm finally meeting the woman who owns the heart of Sadik Qadir Ellis. And she's beautiful, too!"

"She is beautiful," I finally cut in. "Did you expect anything less from me, Julius?"

Bilan giggled nervously.

"And she has boobs!" Julius announced at an excited, yet cautious level. "Babe, you see she has boobs!"

Bilan's attention went down to her cleavage, as did mine. I regretted it right away. Bilan's body had been off limits to me for what felt like an eternity. She glanced up at me, continuing with her nervous laughter. I understood: Julius could be a lot to deal with on this matter. He'd been wanting to meet her since I told him about her before the Pixie concert. I'd left dinner with him to attend.

I was now uncomfortable. Bilan was still chuckling.

Julius issued me one of his silly ass, goofy ass expressions. "You ever tell her you really like her?"

This motherfucker...

"As a matter of fact, I did," I answered, playing his game.

"Oh, right! You did when you went from zero to sixty with pursuing her as a thirty-nine year old man who can't control his emotions! I forgot!"

Bilan's laughter turned serious. No longer was it an uncomfortable titter. Her eyes went wild as she gazed up at me again. "He *is* your best friend."

My brows lifted in warning. "He absolutely is not. He's a goddamn pain in the ass, as you can clearly see."

Keisha was cackling, too. Of course, he'd try this shit at something as serious as a fundraiser for his mayoral campaign. Maybe I should have come alone. Bilan didn't exactly want to be in public with me, and Keisha was extending Julius' leash too much tonight, of all nights with Bilan here.

"He's my idol." Julius' humor began to clear from his tan face. "I'm learning to be grateful every day." His arm swept around Keisha's shoulder. "But I swear, if I didn't have my life, I would want his. As self-deprecating as that sounds, it's a proud flaw I'll take to my grave. That's how much of an upstanding cat this guy is." He tossed his chin my way. "The only things I wouldn't trade are the love of my life and my babies," he attempted clean up. "Those are the only elements keeping me from jumping from my skin into his, and kicking his 'too cool for school' ass out."

Bilan *awww*'d, falling for his shit. While Richards had copped to this on many occasions—most were when drinking heavily—I was in no mood for the embarrassment in front of Bilan.

I was grateful when one of his team members broke up our little cypher, telling the Richards it was showtime.

"We'll see you afterward." Keisha asked, "Right?"

I took Bilan at the shoulder, guiding her away. "Don't count on it."

Julius sucked his teeth, Keisha laughed, and Bilan made a sound of disapproval. We hadn't gotten far when the Riccis were upon us.

"Holy shit!" the wife, Carina, cried, charging toward Bilan and yanking her from beneath my arm. "Where the hell have you been?"

My regard met Vinny's, who swept his away uncomfortably. What Bilan didn't know was about the whispers of her being kidnapped, thanks to Lamont's reaction to hearing from Carina the van Damien had forced her into had pulled off. The Riccis were smart enough not to shout their theory loud enough for law enforcement to hear. As a gesture for peace of mind, I sent Rory by to tell them Bilan was fine. I didn't offer proof, so understandably, they still worried, which is why I chose not to be offended when Carina's ass made a big deal about seeing Bilan.

"You were giving me a fucking heart attack, Bilan!" Carina continued to cry. "What the hell's wrong with you?"

Bilan's eyes swiped to me briefly before asking, "What did I do?" She was sure to giggle, downplaying the dramatics.

"You left in that van, and I haven't seen you in over a fucking month." Carina's hands went to her waist. "You have any idea how worried Nicky's been?"

"I'm sorry," Bilan breathed, appearing sympathetic. "I've been away, traveling...acting my age!"

Carina's suspecting eyes rolled over me. "Traveling where?"

Bilan's shoulders lifted as she took in a deep breath. "I booked a plane ticket to the Midwest, and that's where my expedition began. Didn't you always tell me to grow the hell up?" She paused for Carina's response. She gave none. "Well, I did. I refused my fiancé's advice and booked a one-way without a 'return to receiver's' date."

Carina's gaze and posture didn't lighten.

Bilan shifted to glance around her. "Hey, Vinny!" she tweeted innocently as she waved.

"Hey, Bilan." Vinny nodded. His hand gestured frustratingly to his wife. "You know she worries."

"It's okay. It's why I love her." Bilan reached up and cheek-embraced Carina.

Through the speakers in the room, it was announced the dinner was about to begin.

Bilan turned to me, handing over her flute. "I guess I can't handle alcohol tonight. I need the restroom again. I'll find my way to the table."

I watched as she threaded through the crowd for the door. Then my attention went to her champagne, Carina's gaze burning a hole in me had my head lifting. Her eyes then went to the flute before she walked off.

Her hand was in mine beneath the table, and she was unbelievably close. So close, I could feel her firm tits vibrate when she laughed. So close, I could smell the perfume of her hair, along with the scent of burnt hair from whatever implement used to curl it. So close, my dick was semi-hard. I hadn't had her this close since before she fled the state. If I would relax into it, my mind could forget our current abridged romance.

She'd been an entirely new being these past thirty minutes or so. Her laugh was breathy, and her expressions engaging. Bilan didn't miss a comment at the table throughout the entire dinner. Especially those addressed to me by Sofia. It didn't take long before I knew. I could discern Bilan's, so far, impeccable intuition regarding my past conquests.

"This has been a wildly successful event, guys," Keisha commented to the table. The room was packed, tables filled from wall to wall. We'd still been able to engage in conversation over the music and other competing voices from all over. "I can't believe we exceeded the goal."

"I can't wait until the first day of business," Rodney, Julius' campaign manager, predicted. "Nothing else matters."

"Shit! We're really going to do this," Ebony, a Paterson council-woman, snickered. "Yo, we really have a shot of finally getting shit done in this city before my grandfather dies." She smacked the table.

"The fact that you're acting surprised is jarring, Eb," Julius scolded on the low. "Of course, we can win this. There's so much to do."

"So much to fucking clean," Sofia added, rolling her eyes.

Bilan's grip on my thigh tightened.

"All I'm saying is I'm tired of family who visit home being shocked and, quite frankly, disgusted by what Paterson has turned into. My grandmother could have left with her siblings, all fleeing back to Georgia. But she's stayed because she believes there's still hope for Black families to plant and be successful at growth and wealth in Silk City."

"Where do we start?" Rodney asked. "Like Sofia said, there's so much cleaning up to do. Where would we start, Jules?"

Julius tossed his regard to me. We'd talked countless hours about the needs of Paterson. Instead of sports or girls, we talked hope for Paterson and plausible ideas of change.

"First, I need to secure my senior advisor to prioritize the action points."

Sofia's eyes fell to her cocktail glass on the table. She'd been vying for the position of being Julius' top aide since he shared his endeavors of gaining the seat. She was one of the brightest minds around him, loaded with stamina to take on his opponents and naysayers.

"Your biggest talking points are about restoring self-confidence in the residents. It's so broad," Brittany noted.

"Because the problems of our city are," Julius countered. "We have issues, from the bottom to the top. From the young to elderly. From housing to businesses. I will have made efforts in each of these areas by the time I'm done as mayor."

"Yeah, but I can't wait to start revealing the specific agenda," Brittany pushed.

Shots fired...

Even Tom, seated between Brittany and Bilan, coughed uncomfortably.

"There is a very specific and comprehensive action plan in place for this party," Sofia scoffed. "I'm hearing there are two others still considering tossing their hats into the ring. But one of the priorities is the aesthetics of the city. If the place isn't clean and appears safe, there's no confidence."

"So, what is the plan for that?" Tom asked.

By the time my eyes landed on Julius, his were on me, and they communicated.

"Bringing in developers to build better housing," Sofia answered. "Making the prospect of having a business here attractive for entrepreneurs. Bring in more medical services to improve access to care. These components will make the city more attractive to the right people, who want to come and buy property here."

"Oh, my god," a white woman at the other end of the table chirped. "That will be amazing."

"No, it wouldn't," I remarked, bringing my drink to my mouth.

Young Brittany scoffed. "Why wouldn't it be? She just painted a beautifully improved Paterson."

My eyes were on Julius as he sat back, grinning.

"The picture she just painted was a perfectly gentrified Paterson. Bringing new people or businesses in shouldn't be the goal. In fact, it should be frowned upon. Working with the current residents and businesses as well as budding businesses should be the focus."

"It doesn't have to be exclusively new people buying property," Sofia predictably argued. "Ebony just mentioned her relatives who moved away. We can make this city attractive enough to restore the image of neighborhood and community that appeals to them. It would totally eradicate the reasons they left."

"Again, what about the ones who are still here, like Ebony?" I asked.

"I own a home," Ebony answered. "I'm right on 17th Avenue."

Bilan's grip on my thigh tightened again, this time, her nails denting my skin.

"So, why not own another? An investment property. Why not

eliminate the nonagenarian ass Italians and shady ass Puerto Ricans owning these centenarian properties that are outdated and in poor condition, and renting them out at market value? Why can't those who are there...were born there, be equipped with knowledge of property investments? Why can't they be assisted in learning how to create the businesses they've been pregnant with for years?"

"Who?" Sofia spat. "Who there without those opportunities wants them?"

And this was where her pontification got heated between us. Sofia had strikingly gorgeous features: almond eyes, full nose, and broad lips like an African. She had sex appeal, and she could give head for hours. She was educated, articulate, witty, and informed. I knew this because it was those qualities that compelled me to invest in her education. I paid for her master's degree at *Columbia University* years ago, and she wasn't my girl. Sofia wasn't even a regular fuck all three years of her time in graduate school, either. She was champion for urban development and wanted to make her mark one day locally. How could I not provide her that opportunity?

But we struggled as friends. Sofia wanted to be my woman. And I couldn't bring her home to my mother. With her politics, Irene would chew her young, untried ideologies up for dinner. Sofia was for the development of the disenfranchised, but only that of her own people. She was a Dominican sister from Passaic, one who could articulate poverty and subjugation, but couldn't identify with the plight of a Black man. So basically, I paid for the empowerment of brown people in Paterson...and Passaic.

Bilan's soft hand journeyed up my thigh toward my growing erection. My attention went to her. Her eyes widened, lips parted. I had no idea what she was hinting at, possibly for me to disengage with Sofia. Perhaps the entire discussion. I didn't know.

"People who look like Julius," I explained. "Men and women who look like Tom, Brittany, and Keisha." I pointed. "Contrary to what most believe, many of those Black men on the block, in the barbershops, carrying your mail, collecting your garbage, and selling their legitimate products on the streets would kill for an opportunity at owning a legal business with a storefront. Many of them have been looked over these past fifteen years while the city turned from black to beige. The loans given for businesses have gone to Hispanics, Bengalis, and Middle Easterners."

"So, we're going to be racist in our approach to politics in this city?" Sofia's question was directed to me. "Because the last I knew, growing up poor in an urban city, opportunities belong to those who go after them. Nothing's given."

Bilan's fingers tightened over the head of my cock, stroking in small, unnoticeable movements, but powerful efforts. I was turned the fuck on and irritated at the same goddamned time.

I pivoted in my seat, positioning myself to block off as many as I could. Unfortunately, Tom couldn't be in that number. I shifted close to her face, an intimate proximity. Her eyes were dark and heavy, mouth ajar when I whispered. "Are you having fun?"

A wrinkle formed in her forehead before a smile blossomed in her eyes. "Are you?" she murmured.

Bilan was dallying with me.

"I don't know why you're doing what you're doing, but I know it has to do with her." I was sure to keep my voice low, but the crisp enunciation of the beginning and ending of my words could be heard, I was sure. "I distinctly recall telling you back in May, in my bedroom at my parents' home, not to make me powerless using sex. Do you recall that?"

I'd be damned if an amorous leer didn't spread beneath her half-mast eyes.

"I may need a memory refresher," she uttered.

I gazed at her, almost not recognizing Bilan—at least not the post-kidnapped Bilan. Did jealousy control her libido? I was so fucking desperate for intimacy of any kind with her, I'd allow it. It wasn't right, but shit, neither had things I'd done to her been.

My eyes roved from her eyes to her lips, to her eyes again. "I'm not a fuckin' toy, Bilan. You want your space, your liberties to make your own choices. This ain't what you do to express it."

I backed away slowly, not wanting to give off the impression we were fighting. My dick throbbed and body heated dangerously. I hadn't been this aroused in well over a month.

I placed my elbows on the table. "No," I finally answered an expectant Sofia. "but what I hope he's not going to do is serve another term, or several, where the process of extinction of Blacks in Paterson has become the one issue overlooked time and time again."

She snorted, jaw swinging, expressing her temperament. "Is your argument, the idea of making the city aesthetically pleasing is pushing Blacks out, Ellis?"

"The most significant sign of gentrification is the housing market." My brows lifted. "How much are the homes? The property taxes? These elements aren't in Blacks' favor when you raise the number to attract a different class of people is all I'm saying, sweetheart."

That claw on my thigh earlier was now on my dick. I grunted, pushing back in my seat. Bilan pushed back at the same time.

She smiled to the table. "I need the ladies' room. Excuse me."

I stood from the table and followed her, my hand at the small of her back as we ambled away from the table.

"How necessary was that?" I gritted.

Most were still in their seats, finishing with dessert at this point. A few faces I recognized waved from their tables. I reciprocated while in step with her.

"Watching you and your ex paddle your balls back and forth excited me; what can I say? By the way, never call me sweetheart again."

"We're at a mayoral fundraising event; policy rhetoric occurs."

She raised her index finger and thumb. "But it can be miscon-strued as pomposity when the fiancée's there to witness it all," she whispered before jetting out of the nearest door.

I stopped, lost to her words. Confused by her actions. My fucking dick was still returning to its resting state, thankfully. I tried figuring out what that was all about. She turned from an ex to a part-ner, to an affectionate lover, to a vixen, to angry fiancée all in the span of this event. It was eerie. I didn't like the game.

"Hey." I glanced down to find Carina Ricci, someone I was in no mood for. The Riccis presence here was no surprise. Their racists asses were sure to participate in the political processes of the city because they made lots of money there as one of the largest diners in the state. I was glad she kept her cool earlier when speaking to Bilan. Carina knew I had Vinny cut Bilan's hours, unbeknownst to her, this summer. She was looking in the direction Bilan had just gone. "How long is she going to keep it a secret before you tell everyone?"

"Come again?"

She stepped closer, lowering her voice. "I know she's an extremely private person—good girl, though. The baby. How long are you guys going to keep the pregnancy a secret?" I blinked hard, face tight with confusion. "I knew she was pregnant when she came to Nicky's birthday party at the diner. She didn't tell me, but I knew. Hey," She gave a dramatic pause. "I know my Bilani. She's weirdly private, but cute as hell. I don't know how long you guys can hide it. She looked it in August: tired and sickly in the face, but glowing skin." Carina used her hands to explain. "She don't need bronzer powder. Her hair is even thicker. It's like a sheep's coat now. And those boobs! Look how high they're sitting in that gown. That ain't no undergarment. You know what I mean?"

Utterly speechless, I gaped at her.

"Oh, shit! There's my husband waving at me. Well, whenever you guys decide to share..." She began to stalk off. "*Congratulazioni!*"

My gaze followed her to her seat. I stood along the wall, near one of the ballroom entrances in a fucking stupor. This was the third person asking if Bilan was pregnant this week. Kimmy mentioned her face being smaller, glowing skin, even commenting on how much Bilan had been eating independent of me. I brushed it off as small talk as she dusted the television room while I was in there. Then my mother's call about Bilan's glow, her being and looking tired all day.

My eyes reached to the table, where I could see Bilan's wine untouched. Her wine glass and champagne flute from earlier were virtually full, too. My regard went back out the door. Bathroom. She'd gone to the bathroom just before we left the apartment. Then she went during our heated conversation earlier. But I was under the impression that was just a convenient break from the tension. She went before dinner, and she had to go again. And her mood skipped to extreme degrees while here.

Now, Carina Ricci had just given me the same inductive reasoning. Her skin, her hair, and even her breasts. Had I been that relieved by her being back home that I missed her features and habits? This week, Bilan would get up in the middle of the night, leave the room, and come back smelling like food. Why hadn't that struck me as odd until now? When I found her in the closet the other day, she'd been rubbing her belly. But it was flat: I'd seen her naked the first night she showered at home.

My jaw flexed, nostrils flared wide. There was no fucking way possible a pregnant woman had been in my bed all week long and it had gone unnoticed.

Not Bilan...

I needed to know. Right away. And if she would be straightforward with me simply asking the question, Bilan would have told me already. She would have been forthcoming last Sunday, down in *Macen Beach* when I picked her up. Or the day after. Or the day after that. Or today. She'd been home five days and hadn't mentioned a hint of a pregnancy.

Tonight, I'd find out for sure...

Sick...

I couldn't deny the repulsiveness of my need for him. It was outrageously needed. Paramount desperation.

Summer Walker's *"Girls Need Love"* vibrated across the car as we rode in the back of his *Mercedes-Maybach;* shadows of the night passed over my face as I anticipated my next move. The touch of the leather beneath my misted skin enhanced my aroused state. My nipples tingled, breasts felt heavy, groin churned, and sex throbbed torturously. Visions of having him naked beneath my fingertips, my body intoxicated me. Having his mouth on me.

I couldn't understand what came over me tonight. And while I knew I should have thought this insane need through, I didn't want to stay in my head; not tonight. I needed a break from the stress of my tormented mind. I needed Sadik. His dominance, his ultra-alpha.

My gaze flicked over to him on the other side of the car. The street lights caught occasional illumination on the orange stubbles on his jaw. His eyes the hues of a heated flame. The pulse in my neck beating profusely. I let go of a harsh breath as we turned off Route 22, his high rise coming into view. This was crazy. *I* was being silly. Whatever stupid pregnancy hormonal spike I'd experienced could be relieved by a cool shower and a cup of Taaliba's tea.

The gate rose from the underground parking lot. We pulled into one of Sadik's assigned spaces and, before I knew it, everyone began opening and slamming doors closed. When I stood to my feet, taking my first step to leave the car, I felt the gush of liquid between my thighs. My eyes squeezed closed, silently embarrassed by the manifestation of my depravity.

"You good, B?"

My eyes opened to Rory pulling out a cigarette and propping it into her mouth as she gazed my way.

I was momentarily dazed, until I heard an abrupt subterranean deep tenor utter, "She's good. I'll hit you in the morning."

Sadik's palm slid into mine and with a gentle cue, I followed behind him to the elevator. The ride up was in silence, similar to the car ride, only he stood close to me. His finger stroked the palm of my hand and my eyelids collapsed. The pulse in my neck throbbed, and my thighs clenched. The elevator dinged once we'd arrived, and my lungs gave out.

I trailed behind him with a heaving chest. His scent, the heat emanating from his body...the smooth sway of his shoulders. I had to have him. He dialed in the code for the security pad next to the door. The click sounded and the door popped open. Sadik nudged it wide, treading through the door jamb, and I was on his heels. He stopped to close the door and I continued, easing my grip to release him. Sadik's hold tightened and the moment he yanked on my arm, I knew what he was doing and that quickly decided.

My body glided into him, breasts smacked into the top of his abdomen. Our mouths met sloppily at first, but I pushed from my toes to make the next one hit its target. Sadik's mouth was ready: hot, moist, and champagne-scented. My hands pushed up to the silken skin of his head. The spikes of his face abraded the skin on mine. His big hands pushing into my scalp, threading my hair. I could feel his erection against my belly. My hands dragging down his chest, pushing around his tailored waist and reaching to the wings of his back. Beneath my palm, his spine rolled and he expelled delicious air into my mouth.

Our tongues tousled, lips brushed greedily against each other. My hands exploring all the hardness I missed. The moment I realized he was pulling off his suit jacket, I assisted. Then I pulled his dress shirt from his pants, popping the buttons by yanking it apart from the hem. Our mouths still warring with passion. Before I reached the top, Sadik unknotted his tie. Together, we removed his shirt.

He withdrew his mouth. "If this ain't you opening to me on your terms, you need to make that clear now."

∞ 12 ∞

I could feel him slipping from my grasp and, before I knew it, Sadik broke the nexus and was promenading away. I watched him for a few yards down the hall before it dawned on me to follow him. I reached down to unhook my sandals, then trekked after him. The moment I crossed through the French doors of the master suite, he pulled me into his hard frame. His mouth at the base of my neck, hot hands at my back, unzipping the gown. It puddled at my feet once past my hips. My body instantly chilled. His hands were again on my back, unhooking my strapless bra. My breasts fell, heavy and throbbing. His tongue traced the underside of the left one, setting off a mine-field of nerve receptors. My neck collapsed, sending my head back-ward. I held onto him for balance.

His tongue roved up to my pebbled nipple, teeth scraping its rigid edges. Simultaneously, his thumbs hooked the sides of my thong, pushing it over my hips until it fell on top of the gown. His mouth moved to my right breast, tongue swiping beneath, then the side. I moaned, squeezing into his shoulders. When he kissed my nipple before sucking it into his mouth, I whimpered.

Sadik lifted me in the air, my thighs climbing, then wrapping around his hips. He pulled me up to his waist, kissing me. I felt the air brushing against the skin of my back. Then I was being lowered onto the bed, his hard body descending mine. Soft kisses to my navel had my belly fluttering and hips lifting, and when his lips brushed against the bed of hairs of my pelvis, I dropped back onto the mattress. My hands went to his head, gripping it in a guide.

Then he eased from my grasp, causing me to groan in disappointment. Sadik left the bed, padding into the closet. He returned in no time with something in his hands. I waited patiently as he crawled onto the mattress, straddling me. He gathered my hands above my head. A small piece of rope wrapped around my wrist. Which kind, I couldn't tell in the dim room. But it was rope! Rope only brought two things to mind.

Damien's death and...

My pussy spasmed with deep need, and I pulled my wrists down to see.

"Keep your hands up here, Nalib," he rasped.

Nalib...Nalib. Yessss...

My sex lubed even more at the sound of that name, and that quickly, the fore-memory derived from the material was forgotten. It may repulse me in the morning, but tonight... I deserved each boom bestowed tonight.

"Mmkay..." I purred helplessly.

He moved down my body again, tongue snaking down my neck and onto my chest. My achy breasts were gathered in his warm palms, caressed and pulled together. I watched in the shadowy room as he licked both nipples, then pulled them into his mouth. My thighs opened and hips attempted to lift into the air. He licked, and I gyrated. He sucked, and I lunged hungrily. Sadik tortured me for minutes long, causing my body to react to each movement of his mouth. My head tilted back. I couldn't take it, groin lifting and lifting.

Then he let up. My eyes strained in the duskiness, watching him removing his suit pants and boxers. The way his cock sprang out had my mouth drying. I tried sitting up, if to do nothing but observe closely. But Sadik met me mid-air, easing over me. Mouth capturing mine. He teased me with gentle sucks of my bottom lip. As he settled between my thighs, his tongue toured my mouth again.

"*Uhhh*..." I cried.

Then I felt him. His wide crest swiped over my engorged clit. Sadik rounded his hips, positioning himself at my opening. His aim was off, erection kept slipping away from its target.

"Fuck, baby," he produced a velar cry in my ear.

My eyes closed in shame. This need for a man wasn't natural. I wasn't raised this way. How could I be so desperate under these circumstances? But I was. My pulse beat, abdominals jerked profusely, and hips pushed into his shaft with shameful hunger. He finally used his hand to feed himself to me. The moment I felt him at the opening, my pussy leaped into the air to capture him. Only it wasn't that simple. Sadik met a muscular wall in my canal. I pushed to painful measure, trying to open to him.

"Easy..." he breathed, kissing my neck. The strain in his vocals couldn't be missed. "We'll get there."

I didn't want to be patient or coached. I wanted to be taken and defiled. My wrists yanked at the bow tie with fiery determination. I needed to touch him, to caress his golden skin. The lifting of my hips didn't break, expressing my excitement and simultaneous need. My fist punch toward the headboard with frustrating force, and I felt it loosen.

He began to make efforts into me, but not his full shaft. Already, pleasure mounted in my core. The damn thing wouldn't unravel. My breaths began to fall distressed. Taking pity on me, Sadik reached up and pulled the tie loose. With expedited need, my hands shot down to his hips, anchoring my weight as I lifted higher and threw my sex into him with wild abandon. The walls of my sex swelled and lubricated and stretched to accept this man, even if just marginally. The ache from my forced efforts couldn't supersede the need. The need for this...being who had been the most one-sided, controlling, cozen, dark man I'd ever encountered.

That fact froze my hips.

"Don't!" he commanded powerfully in my ear. "Don't pull back from me again. Not now, Nalib!"

The first tear left the corner of my right eye. "I'm sick."

He grunted. "Nonsense."

"I should be able to manage this need." My hard pants were uncontrolled, hips thrust toward him. I may have had a good three inches inside and my walls throbbed viciously. "I'm sick."

"No, you're not, baby," he crooned into my neck. "You're just not fighting it anymore. You can't fight the force of my need of you."

Need...

I rocked and rocked my hips against him. My sex tight, sopping, pulsating. My nipples stinging with pleasure as they flopped in the air. It was time. I couldn't hold it back if I wanted to. I came. Intense pleasure rolled over me, exciting my thrust. I moved fast and hard, hoping to have him fill me to the hilt before my cresting was over.

"Fuck!" he rumbled, plunging into me with his own wild abandon.

Something inside my vagina broke. Pain seized my core and suddenly, I felt him at the back of my uterus. But it was too late, pure bliss had already imploded and dispersed, reaching places I'd forgotten existed.

Sadik pounded into me as I held my sex up to him for the taking. My lungs sloughed, heart raced. He slowed before suspending over me. His spine curled over, face to my chest as he licked the trail of saliva dropped from his mouth while spraying the last of his hot seeds into me.

He mewled incomprehensible words before his spine straightened, and Sadik pulled out of me. His throbbing appendage dragged heavily, and he rolled off of me and onto the mattress on his back. I lay boneless, chest heaving as waves of satiation undulated my channel. My body shivered, and tears began to fall from the sides of my face. This wasn't the first time he left me stripped, my body bared, and emotions exposed. I felt weak, needy. They weren't adjectives I enjoyed experiencing, especially with Sadik.

Quickly, I was lost to the arrhythmia of our breathing. Once again, alone in my head. How long we lay there muted, I didn't know. Time didn't matter. Only the distance of our bodies concerned me. The waves nulled, and subtle frizzles warmed my groin. Noiselessly, my arm stretched under the darkness of the room, reaching for him. My hand landed on his hip, then pushed until his erection was in my palm. I stroked him from root to tip.

I heard when Sadik's breath caught and knew I'd popped the bubble of his headspace.

"Sadik," I whispered, desperate for him.

"C'mere, Bilan," he croaked, strained.

Without a moment of dithering, I turned to my side and crawled over to him. His standing erection was easy to find. It had been dried of me, but when my mouth encapsulated his length, I could taste my musk. So intoxicated with lust, the foul taste of my essence didn't prevent me from enjoying the silk of his skin over hard muscle. I rolled my tongue around him, fisted from the root, and pushed him to the back of my throat. Sadik lifted, an act of him enjoying my sophomoric attempts. They began slow, then eventually increased, suspending the last few seconds of the thrust. The first few happened quickly; the last were delayed strokes into the back of my throat, causing me to gag.

Even that turned me on, rendering me impatient until I stood on my knees and crawled up his body. I was still a novice. The times I rode Sadik, it had mostly been with his assistance. But tonight, my demanding libido didn't allow for heeding. I grabbed his length from behind and positioned him beneath me before I sank down onto him. My belly leaped at the pressure of him gliding into my swollen-ness. Tenderness struck as his stiffness moved against my sensitive walls. I managed the ache against the throb and moved up and down.

I rolled over him, feeling each inch of his throbbing length. Sadik held me at the small of my back, controlling every stroke I made over him like the true ultra-alpha he was. He held me at the back of the neck, too, making love to my mouth. As I grinded over him, I countered his grip, giving room to my belly against his. My breasts were heavy and bouncing. Nipples peaked and swiping against gravity.

And I felt the churn of my groin, pleasure mounting from that sweet place within. It was a delicious build, a memory no longer so distant for me.

"Sit up, Nalib," he croaked. "I don't wanna come too fast again."

He sounded pained, tortured in a way that selfishly empowered me. As I reclined, straightening my spine, I was reminded of his warning of me weaponizing sex as a means of manipulation. Was that so bad? Was it a crime that in this moment, my body needed him while my heart held resentment for him?

His heavy palms dragging down my breasts snapped me out of my head. My nipples tingled beneath them. When his fingers made it to my peaked apexes, he squeezed them. That single act propelled my thrusts over him. I swelled and liquefied even more around him. Swiftly, Sadik leaped up, capturing my nipple into his mouth, sucking it. His hands grabbed my butt from the back, slapping, squeezing it, and guiding my stroke onto him successively. My spine arched, head rolled back, and I gave into the tsunami of sensations attacking me at the core.

I didn't yell, couldn't speak. I could only hold onto his round shoulders as I hopped over his throbbing dick. Behind my lids, lightning flashed; in my ears, bombs sounded. In my core, an explosion wouldn't end. Then Sadik began to strike me from beneath, his grip on my neck fierce and commanding. It wasn't until his thrusts into me stalled and he groaned that I knew Sadik had come himself.

That was unusual. Other than our first time together, Sadik had never ejaculated so quickly. This was his second time in a row tonight. The first, I could understand. It possibly meant he hadn't been with anyone since me. But this one was strange.

I bit my bottom lip, chest pounded for more reasons than one.

"*Sa*—" I swallowed. "Sadik..."

I flipped her over onto her back before she could whisper another word. Her knees were to her ears and thighs spread eagle. My mouth found her clit, and I sucked on it until her legs quivered around my head. When she was done, I made figure eight shapes in her belly while she caught her breath. I moved back down and did the same on her left inner thigh, then her right. When her soft hands began to caress the skin of my head, I made her clit my focus again. I sucked her fast, wishing I could eat her whole pussy, but my cum was still running out of her and I wasn't into tasting my seeds. Bilan's body vibrated, pussy lifted from the mattress into my face again. She came again.

Before she could finish, I had her on all fours, slipping into her wet folds. I fell in love deeper when her pussy quaked around me. I pounded until sweat dripped and my ass stung from the squeeze of passion. I came with a fury, grunted from the bowels of my damn belly. There was another intermission before I was on top of her again, plunging deep. What began as lovemaking turned into fucking. I'd never come so many times in my goddamn life. Passion put the battery in my back that had me all over her, pulling pleasure from her. Yet no matter how many times I was inside of her, I could feel the wall.

Maybe that was my obsession. My Nalib held back from me even more than she did before. Before, there was a barrier between me and her heart. Since she'd been back, she'd put up one between me and her mind. She'd been more than holding out. Bilan was shutting me out.

It was hours into the next morning that I had to stop. My heart was about to bang out of my chest, and the bed was sodden with her passion and my determination. I released Bilan from my arms, and she rolled right over and into sleep within two minutes. As I waited out my resting heart rate, I couldn't sleep. I felt it all over again; the exhaustion a mere few hours of sleep couldn't cure. I was restless in every way.

Just before the sun came up, I rolled out of the bed and showered. When I returned, Bilan was still asleep, pushing out soft snores. I lay beside her, hoping counting her freckles would lead me to sleep.

My lids blinked, causing me to stir. The dull ache in my arm let me know I'd been on it too long. I turned over sluggishly, feeling sore and drained. Not yet. I didn't want to wake up, not just yet. But I had, which was how I could knowingly resist awakening. My tongue felt heavy, mouth dry. An abrupt growl from my stomach had my hand stretched to lay over it.

Nooooo...

I was awake. It felt like I'd just closed my eyes. As though minutes ago, Sadik had finally released me and I'd rolled into sleep almost instantly. My hips ached. Bad. I was hungry. How much time did I have before I could be at the hospital? The grumbling wouldn't stop. The muscles in my face tightened. Could it wait until I made it to the hospital? The cafeteria had good bagels.

Finally, my eyes opened. They were met with burning ember irises.

Sadik...

My mouth was pasty and I could feel the crust in my eyes. I could half imagine what my breath smelled like. I'd slept with my essence mixed with his on my tongue. Sadik made sure of it earlier this morning when he had me extend it so he could deposit there instead of the back of my mouth, as he typically did. I looked a sight, I knew. Yet he smelled clean. The soft sheen on those lips with the exaggerated cupid's bow wasn't from between my legs. Sadik had showered.

But he hadn't slept. There was no way he could have. I observed tan bags beneath his eyes I'd never seen on him. The veins around his sockets were uncharacteristically darkened, arteries in his forehead were visible and lifted. His eyes were glossed. Had Sadik been crying?

But he smiled.

"My Nalib's pregnant..." He sighed as though it was a painful observation.

I felt horrible immediately. Like a betrayer.

Oh, God...

Tears fell without warning. I nodded, guilt answering right away.

Sadik grimaced as though gut punched.

My tears grew into sobs, abdomen trembling.

He sniffled. "You weren't going to tell me?"

I nodded. My crusty lips broke apart when I quickly—*honestly*—answered, "I was!"

A bawl pushed from my belly, forcing me up against the headboard, where I braced myself. Sadik didn't move. His golden head laying on his open palm shifted up. Mutedly, he watched me trying to breathe.

"I swear, I was going to tell you. I—" I couldn't stop the tears. Just when I thought I'd found a reprieve from it all, it blew up in my face. "There's just been so much going on. You were working night and day. Nicky's party...Abshir texting me to meet him. Damien took me from the diner. Then the rope." My pussy spasmed oddly, a brush of arousal washed over me. "Then I got scared and left. I had to protect my...baby, too." I sobbed.

"I couldn't call you. I had to worry about us. Then I got sick and couldn't leave the beach house. So I stayed...and you came. Then Abshir..." I buried my face into my palms. "It's never been the right time to tell you." I hoped in spite of the blubber between my words, he understood my dilemma.

It took a few seconds, but when I was able to look at him again, Sadik's regard was still on me. He sat up, gaze still on me as he left the bed. I lost his eyes on his way into the closet. And I lost his compassion when he left the bedroom soon thereafter, dressed in a white tee and jeans.

"Hey, sweetheart..." I vaguely heard when I felt soft taps on my shoulder. "Time to get up, Bilan." I awakened to Irene standing over me. She smiled warmly, then gestured toward Abshir. "I'm here. You can go home and get some sleep. I know you and Sadik were out late last night."

My mind went to the time. It was just after three-thirty. I must have fallen asleep while writing a paper. Nurse Gladney was over Abshir, changing his head dressing. I still felt dazed as I glanced around at my things sprawled about, body aching from last night into this morning.

"Abshir's parole officer just left. I made sure he got the paperwork the doctors signed for him," Irene explained.

I couldn't believe I slept through his parole officer's visit. He likely didn't intend to stay for long, but it was his responsibility to see about Abshir with his own eyes. He also needed documentation on his condition and opted to pick it up himself, killing two birds with one stone. How Sadik was able to coordinate Abshir's private care and his compliance with law enforcement without any of them knowing the real story behind his injury was beyond me. And when I came back into town, I fell in line with it so effortlessly, hoping it would spare his life.

The problem was Abshir wasn't getting better. It had nearly been a week since I'd returned from *Macen Beach*, and there hadn't been any progress in his condition for the month since he'd been here.

"Come on, Bilan," Irene gently chided. "My family's Sunday dinner has been prepped for tomorrow, and I brought my office here to get some work done." She began to unpack her things as I slowly gathered mine. "The state makes so many demands on me, but I won't complain."

As she rambled on, I wanted to ask had she heard from Sadik. Had he told her? She didn't give anything away if he had. I hadn't heard from Sadik since he abruptly left the apartment at six this morning. Not that it was unusual. Sadik and I had been two ships passing in the night all week. But this felt different. It was different. He now knew.

Sadik knew he was going to be a father.

Once I was done packing my things, I tried thinking about what I'd do with my time. Contrary to what Irene wanted, I wouldn't go back to the apartment to sleep. I also didn't want to be here waiting for the unknown.

"Thanks for this, Irene."

She was taking over my lounge seat. "No problem, Bilan. I'm happy I can help. Give my handsome my best." Irene hardly looked at me when she spoke.

It was strange...almost motherly the way she swept in, taking all of the burden from my shoulders. My Aunt Astur hadn't been back since the conference with the doctor the other day. And Aunt Franzel hadn't returned at all. She'd called twice, but that was the extent of her support. Irene's help didn't come with contingencies or broken promises. She'd been here every day since the first day of her commitment. She'd text and call me with updates I missed in my absence, and I'd even caught her praying over him two days ago.

None of that mattered to me. Only her making me feel I wasn't alone here. In fact, I couldn't wait for the Sunday where I could sneak over to *Redeeming Souls for Abundant Living in Christ* for a live message to help me along this crazy journey I'd been on. I'd still been watching their services and questioned so much about my religious —and now spiritual—beliefs.

That thought had me sighing. I turned to leave. Outside the room, Rory stood, closing a book. I glanced at the cover of the paperback.

Something Like Love... I read the title in my head.

"You read Christina C. Jones novels, too?" I chirped.

"Huhn?" Rory straightened her back, pushing the book behind her. "Fuck you talking 'bout?"

I shook my head. "Rory, you read romance novels?" It was definitely a romance novel. The cover alone spelled feminine, flowery romance. "You and your boss got a thing for them?"

Her head reared and face tightened. "*What?* I 'on't even read books. S.Q.E. only read important shit."

"Like what?"

She shrugged. "That nigga, Cornel West, James Baldwin..." She snapped her fingers, then tapped her head. "What's the lady's name? Toni...Morrison! Toni Morrison. Her." Her eyes rolled up as she considered it even farther. "I 'on't know. He read a lot of boring shit."

My brows lifted. "Like Christina C. Jones?"

Her eyes fell with shame. I rolled my eyes. "I'm ready." I began to walk off. As I approached the elevator, I was struck with a thought. "Can you take me to my house?"

"Your house?" Rory looked earnestly confused.

"Yeah. You know...the place I lived before your employer swept through my world like a freaking tsunami?"

Rory hesitated. "Why you wanna go there?"

"Because I do." It was time. I'd been back all week and avoided it. Had a new family moved in? Was it yellow taped off from the shooting? What was going on there? "And unless you don't want me to tell the new guy, Johnson, you like romance novels, we should get going to West Paterson."

The elevator toiled, and Rory rolled her eyes this time and mumbled something resembling a string of expletives.

My entire frame was tense as we pulled onto the block, lungs locked with holding air. Each home beginning from the corner looked the same. I even recognized the kids outside playing on a warm September afternoon. But I braced myself for what I'd see once my eyes made it to my house...my old home. Rory stopped the truck, and I realized I'd closed my eyes at some point because when they opened, a long breath expelled, but my already sore body was still tight and frozen.

My parents' house looked...familiar. The aluminum siding was clean, the trees in front were manicured, and the weeds pulled. There were no signs of it being bank owned or the house being in custody of the sheriff's department as I had awakened from nightmares about many times. I stepped out of the truck, stunned by the new appearance. Taking to the stairs, I observed from a closer view. It may have been a stupid decision, but curiosity had me sauntering to the side of the house to get to the back. Dog's kennel was gone, the yard cleared. The back steps looked the same; my ascension felt familiar. But on the way up, I thought to get my keys. That's when I remembered I'd somehow misplaced them last month.

But how?

That thought had me digging into my crossbody; the same I wore that day. Inside were my keys. I pulled out the small key ring holding no more than five keys and, strangely enough, it was there. Without thought, I tried the lock. It was to no avail. The lock had been changed. When I closely observed the door, I noticed it had been, too.

Deflated, I took back down the stairs. Unable to take my eyes off the place, I trekked back to the front. When I noticed the curtains were down, I hiked up the steps and peered into the windows. The place was squeaky clean. From this vantage point, I could see the dreadful place where my brother last lay when I saw him in August. *When I abandoned him, running for my life.* There was no sign of blood or stains at all on the linoleum flooring. The whole place was empty; no cups or folding chairs I'd seen the last time I was here.

My heart felt heavy as I walked down the stairs. The place held no resemblance of the home I grew up in, though the walls were the same colors and the floors were the same material.

When I stepped into the truck, Rory croaked from the front seat, "You good, B?"

It took a while for me to answer, my gaze locked to the house as we pulled off.

"Of course," I mocked. "I lost my family home. No big deal at all, though." Tears pooled in my eyes, but I refused to let them fall.

Long after, Rory cawed, "Maybe you should chop it up with S.Q.E. about that."

"For what, Rory?" My regard rolled to her in the rearview mirror. "He's not God."

...outside of sex, at least...

"That nigga closer to it than any I done seen." She peered directly into my eyes as she declared it.

That's when I knew Rory's words of advice weren't random or out of reckless pity. She meant what she said, and that prospect infuriated me.

∞13∞

It was after one in the morning when I'd been awakened by a harsh snore my nasal cavity emitted. I gazed around the living room, remembering where I'd fallen asleep reading "*African People in World History (Black Classic Press Contemporary Lecture)*" by John Henrik Clarke. It was one of hundreds of books in the television room, and signed to Sadik by Irene. So, I gave it a try.

Just the coffee table light was on, but was assisted by the night-lights along Route 22. The apartment was still quiet, other than the aquatic sounds of the fish tank. Kimmy left hours ago, at eight pm. I didn't exactly want to confront Sadik while she was here, but didn't expect him not to come home at all.

Where could he be?

I could call him. *Shoot!* He had *two* phones. But I didn't want to. I couldn't give Sadik the impression of normalcy. There was nothing ordinary about him, his life, or family. And thanks to him, there was nothing normal about mine, either. There were so many questions I had. Like how he knew I was at that abandoned restaurant that day. He said he got a call. But what did the caller say? And he never answered how Derrick's body showed up in the fire. Why did he pursue me knowing his father wanted my brother dead? It was insulting, at best. He had knowledge—and sometimes, a hand—in all the drama around me all this time, but chose learning about my pregnancy late to be upset with me?

The absolute nerve!

I kicked my legs onto the floor, placing the book and blanket next to me on the sofa. As I stood to my feet, I heard the unclicking of the lock. Sadik was home. I waited for his journey down the hallway. His head came into view from the doorway of the living room before he did. He slowed in the center, finally realizing the lamp was on. Sadik glanced up, exposing his sins.

His eyes were red and glossed over. His frame wobbled slightly, and his posture was mildly curved.

I rolled my neck, hands flew to my hips. "You're drunk?"

A sleek grin cracked on his face. "You're here?"

That delivered a gut punch if I'd ever had one.

"Excuse me? Why would I not be here?"

His head reared, bouncing over his shoulders. "'Cause I ain't the man for you. You don't want one like me. I'm only good to woo and fuck you." His palms lifted in the air and he shrugged. "Apparently, once the layers get pulled back and you see who I am, you run."

"What? Let's not act like you have no culpability in any of this drama—"

"You ran with my fuckin' baby," he reiterated. "My fuckin' legacy! Do you know what that means?"

I blinked hard, trying to strengthen myself. "You know what it means, and you knew where I was. Right?" I challenged him.

"I didn't know you had me in you all this time. I would've handled shit differently had I known!"

"Like what, Sadik? Tie me up with one of your manila ropes?" I scoffed, "That would have been great. First, you murder a man, then you kidnap me. You're no better than Damien!"

He turned to me, an arrogant snicker in his stroll into the living room. "Sticks and fuckin' stones, sweetheart. But what you did is unfuckin'-forgivable. Did you think you'd get away with it? You think I wouldn't have found out? You think I would have let you run off and raise my goddamn child without me? *THAT'S A FUCKIN' ELLIS YOU'RE CARRYING!*"

I leaped. Though not near me, Sadik was close enough for me to smell the hours of liquor intake. Even in his distance, the floor trembled like the ground when a lion groans.

A tear crept into my throat and I tried swallowing it back. "First, I told you never to call me sweetheart. Second, I said I was going to tell you."

"No the hell you weren't! If I didn't come for you, you would have stayed in my house, had my baby with that fuckin' clown. You would have had my speckled face baby with that ugly ass fucka, and nobody would have known because he's got fuckin' freckles, too. Y'all would've been the freckled face family."

As cold as the joke had been, Sadik was unsmiling. I sighed, fighting back another cry as my eyes closed. He believed that. He'd had hours to conjure it up. Again, I reminded myself, I had to fight back. Sadik knew no other way.

"What if the baby had your eyes or hair? How would I have passed him off on Jason then?"

His head reared again. "Oh, you find this shit funny?"

"What are you going to do? Kill me?" My head fell to the side. "You gonna call Rory up and have her handle me? I'm surprised you didn't have her do your dirty work with Damien. But then again, it makes sense. You were jealous. You thought we had something going on."

Sadik ripped out a scurvy cackle. "You...and Damien?" He scratched the back of his head. "You wanted me to believe you had something going on with that muthafucka, and I let you...even let it bruise my ego a few times." He swayed over to me, getting so close, he swiped a lock of hair from near my eye. "Honey, I had a better chance at that blade than you. Damien was gayer than Tracy Martin finally being locked in a room with George Zimmerman. The only thing he wasn't gayer than is Tracy Martin being at Zimmerman's funeral." I swallowed hard. "He never wanted you. You were just insurance, a potential target. Your cute little crush was one-sided. He was never going to exploit your body the way I do. He would have never recklessly shot his seeds into your needy womb the way I did."

"He was engaged," I gritted. "He told me that day in the van."

"To a man, Nalib. His name was Tank. My father executed his fiancé in my face," he whispered so intimately. The words were stronger than the stench of alcohol. "I'm sure that day, in the van, he was excited by the prospect of enacting revenge on *my* fiancée."

I wanted to cry. Could have curled to the floor and cried my eyes out for having my naivety being illustrated once again.

But I didn't.

"And what about Derrick?"

He shrugged. "A mere casualty because he had your sweet pussy before me. Because he had it all."

My eyes ballooned, mouth trembled.

"I knew I sensed darkness in you. I just didn't know how sharp my intuition was."

"I wouldn't bet on that. You had no idea how deep my feelings for you were. You still don't. But the darkness..." His head bobbed up and down. "Your mind couldn't ideate what wrath I would have transacted if you thought you'd give birth to my child and not have me be a part of it."

The first tear fell as he stood centimeters away, hand still adoring me one way or another.

"I knew you'd find out. I knew I had to tell you soon."

"Did you go to the doctor down in *Macen Beach* with that friend of yours?"

I shook my head, face to the floor.

"So how did you know you were pregnant, Bilan?"

"I..." my words a mere whisper. "I took a test a couple of days before Nicky's party."

"And you haven't been to a fuckin' doctor?" I could feel his rage building.

"My appointment is on Monday...with Dr. Clifford. Would I have made an appointment with *your* doctor if I was going to keep it from you?"

Sadik's eyes were glazed over, and not all from the alcohol and lack of sleep. "So you don't know how far along you are?"

My head popped up. That sounded like a motherly question.

"You didn't tell Irene. Did you? Did you tell your family?" Streams of tears coursed my face.

With an impassive expression, Sadik shook his head.

"I don't want them to know—" I spoke over him when he tried to argue with me. "I know what I'm carrying!" I screamed. "I know what's in my belly! I know this baby's life is valued far more than mine and my brother's in the eyes of your family. I know the life of an Ellis resides in me. I'm not stupid or delusional to that fact." I took a moment to breathe. He needed to hear me out. "I've thought long and hard about this for thirty-nine days."

"And I've been thinking about it for the past nineteen hours. I hope you've been thorough in your rational process because you don't eat, Bilan. That could put my baby in danger!" he grounded out.

My eyes narrowed and pulse skyrocketed. "Then that makes two of us in danger." I rounded him, leaving the room. "You're more than welcome to come along, but not your family! I don't want them to know until I'm ready!"

Whoosh! Whoosh! Whoosh! Whoosh!

The rhythm went on and on. That's what I heard from the speaker of the machine as I stood over Bilan, lying on the exam bed. Dr. Clifford's head swung back to me, bringing with it a big ass smile so hard, his glasses lifted.

"We have a baby with a strong heartbeat, folks!"

My fucking lungs deflated and shoulders caved just a bit. Then my eyes fell to Bilan, whose audible sigh rivaled the machine. Her chest heaved as she giggled nervously. She seemed...relieved, too.

"Based on your LMP, everything seems to be on par," he noted as he read a chart handed to him by the nurse. "Your EDD..." he stalled, observing the chart. "...which is your estimated date of delivery, is March ninth. You're in week fourteen of gestation. That puts you in your second trimester."

Second?

"LMP?" Bilan asked.

"Oh." His head swung, realizing his error. "Another acronym; I'm sorry. The last menstrual period, which was about June second."

June second... June second... Where the hell were we June—

Bilan had moved in with me in June. We'd just returned from *Macen Beach* when her parents' home was broken into and Dog had been killed by Damien's crew. I rubbed my tight eyes. *Those days...* The first time I lived with a woman. That adjustment period was likely tough for her, but had been fucking nirvana for me. Leaving for work after a morning fuck. Coming home at night to feed her, bathe with her, fuck her, then talk as we rolled around my bed.

I remembered the one morning she kissed me at the door, bidding me a good day, Bilan could hardly look me in the face when she said she had to talk to me when I got in that afternoon. I could tell something was bothering her, but thought it was her wanting to go back to the diner full time. Before I left, I told her we'd talk. Later that morning, my lawyer called me about strategy, asking to meet for dinner. I contacted Bilan right away, completely forgetting her request to talk...until one of my pity party sessions when I recounted all the bad I'd done to lose her after she ran to *Macen Beach*. She'd never mentioned it.

A tug on the pocket of my jeans snapped me from my thoughts. My regard fell to Bilan, who licked her lips.

"Dr. Clifford asked a question," she murmured.

Ignoring her announcement, I asked, "That morning, when you told me the oatmeal had a strange odor?"

Bilan's eyes bounced around, she bit her bottom lip and nodded before whispering, "I went out that morning you left and bought a couple of tests. I took them the next morning while you were eating breakfast. That's why I told you, at the door, I wanted to talk."

Shit...

I nodded. It was funny how clear signs were in retrospect.

"Well?" Dr. Clifford cut in. I peered his way. "You want to see who's in there? I said, I prefer giving an audio impression before visual in case there's no heartbeat. We have 3D ultrasound equipment. Can get you a few diagnostic images of fetal face defects like cleft lip, skeletal, or neural tube defects."

I couldn't move. Couldn't identify my mood either. I was stuck somewhere between scared as shit, excited as fuck, and angry as hell —at myself.

"Sadik," Bilan called out to me in a soft, beseeching manner.

All I could do was stare at her for a moment. She nodded, an imploring smile on her face, timid eyes. My regard went to Dr. Clifford and I gave a faint nod. The shit didn't feel real. A baby?

My baby?

"Alrighty!" Dr. Clifford gestured to his nurse and she pulled another device over from a different machine. He grabbed it from her and lay it on Bilan's flat, gelled belly. Sound burst through the room. "Okay. Let me see the medical stuff and then we can explore the little Ellis."

I watched as he roved the controller over her abdomen, pressing in some areas. He hummed affirmations every once in a while. We waited in silence. It was incredibly tiny, the bean. I was in awe by the images on the screen. A little chest. Shoulders. A moving arm.

Holy shit...

"Okay," he chirped. "Everything looks good. Let's see this kid's face."

He moved up, beneath her left rib cage and slid down. A head. At first sight, I knew. The little face came into view, and I thought I was going to fall on my ass. Beautiful. Absolutely fucking breathtaking. I was looking at my father's wide nose. My face tightened as little lips came into view.

A puff of air escaped between my lips.

"Sadik," Bilan called in an excited whisper. "That's your mouth!"

Shit...

The baby lay on its side in a fetal position, fast asleep.

"That's the umbilical cord there. Wake up," Dr. Clifford spoke to the screen. "Your dad and mom want to see if you'll be standing or sitting to pee." He used his hand to push into her belly. "Come on. Wake up."

We could see the indentation of his shoves into her womb. They looked deep enough to be painful for Bilan, but she didn't complain. Her eyes were glued to the monitor. The baby stretched, one arm up, looking...real. Real! This thing was real. That was my baby in there.

"Uh!" Dr. Clifford chirped at the same time as Bilan when the baby shifted, rolling onto its back, and—

My motherfucking life...

"And there is the marking of your son, Ellis!" Dr. Clifford announced proudly.

If I could bottle those words, I would. A son. A fucking son!

The tug on my jeans had my head shooting down at Bilan.

Her brows were drawn when she asked, "You okay? Did you want a girl?"

I swallowed, blinked before rubbing my eyes.

"I..." I couldn't fucking speak. My eyes squeezed closed, feeling a lifting from my damn stomach. *My legacy's here...* "I... Ah—"

"Dr. Clifford, can we have a moment...alone?" her tone was soft.

"Of course!" He stood from his rolling stool. The nurse gave Bilan towels to dry her belly. "I'll get a rush on those blood samples for you and write you that script." When he made it to the door, he was sure to express, "Just...for formality sake. We're keeping the fetus. Correct?" His tone was apologetic.

"Without a doubt," Bilan returned, her eyes swiping between the doctor and me.

His attention was solely on me. This wasn't my decision. It was Bilan's ultimately, and I was so fucking relieved she wanted my child. The door closed, and a breath I didn't know I was holding pushed from my nostrils.

I squatted on the side of the exam table, resting my head on her arm. "Do you want to get married in the winter? I can try to arrange something for the fall. I need to call my attorney's office to set up a time to modify my will for my estate to include you, and eventually my—" I sucked in an unexpected breath. "My son. I can call my real estate girl and have her look for a single family today." I glanced up when a thought hit. "If you have a preference for a town or size, let me know."

Bilan was focused on wiping her belly.

"Sadik, how old were you the first time you saw a gun?"

That question jarred me. I took a minute to think. "Maybe five." I was in a room with my father and Uncle Rob, Tiffany's father, what I surmised years later was me walking in on them while they were preparing to roll out to put some work in.

"And how old were you when you held your first gun?"

My eyes glazed over, recalling that incident. "Fourteen."

She began straightening her clothes. "How old were you the first time you shot someone?"

"Fourteen."

She finally faced me. "And how old were you the first time you killed someone?" She spoke so low.

I glanced away, despising her line of questioning. I was so fucking vulnerable in the moment. I'd just seen the features of my first child. My legacy. And she wanted to bring us to a point of nihilism. But I didn't endeavor to create a relationship of dishonesty with her. Even if I didn't think it was best to share everything with Bilan, I needed an open, trusting rapport with her. I wanted her to be my wife.

"Nineteen." I swallowed, regard shifting away.

There was a spell before she spoke again. "So in six years or less, my son will see his first gun. He'll be fourteen or under when he holds a gun for the first time and shoots it at someone. And he won't be of legal age before he kills someone."

My face screwed. "The fuck you trying to say, because my child's an Ellis, he'll be violent?"

"My brother is in a coma!" she yelled. Her mouth balled, lips trembled. "A fucking coma, Sadik! There's a marginal chance of him reviving. Very unlikely. He's shrinking every day. Do you know how he got there? By my son's grandfather and uncle." I winced internally at that blow. "And when Abshir goes, all I'll be left with is my Ellis son. That's it! You have no idea of my predicament right now. You're on the Ellis side. You've been tainted. My son deserves a chance!"

I stood to my feet, lighting her ass with a deathly glare. "You fuckin' mean *my* son! I don't appreciate your insinuation of my family being a goddamn breeding ground for thuggery, Bilan! I won't tolerate that blasphemy."

Her eyes fell, mouth set in a hard ass line as she breathed hard through her nostrils. Bilan was pissed the fuck off, but so was I. This was my legacy we were talking about. What was I without my family? *Who* the fuck would I be without them?

I couldn't remain in the same room as her. I'd say something I'd soon regret. The rules had changed. Bilan wasn't the same Bilan. She was no longer the woman I walked into this exam room with. She was now the incubator of my child. My son. I had to go before compromising the respect ingrained in me to have for the mother of my child.

I left the room.

Johnson held the car door open as we approached. I was the first to slip inside. My thoughts went to the rest of my day. Irene was at the hospital with Abshir. I would need to relieve her soon. She offered to take the morning shift when I mentioned, in passing, having a doctor's appointment. I was grateful for her offering and took her up on it; however, I didn't want to take advantage of her help.

Sadik slipped in right after me. He pulled out his pinging phones the moment he was settled. We pulled off, and I got lost in my head. My regard was outside the window, thoughts on Abshir. If he didn't pull through, how would I pay my final respects? There's no way I'd invite his friends. They were shady. No one I could think of would bring the right energy. Then I realized I was being selfish and one sided. Abshir hung around like-minded people. I couldn't begin to fathom going about searching for his friends—

"Bilan."

"What?" My tone unintentionally sharp, indicative of my mood.

Sadik slid smoothly next to me in an instant, thigh pressing into mine, face glaring. "Who the hell you think you're speaking to like that?"

His heat, scent, and need of me was intoxicating. I wanted him. So badly, I wanted him. But there were too many untethered truths and lies fracturing the thread we'd once been building. So many, but one was the biggest of them all. His family.

I felt my face fold, nose lift in emotional torment. "Just wait," croaked from the back of my tight throat. "Please. Abshir needs to be my priority against your family now. If they knew he was alive, they'd kill him on his hospital bed—"

"Bilan—"

I spoke over him. "I can't deal with Abshir and the baby as far as your family goes. I still have school, and I'm still wrapping my head around being in the mix with a family like yours. God, I gave my body to a man I saw murder another! It's just too much."

He blew out a breath, swinging his gaze in the opposite direction as he muttered, "Family like mine. What the hell does that mean?" He turned back to me. "What are you asking from me?"

"To wait."

"How long, Bilan? What are we waiting for?"

"I can't say how long right now. But I need you to wait before you tell your family about the baby. I swear, I understand the enormity of this occasion for you guys. I do!" Tears pooled in my eyes. "But I don't feel safe around them. Sadik, they almost killed—"

"Ssssssh," he whispered, taking me at the side of my face. His scent. It was the most bizarre thing to be drawn to, but I was. And when Sadik's hands were on me, I felt the protection of a thousand troops. The comfort of a dozen arms. I melted into him. Our foreheads meeting, lips centimeters apart. "No harm will come to you and my baby. I swear on my fuckin' life."

"I don't trust you," I whispered.

"You will again...soon," he sighed in return.

My sex pulsed between squeezed thighs, nipples hardened. "I don't want to."

"You don't have a choice." His eyes raked up from my lips to my eyes. "Now, kiss me, Nalib. You've done enough chipping at my fuckin' ego."

A hybrid of a breath and cry pushed from my throat before our lips crashed. My tongue was in Sadik's mouth before he could meet me halfway. His crisp white tee was balled into my fist, an act of restraint.

Why did I want him so bad?

Why did it take so little effort on his part to render me senseless?

His mouth sopped between the folds of my vibrating sex. My thighs trembled around his head and shoulders. I was ready. My groin was about to implode. I rocked my hips according to his tongue strokes. His big hands cupped my cheeks from beneath, lifting me to his hungry mouth. He sucked and sucked and sucked. The sight of his golden head between my thighs was one worthy of framing.

How did I do this? How did I get here? Just months ago, I had a simple life with everyday issues. Swiftly, a force came through, complicating it at each angle except for one. This connection we had, the harmony our bodies achieved when mating. It shut out all the noise and brought a small space of peace into my mind. I was sick, yes. But incongruently clear about my need. And Sadik's sexual mastery was just that.

I was sick...twisted, enjoying forsaken passion.

"Oh..." emitted in a breath as the lever broke and I orgasmed even harder than the first one.

Sadik licked and sucked successively, creating all the sounds of filth my heart could take as he exploited my clit. Then he stood, mounting me. A distinct predatory hunger in his golden eyes. He grabbed his swollenness in his hand, aligned it with my opening, and plunged into me. Sadik didn't take a gradual approach to his strokes; he began unforgiving thrusts into my core. They were rough, delicious, and reverberating my recent orgasm.

He pounded into me, face screwed, neck muscles flexing. I opened for him more, loving the new sensation. I swear, I could come again. But even if I didn't, the powerful thrusts made my walls cry.

"Sadik!" I cried, the pleasure too raw.

In response, he plunged twice more before abruptly pulling out and splattering all over my breasts and abdomen. A jagged white maze of his semen decorated my torso. My chest heaved as I gazed up at Sadik, his head drawn back, chest lifting and dropping in unrest, too. He was a god. Bubbled chest decorated in ink, broad shoulders, contoured arms, and sweating like a field worker. I was still pulsating; after two rounds of sex, I was still aroused.

When Sadik collapsed onto the mattress, I stood from the bed and headed to the bathroom. The time hadn't gotten too ahead of me. I needed to get back to the hospital. Irene was serving her family dinner tonight and needed to get home to do it. I quickly showered, still feeling the churning in my groin, something that had to be ignored.

I lotioned down and refreshed my eyeliner and lip gloss before heading out to the closet. Sadik was sitting up in bed, on the phone. It sounded like business. I strolled into the closet, able to hear his conversation. It was about real estate. This was strange. All week, we were two ships passing in the night, and this weekend we were help-less wanton companions. The fact of him being one-third of the male Ellis clan hadn't escaped me. I was in *his* closet, pulling out drawers assigned to me, searching rods dedicated to the wardrobe he mostly purchased for me. It was surreal. Conversely, what was not was my glum circumstances.

So when I heard him talk bedroom numbers, square feet, and amenities, that angered me and propelled me to my reality. Sadik was finishing up on his call, I could tell with a realtor.

"Thanks, Jaquana. We'll be in touch." He paused for her response. "You do the same."

Now dressed, I stood in the closet's archway. "What happened to my parents' home?"

Sadik's thick, dark brown brows lifted and his head tilted to the side. My mouth twisted in determination.

He lay his phone on the mattress and turned to place his feet on the floor as he sat on the bed. Sadik scratched the side of his mustache, his regard out the window.

"I bought it."

My heart dropped to my feet. "How?"

"Through a shell company." His feline eyes on mine. "Technically, in New Jersey, I couldn't have purchased it as your fiancée. So, I had an associate go to the sheriff's sale and put in an effective bid to buy it."

My mouth balled tight as I fought my emotions. "So, what does that mean?"

He gave a soft nod, as though he expected my anger on the matter. "When I offered to save it for you right after your gradua-tion, you declined."

"My mother told me not to save it," I explained. "She told me not to use my money on it. To use it to secure a future because the house was cursed and filled with horrible memories."

He nodded. "You told me that the night of your graduation party. And I respected your wishes."

"Until I left."

Rory was right in suggesting I speak to her boss about my family's home.

"When you left, I felt responsible. I'd already had an associate monitoring the process of the foreclosure. When I got the call that it'd gone into sheriff's sale, I had him go to the auction and not leave until he purchased the property. It's been secured."

"For what?"

"For you to tell me what you want to do with it."

"I don't want it." My mother said to let it go.

"Then we'll sell it for you," he decreed. "We'll use the profit for my son."

My neck gave out at that concept. Sadik was raised to uphold Black capitalism. It was second nature. He knew right away what to do with a piece of property that could easily be valued in the neighborhood of a half a million if refurbished. I knew this from previous research.

"Why?" I needed to know. "Why would you do all of that for me?"

His shrug was casual, but the earnest gleam in his eyes was all but. "Because you're mine, Bilan. I'm sorry your orientation has been so rocky. I apologize for not being the nigga from around the corner, or the one you met on campus whom your parents would accept and be proud to join families with. But I've had all last month to cogitate this from every angle. I can't let you go. You say you're sick for indulging me; I don't know what that makes my need for you. I'm sorry, baby. I really am. But I need for you to accept all of me, and that includes my family, who isn't as bad as you've allowed your mind to conjure."

I crossed my arms. "Who are they?"

"Pardon?"

"You said you'd explain everything." I dipped my chin. "Do it. Who are the Ellises? And don't give me the American dream version. Give me their true essence of the American nightmare they've earned. How was your father connected to Damien?" Then a thought struck. "And the moment I sense you're lying or withholding something, I'll—"

Sadik lifted his palm in the air to reject my threat. "I'll explain, Bilan. I'm a grown fuckin' man, too old and accomplished to make up lies. No need for the warning." He took a deep breath, tenting his fingertips as his elbows rested on his knees. There was something to say about a man confident enough to take on this conversation in the nude.

But I was ready—*desperate*, in fact—to learn how I'd intersected with the underworld of the Ellises.

"In the state of New Jersey, there is a wealth of commerce built on illegal transactions and violent crimes. In the lead of the violence were six crime heads: a Russian guns and human trafficker, a Dominican family dealing primarily drugs, an Italian family into distribution of a miscellany of illegal commodity, a Haitian heavily into the arms trade and a little drugs, a Black *gay* man pushing weight and stolen cars, and finally, another African American man with a tenure in drugs and guns wholesale." His gaze was leveled when he admitted, "That's Earl...Ellis."

The Italian family...that was Lia's family. The gay man was, of course, Damien. He was sure to emphasize his sexuality; I was sure to burn it into my brain...and ego. But the Haitian arms dealer was Ricky. It had to be. He was known for his gunplay.

"A few years ago, the violence between the six underground figures was so alarming, it was extremely dangerous. So dangerous, it threatened the income and, most importantly, the safety of the residents of the state. Murder arrests and conviction rates were at an all-time high. One of the crime figures had the ingenuity to propose a union. He called it *The Commission*. It was a structure likened after his Italian forefathers. An agreement to adhere to a set of rules that would allow them all to maintain their businesses and, perhaps, grow them without threat or violence from their most formidable adversaries, which they were to each other. The only bigger rival they all shared was the federal government."

"And not local police?" That struck me as odd.

Sadik shook his head, eyes descending. "Several of the men at this table have a specific and comprehensive relationship with their local law enforcement agencies. Their shared 'bigger fish' is the federal government. Each of these individuals represent million-dollar empires, some just more zeros at the end than others."

"And where does Earl fall into this?" His kaleidoscopic gaze prescinded again. Sadik's head shifted over his neck, visibly uneasy about this topic. "I deserve to know what I'm up against here. The leader of this...'*Commission*' threatened my life! Another kidnapped me. Another's dating my friend. And another is kin to the child I'm incubating. I deserve to have my eyes wide open as I travel this nightmare of a life."

His eyes were on me again, this time green and blazing. "My father is, by far, the richest Black man—person—in the underbelly world of this state. He's built an empire for over fifty years avoiding arrests and/or conviction since his graduation from local police being a threat to now the federal government having a whole unit dedicated to prosecuting him." My pulse raced and stomach dropped like a free fall. "And let's make one thing clear: Salvatore Rizzo may have initiated this agreement, but Earl Ellis' only boss is Irene." Sadik's words were sharp.

However, they were with pride. These were facts he'd lived with, likely his entire life. Clearly, he knew his father's line of work was legally and morally wrong, yet he still held an uncompromised reverence for the man. That was problematic for me.

This!

This mentality of *it's okay we kill and poison people because we're a family* would be passed on to my child. There was no way he could expect me to be okay with it. What mother would? Defeat saturated my sensibilities.

Sadik grunted, hands quickly brushing over his glistening head, then he stood, turning to face me. "I just shared an incredible amount of sensitive information with you. I know you're already dealing with a great deal of moving parts concerning my world. What are you thinking, Bilan?"

I shrugged, brows arched. "How alone I was before you, and how sullen my life has been since your...invasion." I walked off.

"Shit! I don't want you to feel trapped or confined here," he roared, voice just as intimidating as his dick in rest mode. "You still have the privacy and liberties you had before meeting me. You only have to move differently now. You have security, yes. But you're not encaged. I'm not nor have I ever forced you to do shit!"

"You blew into my rather insipid world at breakneck speed and with gripping force, Sadik. You really think I feel the same sense of autonomy I did before you claimed me in Costa Rica?"

From across the room, I caught the darkening of his eyes the moment he processed the occasion. Sadik's cock began thickening, growing in the air. It happened so fast, there was no way it was deliberate. That fact frightened and aroused me to dangerous degrees.

Shaking my head, I turned to leave the suite.

Sick... I was just as sick as the Ellises.

"If you could pack me a couple slices to go," I requested of Candy, who was collecting my plate. "I'd appreciate it."

"Sure, Sadik." She smiled and continued down the table.

When my attention went back to the table, I caught eyes on me. Namely my mother's, Taaliba's, Monica's, and Tiffany's, who was present tonight at dinner. Iesha and Ivana sat next to each other tonight and were busy chatting. My father's gaze landed on me after his plate was collected. It was the unspoken topic raining over my mother's dinner table. Bilan. Why wasn't she here if she had been back in town?

"You know my wife's invitation is extended to your lady, unless there's a problem I ain't aware of," my father inquired.

"It's okay, Earl," my mother tried diffusing the potentially explosive topic. "Really."

"Nah." He shook his head stubbornly. "I'm just asking."

"Mrs. Ellis." Stacy was near the dining room door. She offered a communicative nod.

"Oh!" my mother chirped, rising from her seat. "I have to go," she announced to the table. When she passed me, she noted, "I'll be in my room if you need me."

"Everything okay?" I asked, not liking the jittery manner she'd that quickly transitioned into.

"Yes. It's just..." She hesitated, her eyes cutting beyond me to Monica's side of the table. "Iliza's here. With Stacy's help, I'm keeping her while Lia gets much needed rest. She's not done very well postpartum. Most of the Rizzo family's left to fly Salvatore's body back to Sicily," her tone was apologetic.

Stacy was my mother's executive assistant of the house. She managed the entire staff. She also served the role of nanny for the girls when they were over. So the mention of her name made me curious.

"Who's Iliza?"

When my mother's timid regard went over my head again, I automatically turned. Monica's eyes fell as her fingers curled over the table. She was uncomfortable.

Iliza was my new niece. That's what Iban and Lia named her. I'd been so wrapped up in my own shit, I hadn't met my niece. That thought struck me hard, mentally. It brought back Bilan's position on my family. I'd been too busy constructing the demise of her grandfather; I hadn't welcomed the baby into the family.

Ending the conversation, I turned back to the table. I could feel my mother continuing out of the room. Tiffany took a call from her phone.

"Where is Iban?" I asked Monica.

"Daddy's at work," Iesha answered, attention still on her sister.

Monica's eyes fell away and she rubbed the back of her neck, uneasy.

My father spoke up, "I got him on a job."

"Speaking of which," Monica piped up, a new forced light in her eyes. "My C-section is scheduled. I'm trying to coordinate childcare for the girls so I can focus on the baby. You know the girls were adamant about spending some of that time with their favorite uncle."

"Yup!" Iesha chimed in. "And I get to set the menu with my Kimmy."

"No, you don't, Eshy!" Ivana argued.

"Uhn-huhn! You got to do it the last time!" Iesha cried.

Ivana shook her head. "Let's get back to this." She held her hands in the air, waiting for her sister to do the same.

My attention returned to their mother. "I'm looking forward to it."

"I'll reach out to Rory with the dates for your schedule." Then Monica pushed back from the table. "Come on, little girls. Mommy's tired," she strained, standing to her feet.

I watched as she gathered the girls. Observed the fatigue she exuded. My eyes went to my father, sitting with his elbows on the table and chin on his clasped fists. He had to see what I saw. *On a job my ass*. Iban was likely with Lia. He said she'd been pressing him for things only a wife qualified to get. This likely had been weighing on her shoulders, too. I didn't like what I saw at all. But it wasn't my place to get involved. Monica knew Iban, in some ways, better than I did. I'd have to leave her to deal with him.

The girls ran over to my father with hugs and kisses, saying good-night. They shot over to me for the same, then Tiff.

"Don't forget," Iesha called by the door. "Uncle Deek, I get to be the lady of the house next time. Don't forget!"

"Never, Eshy." Her earnest expression melted my damn heart. "Night, big girls." I waved as they left the room.

Then I found myself at the table with my father and Tiffany. Interesting they were still there, but I understood why for each individual.

"Woman of the house, huhn?" Tiffany smirked. "Being the woman of the house takes more than deciding on the food. Filling those shoes take big feet."

I scoffed, scratching the back of my head.

You have no idea...

"So...work?" I asked my father, referring back to the explanation about Iban's absence.

"Shit go down in my business every day." His words were basically a shrug.

"Any last meetings with your group of friends?"

He knew I meant *The Commission*.

"Got no more friends, last I knew." He turned his head, casually scratching his neck.

I nodded. *The Commission* was still disbanded. This was good news.

"Should there be an attempt for a reunion, it would be in your best interest to decline." My delivery just as casual.

My father's head swiveled to face me, lips pouting and lifted. I issued him a leveling gaze as Candy returned with a small to-go shopping bag.

"Thanks for this." I nodded to her before standing to leave.

"Night, Tiff," I bade, taking off.

"Actually, I need to talk to you," she announced. "Poppa Earl, you okay for the night?"

My father nodded. "Me and the girls going out to the bar in a minute."

"Okay." She stood and traveled over to him for an adieu kiss. "I'll call you in the morning. Thank Irene for dinner for me."

I was already headed out before she finished with her goodbyes.

"So." She trekked after me. "Are you going to the party or not? The RSVP deadline has passed."

"Is harassing invitees a part of the package for your clients?" I joked.

"Funny. Lucky for Ricky, I have access to you."

"I don't think Ricky gives a shit if I'm going or not. We ain't friends." I glanced over my shoulder at her before she caught up to me.

"Sadik!"

I chuckled. "Okay. Let me check with Bilan to see what she wants to do."

"Rory said that last week! You ain't 'talk' with her yet?"

"She just got back into town. Sorry to say, it just hasn't come up. Lots of other important shit to sift through."

"Like relationship issues?"

That broke my stride. "Come again?"

Tiff's giggle was shy. "She ain't here with you at the family dinner, nobody's seen or heard from her in a month."

I swiped my nose. "And how do you know that?"

Tiffany hesitated. "Poppa Earl told me...and Iban mentioned it."

I nodded. Tiffany never understood her favor in my family was with the men and not the women. My mother, Taaliba, and Monica didn't dislike her; they just didn't vibe with Tiffany because she presented herself, all these years, as a prospective in-law rather than daughter. My mother dealt with her daughter and daughter-in-law differently. It was just her way.

I checked my watch for the time. "Tiff, I need to get home now. If Bilan's still awake, I'll ask her if she wants to go and get back to you."

The moment I turned to walk away, she chirped, "Still awake? Wait a minute!" She breathed. "She's at your place...now? Without you?"

"Night, Tiff." I quickly bowed before taking off.

Yeah, it was fucked up that I left her hanging that way. But no matter how clear with her I'd been, Tiffany was being Tiffany. I had no time for that right now.

I was wrong. By the time I made it home, Bilan was turned onto her side, knocked the hell out. From the doorway, I stared at her, hoping a method to making her happy would come to mind.

Her phone pinging up on the bed caught my attention. Bilan didn't stir at the startling sound. Almost as though expecting her to awaken—hoping for her to, I waited. If she woke up, maybe we could...talk. I could kick it with her about this lawsuit shit or about the latest technology project I invested in and had mixed feelings about, unlike my partner. Or possibly the trip out to the Colorado dispensary I'd be leaving for tomorrow for much needed staff restructuring. But she didn't. Bilan didn't stir. I ambled farther into the room for the bed and grabbed her phone.

As I lifted it from the bed, the reminder alert lit.

Jason...

Bilan's phone was password protected. I typed in what I knew it to be, which was her mother's birthday. My jaw tightened when I saw it was incorrect. I tried her birthday, but unsuccessfully. Then I took an impatient moment to be smart about this. What would her password be?

When did she even change it?

That's when it hit me. Today changed so much for the both of us. It was when we learned when our first child—of many, if I could help it—would be born. I gave it a try, typing in 0319. That didn't work. Then I got more specific.

0309

And bingo...

Their texting for today began a few hours ago.

Jason: *i haven't heard from you in days. what the hell's going on up there?*

Bilan: I'm fine. It's been hectic trying to get readjusted and get acclimated to these courses.

Jason: *shit. i forgot about school. #tooworriedaboutyourlife*

Bilan: I'm still breathing. Went to the doctor today!

Jason: *and?*

Bilan: The baby's healthy and gorgeous. He's absolutely gorgeous. And get this: he looks nothing like me.

Jason: *that's too bad for him*

Jason: *wait! you're having a boy?*

Bilan: Yup!

Jason: *holy shit. i want my first to be a boy. a mini me. that fucking ellis gets everything i want. you and your baby. fucker!*

Bilan: Quit Jason. I have too much going on to be engaged in a pity party. If I'm not having one you can't either.

That must have been where she conked out. His last text came thirty-three minutes later.

Jason: *i'm coming home for a few days. please say i'll see you.*

I gazed at the phone for a while, weighing my options. I could have texted him back, revealing my identity, letting him know he had twenty-four hours to live. I could have returned the text under the guise of Bilan being the author and told him to lose her number. I could have called to have my jet juiced, flew to *Macen Beach*, cut his fucking throat, then have been back and showered before Bilan opened her eyes in the morning. Two of the three of those options appealed to me the least. Whether the kid lived or died was of no consequence to me.

The motherfucker knew about my baby before I did. That fact burned the hell out of my ego. I had a team of two keep an eye on Bilan while in *Macen Beach*. I'd gotten reports about her crying on the beach, heading to the boardwalk for food each time, going grocery shopping, running into Jason, and hanging out with his friends. I'd even heard about him creeping up to the master bedroom when his girl and their people had passed out from a night of drinking in my living room. How he'd tried to fuck her, but she turned him away. My finger was on the trigger that night, too. All I had to do was give the word.

This was his corny ass going too fucking far, pushing too much for a man of my resources. He could be dead by morning. Dead. A bullet in his fucking head while I lay next to the woman he fantasized about fucking. It would only take one call.

Instead, I silenced her phone and placed it on the nightstand, then sauntered to the bathroom for a much-needed cool down shower.

"And this muthafucka got everybody coming! Like...every fuckin' body."

"It's his forty-fifth birthday, Randi. This is obviously a big deal for him." I knew very little about Ricky. Truthfully, I was baffled he'd want to do something that would bring so much attention to him. "How many people did he invite?"

"Like four hundred!" she exclaimed. "He even got a boat of fuckin' family coming from Haiti!"

My face tightened. "Randi, you must forget my parents and grandparents traveled on that same proverbial boat. I think it's time we say plane."

"Man, what the fuck ever. You know what I mean."

Something wasn't right. Randi seemed really annoyed. "Why is this bothering you so much? Are they all staying at his place?"

"Some, but his place ain't all that big for all of them muthafuckas. *I* ain't staying there when they come through. No fuckin' way."

From the corner of my eye, I saw Rory standing from her chair. She took off to the elevator. I'd been sitting outside of Abshir's room since Randi called, not wanting to hold a telephone conversation in there.

"Where are you going to stay?"

"If you was still at your old place, I would go there. But I 'on't know now. Maybe I'll get a damn hotel room."

"I don't get it. Why not just stay at his place as you normally do?"

"'Cause this bitch got his lil' girlfriend from home coming."

My eyes ballooned. "Girlfriend?"

"Yeah, girl. You know how Haitian men are!" *No. I don't, actually.* "He got a whole ass wife back home. I told you he got kids, too—two of them muthafuckas grown. One live in Canada. The other one in Europe some damn where."

I was utterly stunned. Vaguely, I recalled her mentioning a child back in Haiti, but not a whole family. So Randi was a side piece? Why had Ricky been here all these years, leaving a family behind?

"Why the fuck you so quiet?" She laughed. "I know you ain't surprised, Bilan. At least, I hope the fuck you ain't. You fuckin' a damn boss now yourself. Shit may be new now, but trust me, give it a few more months and that man'll be back on the prowl for something new. And it won't be that he wanna be done with you. Men like that just get they needs met from a variety of women, just like they do they money."

I considered that for a moment. Earl and Iban were from that "*Commission*" type of world, like Ricky. They had multiple women and it seemed all the women, to some degree, accepted infidelity.

"I'm just..." I couldn't find the words, my hand rolling in the air. "I didn't know he was married with a family."

"Yeah, well. Anyway, I'mma be there stuntin'. I got this *Fendi* jumpsuit I'mma rock. I'm going to *Short Hills Mall* today to cop me the dope ass *Ase Garb* strappy sandals. I dare that bitch to look better than me. And I wish she would act like she want smoke. I'll drag her dusty ass all around that club."

"You'd fight at that man's party, Randi?"

"Hell, yeah. If that bitch wanna shine, let her do it on the floor."

"But his family will be there. It'd be a mess."

"And I got my cousins from Brooklyn coming. Haiti ain't fuckin' with *Pink Houses*! *Shiiiiit!*" she swore. I shook my head. "I hope you gon' be there, too. And you betta not let shit happen to me."

I cringed, then my head rolled back. "I totally forgot to ask Sadik about it. I swear, I'll text him as soon as we hang up." I made a mental note. "But I can tell you now, I can't take part in no physical fights."

"Why the fuck not?"

"Because I'm fourteen weeks pregnant." I stretched my cheeks sheepishly.

"What the hell is fourteen weeks in pregnancy months?" I heard the shock in her voice.

"About three months and a week. I'm in my second trimester."

"You ain't look pregnant when I saw you!"

"I know. It's something I've been keeping to myself for a while now."

"Bitch, but me and you 'posed to be riders!"

"I know. It's been a crazy time, like I told you and Tasche. I hadn't even told Sadik."

"Man, fuck Sadik! I'm 'posed to be your best friend."

My eyes squeezed shut. The amount of apologizing I'd been doing to this girl was mounting.

"I know," I sang again. "I'm just the type of person to keep things in my head before I share them. You know this about me, Randi."

"Pregnant or not, you better come looking your best. 'Cause this'll be at the girl, Tiffany's, club. *And* I been meaning to tell you I heard her and Sadik used to fuck around." My heart dropped as though this was new knowledge to me. "And this came from a tight ass source."

"Really?" I murmured, oddly playing dumb. Then I noticed two figures approaching. It was Rory and a woman carrying a duffle bag. "Randi, someone just came in. I have to go, but I promise, I'll text Sadik and ask what he's going to do with the invitation."

"Nah. Fuck that. You tell him you gon' come."

I rolled my eyes. "Okay. I'll be there."

I tapped to end the call.

"Yo, B, this Imani," Rory introduced. "Imani, this Bilan, the boss' fiancée." We shook hands as we greeted each other. Rory explained to me, "She do massages for pregnant people. S.Q.E. got her to hook you up."

Sadik left town yesterday for his marijuana dispensary in Colorado. He'd be away for another three days. While I appreciated the distance from him so I could think independent of his alluring scent and heat, I missed him for those same reasons. I only wanted Sadik's sex and nothing more. In fact, I'd even changed his profile name in my phone to reflect that.

My eyes bounced around the sitting area. "Here?"

"Yeah," Rory answered, voice unnaturally deep.

"There's no space for that."

Abshir may have had an end room with a row of chairs conveniently outside of it; however, there were other patient rooms just a few yards away.

"Nah." She pointed behind her. "There's a prayer room, or some shit down the hall."

My chin dipped. "A prayer room?"

"The fuck," Rory croaked. "This some form of...meditation. Ain't it?" she posed to Imani.

The Imani woman nodded with pouted lips. "That'll work. This *will* be a form of meditation. And it's only the scalp. Mr. Ellis said you're just out of your first trimester, and he'd like more time before you get a body massage."

Of course, this was thought out thoroughly by him. I was in no mood for a massage or new energy around me, but didn't want to be rude. It was only a scalp massage; that shouldn't take too much time. Plus, I was done with my online quiz before the six pm deadline.

"Okay." I sighed. "Can I meet you in there in a couple of minutes? I need to send a few texts before I forget."

"No problem," Imani granted. "That'll give me enough time to set up."

"I'll walk you over there." Rory turned to lead the way with Imani following.

I went back to my phone and texted my trainer at the gym, something I'd been putting off for too long. As weird as it sounded, I felt my body weakening. My next text went to Sadik.

Me: So this party Ricky's throwing...

Nearly two minutes later, Sadik replied.

My Lover: *What about it?*

Me: Randi wants me to go.

My Lover: *Is that something you want?*

Me: She's been a support to me. I want to be a support to her. You've been invited.

My face balled.

Really?

My Lover: *Okay. You can't go by yourself.*

Huhn?

Duh!

Me: Where do I go by myself?

I sprinkled in sarcasm. Rory always shadowed me.

My Lover: *Meaning I'd go too.*

I rolled my eyes.

Me: Of course. It's your invitation.

My Lover: *Well I guess we'll be going on Saturday, Nalib. Enjoy the scalp massage.*

I groaned as Rory strolled back into the area. That reminded me I was being waited on.

My phone chirped just in time.

Dimi: *hi belon long time no see im still at gym 2mr is good*

That tickled me. My trainer was the worst texter ever. But he was good at fitness, and that's what my body needed. I rolled my neck after standing to my feet for my scalp massage. My "everything" felt tight. If I was going to finally focus on my pregnancy, fitness had to be a part of it.

As I ambled into my two-bedroom condo, just outside of Colorado Springs, I remembered to call Rory back. I split from Johnson, who stayed in my spare room, and kept towards the kitchen for a beer as I called her.

The phone rang twice before she answered.

"Yo."

"What's going on?"

"Just wanted to follow up on Dominicana."

"Hit me."

"She bitchin', still saying she gon' fuck one of our people since we fucked her mans."

I nodded. Lopez had been aging, but his temper was still with stamina. He was an emotional man, always crying, always complaining. The man used too many words just to say he was angry. Men like that were intolerable to personality types like my father's and mine.

I'd known him and his family since I was in college. My father used to supply their guns until their determined period of time was up. They were respecting colleagues, and not necessarily friends. He even sent his kids to *Ellis Academy*. But as families, we'd never shared meals or occasions. It was primarily business. The fact that he wanted to go to war with my father over a low level, who was explained as having disrespected my lady, was disrespectful. We'd even shipped the little fucker's body to Lopez after digging him up. That was a rare courtesy.

"What do we know about her movements?"

"She taking her loved ones back home for a celebration, or some shit. I think it's somebody's birthday."

I considered that for a second. Lopez was taking his family back home to the Dominican Republic for a family celebration of some sort. I'd been monitoring him to gauge when he'd strike.

"Okay. Let's stay on top of her. That bitch is moody as hell."

Rory laughed. "The fuck I know."

"A'ight. I know you're finishing up at the hospital. I'll let you go."

She scoffed. "I ain't at no fuckin' hospital."

"Well, where the fuck are you?"

"Fuckin' in Hawthorne."

"What the fuck're you doing in Hawthorne?"

"Bilan at a gym."

My hand froze over the laptop keypad on the countertop.

"Gym?"

"Yeah. That's the real reason I hit you that last time. She had me bring her here, but ain't want me to go in with her. When I said I needed to run it past you, she flipped the fuck out on me. Said she wanted to go work out alone and didn't need me with her to do it. I ain't argue with her. I saw it was a big ass window in the gym. I can see her now, so I do have eyes."

"But you ain't got speed," I articulated her dilemma.

If someone wanted to take Bilan again, it would be an increased chance of a successful snatching because Rory didn't have quick access to her like she did in a hospital or a store. After Lamont's fuck up, I made it clear Bilan had security in close proximity at all times while out.

And since when the fuck did Bilan work out?

"But peep this shit. Guess who her trainer is?" I played no guessing games, and Rory knew this of me. "Fuckin' Russian ass Dimitri, Popov's old shooter."

Dimitri...

I remembered him. Had even wondered what happened to the man. The Lopezes stopped getting their guns from my father and went directly to the Russian man my father wholesaled from. Popov was the largest arms distributor in the Tri-state area. He was a member of *The Commission*.

Was she purposely being errant? Why would she wait until she was pregnant to work out? Had I been too explicit in explaining she could do what she wanted to do? Was this Bilan's way of testing her boundaries.

Fucking Dimitri, the Russian!

My eyes closed to a squeeze. "I'm on my way home."

"One, two."
I punched, grunting.
"One, two."
My fists met his padded mitts.
"One, two...swing."
I delivered two blows and ducked from his swinging arms.
"And one, two!"
We went on and on until my arms dropped in exhaustion.

"Ah, huhn," he hummed, heavy accent detected even in melody. "This happens when you stop work, Bilan."

Heaving, I nodded hard. "I know. I know." God, I knew. It had been over three months since my last time here. Pre-S.Q.E—*as Rory referred to him*—I'd be here at least three days a week. However, when I moved in, I opted not to have Sadik's security, Lamont, breathing down my neck here. Dimi didn't seem like the type of man who would take too well to that form of intimidation. Then the drama happened before I could figure out a way to work it out.

"Let's try it again," he ordered. "Remember to look at my shoulders more than my face. You cannot read my mind, but you can follow my punches from my shoulders. And do not lock your eyes. You need them everywhere. Don't rely on the rhythm, Bilan. Focus on your offense. Use all senses, not just your eyes on mine." I nodded my acknowledgement. "Now. one, two," he continued his commands.

We did another round of combos, including blocks, thrilling and exhausting me in equal measures. When we stopped, I was out of breath and drenched.

"Fifty!" he pointed to the rubber tiles, commanding pushups.

"Fifty?" I shouted back.

Dimi nodded, big, tall, pale body looked to be made of steel. He was over six feet and had to be at least two hundred pounds, solid muscle. When he crossed those brawny arms, I knew he meant business.

So down to my knees I went, beginning the count.

My arms burned, and I could feel my core strengthening. God, I loved this place. I felt stronger each time I left. The first thing I did when I arrived yesterday was make sure Dimi knew about my condition. Protecting this baby was paramount. I'd even been eating better...more frequently. After working out yesterday, I knew I'd come back today. Tonight, the place was empty.

This gym was a godsend. A refurbished warehouse in Hawthorne with floor to ceiling windows facing the front of the building. It gave off a New York City'ish feel. Tasche told me about it a while back. One of the girls at the club came here to learn how to defend herself against drunken men who can't take no for an answer after hours.

Dimi charged pennies, practically giving away his services for free. He wasn't friendly, but was knowledgeable and fair. The only time I'd seen him come to life was when his wife and their toddler, Zoya, came around. His eyes lit in a way that chased his darkness away.

"Up again!" he commanded. With little grunts and strains, I was on my feet. "Get in that Caddy and let's go."

I obeyed, getting into position with my fists in the air. Body aching, mind alive.

This is what the doctor called for.

∞**15**∞

"I'm here," I told Rory via telephone. "We're pulling up now."

"A'ight. I think I see ya lights," Rory informed. "Yeah. That's you. Cool." The call disconnected.

As we pulled up on the block in Hawthorne, mostly taken up by a warehouse on one side of the street, I recalled a girl I used to know living about a block away. It didn't take long for me to notice the big windows of the second floor. The car came to a stop across from the warehouse, and Johnson cut the engine. I peered straight into the building, recognizing her.

"Damn," Johnson breathed in the front seat. "That Bilan spittin' those 1-2-3-2s like that?"

I sat up in my seat, unbelieving my eyes. Bilan was dripping from sweat, throwing a jab-cross-hook-cross combo, looking determined and practiced at it, too. And there was Dimitri. He paced around her, eyes meeting her directly. I could tell he hollered a directive and Bilan responded as he told her to. She was...trained. And by another man.

I felt a gut blow when it was clear he barked a command by the way his chest vibrated. Bilan immediately began to run laps around the room. His eyes followed her closely. Dimitri blew his whistle and Bilan laid on her back on the floor with her legs in the air, near a tractor tire. Dimitri stood the tire up, then pushed it against the bottom of her feet and pressed his weight into it. Bilan performed leg presses under the weight of the tire and Dimitri standing in the rim.

I took a deep breath, feeling my body mist beneath my suit.

"I've seen enough, Johnson," I grunted.

Within seconds, we were pulling off.

My hands pressed into the dark gray glass walls of the shower. The hot water spewed into my back and shoulders, aching muscles and tendons relaxed. The pressure was perfect and the temperature couldn't be any better. After standing there for a few minutes, I backed away, not wanting to create too hot an environment for the baby—if that was possible. My body instantly cooled, and I took deep breaths to clear my lungs with the steam.

I felt incredible! Sore, but incredible. It was hard to believe I worked out two days in a row. Dimi told me to give my body a break for a day or so before coming back. He said he wanted to keep the baby in mind. As soon as I got in from the gym, I scarfed down a bowl of seafood macaroni salad Kimmy made for me. She knew it was one of my favorite dishes of hers. Then I limped to the back of the apartment for the master suite and shower.

This was just what the doctor ordered—

A cacophonous crashing of glass onto the floor had me leap from the wall. I stood frozen in the center of a glass box, feeling like a fish in a bowl. My full body shook, heart galloping. I was here alone. Kimmy was gone for the day, Rory was in her place downstairs, and Sadik wasn't due back until tomorrow. I dropped my face, loosening the tension in my neck. This was ridiculous. Sadik lived in a secured building. There were guards monitoring the place on foot and through surveillance. Something had broken out in the apartment, and I needed to see what it was.

After turning off the jet sprays, I stepped out of the shower and grabbed my towel. I made quick work of drying my hair, then my body before wrapping it around my vibrating frame. Hesitantly, I ambled toward the door. On my way there, the power was cut outside of the bathroom. The bedroom lights were off and, from what I could see from the door, the one in the hall was out, too.

Taking a deep breath, I swallowed and pushed myself out of the door. The moment I crossed the threshold, a punch was hurled from my left side. With second nature instincts, I ducked, quickly moving from arm's length. Whoever it was stood in the shadows of the darkness in the suite, but I could make out a body. It was taller than mine. I backed away toward the French doors for the hallway. That's when a man lunged forward, throwing another punch. I countered it without thought. *Oh, God, I'm going to die!* But I missed. It was enough to get him to back up.

Foolishly, I got into my Cadillac, the fight stance I'd been taught for years. He didn't move too quickly, but eventually he charged again, causing me to duck. My towel fell to the floor and I was naked. Ignoring that disadvantage, I came up quickly and counter-punched him. It landed square in his palm, something I was accustomed to from class.

Oh, God, I'm going to die...

I threw a fake punch with the left and landed the right

awkwardly on his shoulder, but with a bit of force. It was like hitting a brick wall. However, it was a move of bravery. The room went quiet and my pulse screeched in my ears. I didn't stop, throwing another punch again, this one landing near his neck.

"...*bitch can fight!*" he screeched lowly, hardly giving me the opportunity to hear all of his words.

He backed farther into the room, near the closet, almost in search of something.

Oh, God, I'm going to die!

I took that opportunity to run. My legs took their time to move succinctly, but eventually they were in sync. *Why?* Why would I leave the bathroom in suspicion without my phone? If I could make it to the front of the apartment, I could use the phone to call security. The apartment was dark, the power off all around. All that could be seen was the incandescence of the moon, gleaming through the floor-to-ceiling windows at the end of the hall. I was just at the living room entrance when I heard a distinctive whip against the marble floor.

My feet slowed and body halted on a smooth stop. With eyes wild, breathing frantically, body trembling, I froze with my arms half in the air. I'd heard that sound successively at one time, burning it into the meninges of my brain. It was a rope.

A manila rope...

"You got a whole fuckin' skill set I never knew of," a minatory rasp informed. "I guess you're full of goddamn surprises for this love sick ultra-alpha, huhn?"

Sadik.

My eyes squeezed closed and a gut-wrenching cry shot from the bottom of my belly. My sob bubbled in silence before spilling an audible wail. I hurled over, one hand to my chest as I cried, wobbling to the sofa. I lay my other hand on the back of it for support. My legs felt like they would give out on me. How could he scare me senseless like this? What was he thinking?

The sound of another whip to the floor had me stand, spine straight. Something came over me. In an inexplicably short period, my emotions went from scared, to relieved, to...angry. Adrenaline doubled, tingling my nipples and creating a throb between my legs that quickly. No longer was I under duress. I was safe...and being mocked. That was wrong. It was wholly unfair. I turned and charged in his direction with my hands in the air swinging, but not like the maneuvers I'd learned in class. Like a girl off the block, wanting to stomp a hole in her wayward man.

"What are you going to do with that rope! Are you going to kill me, Sad—"

A fast whip rented the air, and my wrists were caught in a layer of rope that quickly multiplied. Sadik was on me, swinging it from a closer proximity before I could think to counteract his efforts. I swung my arms to try and break loose from the rapid leashing around them. They were over my head as he backed away. I continued to fight, though I couldn't decide how to satisfy my anger over my desire and sudden sexual needs. All I knew was I had to get out of the rope and to Sadik. He would pay for this.

"Stop fighting," he warned. "You won't break loose, but you will tire yourself and hurt—" He couldn't continue.

That enraged me, incited my derisiveness. "Hurt what? The baby?" I screamed at the top of my lungs, my knees now meeting the armrest of the sofa. "Come make sure I don't, you asshole! Why are you all the way over there?"

I was teeming with an overflow of adrenaline. Seething from being naked and assumed helpless, all because of his insecurities!

"You're mad because I won't break!" I continued. "You're mad because I'm not where Ameerah, Tiffany, Sofia, and God only knows how many more women are with pining over the ultra-alpha! No! I won't be one of them. I will protect everything: my baby and my heart. You may have gotten to me...put a baby in me because of my credulity, but my heart was never up for grabs!"

In my angry spewing, I didn't have the sensibility to process his long lunges in my direction until he was upon me. Those feline eyes were an unusual yellow, the blond spikes in his face glimmered sharply. Sadik crowded me, his scent attacked me, and I was angry all over again. My chest rose and fell, groin churned. I lowered my arms and with them tied together, I slapped Sadik with all the force I could. He tumbled backward, palm to his jaw. Slowly, he peered at me.

I stomped my foot, the sting from the blow not a present concern. "What are you going to do?"

It took a singular movement for Sadik to be in my face, glaring down on me. His movement so swift, it startled me. Now, with him this, close...this angry, I cowered. And not because I feared him hurting me. But because there were facets of this man I stood no chance against. Sadik was supreme. His entire countenance arrested my better senses and I instantly became deluged with hungry need.

His shoulders were broad, his posture threatening, his breathing rough as he flexed over me, inflated. His eyes delivered reasonable threats I couldn't deal with in the moment; the adrenaline wouldn't allow. I wanted his dominance, though. I needed his regulating ability he'd always used to make me feel safe. And now, his harsh cologne-infused breaths were crashing into my face, his heat permeating my body. It all reduced my fight.

"Deek," I beseeched in a cry before reaching up and falling into his lips.

I didn't wait for him to join me. My tongue pushed into his contracted mouth and my legs rose, climbing to his hips. While I balanced myself, using the placket of his dress shirt in between the buttons, my pelvis lifted and I rubbed my greedy sex onto him. Dry humping never felt so good, but I tried communicating my need for the real thing.

Sadik growled in a manner incongruent to my need. I could feel his body flex against mine. Felt his hands raise aside my bare hips.

"Don't hit me again, Nalib," he croaked. "I've got fuckin' feelings."

And his mouth crashed onto mine, his tongue more powerful than mine. Sadik invaded my mouth, slammed my pelvis into his erection. He tilted me over the armrest where I lay on the sofa. My arms were pushed over my head, where they could be of no use. The buckle of his belt clanged in the quiet air. His zipper had my thighs widening. My thrust into his pelvis began before Sadik could pull his pants down. But when they were, he positioned his erection at my sex.

And...

"Oh!"

The first thrust inside me was without patience. The delicious forceful entry had my heels digging into the armrest, lifting to meet more pressure. He plunged into me with fierceness; I met each angry one. The sounds of his lunges were spongey as I soaked him in with gusto.

He began to grunt. Those grunts grew louder and rhythmic. I was charged, my sex animatedly obliging each plummet he delivered. There was no movement but ours, no sounds but that of our slapping pelvises. It didn't take long before that undeniably beautiful sensation began to blossom in my groin until I exploded.

"Sa..." My lungs sloughed. "...*DEEK*!" I couldn't endure the onslaught of bliss, breathe, and speak at the same time.

And Sadik went on and on, grunting in my ear as he stroked long and unrelenting. I could feel the ridge of his mushroom head each time he pulled to my rim and thrusted back in. It was delicious. This was remedial. Calming away all the unrest and allowing me a singular focus. Isolating emotions and sensations.

He stayed at it, and I rolled into another release. This one not as powerful as the last, but far more emotional as I clawed into the sides of his abdomen. When I was done, Sadik managed to roll me onto the floor, where he took me from behind. His stamina was as enduring, strokes as strong. And we rocked into each other until he collapsed over me, satiated and rung out.

Completely drained, I was kept awake by his flying heartbeat against my back. His dewy skin suctioning into my own. This was madness. It was sick. This was a life I never knew. A chemistry I didn't understand. But it was all very real.

I dozed off. Didn't know when, didn't know how. But the luxury of his heartbeat and warmth lulled me. I felt the moment he lifted from me, causing me to stir. While on my knees and my elbows burrowed into the cushion of the sofa, I pushed my leg out, stretching it while half sleep. Then Sadik grabbed me, arranging me in a position he could carry me into the master suite, where he lay me on the bed gently. I rolled over, not caring about the stickiness between my thighs. I was carried into siesta by the Sadik-stained bedding...and the man himself.

My bladder awakened me. It was heavy and threatening. Quickly, I left the bed and hurried into the bathroom to relieve myself. My eyes gazed down to the dried texture between my thighs and I groaned. Instead of getting back into the bed for more sleep before I had to be up and out, I needed to shower instead. After wiping, I flushed the toilet and toiled into the shower. My mind still not fully roused. The moment I began to rinse off, memories of last night's mayhem came crashing in. My eyes opened anew. I gazed around the room, recounting the events.

When I stepped out of the shower after turning the water off, I noticed my phone being in the same place. I dried off, tossed on a robe, then quickly brushed my teeth and washed my face. The power...was back on? It had never gone off in the bathroom. Once done, I made it back out into the suite. I tried a light switch and saw it worked fine. My curiosity had me opening the door and traveling out into the apartment. I heard sounds, distinct scratches of glass. The living room was empty. That led me to the kitchen, but movement from the dining room arrested my attention.

My jaw dropped. There, in the center of the room, were Sadik, Kimmy, and two people I didn't know, sweeping up glass. And when I say glass, I don't mean broken stemware or a bottle. The gorgeous intricately designed crystal chandelier was no longer hanging from the cathedral ceiling. The glass table was gone. All ten chairs had been stacked and moved against the walls. Sadik was bent over in slacks, a wrinkled white dress shirt, and *Timberland* construction boots, assisting in the cleanup.

"What happened here?" I demanded.

The two male strangers stood, alarmed by my aggression. They gazed over to Sadik for direction. Kimmy's lifting from her industrial broom got my attention next. Her eyes widened before they retracted and warily reached Sadik before falling back down to the task at hand. Sadik glanced my way, but he continued sweeping.

"Sadik, what happened?" My brain kicked in, and regard swept the hallway and what I could see into the kitchen. There were no lights on, but not unusually: it was just after eight in the morning. So I stepped closer into the archway of the kitchen and tapped the light panel. It lit right away. The time on the microwave was on, too. As was the slow cooker. The power had been restored.

Unless it was intentionally cut...

My face lifted into a pout as I pivoted around to the dining room.

"Sadik!" my tone firmer.

"Yes, Bilan," he replied without his eyes while continuing to speak.

That quickly, the atmosphere in the room had changed. The others were visibly uncomfortable.

"We need to talk," I informed. "Alone."

I could perceive his eye roll as he exhaled roughly before dropping the broom.

"Excuse me," he murmured before sauntering toward me.

On his approach, Sadik didn't stop, he ambled down the hall. I followed him back into the master suite and closed the door behind myself. Sadik turned to face me, swiping his nose.

"What happened to the chandelier?" I asked.

Sadik's gaze was empty as he stood motionless. "What do you want me to say?"

"I want the truth!"

"You know shit about the truth. Not a damn thing about transparency!"

"What does that have to do with you cutting the power and scaring me out of my mind like that last night?" My eyes bounced around and a wild thought collided. "Did you do all of that...break that colossal chandelier, your dining room table, and shut down the lights just to express your anger with me?"

"At least I didn't run out of town." His answer brazen.

Sadik all but admitted to it.

I grabbed my head, not believing this. It was childish, at best!

"Are you kidding me right now?"

He shook his head, and softly he answered, "No, Bilan, I'm not."

"Then what is going on?"

Sadik took a deep breath, switching the weight on his hips and rubbing the stubble on his golden head. "Bilan, I've been under an unbelievable amount of stress lately. More than I care to get into. Just when I thought I had itemized, at least the important issues, in their respective places, you tell me you're pregnant." His eyes closed and head shook.

I swung my arm backward toward the door. "So, you do this because I'm pregna—"

"No!" he barked. "Hell no!"

"Then what is it?"

"I'm fuckin' trying to explain, dammit!" he groaned.

A virile man in an Italian designer dress shirt and pants before me, unable to explain his temper tantrum.

I crossed my arms. "I'll wait."

"Don't fuckin' patronize me, Bilan." His glare deathly. "You won't win."

"Then talk to me. Tell me if the Ellis I need to watch my back from is the one whose bed I sleep in at night!"

"Don't be ridiculous."

"Ridiculous?" I snorted. "You fought me last night!"

His head lifted, face hardened. "I would never in life lay a hand on you!"

"I can't vouch for that after last night, Sadik!" I shouted. "What would you have done if you'd actually hit me?"

"I wouldn't have hit you." His tone was dismissive. Sadik even waved off the notion. "I wasn't trying to."

"Those were real punches, Sadik!"

He repositioned his stance, hands on his waist. "They were the slowest jabs thrown since I was in elementary school."

My brows shot up. "Should you be throwing anything fake at a pregnant woman—a woman?"

"Should you be working out while pregnant?"

"Sadik, of course, I can work out. You didn't know women can work out when pregnant? Some can perform some form of exercise until they walk into delivery! You don't have any women to bounce your ignorance off of?"

"No, seeing that I can't say shit to my mother!"

The strain in my neck suspended and my face dropped.

That's what this is...

"You're angry at me because I'm becoming a wedge between you and your family," I murmured, surmising it all.

The Ellises may have been dysfunctional in many ways, but they were a tightly woven group. He'd told me this after the Pixie concert.

Sadik scoffed. "Nothing comes between us. I get you don't understand it because of the unfortunate circumstances of your family, but they are my anchor, my identity. They're attached to my purpose."

He practically admitted to that, too.

Guilt encased me. "I'm not asking you to choose here."

"I think I've been past the point of choosing with you, Bilan." He turned away, mumbling. "It's what fuckin' rabid curiosity gets you."

"What?" I leaped in place. "What did you say?"

Sadik turned to me, irises green and dark. He closed his eyes, squeezed them before clasping the bridge of his nose.

"You said rabid curiosity. What does that have to do with you choosing—"

"Just drop it, Bilan!"

"No! You don't get to refer back to when you were trying to fuck me"—I shouted— "because let's be clear, that's all your pursuit was. Maybe after seeing I wasn't that type of woman, you found something more interesting to make you wait. But you don't get to forget how you 'chose' to pursue me after running into me at a diner when you were on an errand boy run for your cheating brother and his mafia princess mistress. You could have left and acted like the high prince of the Ellis throne you are. You could have forgotten about me and found someone better suited. This is no love story where you feel love at first sight—"

"You think that's what happened?" he screamed the hot tempered-Sadik yell. It also was no less intimidating than the first time I'd experienced it. He turned to me on approach. "You think the first time I'd laid eyes on you was that night in the diner, with Lia?" His scoff was sinister, a flash of Iban Ellis in the beautiful presentation of my Sadik. It was there. The genetic monster only demonstrated by an Ellis. "Honey, I knew you were reasonably green to the deleterious dealings of my world, but you're an exceptionally bright woman. I thought smart enough to know nothing I fuckin' do is random."

My eyes ballooned, lips trembled. It was here again; that darkness I'd always sensed in Sadik.

"What are you saying?"

"I'm saying I knew Bilan Asad-Yasin existed long before the night I volunteered to take my brother's 'mafia princess mistress' to her racist ass father's party. I knew she wanted your desserts—I volunteered to do that, too, by the way. It was why I endured hours with her racist as fuck family and friends. All so I could 'run into you' and appear to only want to fuck you."

My mouth moved to speak, but no words. Sadik wiped the side of his mouth, chest heaving. His face was reddening with anger before my eyes.

"*I'M A FUCKIN' ELLIS, BILAN!*" he roared, slapping his chest. "My intelligence, hunger, and prolificacy is superior to my brother's and sometimes, my father's. I'm the chosen one to his throne. You know why?"

A tear fell. I shook my head, wiping it away.

"Because when some goofy ass runner boys rob my father's warehouse for a few keys of coke, and by sheer luck kill his men and get away, it's my talent to have their names in an hour. It's of my resources that, by the next day, I have their addresses, mother's name and occupation, siblings' ages and hobbies, a copy of their father's death certificate, and that of all four kids involved. When the ring leader is arrested, I have each court date he's been given.

When he's tried and convicted, I have the prison he'll be assigned to, to serve his time. I know his cellmate. I know when his mother is diagnosed with pancreatic cancer. I know when she can't afford the mortgage anymore." He advanced slowly toward me.

"I know when two of his assailants take off, leaving town. Just like I knew where my fiancée ran to within a day or so, so had I my father's thieves." His head fell to the side, the muscles around his eyes relaxing. "So, my beautiful Somali girl, yes, I knew who you were before walking into that diner in March. I knew where you studied. I'd been on your campus when you got off the bus for class once. I knew who your two closest friends were, like I knew you were planning to go to the Pixie concert.

"I knew you were alone before you shared it with me. I knew your shoulders were weighed before you got drunk at your graduation party and spilled those unsavory truths about yourself. I was at your mother's burial. I remained there on that rainy day when everyone else left and you sat on your knees, motionlessly staring at the hill created when the last of the dirt was thrown over her casket."

My heart fell from my chest and bile shot from my belly. I was able to manage it down. I had to. In my new world, the bottom could drop out at any moment. But eventually, the will to remain strong was overcome by viscous emotions, remembering my mother's burial. It was hard leaving her in the cold ground. It felt betraying. She was my mother, the one who cared for me, nurtured me. Leaving her in the rain didn't seem like much reciprocity. So I stayed...until the sun fell.

After calming myself, I rolled my head up to see Sadik's glaring countenance.

"And with knowing all those events, my stupid ass doesn't know when I impregnate the only womb I'd been fascinated with filling. Just like I had no fuckin' idea she was being trained by a known Russian assassinator, one of the most dangerous in the Tri-State in the past two decades."

I swallowed back stupid tears. "So this is all because of who trains me?"

"No, Bilan. It's about who trained you. As in past tense."

"What?"

He shook his head. "No more. Last night was your last time working out with Dimitri Sokolov."

"So you dictate who I work out with now?"

"No, Bilan! I'm just telling you who you won't be working out with moving forward."

"So I have to find someone else that good?" I tossed my arms in the air, slapping them against my outer thighs. "Great! Got any recs for a replacement, Mr. Prolificacy?" I asked as he headed toward the door.

Sadik glanced over his shoulder, voice controlled. "I'm available to supply any need you have. I can teach you self-defense better than anyone." His hand gripped the doorknob. "You're the mother of what will be my greatest investment. It's in my best interest to sow well into you."

My neck whipped hard and eyes flashed wide. "You know how ridiculous you sound?"

"Well, ridiculous is me."

Sadik left the room.

Johnson opened the door, and Rory strolled inside of *La Cocina* in Newark. I meandered in after her. It was my first time in the Dominican restaurant belonging to Luis Lopez. I knew it wasn't his first restaurant, or his most recent. He'd been doing well, moving up from bodegas to eateries between Passaic and Newark.

He sat at a table in the corner, sipping on a tea cup while a cigarette burned between his fingers.

"Smells good!" was my manner of greeting him as I made my way to the table.

"Well." He splayed his palms in a shrug. "It ain't as fancy as the import/export business, and may not be as big as the laundromat or... liquor store money, but..." He shrugged again. "It's mine."

"That it is," I agreed, taking a seat across from him at the tiny table.

"How can I help you, Ellis?" He turned to face me in his chair. "Even though it's about the business of me and your papa."

I nodded, lips pouted. "*Sí.*" My eyes rolled toward the ceiling. "*Siempre lo es.*"

It *always* is.

He sighed, clucking the roof of his mouth with his tongue, then mumbled, "Here we go with the bullshit."

"Doesn't have to be," my tone more congenial.

Fucking Dominicans were sensitive ass bitches.

"You killed my—"

"I murked a goddamn kid who threatened my lady. Period." I swiped my hands in a crossing fashion over the table. "Now, I've already sent my apology to you via Palmer for having the shit be so messy. But what will never be a regret is addressing any man who makes my woman think his cock is going to be in her mouth. Fuck that." I made sure to peer him directly in the eyes. This was non-negotiable. "But I am here to offer the same apology face to face, as a man. I had no idea he was yours, Lopez."

"My goddamn niece is fucked up about this shit." His nose lifted and nostrils widened, lips tightened, too. "You expect me to take my balls in my hand to her, saying I can't get back at the crew that killed him?"

My brows hiked and I tilted my head slightly. "I can't tell you how to explain his depravity to her. But I can tell you this shit won't end well."

Lopez's face lit up with humor. "Oh, really?"

I nodded, expression confident. "It won't, and you know this.

Yeah, you may have shot two of my father's low levels and, as a result, they're in police custody, but that's a small victory in battle. You know we have an endless army, from the top of the Garden State to the bottom."

"Oh, I know. I followed the war with the Italians. That was fucked up how Double E Bags distracted Rizzo with the street war so he could take him out. He broke the fucking rules, and he knows it—you know it, too." He sat back, pulled on his cigarette.

I chuckled. "That's all conjecture, Lopez. Is that what this is really about? You and those other dumb fucks think Double E violated the terms of *The Commission* rules?" I laughed, thinking about the *FED* snitch. "You got more to be concerned about as a unit." Unless Lopez, here, was the informant.

"Listen, kid—"

A harsh, yet genuine chortle pushed from my lungs. "Kid? Lopez, you're about fifty-seven years old. Let's not whip our dicks out on this table. And you don't want to run our numbers either. You got the head start, and without Double E's money, I've jumped over your head years ago. Let's let the *only* kid in question rest in peace. *Bueno?*"

Lopez shifted over the table, irritated. "You know, the only reason I got a bit of respect for you is because you showed heart with Williams. That shit was tight. You handled that like a few of us wanted to, but couldn't. But don't push me with the disrespect about my family, Ellis."

"Cut the street war," I offered again.

He sat back in the small seat, stretching his arms wide. "As the kids say, I got time." He laughed.

"And we have soldiers and stamina you could only dream of," my tone was even as I pushed my chair from the table, signaling the close of this attempt at peace.

I stood to go.

"You know," Lopez was sure to speak loud enough to gain my attention. I shifted to see him. "...you Ellises move like y'all some Wakanda mutherfuckers. Double E always had this chip on his shoulder, like his operation was better than everybody else's. Yeah, he been doing good...expanding his organization all these years, but he don't like to follow rules. I told Rizzo that shit when he came to me about doing *The Commission*. Since I've known that dude, I try to stay out of his lane, even sent my kids to his wife's schools to support him." He nodded. "I been respectin' his moves. This time, he went too fucking far, my man. The Ellises ain't the only family on the block."

I scoffed. "Nah. But we are the premier family on the earth. It's the Earl Ellis way. Are we perfect? No. But we walk with a manner of elegance and pride. My father wasn't happy to learn about your great-nephew, Lopez. But a man of your lifestyle and reputation cannot fault me for protecting my lady." I issued a stern gaze. "See, I've apologized through the proper channels and now, in your home, to your face. You're refusing the hat of humility I've removed from my head." I shrugged with my brows and mouth. "I guess, at this point, you'll be reminded of why the Ellises are premier."

I finally took off, leaving Lopez with a non-negotiable warning. It was the Ellis way.

∞ 16 ∞

Bilan

"Our Father in heaven, hallowed be Your name. Your kingdom come," I whispered from the side of Abshir's bed, kneeling from the floor. Eyes closed, palms meeting, and fingers intertwined. "Your will be done on earth as it is in heaven. And...forgive us our debts, as we forgive our debtors. And do not lead us into temptation, but deliver us from the evil one. For Yours is the kingdom and the power and the glory forever. Amen."

That was the prayer Bishop Carmichael used often. He'd been preaching a series on "How to Pray." He was sure to explain this was the formal, official prayer, but the most common and just as effectual ones were those from the heart, lacking articulation. He said the ones that were more or less groans could even be clearly interpreted and felt by Him.

I wasn't crying, neither was I groaning when my aunt and cousin stepped into the room, but my heart was genuinely beseeching.

I rose to my feet, caught off guard, yet expecting her.

"Hey," I greeted nervously, sweeping down my clothes.

I knew Aunt Franzel was coming, but had no clue Joslyn, Aunt Auster, and Angela would be with her. Their expressions were sober, neither of their regards meeting Abshir.

"Hey, honey." I met Aunt Franzel at the foot of the bed, not knowing how to greet her. Her eyes roved around. "We here alone?"

I didn't catch her drift as my eyes followed her path. "Yeah. Just me and Rory out there."

Irene wasn't due for a few hours. She'd been so good with keeping a vigil for me. She even brought some official from her church to pray over Abshir again—with my permission in advance. She had been growing concerned with his lack of progress, too. Irene may have been an Ellis, but she was a supportive one. She came, didn't badger, and asked no questions outside of his update since her last shift. The other day, she asked about my mother, wondering what type of person she was. When I did my best to explain, Irene said she wished she could have known her. She'd wish my hooya was here for Abshir, me...and her to help her get to know me better. That desire stuck with me.

"Oh, okay." She nodded. "How's it going?"

I gesture toward my brother. "I don't know how to answer that."

"Well." She glanced around. "That's why we're here. As your aunts, we realize you may not have been brought up with the proper rituals and understandings of our beliefs. And what I mean is, you may not know that under our Islamic faith, we don't believe in life support."

I wasn't quite aware of that and didn't get her point.

My regard browsed the assembled group. "Okay."

"With that being said, I—*we*—believe, as your family, you should have the doctors discontinue the life support."

I didn't know what I was expecting, but that wasn't it. This past week alone had been a whirlwind, and let's not forget about the speed of my life over the past six months.

Admitting that was conceding that my family—those I'd shared a home with all my life—was all gone forever. I was now alone. Permanently. Yes, I had other biological family, but none who I had shared pain and doses of happiness with. These were the last days. Abshir was en route to the next life with our parents.

"Oh. I don't think that's his status anymore," I began to answer, voice unwavering so far. I pointed above his bed. "I guess you haven't noticed the additional equipment in here. Abshir's kidneys have begun shutting down. The doctors just left."

"Doctors?" Aunt Astur parroted.

"Yeah. The renal specialist and neurologist. Ironically, they were both in and available this morning. Abshir has been the patient causing the most trouble in this wing." I tried for a smile, one that was forlorn, but helped me.

What I wouldn't share was just how popular Abshir was this morning. As I spoke with his doctors about Abshir's grim prognosis, a police officer came in. He was doing more than a friendly check-in on Abshir. Apparently, in the short time since his release, Abshir sexually assaulted a woman. And from what I could see, it was more damning than an allegation. He played me a recording—unauthorized—where Abshir's face and body were clear as he was aggressively grinding on a woman who could have been in distress.

But of course, I'd never share that with my aunts and their daughters.

"We're sorry to hear that." Joslyn was the first to speak up. "You may not remember the proper burial procedure, but the elders in our community have to resume care of his body."

"No embalming," Aunt Franzel interjected.

Joslyn shook her perfectly straightened dark, long and layered tresses. "No embalming. I'm sure if you tell that nurse this in advance, they'll be familiar and allow the family the body."

"We don't traditionally do funerals or repasts, and I'm sure doing them will only overwhelm you anyway. So, no need for that."

Before I could process that information, Aunt Franzel asked, "And they still don't know what happened to him?"

I froze at that question. "They" didn't know, but I did. No justice would be served in the murder of my brother, neither would it be in the rape of that poor girl Abshir took advantage of.

Oh, God...

"You know, I told this boy a hundred times to stay outta them streets! If you live by the sword, you die by the sword!" Aunt Astur supplied through gritted teeth. "I told my brother, Asad, to be harder on him! He should be at the mosque...be with family, learning the right way!"

Aunt Franzel hummed her co-sign. Angela rubbed her mother, Aunt Astur's, back.

And here it is...

I refused to cry. Crying got nothing resolved but public weakening and embarrassment. It, to me, seemed like something my father's family likely thought was in my father's share of DNA.

To them, *this* seemed likely an event in my father's legacy. Defeat. It's how he went. My mother went unsupported in her slaughter of pancreatic cancer. Now, Abshir had succumbed to his greatest disloyal ally: the streets. It was the only thing he championed.

That summation crushed me.

The moment he stepped into my brother's hospital room, I saw an antiquated version of him and knew I'd remember him in my heart forever. It was strange, but in that instance, as he pushed through the door, his kaleidoscopic irises were on me, those lips fixed into a grim line, I got a flash of my forever. Sadik paused momentarily to request my permission before his strong arms encased me, pulling me into his chest, where I felt as light as a feather. A huge contrast to what I'd felt most of my life. Sadik's arms were comforting, his hands resourceful. When Irene entered the room just after him, I lost it.

How was he able to do this? After the police officer and doctors left, I sent a text to both of Sadik's phones, rambling about my morning, admitting I couldn't do this anymore. I couldn't stand the pressure. He only responded, "I'm here for you" from one. And now, I knew how. I drank in his heat-scented cologne as I sobbed quietly into his chest.

Vaguely, behind me, I could hear voices of concern. Irene answered them by demanding they let Sadik do what he could effectively do.

Then I was being ushered out of the room. My eyes were closed as I clenched his dress shirt, but I could perceive the movements. I heard a door close and was urged to sit. The separation was too long, but I was soon in his chest again.

"I can't do it!" She finally sobbed out loud. "It's too much: rape, an Islamic burial, no embalming, finding elders—"

"Baby, calm down. You're going to hyperventilate." I tried a soothing tone. It somehow came natural to me with her. "I'm here."

"Sadik!" she cried. "I can't do it! Let's go away. Let's...go back to Costa Rica before all the drama." I shushed her, rubbing her back. "Or use your money to get me back to when I was a little girl. I just want my hooya back! Aabo knew how to handle him! I swear, I'll wake up every day again as a little girl to escape this nightmare! I'm all alone! I wasn't alone when I was a kid."

"No, baby," I cooed. "Then I wouldn't have my future wife, and we wouldn't be expecting my first son."

It took a few seconds for her to process my words, but when she did, Bilan stopped groaning. She pulled away and met my eyes. Her diaphragm wouldn't slow, but her brain did for a moment.

"I..." She hiccupped, face swollen, eyes red. "I don't know what you see in me. Why do you want...me so much?" she managed.

I tried smiling, the answer so easy. "Because you're human, vulnerable, resilient beyond anyone I've ever known and, most importantly, mine."

The tears wouldn't stop. "Not like this when I'm weak." That made her cry even more.

"When you're weak. When you're strong. When you're afraid. And when you're angry." I took her at the chin, aligning her gaze with mine. "You're mine either way, and we're going to get you through this, Bilan. This won't be another event you have to tackle alone."

I didn't like her in pain—hated it, in fact—but I could use this point in her vulnerability to show her I'm the man she needs. I could support Bilan, nurture her, and give her something she could barely recall having: family.

I could do this for her. And I would.

"Shit!" I yelped, fist raising to my mouth as I watched the field fixedly.

"Fuck me! Fuck me!" Iban yelled, attention on the same play. "Fuck me!"

When Bailey kept running with the ball, dodging everyone coming his way until he made it to the end zone, Iban and my father jumped from their seats.

"Shit!" I whispered, sitting back and stomping my foot.

"My man!" my father cheered. "TB! That's a Jersey breed right there!"

"And you saw the way he threw that fuckin' full field pass to Amare," Iban shared just as riotously. "And that nigga caught that shit the way I be catchin' pussy?" He punched the air. "*Whoo!*"

"That kid is a fuckin' beast!" my father shouted to us, then he turned back to the field. "A fuckin' beast!"

"The best fuckin' QB in the league!" Iban declared, *Corona* bottle in the air. "On God!"

"Yeah." I chuckled, kicking out my feet. "Yo' ass wasn't saying that in 2016 when they announced the *Kings* were reacquiring him."

Iban rolled his eyes, taking his seat. "Yeah. Yeah. Yeah."

"You said he wasn't a good investment," I continued to tease him.

My father sat down, laughing just as I had been quietly.

Iban took the short set of steps to the interior of the lounge and headed to the counter for the tin bucket of beers.

"Shit." He huffed, pulling out a fresh bottle. "I still can't wrap my head around that shit. I couldn't put my money on no nigga that was locked down to come back into the league. We ain't got the facilities or equipment they got in the league *or* as a free man, period. Just 'cause I was the only one in this family betting against TB don't mean I was the only one in this damn world that ain't believe he could pull it off." He resumed his seat on the other side of our father.

"Yeah." I hummed, not agreeing. "But you gotta keep in mind, Bailey didn't do an excessive amount of time. He only did like eighteen months." I shrugged. "Some talent is God-given."

"Yeah," my father chimed in, leaned over his knees. "That was all God. Every muscle in his body was hand-placed and blessed by the Father hisself." He nodded, eyes locked to the field.

Half time had begun, the players running off the green.

Iban did an air toast. "True that," he agreed.

Then dad sat back, humming contently. His eyes below, still on the field. "Damn, it feels good to be out here with my boys again. It kind of reminds me what's important in life."

Iban reached over our father's back and offered me a fist bump. This *was* nice. Like the old days. Sun was out, breeze was nice, and the energy was right. Since I could remember, my father would take us to see the *Connecticut Kings* play. We'd even go to their away games if it suited him. He'd been a season suite owner for years. This was our "Ellis men's time" before Iban and I were quite men.

"I hear you going to Haitian Ricky's party." Iban's regard was on me.

Oh...

My attention went ahead again. Blame it on the *Mauve*, but it took a while to process his words. I didn't fuck with Haitian Ricky. None of us did, at least outside of *The Commission* for my father and Iban. I bluntly didn't fuck with him at all. I could count on one hand the times I'd actually seen him.

I sighed. "Not something I'm particularly interested in, but... politics. Yeah. My lady wants to support his girl."

It was still strange as hell that nigga was having a party. And he'd invited me. If it were left to me, I'd leave his ass hanging. But my Nalib... She made a request, and it was my duty to bring it into fruition.

"First, I thought your lil' lady was having a problem with the Ellis family since she done been back in town and ain't come to my home or to my wife's table yet." My father shrugged. "But seem like everybody in the family done seen her but us." He gestured between himself and Iban. "So maybe it's the men in the family she got a beef with."

My brows lifted. "You didn't start that beef? Both you guys...you didn't hand-deliver it yourselves?"

Iban waved the concept off.

My father shrugged. "I know." He sighed, shaking his head. "You make a good point. Listen, I know it got fucked up last month—I still ain't hear nothing 'bout his funeral, by the way. I got Palmer looking into his parole officer."

"Don't even waste your time." I took a deep breath. "What's done is done."

"Yeah," he sang, sighing. "I got bigger fish to fry. Lopez still tryna square up with me in the streets. My men are tired from the victory with the Rizzos, but they soldiers, too. We fight till we win or die." His tone was final, yet weary.

I was fed up with the Lopez bullshit and could only deal with one thing at a time. That "thing" was my future. Bilan had to be my priority, until this thing played out with her brother.

My father sat back, eyes still out on the halftime show below. He took a sip of his brandy, then sighed. "I'm getting too old for this shit. Health declining..."

"It's time for you to retire. You need to hand the shit over." Iban shrugged, bringing the beer toward his mouth. "You 'on't wanna hand it over, I 'on't know what to tell you." He took a sip.

My father's regard was hotter on me than the sun. I glanced away. I was only one person. My focus had to be my fiancée and baby.

That's when I peered over to my father, who had returned his attention to the cheerleaders on the field. I had a fucking baby on the way—my first—and I couldn't tell my father he was expecting his first grandson.

In due time...

We finished out halftime, then the game without further discussion on the topic. I'd just have to apply patience.

It's here...

I turned in the mirror for my profile as my gaze swept over my full frame, from top to bottom. My baby bump had finally—inarguably—arrived. My perpetual little flab had grown into an expectant pouch. What was strange was, my frame had still been smaller than it was a month ago, although I'd improved with meals.

My gaze traveled over to the countertop of the island in the center of the two-story, walk-in closet. Among jewelry and undergarments was a purple leather corset. With my regard still on it, I backed into an upholstery chair in the corner.

"How am I going to pull this off?" I whispered to myself, hand cupping my mouth.

Tonight was Ricky's party, and I had less than an hour to finish getting ready. I'd had plenty of time. My hair was done first thing this morning, thanks to ShawnNicole. I'd just finished showering and doing my makeup. It was now time for me to get dressed and meet Rory downstairs. But something didn't feel right. Why was I going to a club to celebrate a man I didn't even know? I was pregnant and...lonely.

Irene was up at the hospital with Abshir. It was close to visiting hours being over, so she'd be leaving soon. Sadik was up in Connecticut for the day with his father and brother at a *Kings'* game. Of course, the Ellises would fly to another state just for an event. That was how he wooed me on our first official date. They were on their way back, and Sadik would meet me at the party. I hated to admit to myself how I missed him. He begged me to come with him, offering to take his own jet for the two of us and have me spend the day at a spa while they attended the game. It seemed like a lot of special arrangements needing to be made instead of him being able to just chill with his father and brother. I'd already caused a wedge with my conspicuous absence and hidden pregnancy. My decision didn't feel good, but felt right.

I sighed deeply, standing to "attempt" a leather corset over a new baby bump. Something about this felt so wrong.

"*You know there's nothing...nothing...nothing I would not doooooooo. Uh-nooooo! Before I let you gooooooooo!*" We sang to the track the deejay spun, but Tasche was louder.

Her arms swung into the air, hips dipped and swirled as she did. I could only give arm action. The music had been great! Then the deejay blended the song into a Wally track. It was the one featuring Young Lord and Jay Z.

"Boo!" Randi roared, but her voice didn't travel outside of our VIP section. "Fuck Lord!"

I rolled my eyes, fighting my grin.

Young Lord...

Every time I heard a Young Lord track or saw him on an interview, I was always reminded of how Randi told me he used to sweat her for years, but she never gave him play because she heard he had a lot of kids. Then he blew up and came back to Jersey for a visit and she finally slept with him. Randi said she hadn't heard from him since. She called the number he gave her a hundred times until finally, some lady named Touchie answered and cussed her out. Randi went down to The Main in Paterson to confront her, but when she saw the size and the countenance of the woman, she backed off. Of course, she didn't tell the whole story, but I knew my friend. Randi wanted no smoke with those Main girls. They were brutal.

The crowd went wild with the switch. It was an upbeat track; compelling and clever, yet simple. It had been in heavy rotation for almost two years now on the radio. All the kids came into the diner reciting the lyrics, some doing a dance inspired by the song that caught on fast.

Tasche ignored Randi, knowing the story herself, and began singing Wally's part. The song title was *"The Greatest Love Tragedy Ever Told."* It was a personal account of the three rappers' deepest love lost or conquered, but all included pain and tragedy. Of course, you couldn't get rappers to pour their hearts out over a beat, but their creative minds made each verse absorbing.

Wally spoke about his first crush from second grade. He'd steal from the local bodega to feed her lunch every day, but never told her he liked her. He beat up a kid who pushed her down on the playground. The verse turned tragic when she stopped coming to school, and Wally and his classmates later learned she was killed by her father, who had been sexually assaulting her for years.

Young's verse was next. He spoke about a college sweetheart he almost lost to a local gang with a sex slave ring. The girl was naïve and, instead of telling Lord how she felt about him, she went out to a party and got roofied by the guys from the gang. He said by sparing her that tragic experience—he never said how—he saved his own life.

"*In the streets, they never teach to love nothing that ain't green...*
But for shawtie I had a heart that 'a beat mean.
Made my head spin and my dick hard...
She tossed my heart away, but I never went far.
Loving my babies and giving me a family was her super power...
If I let 'em take her, y'all wouldn't know 'Sunset Showers.'"

As if on cue, I glanced over to Randi, who had her ears covered. I couldn't help but laugh that time.

Hov's verse was next. It was controversial because this track was released before his "*4:44*" album, so his transparency about infidelity in his marriage on "*The Greatest Love Tragedy Ever Told*" was a precursor to his coming disclosure and a confirmation to his wife's "*Lemonade*" album.

And Tasche knew each lyric. She put on a show performing it. She had the attention of several men below on the floor level. One handed her *another* drink.

"Awwwww, baby," she sang. "Thank you!"

He nodded before moving on. The place was packed, but without an overwhelming shoulder to shoulder look on the dance floor. I had to give "Tiff" her just due. This club, *Pulse*, had a different vibe from her other, *Energy*, but both were classy, spacious, and contemporary. So, yeah...she was a beauty with body, educated from one of the top —if not *the* top—HBCUs in the country, and a former lover of my...

I didn't know what Sadik was. My eyes glanced down to the engagement ring I decided to wear tonight, though not quite sure why. Then again, if I would be honest with myself, it was because I knew I'd see Tiffany tonight and wanted her to see it. It was childish. The woman had never done anything to me but be a trophy of a bad ass Black woman. I rolled my eyes under the purple and white strobe lights. That's when I noticed a drink in my face. My gaze shot up to Tasche. It was the one the guy had just handed her.

I sucked in a breath. "You know I can't have that!"

She laughed, placing the plastic cup on the table. "I'm just fuckin' with you because you shoulda told me before tonight, yo!"

Guilt washed over me as she sat next to me. My eyes went to Rory, whose back was to us, and it didn't appear she'd heard.

"I'm sorry, Tasche," I tried.

"You keep saying that shit!" Randi hissed on the other side of me. "You done changed. I knew this shit was gonna happen. That fuckin' Sadik!"

"I wouldn't say all that," Tasche defended me.

I didn't need it, though. My face folded. "And what makes you the Iyanla Vanzant of my life?"

She spat a laugh. "We all know I got more experience fuckin' with dudes like Sadik than you. Don't get ya panties in a bunch. I'm just trying to say, you been actin' funny style since him."

"Funny or just protective of the details of my life?"

"So you admit to keeping secrets?" Randi challenged.

"No. What I'm saying is when you get the type of man you're supposedly "well versed" with, you can't run to your friends with every little detail. I've been transparent about the important things."

She brought her drink to her mouth and rolled her eyes. "What the fuck ever. Just as transparent as them big ole titties spilling out that damn corset." My eyes and hands shot to my cleavage. The corset had presented them ample, something I didn't expect. "Your fiancé going for that? Niggas like him don't like shit like that. They hella possessive."

"If you would shut the fuck up, you'll see Ricky with that bitch, yo," Tasche warned, tossing her chin in the direction of the two.

Ricky had his arm draped around the back and waist of his wife. I'd been here, at the party, for just over an hour. As soon as Randi saw Rory and me come through the door, she took deep lunges my way, made a show of greeting me, and walked me over to Sadik's VIP section, just off the dance floor. Tasche came not too long after, and Randi filled her in on who was who.

I couldn't get a distinctive look of her face, but could see Ricky's wife was a caramel complexion, small frame, and decent style with six-inch *Ase Garb*'s Zara sandals on. They were the latest rave. All the celebrities were wearing them. When I saw them at *JAGMisha*'s in the summer, they were priced at $1600. They were an obvious purchase from her husband, Ricky.

We watched as Ricky introduced her to people on the floor. His eyes skirted past us, or more specifically, Randi, but landed back to the woman in his arms.

"I guess I'll be staying at your place a few more nights, Tasche," Randi sulked...in her protective way. "Fuck niggas!"

"Get moneeey!" Tasche jumped to her feet. She reached back for me to dance with her. "Come on. Let me see you two-step in those dope ass *Ase Garb*'s!"

It was difficult to acknowledge I'd worn the same sandals as Ricky's wife tonight. Hers were gold and mine were the same purple leather as my corset. To escape Tasche's stupid blurt, I jumped up and danced with her. One of Brielle's women-themed songs rang out in the place, so it felt appropriate. And it felt good. Of all the crying, stressing, and sulking I'd been doing for the past month or so, it felt great being silly with my friend again. Tasche could do that. She was a spirit booster, and I loved her for that.

Eventually, my arm swings slowed to a full body sway as I gazed the room. Ricky was nowhere in sight, but Rory stood guard just a yard away at the opening of the VIP section. My eyes continued to people watch, until I felt this indescribable pull ahead. It took no time to understand why. Sadik stood there, two of his security on either side as his feline gaze penetrated me. One hand in the pocket of his pants, and the other at his chin as his thumb brushed against his goatee.

And my god...

He did something I hadn't seen of him in so long, I forgot how much of an aphrodisiac it was. How fluently it spoke to my libido. His full lips parted as his tongue swiped the inner lining of his bottom lip, back and forth. A soft breath escaped my lips.

"Oh!" Tasche sang. "Look how he looking at you, yo. Look, Randi. Dude gon' fuck her in here. Let me move my shit. Matter fact, I gotta pee. C'mon, Randi."

"I need a minute," Randi dismissed her request.

Tasche crossed over me to sit on the other side of Randi. I hated she broke the eye action I had going with Sadik. It had been another visceral connection we'd shared over the past thirty-six hours or so. My mouth watered as he gaited toward the VIP section. I couldn't tear my eyes from him if I wanted to. It annoyed me that he stopped when Rory had to speak to him. His golden eyes went between her shoulder and me as she whispered to him. When he replied, his multi-hued irises were locked onto me again. Even from a yard away, I could smell his alluring cologne.

Then he was on his way up the stairs. Only one person followed him. Rory.

Ugh!

Sadik promenaded over and feather kissed me behind my ear, down to my neck. He then whispered, "How are you feeling?"

Those simple words were a kind gesture. He didn't say "Hi" or "What's up?" He asked how I was feeling. The trickled sensation of delight on my spine was unfair. I couldn't look him in the face. Neither could I fight the smile trying to spread on my face, though I tried.

"I didn't think you'd come."

The air from his snort reached my face. "There was no fuckin' way I'd have you here alone."

Finally, I peered up to him. "Rory's here."

"Rory's good, but Rory ain't me."

My face heated and I gazed away. "That she isn't."

"And you haven't answered my question. How are you feeling?"

I nodded. "Good, actually."

"You look fuckin' fantastic," he groaned, swiping his nose against my shoulder.

I couldn't shake the goofy grin. "Thanks, Sadik."

"You're welcome, Bilan."

"How was the game?"

He took a deep breath, standing erect. "The whole day with my guys was fantastic. Nostalgia live and in color."

I smiled up at him. "I'm glad you had a good time."

∞17∞

Her smile was warm as she peered up at me with unfeigned regard. "I really am."

I reached down to peck her mouth. "Thank you." Then I glanced beyond her to finally speak to her girls. "Randi." I nodded. "How are you, Tasche?"

"Hey, Sadik!" Tasche greeted. "Good to see you, sugar."

Randi only offered a flash smile as she sipped her drink from a small straw. I sat back with one arm around Bilan, feeling a touch of exhaustion. It had been a long day. I'd been up since five this morning, starting with a workout, then the ride to *Elliswoods Palace* for my father's jet to Connecticut. I swear, I had no desire to be here. By the looks of it, Bilan wasn't exactly partying herself—not that I expected her to while pregnant.

As her girls left for the restroom, she texted Nurse Gladney for an update, then turned to me and giggled.

"Would they notice if I left?" Her laughter was lyrical.

"We can stay at least an hour then go." I traced the cleavage of her leather top.

I could use the grip of her tight pussy while she was bound and screaming tonight. Those were desires I'd suppress until she was in a better place emotionally.

"Sadik!" my name was boomed over the music.

I stood, reaching over the railing to take Ricky's proffered hand and give him dap. "Happy G-Day!"

"Thanks, man!" His eyes skirted around. "Did you get the *Ace of Spades* I had sent over for you?"

I glanced around, too. "No, but I see this bottle of *Mauve* here. Much respect."

"Looks like Randi's greedy ass done drank it all up," he grumbled in a way it was clear he was displeased. Then he addressed Bilan. "When she get back, tell her to meet me by that bar over there." He pointed.

While Bilan may have been clueless to it, I knew his request for Randi's presence was because I'd now arrived.

Bilan nodded, I could tell not exactly comfortably.

Ricky took off and I surmised in her ear, "You don't know him."

She shook her head. "I've seen him maybe three or four times in passing. Never even been to his place. He's...weird."

I loved her greenness in this circle so much, I found myself stroking her cheek with my index finger.

"My mother said Ab hasn't—"

"You finally showed?"

Below, just where Ricky stood, was Tiffany. She sported a new wig, making me think twice.

"Wouldn't miss it for the world," I replied wryly over the music.

"Yeah, and giving my security hell is whack as fuck," she griped.

I shrugged. "It's the Earl Ellis way. I go nowhere empty handed."

Her security wanted us to lose our guns. I wasn't having it.

Fuck that...

"You look cute!" Tiffany's pitch was high, phony as hell as she addressed Bilan.

Bilan's ballooned eyes swung to me. I regarded her with patience for several seconds before lifting my brows.

She returned her gaze to a mildly grinning Tiffany. Her pitch was hiked, too, when she offered, "Not as cute as you!"

Tiffany's eyes cut to me, stunned. And I knew in that moment the period of peace between the two had been breached. It was a gut feeling.

Tiffany emitted a nervous chortle before she shifted her stance, straightening before speaking to me. "This is your second time here. You ain't see much a couple of weeks ago when you stopped by. Let me give you a proper tour."

Bilan's soft hand brushed across my thigh in response. She clawed me in plain view of Tiffany.

And there it was.

"Not tonight," I told her. "We don't plan to stay long."

"Ricky said you needed more champagne, though."

I shook my head. "We're good. The ladies got started before me."

Tiffany appeared uneasy. She hadn't adjusted to the new rules. Perhaps we should have established them together.

Her eyes swept over to Bilan before returning to me. "I'll hit you later."

Before she turned to take off, Tasche was speed walking our way.

"So, you were at your ex-lover's club a few weeks ago?" Her eyes narrowed, seduction in them.

My Nalib was goading me into a fight. It was cute. I leaned over and whispered into her ear. "I miss sucking on your fat pussy, Nalib."

Before she could react, Tasche was upon us, crossing over Bilan.

"What's wrong?" Bilan asked.

Tasche picked up her purse from the bench before whispering something in Bilan's ear.

"Oh!" Bilan remarked before standing. "I'll walk you out."

I grabbed her arm, protesting her decision to up and leave. She quickly reached down and whispered, "Her period came on unexpectedly. She's a heavy bleeder. I'm gonna walk her out to her car."

Rory's big eyes were locked on us, sensing Bilan's exit.

"No."

"Sadik," was all she said.

"No."

"It'll only be a minute. I don't want her feeling alone in case she has an accident. All these people around. No one will bother little ol' me."

I shook my head. Rory tossed her chin. "I'll send a man with you."

This was hard. I had to be sure to make Bilan feel she was free of shadows and danger. But in here, she wasn't. I had no idea what dumb ass would try her while doing a simple girlfriend task.

"Sadik!"

"Johnson!" I barked. He turned to me, and I tossed my chin to gesture for Bilan. "I think she needs to go," I reminded Bilan.

Releasing a huff, Bilan took off down the stairs. I watched them until they disappeared into the sea of bodies on the dance floor.

Rory sat next to me. "Luiz, one of Lopez niggas, here."

"At Ricky's party?" I asked rhetorically. She sat muted as I considered the possibilities. It could be plausible that Ricky was cool with someone in Lopez's camp. But even the concept of being here at Ricky's party was particularly odd. "Go have Jamil ask Tiff about the emergency exits. See where the nearest one is to here. We'll be leaving in thirty minutes anyway."

She got on it right away. I sent a text to Johnson about pulling the car around once he delivered Bilan back to me. I'd never been a paranoid type of man, always preferring calm for cogent thinking. This was that occasion when I remembered I had to teach Bilan how to shoot a gun. I recalled her having one at her parents'. It was a small piece-of-shit pistol. She had to learn how to arm herself with a real gun.

Bare legs crossing in front of me had me peering up. Randi wobbled past to her things on the bench. She went for a cup left on the table and tossed it back.

"Yo, Randi," Rory rasped loud enough to capture her attention. "Your old man want you by the bar." She pointed across the palatial room.

Randi waved her off dismissively. "Nah. I get it." Her eyes met me. "Sadik don't want me over here while he with Bilan. Fuck y'all."

My head swung back and brows hiked. She didn't sit, but pivoted, making it clear Randi wasn't going to stay. She began my way to leave the booth. Her index finger was pointed toward me, eyes pink and lipstick smeared outside of the lining.

"I know what the fuck you doing to her. You fuckin' with her head. B ain't that kind of girl. She 'on't know how to fuck with niggas like you."

I couldn't help my grin. "And you do?"

"Don't fuckin' act like you don't remember me!"

"And you shouldn't believe you *know* me."

"Yo, Randi," Rory shouted again. "Your old man want you by the bar." She pointed again. I lifted my arm pointing, too, as I looked her square in the damn face. "Ah, fuck it. Here he come!"

Randi turned first, then I looked myself. Ricky was charging toward us. Rory postured up, ready. I didn't move, but had my next one in mind. Randi began to shuffle out of the booth. Before she could make it to the last step, Ricky had yanked her up. Rory stepped aside as to not interfere.

"I was fuckin' coming!" Randi protested, trying to stay on her feet. "They just fuckin' told me—"

"How fuckin' long it take you to pee?" he demanded. "Huhn?"

"Why the fuck you care when you got your fuckin' wife here?" As Randi barked back, Ricky tossed me an expression of contempt.

It was a far cry from his friendly veneer during our recent encounters. I knew what that meant. I lifted my palms in the air to message my defenselessness. I could give a fuck about a dried up ass Randi. That bitch had too many miles on her pussy by her eighteenth birthday, so I could imagine where it was now. Ricky's scowl continued as he cut through the thread of people, dragging Randi behind him.

"That fuck nigga!" Rory called out as she walked backward up the stairs next to me. "Here go B and Johnson right here."

Bilan, indeed, was on her way. Her arm covered her midsection as she strutted underneath Johnson's extended arm, preventing people from bumping into her. When she hit the small set of steps, I stood. I sat down after her.

"That took a while," I spoke in her ear, caressing her arm.

"She parked like two blocks away," she provided while going through her small purse. "It's chilly out there."

I rubbed her arms, enjoying her chiseled cheeks, though I could hardly see those freckles. Bilan's beauty was truly remarkable. "You ready to go?"

Bilan's movements froze and she peered up at me. "You're ready to go, too, huhn?"

"I won't rush you. Your call." I tried to soften it with a smile.

Her expression mirrored mine. Then Bilan gazed over her shoulder before leaning into me. "When Randi comes back from god only knows where she is, I'll tell her I'm tired."

I nodded. Fair enough. Rory got my attention and tossed her head to the left of her, where I was able to spot a dimly lit exit sign ten yards away. I acknowledged her, then turned my attention back to Bilan. She slid closer to me, her eyes soft as she chewed on the inside of her mouth.

"I've been meaning to ask you a question."

"Go for it."

"Do you want me to pour you a few thumbs of brandy?"

My forehead raised and I snorted, "Do I need it?"

She returned back into my ear. "Maybe." I nodded, inviting her to continue. Questions be damned, I was thrilled to have her this close to me. "The night Damien took me from *Michelle's* and I went back to my parents' house, I didn't have my key." My fingers drumming the back of the bench froze, abruptly arrested. "But when I went to check on the house the other day, it was there—didn't work, but was there." Bilan hesitated, and I nodded to encourage her to finish. After a few beats, she did. "Did you take it?"

Bilan pulled back to see my face. I moved to speak in her ear.

"Can you handle the truth even if it's ugly?" I withdrew and watched her nod. Her lips trembled, then she closed her mouth. I moved to her ear again. "Yes. I did take the key, then returned it."

She wasted no time pushing her face to the side of mine. "You stole my key to kill my brother. That's insane, Sadik." I could hear the tears in her voice.

When she pulled back, I could tell she fought not to let them fall from her eyes.

I pulled her by the neck and the back of the head to my face. "My life is complicated, baby. I told you this." I found myself hesitating. "I didn't do it, though." I hesitated again, detesting the urge to feel regret for something I'd done in the Ellis name. But for her, I did feel remorse. "But I went there to do it because I could separate it. I could see Ab's commitment to his hustle, and had to measure that against my father's position. It's the game, Bilan. It's the streets."

She moved to speak in my ear. "But you're not the streets. You're not in your father's line of work."

"But I am in his world. I'm his son."

She moved fast to return. "You're better than he is! So much of a better man!"

I shook my head. "Bilan, I'm just a different man. But I'm still an Ellis."

She snatched her neck from my grasp, turning away. I could tell she was stewing on my confession, one I wrestled with each day since I fell in love with her.

Then Bilan returned to my ear. "So my son is supposed to wear the badge of murderer? Huhn? Am I supposed to roll over, turning a blind eye to his grooming to the world of darkness, like Irene and Monica? Or is it already in his DNA to kill?"

That wounded me. As I shook my head, I peered into her wet eyes as the music blasted around us. I wished I could explain my heart. Snatch it from my chest and dissect it with her. For her. I'd do the same with my brain to show her it was all wired for her. I wished she could see. I wanted her to see the demands of my world. Needed her to understand my limits: hard and soft. Wished she could learn my temperament to eradicate that slither of fear of me I smelled on her.

I pulled her to me. "Why didn't you tell me Ab threatened to have you suck his boy's dick?"

When I withdrew, I could see the blood drain from her face.

I must have gripped her neck too hard when I pulled her to me this time because Bilan grabbed my arm. "Why should a man live after threatening his sister—my woman—in that debaucherous manner? Hmmm?" I hummed forcefully in her ear. "You're mine, Bilan!"

"No, I'm not!" she screamed as I maintained my grip.

"You are. And while it saddens me to bring this darkness, as you call it, into your world, losing you would remove the light I've been searching for damn near all my life. You are my light. Killing Damien was a small piece of my darkness I had to display to keep my life lit with joy and satisfaction only you could bring!" My pulse quickened and tone morphed into a gruff as I admitted, "It took me thirty-eight years to find a woman who could appeal to me beyond a trip to *JAGMisha*'s and fuck-a-thon on a tropical island. Took nearly four decades for me to feel something each time your eyes are on me. I may be your definition of dark, dear, but your light is so bright, I'd kill Damien, and now Ab, a thousand times to keep you safe. And now, you're carrying my legacy, my child I plan to worship almost as much as I do you." With force, I let her go, snatching my arm from her straining neck.

Bilan's frame sprung backward, and her regard on me turned wild, pupils dilated.

She'd seen it. A demonic pull I'd fought for years to extinguish easily flared the moment I realized someone had brought her harm. When Ab mentioned his boy's dick in my Nalib's mouth, death was the first whisper in my soul. I didn't think twice giving the order. It was then I knew Ab would die, too, but not until my intrigue of their dynamic—more information on Bilan—had been satisfied. Nonetheless, his hate for his sister had sealed his fate.

And now she knew. She knew the ugly. She'd experienced the unremitting demon. It didn't matter how I'd kept the thrill of taking Damien's life to a minimal while doing it. Didn't matter that because she was there, as I killed him, it was quick with little pain. That wouldn't be credited. It wouldn't be noted that he had to go when he put her life at risk. All she wanted to see was a murderous family. And I couldn't change it for her, even if I wanted to.

When the first tear fell from her eye, a zip above my head popped my bubble of awareness.

Another zap.

"Shit!" I pulled her onto me as I dropped to the floor.

"Sadik!" she screamed.

"I'm sorry, baby!" I gazed around, hearing all the screams. "Someone's shooting. Please guard your belly, okay?" I asked helplessly.

"Boss!" I heard Rory down near the steps.

I turned over to lower Bilan onto the floor. Then I pulled my gun from my waist, checked the chamber, then cocked the hammer. Next, I reached for the silencer attachment and quickly screwed it onto the barrel.

"C'mon, boss!" Rory shouted. "C'mon! I got Bilan!"

No way I was giving Bilan to anyone. Quickly, I lifted to peer over the table, hoping to see a shooter, but all I saw were bodies in disarray.

"We ain't got time for the door, Deek!" I recognized Jamil's bark.

The door. If they opened it, it would flood with bodies trying to fit through and we'd be stuck. I rushed to my feet, stayed low, and lifted Bilan.

"Come on, baby." She struggled to her feet. "Let me get you out of here."

We moved a few feet before I realized she'd left her purse.

"Cover her!" I shouted to Rory and quickly ran back to grab it. Two zaps over my head that quickly had me moving in super speed. Jamil and Johnson were at the bottom of the steps, waving us on when a silver flash caught the peripheral of my right eye. The Lopez gang tattoo above his right brow identified him.

While in movement, I could tell Bilan saw the olive skinned man with thick, dark curly hair aim his gun our way, too, because she froze. With no time to consider if I should deal with her or address him, I pulled my gun up. It was a tricky aim because of the fleeing bodies between us, but I caught a crosshair and took the shot.

Bilan screamed hysterically when she saw him drop backward

without the warning of a popping sound from the gun. She wasn't the only one. The whole place was up in panicked emotions, though I doubted many saw why the guy went down. It had been years since I'd experienced this level of mayhem. It was why the Ellises partied together and exclusively.

"Come on, baby!" I screamed, then lifted her by wrapping my arm beneath her breasts.

It didn't take long for her to begin walking on her own. We made quick work of hightailing it to the door. Jamil kicked it open as Rory took cover over Bilan and me. We followed him from the side of the building with Rory behind us as Jamil communicated with Johnson about his location versus ours. All around us, people were running and screeching cries of fear.

Within seconds, the *Maybach* could be seen and heard screeching to a stop. We took off to the car and made it inside without incident. Only, the five of us had to squeeze inside, which were more bodies than I preferred.

"Are you okay?" I asked Bilan. She nodded, eyes ahead. My hand went to her midsection. "The baby?"

Bilan nodded again.

"Rory, where are you parked?" I asked as I unscrewed the silencer and decocked my gun now that we were in the car.

"Around the corner."

"Take her to the truck, Johnson. You two take the truck back to my garage," I ordered with my hands rubbing down Bilan's cold arms and back. She was shock-still in the center. "Breathe, Bilan. Just breathe."

She wouldn't look at me, only stared straight ahead. That was a glaring contrast to my security, whose heads were swinging left and right.

"Man, what the fuck was that?" Jamil barked.

"That was some fuck boy shit," Rory grasped, glancing all around.

"Man, listen!" Johnson started. "I'm glad you brought that potato for ya Glock, man!"

Johnson was former law enforcement and knew the implications of firing in a room full of civilians. Them not hearing what would traditionally sound like a gunshot helped the shot go unnoticed by most.

When I checked on Bilan again, I saw her eyes below where I stowed the gun parts. *Shit...* I didn't want to fight about this. Here we were, in another situation where I had to show her the ugly in me.

And right after our fight a few minutes ago...

I decided then and there to not demand anything from her tonight. I wouldn't expect much either, just for her not to run.

We stopped at Bilan's *Range Rover,* and the car quickly emptied. Rory jumped in the front, and adjusted the driver's seat as she pulled off. I then pulled the magazine from the Glock and put it and its pieces into a compartment underneath the passenger's seat. When I pulled upright, I found Bilan's eyes on me again. Ignoring it, I sat up straight, smoothing down my clothes.

Bilan never moved from the center of the backseat. I wasn't sure if that was a sign of companionable quiet tonight or of the unrest still brewing. My cell phones were still vibrating with fury in my pockets. I pulled them out and began to address what I could via text messages. One was from Tiffany, asking if I was okay. She'd sent several already, saying she was fine and locked down inside her office with security.

I sat back groaning internally. Bilan and the baby had been my single and most significant priority. In my frantic efforts to get out of there, I never considered Tiffany's safety.

That's fucked up...

I closed my eyes. This shit was a close call. I wanted to ask her about the baby again, but was afraid of getting something more than an answer. So I'd shut the fuck up and answer these texts about the club shooting from Tiffany, my team, and my lawyer. And that's what I did. The process was longer than I expected because at some point, my thoughts got lost in them when I was discussing Ricky's guest list with Tiffany. I also needed to know if her surveillance cameras picked up my shooting...without saying it was my shooting.

A soft, warm hand slid over my thigh, snatching my attention completely from the conversation. My head shot over to Bilan to find her still gazing straight ahead. Then her little hand pushed over to my crotch, awakening my dick. I peered down and watched her loosen my belt, then pants. Rory's attention, in the front seat, was straight ahead.

Before my regard could drop back down to her one-hand work, Bilan was pulling my dick out. Her aggressive touch was painful because my pants were still up, but I couldn't blurt that. I quickly adjusted my pants, just slightly to end the discomfort. Her small palm jerked me with boldness. When I turned to communicate to her in some form, Bilan beat me to it. She swung her torso over and pushed her damn tongue down my throat. I was in trouble, but I didn't stop her. Neither did her fisting stop.

We kissed wildly as I tried following her lead. Who was this woman? Something had come over Bilan.

"Sadik," she cried in my mouth.

My breathing was ragged. "You okay?"

"I need you," she squealed. "Let me put my mouth on you."

I peered over her and saw Rory was now looking at us. My dick was inflating in her hand by the stroke. The last thing I needed was Rory seeing me fucking my lady. She'd seen enough of my recklessness in the past with women not even half as significant to me as Bilan. She wouldn't catch this one.

"Bilan," I whispered breathlessly in between kisses. "Rory, baby."

She pushed her tongue in my mouth again, and I could feel my damn balls jerk.

"Bil—"

She wouldn't let me speak, but her ass did swing her legs over until she was straddling me.

"Sadik," she cried, kissing me again, stroking my dick fluidly. Now, Rory could only see her dry humping me. "I'm so horny." Her timbre was as though Bilan was crying.

"We're almost home, Bilan." My hands gripped her thighs.

She dropped to my mouth again. "I'm sick." She'd said it again. "You make me sick like this," she alleged, stroking me. Her tongue swiped into my mouth, leaving me teased. "You kill a man with a rope in front of my eyes, my nipples get hard. You tie me up with the same implement, I lose my mind in sensual need. And tonight, you—"

"Shhhhhh!" I urged her not to say it.

The fight not to enjoy her hand job was now becoming painful. Her breasts at my neck, her breath hitting my face while her grip on my cock felt mastered. I could feel the strain of the fabric of her tight pants on my thighs. I wanted to fuck her. I needed to fuck her. This quickly, Bilan had disarmed me.

"Sadik—"

"Nalib, shut the fuck up!" I whispered forcefully, thrusting into her two busy little palms. "I'm about to—"

"I want to feel you come in my hands," she panted. "Deek," she purred as though begging, thrusting her hips.

"I'm cum..." I couldn't speak.

My balls warmed, goosebumps lifted all over, and heart felt like it would beat right out of my fucking chest as an orgasm quaked through me. I could hardly breathe and, to make it worse, Bilan pumped her tongue into my mouth, silencing me.

"Yesssss," she breathed into my lips, fondling my dick with reverence.

Completely immobile, I couldn't move. My lungs were about to burst. I lay my head back with my eyes closed. She rested her forehead against mine, sweet breaths hitting my face, only further torturing me.

After a while, she sat up, tapped a center console, and grabbed several napkins. My eyes were still closed as Bilan cleaned the mess she made. My mind swirled with what in the hell just happened. It reminded me of her arousal at the fundraising dinner, when she witnessed Sofia and me battling public policy.

When she lifted from my lap, I could see we were turning into the garage. I went about straightening myself, though I couldn't get my head to stop spinning. Rory pulled into a parking space and I opened the door before she cut the engine. I reached back for Bilan's hand.

"I'mma stay behind and wait for the truck, sire," Rory jibed, making me think she knew what had just happened. "Jamil text me. They stopped at *B-Way Burger* for a bite. Shouldn't be long."

With one hand locked with Bilan's, I used the other to wave my acknowledgment as we headed to the elevator door. When the car arrived, Bilan stepped on first. I followed her, selecting our floor. Silence rang between us. On the ride up, Bilan held onto the railing as she removed her sandals. She toed over to me, lifting from her toes, and kissed me again. I took her at the small of her back, stroking her ass. Her shoes and purse on either side of her shoulders as she fucked my mouth.

The elevator dinged and the doors opened. I let her go and got off first. I could feel her behind me on the way to the apartment door, until I couldn't. I punched in the code and opened the door. When I turned back for her, Bilan was standing straight from pulling off her leggings and panties. Her shoes were left just outside of the elevator and her purse was in one hand, clothes in the other. As she toed inside, my cock swelled again instantly.

I slammed the door behind us.

What the fuck is this?

Bilan dropped the contents of her hands on the floor and jumped me, pushing me against the wall. Her tongue toured my mouth hungrily, hands gripped the crown of my head. She moaned, throwing her pussy into me. Her movements fast and as aggressive as they were in the car. She let herself down without leaving my mouth. My belt was unbuckled, pants were unzipped and being pushed down my waist.

Before I could blink, her mouth was on me, hand cupping my balls. My head rolled against the wall, brain fucking loose from my spine. But I had to gain some control. I'd already come in her hands, I couldn't come, this time, in her mouth. I pulled her head away as I reared my hips. Reaching down, I prompted her to stand and lifted her to straddle me again. Right away, Bilan's mouth connected with mine. Her kisses were nasty: forceful, seductive. So fucking arousing.

I walked us down the hall and into the living room, sitting on the sofa gently. Bilan wasted no time climbing onto my dick. She ground her way down with lost patience, arms stretched to cup my shoulders.

"Help me, Sadik," she cried, eyes half-mast, jaw relaxed.

I reached to the back of her leather top for the zipper. Bilan, sensing my search, lifted her left arm, exposing the zipper. I pulled it down, releasing her almond breasts, toffee and pebbled at the apex.

Fuck...

"Oh!" she moaned, head tossed back as her hip thrusts deepened.

My ankles vibrated from my phones in the pockets, but nothing could disturb watching my fiancée fuck the shit out of me on the couch with a city highway in the backdrop. Her neck exposed, tits bouncing at a particular pace and rhythm, and thighs squeezing almost as tight as her pussy around me.

So, this was what love felt like. It was what longevity looked like. Because I observed the erotica hopping on my lap, all I could see was my forever. Maybe that's what Bilan saw the other day in the hospital when she said she saw an older version of me. She was my light and in the moment, the only regret I had was not having eloped this summer. Then I remembered Bilan wasn't ready. She wasn't even in love with me yet. But I'd wait. Just like now, I focused my mind away from the suctioning game her pussy was wreaking on my throbbing cock. I swear, if Bilan wasn't carrying my baby right now, she would have been by the end of the night.

"Oh, god!" She screamed, thighs tightening, pussy quaking, and drives onto me quickening. "Sadik!"

Grabbing her by the ass, I thrusted with her. "Get it, Bilan." My mouth latched onto her nipple and I couldn't tear my eyes away from her face, hating I couldn't take in her full frame. Bilan's movements from the beginning of this tryst were feral, the brashest I'd seen of her. And as I began to explode with her, jetting hot cum inside of her, I knew there was a cryptic cause to her spiked libido tonight.

"Fuck, B!" I groaned, rocking up into her core.

Whatever turned my lady on, I'd be there to help sort out. I just hoped my arms were capable. We rocked into each other, crying out in ecstasy together. Her claws on my shoulders, my clasps on the fat of her ass as we held onto each other while floating above the fucking Earth.

Her breathing was wild, moans persisted even after we both sat languid, bodies drained. Her chest heaved, head rocked while extended back each time she groaned. It went on so long, I opened an eyelid. Bilan was crying.

What the fuck?

I shot up, taking her at the back of the head to pull her up. "Bilan!" She came up with tear tracks at the side of her eyes. "What's wrong?" I asked, rearranging her body to lay across my lap horizontally. "Talk to me, Bilan." I removed the panic from my voice.

I needed to stay ahead of her emotions in order to calm her. Neither would I fault her for expressing her feelings during this adjustment period. Instead, I would provide the comfort and patience she needed. Bilan was strong. I'd seen enough signs of it to be convinced.

"I was almost killed," she wailed, "again!"

I rocked her in my arms, leaving enough room for her small belly. "But you're still here with me. I swear on my life, until I'm no longer here, I'll protect you. With every fiber of my being, I'll provide you with any resource I can find to keep you from danger."

Her soaked pink eyes peered up to me. "And what if the danger is you?"

"Then, I'd have to protect you from me. That's one of many roles. Your friend, your lover, and your protector."

I watched a few more tears fall as I combed the back of her head with my fingers. Bilan closed her eyes, breathing began to even out, and the crying subsided. When I thought she was about to doze off, I kicked off my shoes and pants, then lifted us from the sofa.

Tonight, I held my fortune in my hands. My light, legacy, and future. I walked us into the bathroom where I stripped the rest of my clothes off, ate my lady, and washed us completely. On our way to bed, much of Bilan's weight was on me, as was my own exhaustion.

My last thoughts were just how I'd devastate the Lopez empire.

Turning over on my pillow, I heard it again. My eyes popped open wide. Then I jumped too fast from the pillow in search of my phone on the nightstand. My pulse elevated as I read the name of the hospital I had programmed into my phone.

"*Hel—*" I swallowed involuntarily. "Hello..."

"Bilan?"

"Yes."

"It's Nurse Gladney. Abshir had a rough morning. As you know, his vitals have been weak and organs began shutting down. He suffered a heart attack, honey. It's called acute coronary syndrome and happens when the arteries that carry blood, oxygen, and nutrients get blocked. The heart didn't get enough blood supply. Between the kidney failure and wound from the head injury, his body could no longer keep fighting. We lost Abshir at 4:07 this morning."

I glanced at the clock. It read 4:48 AM.

My eyes closed and I dipped my head, my curled index finger pushed into the side of my nose to distract from the cry threatening. I knew this day would come. The medical staff had been very clear about Abshir's prognosis. Had he been at any other non-level 1 trauma care facility, we would have likely lost my brother before I returned to Jersey.

This time, memories of pleasant days past didn't flood my mind. This time, being told he was gone, my mind simply didn't function.

"Thanks, Nurse Gladney."

"I'll be here until twelve if you need me, Bilan."

It took several seconds to return an empty, "Okay."

The line disconnected, and my eyes focused on one of the golden hooks of the blackout window shade. I dropped my hand holding the phone. The air stilled, the room soundless. My ears insulated, feeling pressurized.

Where to start? Who do I call?

Warm palms were at my shoulder. As he shuffled closer, the heat of his bare frame rivaled the coldness casing my skin.

"I'm here," were the two words his morning timbre uttered.

What did that mean? I knew he was here. He'd always been here. But what did that mean for me, a woman who had to put to rest a brother murdered by his family?

A sob struck my core, causing my shoulders to cower. But the tears remained at bay.

"Sadik..."

"Call my mother," his gravelly chords produced.

I shook my head. Irene had done more than her share. "*I...*"

"Bilan, call my mother."

My eyes closed in frustration. "She's a Christian. We're—Abshir's —of Islamic faith. *I—*"

"Call my mother. She'll know what to do."

The confident finality in his voice was what allowed the first tear of bereavement to fall.

"Bilan?" When I turned behind me and found my Aunt Franzel leaning through the screen door onto the patio off the kitchen, I forged a smile. "You sure you're not ready to eat?"

My nose turned up at the mention of food. "No. Not quite yet."

"Young lady, this woman has arranged a spread just for us," she retorted, head landing to the side.

She had. Irene hired a Somali chef for foods she thought my family would be familiar with and enjoy. On top of that, she, herself, had prepared several soul food dishes.

"I will. Later." I widened my smile.

She sighed. "Okay." Then she retreated into the kitchen, closing the door behind herself. My regard returned to the view of the wooded area nestling Sadik's apartment building. The trees made me feel hidden so I could sort my thoughts.

My mother opted to have my father's funeral at a funeral home.

A few of his old customers attended, but not much. His sisters came, but with reservation. However, not all of my cousins paid their final respects. That hurt my mother and me. She never forgot the lack of support by his family. She was an only child and didn't have family of her own to shoulder the burden.

When my mother passed, two of her closest friends, also her coworkers, were extremely helpful in planning her American funeral. One had arranged to have it at her church on a weekday and, thankfully, they did not charge. Not many attended. My aunts and their families refused to go to the funeral portion, only opting for the burial because of the facility. The women were even nice enough to have a repast. None of the family made it because I stayed behind, unable to leave my mother's body in the ground for hours.

It was the day after I got the call about my brother's passing. Aabo was dead. Hooya was dead. And now, Abshir was gone, too. Life could be so cruel, so empty. My hand dropped to my belly hidden beneath the duster I wore over my dress today as a thought occurred to me. My son would never know them.

My phone vibrated on the glass table next to me.

My Lover: *It's after 3. Why haven't you eaten?*

Me: I'm not hungry.

I rolled my eyes, tossing the phone onto the table.

The door opened again. It was my cousin, Mimi, stepping out onto the patio.

"Hey," I greeted.

"Hey, girl!" She giggled, moving to an adjacent patio seat. "Why you out here by yourself? You okay with the ceremony? Mommy said it was your first."

"It wasn't my first. My first was cousin Charles."

"Ohhh!" she resounded. "I forgot all about him. Aunt Franzel took that hard."

Aunt Franzel had a son who died from chronic asthma when I was about twelve. Charles had to be eight at the time. My father took it hard.

"The ceremony was good. I learned more today about how it's done in Somalia."

"My mom took us back to Somalia for grandmother's funeral," Mimi recounted, a memory I recalled. We couldn't afford to go, but aabo did send money back to bury someone he wasn't related to. Mimi was referring to her father's mother. "I can't believe how they were able to pull off the rituals and have elders from the community do it, along with my father and uncle."

When Sadik told me to call his mother, it wasn't to throw me on her. Apparently, he'd told her I mentioned our Islamic rituals, and she immediately reached out to friends she had in the faith. One was a sheikh. They generously took custody of my brother's body from the hospital, along with my uncles, and prepared his body by washing him, praying over the body using verses of the Quraan, rubbing his body down with Karfan, and using Adar perfume. I'd learned all of this just yesterday, when the sheikh called to inform me of what would happen. At the burial, the women stayed behind observing as the men took care of his body, from the hospital to the grave.

"It was an experience," was all I could offer to keep this conversation surface level.

Reciting the *Janaaso* was done with mixed feelings. It was the final and goodbye prayer. While performing it with my family, in my heart, I begged Abshir to get messages to my parents. It was difficult not to break down.

"Well, I'm glad you and your in-laws were able to keep with tradition this time. Hooya's happy, too."

"I'm not married yet, Mimi," I corrected just as the sliding door opened again.

Sadik stepped out onto the patio with a plate of food and a bottle of *Fiji* water. He managed to close the door behind himself and slip behind me on the chaise lounge as I scooted up, making room for him.

"Mimi, right?" he asked with a soft smile.

"Yeah." My cousin smiled—rather blushed. Was she crushing on him *that* bad? All day, she and Joslyn couldn't keep their eyes off of him. They snickered and whispered, too. And they weren't alone. My aunts couldn't keep their eyes off of him either, only they weren't as immature about it. And the fact that they were still here, all in Irene's face, spoke volumes. I thought they didn't participate in repasts. I hadn't seen my aunts this engaged around me since I was a kid.

"I was just telling Bilan how you and your mother did an awesome job here. My *hoo*—mother and aunt are damn blown away."

Sadik placed the plate and water on the table and reached for a fork. "Anything for my Bilan." He scooped turmeric rice and brought it to my mouth. "I hope your family was at least comforted by the rites today. It was important for us to provide you all that."

My eyes flew to Mimi and I cringed. Why would he do this?

"Sadik," I murmured, not wanting to blurt what I really wanted to say.

"Nalib," his smooth alto produced in a way I wasn't confident my cousin couldn't pick up. "It's not just you to be concerned about."

I turned my head in the other direction so she couldn't see my face. "You've got to be kidding me."

Sadik switched hands with the fork. "Does it look like I'm playing?"

With flared nostrils, I parted my lips. Sadik quickly pushed the food into my mouth and I ate. When I turned back to my cousin, she pretended to be reading on her phone.

"So, what are you going to do now that you don't have to be at the hospital every day?" Mimi asked, eyes slipping back to Sadik.

"I thought we'd go away," Sadik murmured, mostly to me.

"Go away?" I asked, astounded. "Go away for what?"

"To help with the grieving. A new climate. Beautiful terrains." He reached down to my ear. "An ocean for skinny dipping."

I lost my breath at the flash memory of Costa Rica.

Did I just giggle?

I think I did. This was embarrassing...inappropriate. So Sadik to spike my arousal hours after burying my brother.

"We can't jet off to Costa Rica," I squealed harshly from the company we were in.

"I was thinking the Caribbean," he corrected. "There's this small exclusive island I want to try near Puerto Rico. *St. Justin.*"

"Oh!" Mimi piped up, eyes wide. "That's where Trent Bailey and his wife honeymooned!" She was bubbling over in excitement. "That blog, *Spilling That Hot Tea,* posted pictures of them there!"

My brows shot up.

All Sadik uttered was, "Interesting."

"So, when's the wedding?" she trilled, clearly uncomfortable and intrigued at the same time.

"Soon," Sadik answered right away.

I swallowed my food. "That has yet to be determined."

When I rolled my eyes up to him, Sadik had the next forkful, this time of collard greens, waiting for me.

"Thanks for this, Queen." I kissed my mother's cheek as her assistant and Bilan watched by the door.

She was all packed up. Kimmy and Bilan washed her fancy china and other dishes she transported her food here in. Her assistant, Kema, a young twenty-something-year-old, held the rolling cart filled with my mother's things.

"Oh, baby," my mother sang. "you know that's what I was born to do. To have your back." She nodded firmly.

"That you do." I smiled. Then I asked Kema, "You sure I can't help you out with that?"

"No." She shook her head. "I'm fine. It's my companion."

I nodded, conceding.

My mother then turned to Bilan. "Is there anything more I can do for you?"

Bilan didn't answer right away. Her face lifted into a crooked grin and she bit her lip. I took to her side, placing my hands on her shoulders.

"Yes. You can, actually. But first, I want to say thank you so much, Ms. Irene." Bilan's shoulders lifted. "For everything. I know you're Sadik's biggest fan, but I'd be remiss if I didn't acknowledge your sacrifice of time and confidence. Thank you for sitting with my brother this week. Thanks for pulling off his funeral in less than twenty-four hours. And thanks for the kindness you've shown my family. More specifically, I appreciate you making them feel like I belong somewhere."

I squeezed her shoulders in encouragement. That was a mouthful and, I was sure, difficult to admit.

My mother took a step closer to us, her forehead tightening. "Honey, my child says you belong to him. That means you belong to me, too. I saw what those weeks of you being away did to my son. I'd never seen him that dismal. If I can do more to guarantee those days do not return, I'm going to do it."

Bilan's shocked regard rolled up to me behind her.

"And Bilan," my mother continued. "I meant what I said about wishing I knew your mom. I'd used her divine maternal knowledge of you to get to know you better. I wish I had her approval to envelope you into my family."

Bilan glanced up at me again. "If there's a way, I can assure you, your son has already sought out both my parents' approval and has gotten it." There was a bite and air of confidence in that statement.

She rolled her eyes from me back to my mother.

"So tell me." My mother's laced fingers dropped below her belly as a show of humility. "What can I do for you, Bilan?"

Bilan snorted. "You think you can point me in the right direction for a job at *Ellis Academy*?"

I couldn't trust my damn ears. Bilan was interested in one of our family's businesses? She was adamant about not doing exactly that.

My mother's surprised regard was on me before it returned to my lady in front of me. "Baby, I'd be more than happy to send you a list of openings. If there's something in mind you want, but don't see, we'll create a role for you."

Kema was already pulling out her tablet.

"Thank you, Ms. Irene."

"Oh, no!" My mother's neck rolled with sass. "I'm Mrs. Ellis around my subordinates, but in your home, we have to come up with something more intimate."

Bilan nodded. "I'd like that."

That short exchange brightened my day. I may not have been able to get her to fall head over heels for me yet, but Bilan had shown signs of settling into my life. That was a major play on the board.

We walked my mother and Kema out, watched them board the elevator, and waved them off as the doors closed. Together, we trekked inside the apartment, hand in hand. Such a quiet moment in a somber day. I didn't know what was ahead for her, I only knew I'd be there to endure it with her.

She closed the door behind us, and I kept down the corridor.

"Sadik," she called behind me. I turned back to her, shifting my body with curiosity. Bilan took a deep breath and blew it out slowly while nodding. "It's time."

"Time for what, baby?"

"It's time to tell your family you're expecting."

As sweet as the words, Bilan's expression didn't match them.

"Are you sure?"

She nodded. "It's time."

I found myself nodding, too, as I reached for her hand.

A pinch of pleasure lashed my core. I stirred at the slithering sensation accommodating it. My right thigh lifted and hips shifted forward, and a hum of contentment pushed from my lungs. My mind went between roaring waves on the sands of *Macen Beach* to this growing need in my groin. When the sounds of lapping exceeded those of the waves, conscientiousness broke through and I realized the beach scene was a dream. But those delightful strikes of bliss were my reality and my hips began to buck.

Sadik...

He'd been out of town and must have returned last night...this morning. I passed out rather early, extremely tired since burying Abshir four days ago. It was the second night I could sleep soundlessly and needed help awakening.

But this kind of help...

As I rocked into his face sandwiched between my thighs, my breasts felt weightier...in a beautiful way. An erotic way. His hands squeezing my cheeks, pulling me into him, incited my climax, stirring my groin even more.

Then he pulled away.

"Wake up, Nalib," his morning chords hoarse. "I see you forgot the no clothes in my bed rule."

I could feel the head of his cock in search of my opening. I groaned, partially in response to his rebuke and wholly in anticipation of him entering me. It was only a t-shirt, one I could barely fit these days. The smooth, bulbous head slipped around my sex, missing the mark. With my eyes still closed, I helped him by lifting my hips. He pushed inside of me, lighting more than my body on fire.

"Damn, girl," he grunted.

I soaked him in, feeling him heavy and pulsating. Together, we moved in sync. Suddenly, I was at the beach again, isolated, safe.

This was beyond a sensual play and physical connection. It was undeniable, indelible soul-binding. I belonged to Sadik. Never again would I touch any area on my body and not be reminded of traces of his hands or mouth. I was now branded by him.

This session was short. After a few short minutes of hip rolls, skin clawing, and his teeth scraping the skin near my collarbone, my climax arrived, prompting Sadik's. His deep breaths into my neck, the way he held onto me with hopeless desperation—it all made me lose myself to him with reckless abandon.

My body went immobile, posture languid against his. Sadik stilled a spell after. We waited for our lungs and heartbeats to do the same.

"You missed me," he graveled, smile tired from exhaustion as he closed his eyes.

"What makes you think that?"

"Your pussy never lies to me, Nalib."

"Really?" I giggled, trying not to breathe too much of my morning breath on him. "That can go both ways, buddy."

"Oh, I don't deny it at all."

"So, you've missed me?" My smug grin was more bashful than his.

"You belong to me, how can I not?"

"That doesn't answer my question."

"You in love with me yet?"

That knocked the humor from my face. Where did that come from?

He snorted, his cologne pushing from his nostrils. "I guess that's your answer." Then he ducked his face beneath my breasts.

"That's not fair." I hated witnessing his confidence being vacuumed from his usual dominant persona.

His head lifted, and he declared with confidence, "It is." Sadik kissed the center of my chest. "It's time for us to talk about it."

"About what?"

"About the shit storm I've brought to your life. Exactly what you've said."

I wet my dry lips, hesitating. "Why do you want to talk about that?"

"Because no matter how weak it sounds and how much it compromises me as your lover, I need you to love me in return," his words delivered so softly.

I was jarred, couldn't speak.

Sadik lifted his arm and traced my shoulder with the pad of his middle finger. "I want you to want to be here, not feel like you have to."

"I don't!" I answered too quickly; I needed to clarify. Then I swallowed, trying to gather my thoughts.

"You haven't been back two weeks yet," he argued.

"I know. And a lot has happened in the past week and a half, trust me. I've lived it."

"So, what's changed to make you feel you want to be here and aren't obligated?" His hazel irises implored me.

"Why do we need to talk about it?" I could feel him deflating inside me.

"Because it's what grownups do, Bilan." I rolled my eyes away, feeling slighted by that hidden accusation. "It's also not lost upon me that you've experienced trauma before me and...because of my complicated world, since me."

"What trauma before you?" I challenged.

I could perceive his head push deeper into the mattress to express his disbelief. "Do I need to remind you about your meltdown at your graduation party?" I cringed at that memory. "Not to mention, your eating aversion. You'd also been alone for some time before I came along."

"I've had friends around before you, Sadik," I tried.

"Bullshit. Randi and Tasche don't count. Your day to day life was pretty solitary. Your friends and acquaintances were in passing." He lifted a brow. "Much like your eating."

"I ate—eat—okay!" That quickly, I was annoyed. Sadik didn't waver from his expression. "Okay. You wanna know about my issue with food?" My tone was harsh.

"I'd love to." His tender eyes were now narrowed and concerned. Anxious.

"Back in those days, when Abshir would bring his trouble to my parents' restaurant, one day, a guy—older guy, but younger than our parents—came in the back with his boys. They pushed their way into the door after we'd closed for the day. Two had guns. One had a bat. This was before the time when they threatened to kidnap me. They demanded money from my father. I guess they thought, like so many others, since he had the restaurant, he had money, too. When they went through the register and found nothing, they ransacked the place looking for a stash that didn't exist."

My stomach began to churn at the memory, nausea creeping up my belly.

I swallowed back silky, tart'ish saliva and continued. "Abshir had broken into their boss' home and stolen jewelry and electronics, and my father was expected to reimburse him. After so many times of telling them he didn't have it, they began taking things from the fridge and pantry. And one...the leader of the pack..." His image flared in my head. Tall with a colorful *Grambling University* sweat suit and black leather boots. The gold cap on one of his two front teeth was distinctive. "He said they wouldn't leave without making my father pay in some way."

My eyes closed as I tried to let the nausea wash over me— begging it to.

"Nalib," Sadik called out to me gently.

"They took a tied trash bag we had next to the door to go out to the dumpster that night." My tongue seemed to have swelled, chopping my words. "He opened it up and dumped all the trash onto the floor. He told us..." I tried swallowing again. I could feel Sadik's thumb swipe my wet temple. "He told us to eat the..." I began breathing hard. "He made us eat off the floor. Scraps from the—"

"I got it," Sadik whispered, pushing himself up the bed and pulling me into his chest. "Say no more."

"I eat," I tried over harsh breaths. "I ate when I needed to. I just did it..." This couldn't be another occasion for tears. I was over being sad. "I guess I did it on the run. While in transit. Sometimes, the thought of sitting down to food...it just..."

"We'll work through it." His embrace was meaningful.

"How?"

"I'll figure it out. But now, it's paramount."

The baby...

I could feel the nausea lessening, my body relaxing.

"Shit..." he swore beneath his breath. "I didn't know this would upset you."

I nodded against his chest, eyes opening slowly. "Why does it sound like you're apologizing? That's something I should've told you long ago."

"Because you've been through so fuckin' much, which is why I need to know if you're here because you want to be."

I now understood.

"Am I angry about your family killing my brother? *God!* It sounds cinematic—" That brought Pastor Carmichael to mind. "I'm very angry. But I don't feel as betrayed by you as I did at first."

"Why?"

"Because, I'm slowly coming to accept the paradox that is Sadik. I don't pretend to understand it, but this week, I've seen the dichotomy of you. There's the Sadik I met: cultured, stubbornly seductive, generous, needy, intentional, and intellectual. And then there's the one Earl and, possibly Irene, created: calculating, avenging.

He cracked a seductive smirk. "I think my parents created these looks."

"You're deflecting."

He kissed my nose. "I am. To keep those bad attributes at bay in that beautiful mind of yours."

"My point is, you've shown me support in ways I didn't know really existed." Not to mention, he saved my life. Twice. *Cinematic...* "You and Irene were more than what I needed during a difficult time."

He kissed me chastely again. God, the simple act held too much comfort. "That's what family does," he explained too simplistically.

"Not kill to cause this type of loss?"

His slow caress on my arm ceased. After a spell, he husked, "Are you going to be up to tonight?"

Dinner with the Ellises tonight. That was how we were going to share the news about my innocent baby to his family. Whether I liked it or not, it had to be done. The sooner I could gauge their reception, the better I could plan if I'd stay away from them the remainder of my pregnancy, especially when I was too far out to...run.

I shook my head, then nodded in correction. "Yes!" I blinked successively. "I have to be. It's time. I asked you to give me time to deal with my brother. You did. It's done." I began to back away. My bladder was filling, and I needed a minute alone. "Let's do it."

I left the bed, watching Sadik sit up on his elbows.

"Where are you going?"

"To do those womanly things a girl does before going to meet her murderous fiancé's murderous family to tell them she's carrying their lineage."

His brows pinched, and those irises darkened to a green. I swear, his eye color changed according to his mood. "That's not funny, Bilan."

"Neither is the current state of my life, Mr. Ellis." I closed the bathroom door.

Cinematic. Ezra Carmichael called that right...

"I see you still 'on't eat," my father commented from the head of the table to Bilan.

The entire room silenced. Chatter from all but the girls vanished. My mother's typical expression of concern surfaced. Taaliba froze with her body angled from handing Candy her plate. Iban glanced up from his murmuring with Monica. The energy in the room suspended.

Bilan's expressive eyes shot to me first. I sat quietly, waiting with practiced patience. Then I lifted a brow. Bilan had to assert her own demand for respect, even at this table.

She managed a feigned giggle. "I'm saving my appetite for the apple pie Irene made."

My father's response was a deep stare as his tongue roved over his top teeth with a closed mouth. The tension was thick, and my Nalib contributed to it.

Since we'd arrived, she'd been conversable with my mother, sister, sister-in-law, and nieces. While that was quite a number of people, she virtually ignored two. My father tried engaging—or possibly prodding—twice since our arrival. It wasn't genuine, which was a lot for the leader of my pack. Bilan would reply, but move on to the next person. Iban didn't engage her at all after acknowledging her presence. It was his typical cold manner reserved for most outside of this family. I could feel Bilan shake like a leaf beneath me during their encounter, but I remained silent.

This was because Bilan had to demand respect from all or get run over. How else could she act in my proxy, as my wife, should I become incapacitated, or simply need assistance when overwhelmed?

My father grunted in response.

"Well..." my mother sighed excitedly from the other end of the table, her hands gripping the edge. "We've all been busy, running hard recently, myself included. Nonetheless, we *really* must discuss our holiday plans. The hour is calling late, and I have to begin my arrangements. I hope you're not in a rush to go." Her eyes were inarguably on Bilan and me.

Bilan peered over to me, and I regarded her in the same manner.

She turned to my mother. "I'm absolutely in no hurry." Her claim was delivered weakly, but she answered.

"Great!" My mother slapped her palms together. "Then we can move to the courtyard. I have the desserts set up out there. Jimmy should have the heating lamps going already. Let's meet there." She stood from the table, prompting us to leave as well.

"How are you feeling?" I asked when joining Bilan's side.

"Like if I had food in me, I wouldn't be able to keep it down," she murmured, mouth hardly moving. "Your brother is evil personified, and you father's more intimidating than Denzel Washington in *American Gangster*."

I chuckled. "He's not that bad." My hand reached down to her ass.

"You say that because you can be just like him."

That made me laugh as we neared the door.

"I need a word with you and your brother, Sadik," my father called from behind me.

I acknowledged him as we strolled out into the hall. The girls caught up to us, racing to the door leading out to the courtyard. Bilan found their child play humorous, her eyes lit with awe watching them go. They cut the corner, leaving our sight.

"Gotcha!" Taaliba playfully growled as she grabbed the side of Bilan not attached to me. She walked with us. "He's had you to himself for over a week now. I need some girl time before I leave."

"Where are you going?" Bilan wanted to know, and so did I.

"India," Taaliba answered.

"Where in India, and for what?"

"West Bengal. There's an herbalist out there that finally approved my apprenticeship." Taaliba beamed, proud of her latest pursuit.

"Wow!" Bilan nodded, appearing impressed. "That's pretty cool. How long will you be out there?"

"Five weeks, and I can't wait."

"Alone?"

Taaliba's eyes skirted to me as we came to a stop at the door leading to the courtyard.

She pulled at Bilan, forcing her to leave my arm.

"Let's talk about this without the ears of an Ellis man," Taaliba proposed, suspicious eyes on me as she did.

Bilan didn't look back as they continued onto the stone walkway. I watched the back of her fluffy skirt bouncing as she sashayed in burgundy suede *Louboutin*s. Her calf muscles were pronounced, skin luminous.

"She's not going far," Monica teased, passing me.

"Y'all go on ahead and let us talk back here for a minute," my father requested. "We'll be right there."

One of the staff approached my father with a tray of cigars for his selection as Monica separated from Iban. We waited while he lit his cigar, blowing a great cloud of smoke into the air.

"Lopez wanna meet," my father shared before taking another pull.

"For fuckin' what?" Iban demanded.

"Negotiate," he answered.

Iban's face balled tight. "That fucker know it ain't no negotiating after you try to murk a Ellis."

"He also knew he wouldn't win the war when he took it on," I countered.

My father's regard rolled over to me. "So, what you think?"

"About meeting with him?" I asked. "I don't. There's nothing to think about other than why meet with someone suicidal?"

Iban snorted. "That's what the fuck I'm talking 'bout. Lopez a dead man. He know it. My body count on his crew 'bout to be twenty in the past five days. That nigga know what time it is."

"Did he only ask to meet with you?" I asked.

I wondered if Lopez was the *FBI* snitch.

When my father nodded, that momentarily canceled my suspicion. "What are you thinking, son?"

I shrugged, hands in my pockets. "How the fuck did his men get into a member of *The Commission*'s party without their permission?"

Iban's full body turned to face me, and my father's arm dropped.

"The fuck, bro!" Iban barked.

"Ricky and Lopez," my father considered out loud. "Ricky don't say much at the meetings. Never really did."

"And yet, he throws himself a party."

"Shit!" Iban spat.

"Ricky with Lopez?" My father tried the theory out for size again, cigar forgotten about.

"I'm not sure," I tried explaining. "There're just several variables I'm considering. The bullets were just over our heads, and that's not something I can excuse as an accident."

"I'm gonna take the meeting with him," my father shared. "See what he know and what he's thinking."

I shrugged, lifting my lips and flicking my neck. "Do what you must."

Sounds of little feet beating the travertine pavers caught my attention. It was Iesha and Ivana running toward us.

"Daddy, Papa!" Ivana shouted, out of breath, bearing the biggest beam. "Nana said get your butts there now!" She laughed.

"No, Nana didn't!" Iesha disagreed with humor. "Nana said to get their hinds here now!"

Both girls found that funny.

"We're coming," their grandfather couldn't hold his laughter while trying to speak.

"Race you back!" Iesha challenged her sister.

Giggling, they took off.

I began first toward the center of the courtyard when Iban muttered while on his phone, "I'll meet y'all down there."

Wordlessly, my father and I proceeded. The women were seated around a glass table topped with sweet goodies and beverages. The gas heat lamps were, in fact, out, creating a balm of heat. The ground lighting provided a nice glow against the purple skylight.

I took the empty seat next to Bilan as she talked with Monica to the right of her.

"You took my seat, bro," Taaliba protested playfully.

I pretended to look around. "I think I'm right at home here," I returned.

"Asshole," she hissed before ambling to another seat with a donut in her hand.

"Sadik," Monica called over to me. "I told Bilan about you keeping the girls when I deliver. I hope she's ready." She chuckled.

"When's the delivery date again?" I was sure she told me, or Rory told me when Monica had reached out to her to put it on my schedule. That was when my mind was fogged with details of getting my life together or, better yet, getting Bilan back in my home.

"October seventeenth," she answered.

I pulled out a phone to be sure Rory had it on my schedule. "You good with that, champ?" I asked Bilan.

"Can't wait," she replied swiftly. "I'm already thinking of recipes to teach them. Manis and pedis, too!"

"Oh!" my mother chirped in the manner I was conditioned to recognize as her shock. "I wasn't expecting you, dear."

It was Tiffany.

"Wow," she emitted nervously. "Can I stay?"

That was a ridiculous question. Tiffany didn't attend each dinner or family event, but she was a familiar attendee. Even with that being the case, tonight wasn't a good one for her random pop-ups.

"Sure, you can! I just didn't know you were coming," my mother explained.

"Okay." Tiff's discomfited smile couldn't be broader. "It's just that Poppa Earl told me to stop by tonight."

"Yeah." My father took a seat next to my mother. "Irene said we were finally talking about these holiday plans."

Tiffany's eyes swept over to Bilan, whose hand went to my thigh, pulling it closer to her.

Shit...

∞19∞

"Okay!" mother closed the discussion on a pleased sigh. "So, it's settled: Thanksgiving in Antigua and Christmas in Aspen! I'm excited already. Kema and I will get started on the accommodations first thing tomorrow. Let's hope Monica and the new baby can be with us in Antigua." She fixed her eyes on Monica. "It wouldn't be the same without you, honey."

"Let's hope all will be well," Monica replied.

"I'm claiming it will be," my mother encouraged. "Everyone else should be fine."

"I don't know about me," Tiffany replied apologetically as Bilan fed me a slice of pie. "Thanksgiving falls on my birthday this year."

"You had plans already?" my father asked.

"Not really, but I was thinking of doing a trip with my girls since... You know."

Since she broke up with Larry.

"Well, you know you're always invited," my mother provided. "There'll be room for you if you decide to spend your birthday with us."

Tiffany smiled, mouthing, "Thank you."

"I want the new baby to go swimming with me," Iesha yawned.

"I wish it was a boy," Ivana shared. "I want a brother. Somebody to kill the sharks with."

We laughed at that. My gaze found Bilan's. I lifted my brows, asking if she was ready to break the news. This was a segue. In response, Bilan bit her bottom lip and her eyes fell. She was nervous and I could understand that, but it was time. Even she'd said so. It had to be done.

"Funny you say that, Ivy," I began, suddenly feeling uncharacteristically nervous. "I can't help out with a brother..."

Monica took lead in the group laughing. I guessed it was a good distraction before I went all in.

Then Bilan stood. She pulled the sides of the denim hiding her small belly behind her and rubbed. "But maybe a little baby boy cousin to boss around would do until then."

"Oh, my god!" Monica trilled, hands going to her mouth.

"Holy shit!" Taaliba was out of her chair and on Bilan, bumping my leg when reaching over me. "This is fucking awesome!"

I leaned back and somehow caught the reaction of my queen. Tears. She was on her feet, fists balled in the air, eyes wide as tears fell from her face.

Monica joined Taaliba in hugging Bilan. I had to grab the small plate Bilan held before it fell.

"Ms. Bilan's having a baby?" Ivy asked. Her eyes, too, were wild with excitement.

"Ms. Bilan's having my baby," I amended.

She began to jump up and down in place. "Iesha, Uncle Deek's having a baby!"

Iesha didn't share in the happiness. She crossed her arms and sat back in her chair, pouting.

"What's wrong, baby?" I asked, wounded.

"You ain't married yet," she retorted, eyes fixed straight ahead.

Before I could respond, a heavy slap hit my shoulder. "If I wasn't so happy, I woulda kicked your ass all around this damn compound, you hear me?" His unbridled smile almost foreign. He held his palm out.

I stood, accepting it. "Congratulations, son. This shit right here..." He was choked up, pulling me into his arms.

"Thanks, sir." I returned his tight embrace. "My pleasure."

"Shit!" he grunted releasing me to return to his seat.

My mother was still frozen. I decided to address her, so I sauntered over and pulled her into my chest. She howled as soon as she landed. It was just a croak, but a gesture I felt in my belly.

I whispered in her ear, "You were right, and I was wrong." I squeezed her tightly. "Again," I amended.

"I'm so happy," she bawled.

Then I felt a soft hand at my back. Bilan had come over. She pulled my arm from my mother to duck inside our enfold.

"I'm happy for you, Ms. Irene," she murmured.

What a sweet thing to say. That tugged at my emotions. My lady wanting to please my queen gratified me immensely. Apparently, it did my mother, too, because she peered up and found Bilan with us. She wrapped her arms around my lady and cried silently on her.

"I wanted to tell you, but I hadn't told Sadik. And I was afraid and untrusting." I heard the tears in Bilan's whisper that didn't reach further than the three of us. "I think I know how happy this makes you."

"You have no idea, baby," my mother declared loudly. "Thank you so much."

That's when I realized how real this was. My mother never reacted this way before. She was a heavily expectant grandmother for both my nieces, buying out several baby boutiques to prepare for their births. But I didn't recall seeing her this emotional at the announcement of their births.

What shook the core of me was when we all backed away from each other, catching my father wipe his eyes. It was the same time I noticed my brother walking off, toward the house.

Taaliba and Monica engulfed Bilan again. It was nice to see her doted on.

"So, y'all getting married? Moving in together? What?" my father inquired.

That reminded me I'd never told my family Bilan had moved in back in June.

"Bilan's moved in," I shared.

As I returned to my seat, my eyes brushed against a sitting body. *Tiffany...*

In that short period of time, I'd forgotten about her. And that quickly, I felt fucked up. Not because I'd done anything wrong, but because I genuinely cared for Tiffany and her feelings. I didn't jump to address her. Instead, I waited for the group to start to disseminate.

"I have to go to the restroom." Bilan tapped my knee. "I'll be back."

I watched her take off with Monica. Taaliba had already left to take a call. My mother had been back and forth with her staff to clear the dessert table. Stacy had taken the girls inside to brush their teeth from dessert. This left my father and Tiffany, who sat engaged in her phone since my announcement.

"Tiff," I called over to her. She glanced up, acknowledging me. "I can make the girls trip happen, if you like."

Her brows met. "How?"

"I can have Rory make some calls." A memory shot to the front of my head. "A friend of mine...Dawn, from the Turks and Caicos, has been trying to get me to buy a unit out there in one of the resorts she manages." I tossed my head to the side. I haven't had the time to go entertain her. I can send you in my proxy. Y'all can take the jet."

She exhaled, dropping her phone into her lap. "That your way of apologizing for this fuck boy shit?"

My head pushed back and lips poked. "Pardon me?"

She shook her head, then tossed her phone into her pocketbook. "Don't fuckin' even worry about it. I'm good." She stood.

My father jumped from his seat. "You sure, baby girl?"

Tiff rolled her eyes, shaking her head. "Yeah. I'mma have a drink while they bring my car around."

"Don't leave. Let's talk." My father's tone, posture, and words were beseeching. "We family. We can talk this out. Maybe some things was said that was misunderstood..."

Tiff's hand shot into the air. "I'm thirty-six years old. I understand what a man does with me."

"Fuckin' don't mean shit, Tiff. You know that." My eyes narrowed and head shook.

"It's about more than that, and you know it." The look in her eyes concerned me.

She appeared betrayed, and I didn't totally understand why. Yes, I knew Tiffany's interest in me exceeded mine for her. However, I never promised her more than I gave. I'd been very specific with her as to not create expectations I couldn't deliver on. Tiffany had never been an option for me. It was why I handled her particularly.

"C'mon, baby." My father used a calm timbre as he approached her, his arm reaching out. "Let's go to my study. Diane's got the fireplace going already. We can talk about this in there."

I didn't catch her response because my phone rang, the one I knew must be answered at this hour. As they walked off, I turned my back.

"Yeah?"

"Done."

Jamil's swift one word report wasn't lost upon me. Another member of Lopez's crew at *Pulse* that night had been collected.

"Have a good evening." I disconnected the call.

That's all I needed to hear to know what my plans for later tonight would be. First, I needed to put my fiancée to bed before going out to extract information.

As I began toward the house, it dawned on me that Bilan's courage soared infinitely when stealing my thunder with the announcement. The woman had a sharp jealousy streak I needed to finally acknowledge and better manage.

It could flare at the wrong time.

I flushed the toilet and moved to the fancy vanity in the bathroom, turning on the faucets to wash my hands. As I paid myself close inspection in the mirror, I could see my eyeliner running a bit. I was tired. Nothing more would satisfy me than to snap my fingers and be showered and in the bed with Sadik. I decided on my way in here to have a slice of pie packaged to go before leaving tonight.

I dried my hands, then adjusted my clothes. This dress was casual cute, but could be formal chic without the denim jacket. I wore it to camouflage the swelling of my midsection. The timing had truly been perfect. I'd been growing by the day, it seemed, in the waist. My belly was still but a pouch, yet at a size only pregnancy could explain in relation to my body build. The high heeled *red bottoms* helped façade my secret as well. Man, did it feel good not having to hide my truth anymore. Now, everyone most crucial to the knowledge of this pregnancy knew. That was a huge weight off.

A deep sigh left my lungs as I flipped off the lights to the bathroom and opened the door. Just as I turned in the hall to begin the trek through this mammoth place, a leggy figure leaning against a column across the gallery startled me. I jumped in the air, grabbing my beating chest.

"There are better ways to get my attention than to wait on me in the hallway," I panted out.

This felt like déjà vu.

Panic loomed over me, threatening. But immediately, I decided to reject it. I had to start somewhere. Iban had decided poking season would continue so soon. I had to fight back.

His leer was carved out by Lucifer himself, convincingly evil.

"I ain't think bitches like you get scared."

"I'm human." How else would I respond to that?

"A hoe?"

"Excuse me?"

He pushed off the column and paced toward me, shrinking me by an inch with each step. His tongue wet his lips, eyes narrowed in seduction.

"I know what you like. Know what you need, too," he informed.

I swallowed hard, then cocked a brow. "I could use a laugh. Haven't had one since you and your father killed my brother."

"That's the thing." His index finger stabbed the air repetitively as he chuckled. It was still shocking—baffling—how these Ellis men could look so debonair while terrorizing people. Iban's navy blue suit fit his frame perfectly; the jacket's sleeves pushed up his arms. The V-neck white t-shirt exposed the top of a tattoo at his carved chest. His light brown irises were lit wickedly, his orange hair low and tapered with precision. "I'mma give you more options than he had." He stopped inches away. "I can get you a bag to get the fuck lost forever. Or I can put you in a box and lay you next to ya whole family in the ground." He gave a dramatic pause that worked.

He just threatened to kill me and, for the first time in my life, I was being threatened by a known murderer. He'd killed before.

He kills!

Life wasn't viewed in high regard to people like him. Iban knew violence, not compromise.

I switched postures, engaging in the best acting of my life. The muscles on one side of my face lifted. "Cut it out. No harm will come to me without your brother's consent, and you know it."

He snorted. "Why you think? 'Cause you pregnant?"

"Even if I wasn't carrying his baby, you'd never lay a hand on me. And you know why, Iban. It's because your brother for real, for real loves me. You know just like the rest of your family, Sadik has never been into a woman like he is with me." *God, let that be true...* It's what I'd gathered from my first visit here to *Elliswoods Palace*. "The baby only furthers my security. You need to get over whatever issues you have with me. I've accepted the sick, villainous ways of your complicated family. Surely, you can figure out a way to get along with my simple ass. No one else is holding back on rolling out the welcome carpet but you." I gritted my teeth, feeling a surge of anger out of nowhere. "If I can sleep with a man every night whose family killed mine, you can figure out how to stop trying to intimidate me!"

Iban laughed, unaffected. "You wanna kitty."

My face folded. "A what?"

He scoffed. "A kitty. It's what we call it in the pen. When a new inmate come in, he ain't got no commissary. Depending on the day of the week, he may not have no good shit to eat for days. So the set he rep put together what we call a kitty. Food, snacks, deodorant, tooth-paste, drinks...shit like that." He nodded. "Guess you could call it a welcome package to help him start his bid. That's what you looking for from me." A nasty guffaw pushed from his belly, it seemed.

Iban expressed his guileful humor in my face. "Sorry, young bird. I was that nigga that plotted on a nigga's exit, not his coming. I'm the enforcer, remember?" His face morphed into an ugly glare in less than a second. "When it comes down to the Ellis name, I'm murkin' niggas to keep the legacy." Those were the same words he used during my "orientation" here the first night I stayed over.

"Why do you think the legacy's in danger, Iban?" I lowered my chin. "Because you know he wants to marry me?" I nodded. "He does. I just don't get what that has to do with you. Why do I pose a threat to you? And now, I'm carrying his baby, and you threaten me? It's your nephew, Iban. *Your* flesh and blood. *Your* legacy—"

"That shit ain't my fuckin' legacy!" he bit out.

His adamancy dazed me. The Ellises believed in family, from what I'd been told and had seen. They were an insulated unit, believing to be exclusive and above the rest. The Ellises were aristo-cratic and had convinced me of it.

"My child won't be Earl's legacy?"

"Nah." He shook his head. "Hell no."

"But Lia's baby is?"

My chin lifted at the same pace as Iban's eyes. They darkened to a new hue of evil.

"Bitch, don't speak about my kids. You 'on't know shit about me or my kid's mother, my wife, *or* my brother, if you wanna keep it a buck. You just new pussy to Deek. That's it. You ain't built to be in this family. You think I 'on't see who you is, staying around knowing what we did to ya peoples? You wanna get some information to go to the law with? Huhn?" He entered my personal space. "Ain't shit you can tell them that'll hurt my family. Deek nose may be wide ass open, but the man know what to keep close to the chest. Fuck what you think. He a Ellis soldier. Don't let his dick game make you forget that shit."

"He's an Ellis soldier," I echoed, blood rushing in my ears.

"You damn right!"

"The regulator in this family."

"You better fuckin' know it," he gritted.

I swallowed, turning away from him to leave. "Then you should know I've got the power."

I watched recognition wash over Iban. "What the fuck you just say?"

I began to walk backwards as I nodded. "Yup. I have his heart and his baby. *I've* got the power, big brother." My words were delivered with confidence, and the wink I implemented was the icing on the cake.

Iban started toward me. In a panic, I picked up the pace. *God, I'd crossed the line...* Before turning to run, I noticed Iban's eyes flash, and his stride suspend. Then I slammed into fleshy steel, startling me again. Stars lit behind my lids and when I was able to open my eyes, I saw a glaring Sadik. Orange irises shooting between Iban and me.

His frame was hot and hard, and the chords in his neck protruded.

The lion contemplated the jaguar.

"Let's go," I whispered, pleading with him. Sadik didn't respond. He remained immobile as I glanced back to his older brother frozen, too. Only Iban's expression was somewhat of guilt. "Baby," I rubbed his arm. "I'm tired. Let's go home." After a parting gaze at Iban, I shifted past Sadik, pulling him down the hall to leave.

"Alright now," my father waved us off, his convivial smile still in place.

My mother, beneath his arm, squealed. "I'll try to give you some time before I start calling about the nurseries and pregnancy photoshoots. We need to do at least two for his keepsakes." She covered her mouth to stop speaking and handed me a paper bag I knew was packed with food.

If I wasn't so fucking heated, I would have laughed the way Bilan did, standing in the door jamb of the entrance of *Elliswoods Palace*. She was ready to go, and I was torn about whether it was best to get her out of here or beat the shit out of Iban for addressing her without my permission again.

But we'd given out our goodbye hugs. Bilan was stiff in my father's arms. The sight itself seemed unnatural. Even my mother wore an expression of unease, now knowing our men killed Abshir. However, if Earl wanted to express warmth to my lady, he damn sure had every right. So, I allowed it. Taaliba, Monica, and the girls gave their hugs and left the foyer for various reasons. Iban never showed, and Tiffany left nearly thirty minutes ago.

My hand was clasped with Bilan's as she stood halfway out the door. Again, I could tell she was ready to go.

"Sadik," my father's paternal boom burst into the air. His chin lifted. "Call me once you're ahhh...settled in."

I nodded, knowing what that meant. He sensed the tension between us and wanted to know what had disturbed the announcement of his first grandson.

"Thanks for dinner, Queen," were my last words before I allowed Bilan to lead me out of the door.

We trekked down the stairs at an unhurried pace to accommodate her high heels.

"You sure he didn't get out of pocket?"

"Sadik," she groaned. "I said he was fine." Bilan didn't break her stride.

Johnson was working because Rory had the day off. He waited at the bottom of the steps with the door to the car open. He greeted Bilan when she reached him. I waited for her to slip inside, then closed the door and crawled in on the other side of the car. She curled herself against the opposite door, resting her chin on her fist as she peered through the window. The roads grew dark once we exited the gates of the compound.

I automatically took to my phones to answer mounting texts and inboxes. The trial for wrongful termination in Rachel's lawsuit had been given a date. My legal team assured me they were prepared. I'd already adjusted to the fact that I'd been airing Rachel out in public. She pushed for this.

As I read through a venture proposal, her hand reached over and pulled my arm over the middle console. I adjusted by sliding closer to the center and continued scrolling through my device, observing columns for comparison.

"Sadik," I heard in a whisper.

Music was flowing, an organ and drum lead by a cat named Sonder. The numbers weren't adding up, which annoyed the fuck out of me. It meant my team didn't suitably investigate the company requesting capital. Why have a screening process if my staff wasn't properly vetting?

"Sa—" My arm was being pulled even more, the tips of my fingers were on the smooth skin of her thigh. "Deek." Simultaneously, my fingers brushed against hairs.

Hot hairs. Moist hairs.

Fuck...

Gelled flesh that could only be one thing.

My neck snapped, head swinging in her direction. Her jacket had been removed and, at some point, she'd slid over to the center seat on the bench. Bilan's head was pushed back into the headrest. Her body slumped, legs wide, presenting her pelvis to the air. Her eyes were imploring me, lips ajar. She was pushing my hand into her pussy, using only the discretion of the whisper of my name.

Shit...

She was aroused. It took no time for the revelation to arrive. Iban had fucked with her. She'd lied.

He fucked up...

But we were in my car and not a limo equipped with a partition. Bilan moved my hand from between her legs. I could see the smoldering of her eyes as she crawled over the center console and onto my lap. Her breath uneven, though she made the task appear effortless. Her hand reached the waist of my jeans for my belt, busying without requests. I tossed the phone and tapped to mute the music.

"Johnson, pull over now." Bilan mounted me, the heat from her pussy already swelling me. "And get the fuck out!"

Her puffy lips pouted, and soft breaths pushed from her nostrils. They twitched on occasion. I never knew that. The balls of her eyes stopped moving ten minutes ago. Bilan was deep into rest now. I lay in our bed watching her, absorbing her.

It had a face.

I'd seen it a lot growing up. My brother was the most intimate case, but I'd seen it from other than him. My partner, Matt, in the cannabis industry needed medication to help him balance it. But I never thought it'd be in my home, in my bed, clawed to my heart like...this.

A purr spilled from her throat; she tensed, then relaxed. It made me wonder if deep in the recesses of her sleep, she was still in fight mode.

Damn, she was a fighter.

The ride home was done in silence. I imagined nearly forty-five minutes of car fucking off a dark, low traffic roadway would do that. She trailed behind me into the apartment building with her head down, almost lifelessly. I imagined that was simply the walk of shame. She'd get over it after a shower and possibly some sort of sustenance, seeing she had little at Elliswoods Palace.

That was until she pushed past me when I opened the door. I watched her pace quickly down the hall, toward the bedroom. I stood in the foyer, poring over mail Kimmy set aside this week. Within the span of two minutes, she returned in workout gear and sneakers.

"Let's hit the gym." Her vocals were coarse.

I stood stunned, eyes blinking.

"What kind of workout did you have in mind?" It was minutes to midnight.

She tossed her chin. "A little sparring."

My eyes rolled down to her exposed paunch. Once again, I found myself blinking. My plans for the remainder of the night included showering and curling around her soft curves until she fell asleep. Then I'd slip out to handle business. I'd, at least, wash her dried essence from my face before leaving. But I was faced with a dilemma and very few options. I had to stay ahead of Bilan or lose my predominant position in this troth. She needed leadership, not adversity.

Bilan taking off for the stairs to the gym forced my hand.

She moaned, rolling from her back onto her side. I still had a view of her against the moonlight shining through the broad windows. It was the most exquisite nimbus of fortune I'd ever seen, other than those moments when I was inside of her, drilling while she was exploding onto me.

"Move faster!" Bilan demanded, returning two hard blows to the pads on my palms.

I shifted, and she followed. I called a different punch combo, lifting my hands. Bilan met them before I could complete the sentence.

"Faster, Sadik!" she barked, sweat dripping from her temples. "You're not going to hurt me or your 'precious' baby!" the line delivered with palpable derision.

She smelled my fear. The pits of my arms spiked with perspiration. I fought for placidity as I ordered a different jab combo.

"Jab, cross, left hook!"

Again, Bilan grunted, finishing the sequence before I finished.

"Arg!" she growled.

Then came a succession of punches I didn't request. My instincts kicked into gear and I threw up blocks against her blows. Bilan had, that quickly, snapped into a rage; grunting, swinging, rushing toward me...on full attack. What she landed was on my arms from my blocks. The rest were in the air. I could have completely ducked from her barrage of punches, but doing that would put her at risk of falling to the floor.

"Bilan!" I shouted. "Bilan, calm the fuck down."

As though my command fell on deaf ears, her sequential strikes continued wild and recklessly, so forceful and unskilled, one of the gloves fell off.

"Bilan!"

She finally let up. Face glossed of sweat, chest rising and falling manically. She pulled the other glove off, then lunged toward me again. This time, she went for the waist of my pants. I froze when she went for my belt. My mind cranked again at the sound of my zipper. I jerked back from her reach.

"The hell are you doing?"

Her head rolled up, a cunning smile stretched her face. "About to blow your mind and cock." She pounced on me again.

I was stunned by the change in her timbral cadence, my reaction was slow again. Bilan had my pants and boxers down with my dick in her mouth before I could stop her without possibly hurting her. Her movements were coarse, rough. This didn't feel right. She wasn't right.

She wasn't Bilan.

My hands stretched, suspended in the air while she bobbed on my dick. There was no passion, no pleasure or seduction to it. I felt nothing, bordering on disgust.

Bilan pulled back and peered up to me. "You don't get hard for me, Sadik?"

"Baby—"

"You claim to want to be everything to me," she bit out.

That dig wounded me. I searched her eyes, trying to find a smidgen of recognition in them. This wasn't the woman I knew; at least not a facet of her I was familiar with.

Then she started again. I tried. I swear, I tried standing in the middle of the gym of my duplex with the object of my desires, to find a reason to get aroused. It had never been work in the past. I could smell the ghost of Bilan and my dick would spasm in my pants. And here she was, jerking me with impatience, and I couldn't get hard. Desperate to end this, I forced my mind to other women...images and unfulfilled fantasies I had in store for her, all desperate to meet her demand. My eyes squeezed, scalp secreted.

Then she stopped. "You say you're in love with me...my friend. Claim to be my protector and lover." She spat. "What lover doesn't get hard when their dick's in the mouth of their love interest?"

My eyes snapped open, head dropped to capture her. If I didn't know better, I'd think she was intoxicated. Her eyes were low, pupils dilated, and breath leaving her erratically.

Anger struck my belly. She was manipulating me with sex again, challenging me with my own pledges to her. Those were my words. My oath to her. I remembered the emotion attached to each of them. The utterance of my commitment.

Within seconds, my erection blossomed in her hands. My unrepentant duty to her as her friend, lover, and protector. That comprehensive devotion had to be when she was at her best or her lowest. It had to extend from health to...illness.

Bilan's mouth moved over me, tongue lashed against me, hands massaged me. And behind my lids were images of her love for me. My sole goal in life at this point. She said she was sick for wanting to be by my side after learning of the complications in my world.

What did that make me when I climaxed in her mouth, knees shaking around her arms?

"Mmmmmm..." she breathed with contentment.

Satisfaction.

She was safe.

We showered off the fears and confusion after leaving the gym, ate the leftovers my mother had the forethought to pack, and sipped Taaliba's nighttime tea in between bites. I disrobed her at the bed, watched her crawl onto the mattress gloriously bare.

And now I watched her rest, identifying the face of...*it.*

∞20∞

"*Account-a-what?*" Tasche trilled.

I groaned, stretching my arms above my head and extending my pelvis as my much as comfortability would allow. "Senior Account-ability Coordinator," I corrected.

"The fuck is that, yo?" pushed from her belly as she lay reclined in the cushioned leather seat while having her toes painted.

We all were. I'd invited the girls out to the spa today. A morning of massages, facials, manicures, and pedicures was just what the doctor ordered. It was suggested by Sadik a few days ago when I sulked about not having hung out with Tasche and Randi since Ricky's party two months ago. After a series of texts between Tasche and me and Randi and me over the past month and a half, it was decided we were overdue for face-time. I'm sure neither woman objected to the other being here, but what they had in mind was probably one-on-ones. That would have been a hefty feat, considering my new schedule. Between Sadik, school, and work—Sadik being in the lead because he'd kept me underneath him a lot since the shooting at *Pulse*—I had little down time.

That had to stop. I wouldn't be one of those women in a relationship, who lost themselves. I mean, I'd watched the man shave his head almost every morning, we'd been that attached at the hip. Sadik had been beyond life, but could vanish just as my parents and brother did. I realized after the shooting I had to be smart about my attachment to him. It had been hard, though. He had seemed to become more sensitive to my next need. Sadik contemplated them. Just like today. When I began rambling about the need to catch up with the girls, he had Rory make an appointment here at Imani's full service spa. She was the masseuse Sadik commissioned to the hospital for my scalp massage. It was a sweet gesture.

"It's basically quality control," I explained to Tasche. "My role is to make sure all schools in the *Ellis Academy* community throughout the state are meeting, not only the state requirements for funding, but those set by the CEO."

"That's Sadik's mother," Randi added.

"Yes. Irene may not participate in day to day practices, but she does set the annual goals

"And you been doing this for two months now?" Tasche asked.

I nodded, then answered, knowing she couldn't see me. "Yeah. It's actually been fun. More than I thought I'd find in my first job in my field."

That's how nepotism works...

But I was tired, and particularly today because Sadik increased the workout sessions we'd been doing in his gym since we were going away this week. It didn't help I was in my twenty-fifth week of pregnancy. My little pouch had transformed into a stiff, vertical watermelon behind my belly button. I had an OB appointment later today after work, and couldn't wait to hear an update about this phase of the pregnancy. I scheduled to work a half day today because the morning was a convenient time for Tasche to do the spa, considering her work hours. She made it clear several times: once she left here, she'd be heading straight to bed.

"That's what's up," Tasche hummed, sounding relaxed. "Proud of you, yo."

"Thanks, Tasche." I smiled, stretching out in my own chair. My toes were done and now drying. "I'm just sorry we don't have more time than this together. Between you just getting off work and me having to be there myself soon, I'm lucky to have this with you guys."

It was the truth. In two days, I'd be boarding the Ellis family jet to Antigua for Thanksgiving. I didn't know how I felt about that. Sadik and I resumed our weekly meals at *Elliswoods Palace* since announcing my pregnancy, and surprisingly, there had been no drama. Ironically, there had also been no Iban. We only attended once a week, as opposed to twice like we did before I left for *Macen Beach*. Each visit, I braced myself to see my arch nemesis, and like an act of God, Iban had been absent. Irene hosted dinner for her family at least twice a week. I'd gotten the impression he was there on other days for dinner. Maybe he was still upset by the salt I'd thrown on his wound left by making the point of his brother's affection for me. Either way, I hadn't missed him at all.

"Yeah... Yeah... Yeah," Randi pretended to be dismissive. "All I need to know is if you brought the damn corset."

"Yes, Randi," I sighed. "It's in the locker." She'd been asking to borrow my purple leather corset since Ricky's party. It was odd having her ask me for clothes. Since I'd known Randi, I'd asked to wear her gear. Her style was fierce. It was my pleasure loaning something to her. "God knows I won't be able to wear it for a while." I snickered to myself.

"Oh," Randi chirped. "Then I need to text yo ass a list, I see." That had me cracking up. "Your shoes, too."

I shook my head. "Not those." Sadik wouldn't have it. "I still wear heels...every day," I made clear.

Sadik liked me in them. He had me pose nude in just *Ase Garb* and *Giuseppe* five-inch stilettos several times, journaling my pregnancy. The last time was last Sunday after church.

And that...

It was my second time going with the Ellises to their place of worship. Apparently, they were devout members of a rather large church. We all sat on the same row, with the exception of Iban and Taaliba. She'd been in India. It was...interesting both times. The pastor was older, a screamer delivering the message. I tried keeping up with him, but was distracted by my comparisons to my experience in the mosque, and the *RSfALC* streaming services I still watched whenever I got a moment to myself. Sometimes, I watched while Rory drove me around.

The Ellises were a Christian family. It was still a concept I was chewing on. A clear paradox, many would agree with. It was something I was hoping to see in action during this trip.

"So, what are you guys' plans for the holiday?" I asked, still not believing Thanksgiving was here already.

It felt like just two weeks ago, I was still waking up to the calming cries of the ocean each morning.

Tasche yawned out loud. "I 'on't know, yo. I may work. This shortie there want the night off. But Lex want me to pull up."

That name drop made my eyes burst wide.

"That sounds nice," I tried sounding encouraging.

"I guess. They just be having mad people over, and shit."

"Like who?" I was curious.

I would be spending the holiday with a murderous family. I wondered were Lex's in-laws peculiar.

"I 'on't know." She hummed. "Last year, Trent Bailey from the *Kings* was there with his family. Yo, that nigga fine as fuck," she chuckled to herself.

"Ain't he?" Randi all but shouted. "That muthafucka can get it, with his convict ass."

Tasche laughed. "I wanted to ask the nigga to bust one move for me. But his wife be on it, yo. Her eyes stay around his ass." She continued to laugh. "That was cool, though. Lex and Ez go to TB's charity dinner he do every year for the homeless, and shit. Lex said this year, StentRo and his family 'posed to be there."

Randi sat up. "Then, bitch, what time we pulling the fuck up?"

Tasche scoffed. "You crazy as hell, yo," she murmured. "Ricky ain't say shit about who shot up his party? That shit was crazy, yo. That club owner better be lucky only one muthafucka died."

"It was one of the shooters, too," Randi shared what had been reported on the news. "You know Ricky don't talk about shit to me. I was arguing with his ass one minute. The next, he was telling one of his boys to get me outta there. Instead of his ass getting me out, he had to go back for muthafuckas."

"His family was over from Haiti, Randi," Tasche reminded her. "What you expect him to do? Leave them niggas to fend for they selves? That woulda been some goofy shit. Straight up, yo."

"Man, fuck them," Randi hissed.

"I'm just glad you left when you did," I tried spinning the story positively.

"Yeah, man," Tasche agreed. "Lex was like, 'everything happen for a reason.' She think God spared me, or some shit. I'm just glad my ass was on my way home. I coulda been on the dancefloor, fuckin' shit up."

I tried not to think about that night. It brought anxiety that could be messy in public. Instead, I tried to focus my thoughts on work. Irene gave me a hefty role in her organization. I was responsible for all the schools in the state. There were fifteen in total, and more underway. I learned quickly about the rivalry between public and charter schools. The underlying and driving factor was funding from the respective school districts and, sometimes, the state. *Ellis Academy* had to be more than compliant for survival. It had to be excellent.

The academy's school accountability was set by the state's statute and the state department of education's regulations. As the coordinator for the entire academy, I was responsible for all aspects of compliance, besides funding reporting. That was someone else's role. My job was to be sure all testing, curriculum, documentation review, classroom observations, and any other requirements set by the various funding and regulating offices as well as the academy's were being met. This took the assistance of a staff, which meant I had several people reporting to me. I didn't approve time off, but was responsible for their performance because it meant the welfare of the *Ellis Academy* community. It certainly came with its share of responsibility. That fact hadn't escaped me since being hired.

"Tasche, I want to check out *Redeeming Souls*. Wanna go with me?"

"Ah, shit!" Tasche carped. "Why the fuck you wanna put my ass through that shit again?"

I laughed. "What shit?"

"Being in church with that nigga, Ezra? The shit's too fuckin' heavy for a bitch, yo!"

"And ain't you Muslim?" Randi asked, knowing the answer. Her eyes questioned me just as directly as her words. "Don't tell me Sadik and his saddity ass family go to church, and now yo ass wanna switch religions."

Tasche hooted. "Them muthafuckas can't be religious. Unless they worship fuckin'...gang bangin', and shit!" She couldn't help her humor.

It was funnier than she knew.

You don't know the half, T...

A salad, fries...crème brûlée from DiFillippo's...
Oooh! Do I have time for that?

"Enjoy your lunch," one of the academy's office administrators bade me in passing as I was leaving for lunch.

"Thanks!" I smiled in return. "Hope yours was good."

"It was. Thanks!"

I continued out the door, still undecided on what I'd eat. Though the baby had been growing and developing on schedule, Dr. Clifford wasn't impressed by my lack of weight gain. Never did I think being a double-digit sized woman would be considered too small. I promised the doctor and Sadik I'd put more effort into increasing my food intake. Rory had been waiting on my meeting to end. When she texted to ask how much longer, she mentioned being hungry, too.

Maybe I'd let her pick where—

I stopped down the pathway toward the parking lot. Next to Rory's miniature fixture in a suit was an uncanny senior version of my lover.

When Earl removed his hat, placing it to his chest, the sun illuminated his eyes, making them translucent. My breathing picked up and mouth dried.

"I come to you in nothing but peace, Bilan," Earl claimed.

That statement was almost believable by way of his debonair appearance. It was clearly a trait he'd passed on to his sons. Earl's tan suit fit his slim frame unfairly well for his age. The white dress shirt beneath his suit jacket was tieless and left the first few buttons undone. Down to his shoes, the older man exuded swag.

But I was at work. In a nondescript building in Boonton, New Jersey. *Boonton!* I'd never been in this township before this job. Sadik told me it was him who suggested a location for his mother's administrative headquarters, which was away from the inner-cities she serviced for safety reasons. It also so happened to be in the next county, north of the one where she lived. And I learned over the summer, the Ellises' command post was in the middle of nowhere.

Seeing a man—who threatened me virtually the first time we met —waiting on me wasn't the most pleasant feeling. Especially when Rory wore an expression of apology. Seeing two staff members coming up the walkway snapped me into action. I continued toward him.

"Hi, Bilan," Earl greeted. "I know it's your lunch break. I was hoping to take you for something to eat. Maybe we can hit the restart button."

I was stunned. Was he serious?

I blinked away my daze, shaking my head. "You wait until a workday to approach me? I'm at your house, at least, once a week?"

"And you've been distant. Plus, it seem like Sadik's arm is too much of a hiding space for you. I wanna see you. The real woman my son done fell crazy for."

He was serious. My eyes flew to Rory. Her expression of regret hadn't changed.

"Rory can follow us. It's a small restaurant just two blocks up the way." He pointed.

My eyes flicked to her again. She took a deep breath, switching weight on her short legs. Rory appeared uncomfortable.

"She's an employee. You a future Ellis. A shot-caller." Earl's tone was pertinacious.

"I'll be right behind you, B." Rory must have heard his uncompromised request.

A sigh of fearful resignation emptied from my lungs.

"Harming you puts my legacy at risk, honey." His honeyed eyes fell to my midsection. "Don't get it twisted: right now, that lil' life growing inside of you is the most precious thing to me. The last thing I need you to be worried about is me harming mine."

A perceptive Earl moved from the doorway of his *Mercedes*, inviting me inside.

Earl made good on his word. Fifteen minutes later, we were a couple of blocks away from the *Ellis Academy* corporate building and inside a modest-sized, quaint restaurant. He didn't, however, mention he closed it out for a private lunch. The dining area could fit no more than maybe fifteen people. The tables were situated along the walls, loaded with different foods. Salads, sandwiches, soups, meat dishes, and pasta from what I could see. Rory and Earl's two security were up at the buffet tables, fixing themselves food.

The senior Ellis and I sat at the sole table in the center of the small room. After getting a lay of the land, I straightened in my seat to finally brave facing Earl.

He smiled, teeth wondrously white and aligned. "You're not going to eat, are you?"

My head shook softly. "You'll understand if I tell you I no longer have an appetite."

"You don't trust me," he observed out loud. I didn't respond. Earl chuckled, revealing charming features I never noticed. He was...rather handsome. *Handsome, handsome.* Oh, god! The man smelled good, too. "I need you to trust me, sweetheart."

"I'm the flower bush in your gorgeous garden that doesn't fit in," I reminded him. "I'm the one pushed onto you. The one ruining the motif of your property." It was the metaphor he used out on the veranda that morning Iban kicked off the tag team bullying session.

A sheepish expression opened on his face, yet in a cool "Earl Ellis" manner. "That was another time. Things was different back then, young lady."

My regard shifted to Rory taking a seat at a table near an adjacent wall.

"It's when I complicated your revenge." I peered him directly in the eyes again, trying not to be blinded by the remarkable similarities in his and Sadik's features. "You sent your goons to kill my brother."

Earl nodded. "He stole from me. Took a couple of my men out. He had to answer for it with his life. I will not apologize for that." He rearranged the napkin on the table. "And what I did wasn't revenge. Ya brother wasn't on my level. What I did was made him an example to any other kid thinking they could take food from my family's mouth."

"A few kilos of coke didn't exactly bring famine to your estate."

His chuckle was affable. Too casual. "No. But being robbed without responding invites other predators, honey. They'll think it's open season on my organization. In my line of work, I gotta be the biggest predator on the block. Can't be kind. Can't be reasonable. I gotta dominate." He shrugged, tossing his head over his shoulder. "It's the only way I know. The way I teach."

Iban.

Sadik...

"And me? You sent them to kill me, too," I murmured, hands trembling over the table. Earl saw it.

"You was a casualty, yes."

"And what am I now? Neutralized?"

His warm hand covered both of mine. Earl lowered his head to meet my eyes. He croaked, "You're the center of my garden now."

My heart fell from my chest. This couldn't be real. "How can I believe that?"

He sat back, smiling. "How's the baby coming along?"

My eyes glanced down to my lap before I could catch myself. Before I could understand he was changing the subject.

I wet my lips. "Healthy," I sighed, sitting back myself. "He's just over a pound and a half...the size of an eggplant."

I watched him dig into the inside of his suit jacket, pulling out a phone. "You skipped over the good part."

"What's that?"

He held the face of the phone over the small table for me to see. "His features. The doctors say he got my wife's blond hair."

I swallowed hard, recognizing my latest ultrasound images. When the face blackened, I surmised that image was Earl's wallpaper. Sadik must have shared them.

"And the fact of him having a close resemblance to you." My eyes fell away.

He did. My son's nose was carved as Earl's before me was. His mouth structure was the same. I'd been noticing it as his features began to form more distinctively. Sadik and I hadn't spoken much about it, but I'd observed it. So far, my son resembled his father. His father shared his grandfather's features. I read babies' features continually changed well into their teenaged years. But right now, not even a blood test could refute what could be seen, thanks to the latest technology.

"That ain't so bad. Is it?" Earl regained my attention.

I shook my head. "Him having someone's features only means he belongs. Belonging goes a long way with me."

"Then why the long face? You look sad," he observed.

I considered that for a moment before my eyes narrowed. "Because I don't know you. I have an idea of what you do for a living. I know your pride's heavily in your family. Other than that, I fear the expectation of my child will be..." My eyes jumped around for listening parties. "...to do what your sons have been trained to do."

Earl nodded his understanding. He then took a swig of water before planting his elbows on the table, nearing me intimately.

"I grew up all over the city of Paterson. My mother lived in Warren County, North Carolina...born and raised. She made it up to eighth grade before she set out to work for a living. Her daddy died... heavy drinker. Her mother, from all memory of her, was a simple woman in the head. She had eighteen children, and that may have helped," he quipped, shrugging. "My mother did odd jobs down there until she saved up enough money to catch a bus here to New Jersey. It's where all her peoples was coming to make a living.

"That was a smart move. What was dumb was getting pregnant with me the first couple of months she was here. My pops was a different story. He was a numbers hustler. His money came fast and quick. It left even faster. Faster than that was his lifestyle. High risk nigga...all heart, no brains. He had his throat sliced when I was eight years old. I came home and found him like that."

My entire frame tensed.

"So my mother lost a lot of her income after that. She ain't have no real education, so she enrolled in school and took shitty jobs where she could find them. We ain't have a place to call ours and lived with people she knew from the south. Shitty ass, shady ass muthafuckas she ran into on the welfare line. We lived in places roaches had more rights than we did. Our food' got stolen while I was at school and she was out looking for work or working. If we slept too hard at night, our clothes got taken. Couple of times, my mother was attacked. One nigga tried to rape her on a floor mattress, right next to me. I was eleven and almost got my ass killed tryna help her fight. But this was the game for us with no daddy and no money.

"Our luck changed when I was maybe fifteen. I ran into a couple of my father's old roadies in the streets. They was still up to the same shit, running numbers for this Italian, Fat Tony. None of them niggas was rich, but they looked clean. One even had this smoking 1962 *Cadillac Seville*!" Earl whistled, lost in beautiful nostalgia.

"Whew! It was pretty as hell. He told me he heard how my mom had been struggling since my pops passed. Even heard how I ain't give her no trouble...I was handling my studies. So, he gave me a job driving for him as he made his rounds, doing his numbers." He laughed. It was a little infectious. "All I wanted to do was drive that *Caddy*! So, I agreed. He taught me how to drive, and from there, I drove him around after school, well into the night. That's how I learned the game.

"Fat Tony started seeing my face. About a year into it, he started to address me directly. One of his runners got killed, caught up. He needed a replacement and asked for me. I ran for him the rest of high school. Then I worked my way up to collecting from all his runners. *Then* in the seventies, Fat Tony broke away from his mafia rules of no drugs and started slanging cocaine."

Earl dropped back into his seat, arms falling at his side as his head rolled around on his neck. "At first it was in small doses...just to get a feel of the market. Well, it ain't take long for that nigga to find out all them rich white people wanted that and LSD. That was heavy back then, too. *Them white people went crazy for hallucinogens*. Well, the demand was so damn high, he had to shift his runners from numbers to drop offs. That's what we called slangers back then. I was one of his top money makers. So that meant more money for my momma. It meant we ate how we wanted, when we wanted. That meant nobody stealing our shit. It meant sleeping with both eyes closed.

"I made a killin'. My name was known in the streets. And not because I worked for Fat Tony, but because some niggas robbed my house one night. They tied my mother up, slapped her around, and ran through our shit. Her furs and jewelry gone. A couple of the stashes I had around the apartment gone. That shit broke my heart. To see my momma so shaken like that. It like..." Earl spent a half a minute considering it. "It woke up something in me. I had to watch them bruises on her for a couple of weeks." He cleared his throat, coughing into his palm while blinking successively.

This seemed hard for Earl.

"In the eighties, shit got real. That's when crack hit. Man, I told Tony I wanted *in*! I went up to his crib on East 38th, right there by Eastside park. Crack was so damn cheap, I could sell it to people who looked like me. Them niggas that couldn't afford expensive ass coke like that. Well, Fat Tony didn't deny me. He gave me a chance at that. I hustled morning, noon, and night. At this time, I was doubling my money. It was so much, I hired two of my buddies. I 'on't know if you know my assistant, Palmer, but him and my other dawg at the time, came aboard. He's dead now."

"I'm sorry to hear that." This time, I was blinking. "How did he pass?"

"The streets. That was Tiffany's father." My eyes fell away. "I know. I see the conflict, and I'm working on the solution."

"It's not your job." I cleared my throat, my hand going to the back of my tapered head. "Besides, there's no problem."

"Sweetheart, I'm Earl Ellis. I know money, business, and women."

I grumbled beneath my breath, hating the jealousy surging my veins. "You went to prison."

"Yes," he exhaled, sitting up.

"When did that happen in this timeline?" I successfully changed the subject to something more palpable.

"Years later. Right after my wife had our first baby. I was in the game for years before then. Some racist ass cops pulled me over one night when I was riding down from Franklin Lakes, where Fat Tony moved to by that time. They ain't like seeing a Black man riding in a *Caddy* he bought hisself. They threw me outta my ride, searched it, and found a few vials of crack on me. Something my stupid ass partner left in there."

"Who?"

"Rob. That was Tiff's father."

Oh, her...

"So, bad luck?"

Earl shrugged. "Kinda. Them pigs knew who I was. They knew why I was in that neighborhood. They set me up. The *FEDs* came in when I was in the county, tryna offer me a deal to flip on Fat Tony. I said fuck them. My public defender told me the max charges and sentences. I knew I was gonna have to wear it."

"Wear what?"

"Whatever time the judge gave me. I was no snitch. It was my first drug charge."

"Did Fat Tony worry?"

"Like a muthafucka." Earl laughed.

"He sent his guys to my court dates. I waived the right to trial and pled guilty. That shocked the shit outta his fat ass."

"Me, too!" I snorted, going for the bread and butter on the table.

Why did I find this story so fascinating?

Earl's smile was disarming. "I'm an Ellis, baby girl. We adjust to our consequences, but we don't fuckin' snitch." He shrugged. "I did two years and five months, came home and made another baby with my old lady. My ace. Sadik."

It was ridiculous how those two syllables made my belly flutter and lungs seize.

"Mmmhmmm," Earl nodded, peering me directly in the eyes, knowingly. I bit into the bread to distract me from his scrutiny. "I already know the kid is special. I prayed for that nigga. He's more than amazing. He's fuckin' me 2.0. The best of my stock."

That admission was heady.

"Sadik's an amazing human being," I murmured honestly. The crap I'd revealed to him subconsciously left me wondering what he still saw in me.

"He's the best thing I've made, young lady. And believe me; I've done some amazing shit in my day."

I smiled at his confidence. "Tell me about it."

He scoffed. "You gonna have to eat something for that. Hell, I need to eat my damn self."

And for the first time, I felt a smidgeon of safety in Earl Ellis' presence.

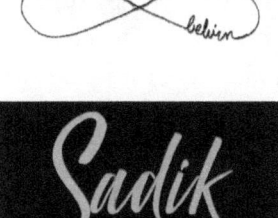

"I never thought this day would come," Abram Murphy admitted emotionally. "For years, I've committed myself to the *Port of Paterson*, knowing each day I did it, my American dream would pay off. As a man half Polish, half Irish, I stand before you a second generation American." The small room of employees, board members, his family, and local press applauded his victory speech. "And to my dock workers here at the port, I will fight to make sure conditions improve for the betterment of your work and all others here." He gave the room a neck bow. "Thank you. God bless you."

A collective clap rented the air of the small room. I took the time to check my phones. Among the number of missed texts was one from Jefferson.

Unknown: *1101 Call*

"Mr. Ellis," Abram called out as he approached me from the podium. I stowed my phones into my pockets as I waited on him. Abram was a rather short man, his head meeting my chin. "I just want to say thank you for being here today." He offered his hand for a shake. "In the wake of the port's loss, it's good to see unity. It means a lot to see the head of the *Board of Commissioners* here in support."

I gave an affirmative nod. "It's good to see the right man obtain this role. You've put in your time. Your knowledge of the port and dedication to it over the years will only prove beneficial to the community."

His palm reached to his chest. "I'll work damn hard to live up to the expectation."

"I have no doubt you will." I proffered my hand for a final shake.

We parted ways after that, my confidence high about this installment. Yeah, Murphy's promotion was bartered for services to be determined at a later time by me to his brother-in-law, Kolwaski. However, he was the ideal candidate, appropriately suited for the job. As I walked out of the building and to the waiting car, I felt good about the occasion.

When I closed the door behind me inside the car, I immediately dialed Jefferson back.

"Yeah," he answered, voice ringing out through the Bluetooth.

"Speak."

"Your name was flagged on a call to the state *FBI* office."

I ignored Jamil's questioning expression from the rearview mirror as he glided out of the port's parking lot. "Speak."

"It was a tip about your possible ties to a company called *TCU, Ltd* used to purchase a home in *Macen Beach*, South Carolina. He claimed the same company sold *Neighborhood Foods*, the grocery stores in New Jersey, to Earl Ellis in 2002."

TCU was one of my shell companies. I created it over fifteen years ago to transfer the purchase of my father's grocery store chain to him, so he could own it legally. Then I unwisely used the same shell to purchase a cape cod across the street from the home I purchased for Bilan and me. That was for my surveillance team to have a place to stakeout while she was alone down there.

I nodded, watching the traffic on the opposite side of the highway. "What's the tipper's name?"

"Jason Anderson."

That IT fucker would look into it to make the connection...

"Enjoy your day."

"Yeah."

The line disconnected.

"You shoulda killed him," Jamil murmured from the front seat.

I took a deep breath, reclining in my seat.

"Good morning, Mr. Ellis," Captain Willie greeted near the stair case of the jet parked at *Elliswoods Palace*. "Welcome aboard the *Ellis Bombardier!*"

At just after four in the morning, the sky was pitch black. The runway and aircraft lighting guided us on the tarmac. In one hand, I had my travel bag, and in the other, I held Bilan's as she hiked behind me. My mother secured him to fly us out to Antigua this morning on my father's *Bombardier 7500*.

"Morning, Captain. You need a signature?"

"No. The senior Ellis has taken care of it all," Captain Willie replied.

"I see you have the best co-captain money can buy." I greeted his son with a nod. "Good morning, Captain Baker. Father/son duos are dearest to my heart."

He tipped his hat. "Good morning, sir. I'm honored for the

opportunity. The sky seems to be fair this morning. Your flight time is three hours and about fifty-five minutes."

"I appreciate that."

"Enjoy your flight, Mr. Ellis," Captain Willie bade.

I led Bilan up the stairs where Mel and another woman from her company stood, awaiting us.

"Good morning, Mr. Ellis, she greeted with a smile you don't usually see at this odd hour. "Ms. Bilan."

"Good morning," Bilan croak from thick, morning chords.

I allowed her to walk in front of me, her head low and covered by a hood. She slowed and turned to me.

"This thing is huge. I don't know where I'm going."

Her lips were too full and promising not to kiss. I reached down and brushed mine against them.

"Sadik," she groaned, protesting. "I'll need to follow you. This thing is gargantuan!"

"You saying my jet is tiny?" I cracked a smile.

She rolled her eyes, grinning. "Men and their toys. Come on. I'm tired."

"I told you to have some tea and take it down early, but you wanted to stay up and fight instead."

We didn't stay at *Elliswoods Palace* last night, which would have been convenient because we were taking off from here.

"No. I wanted to see what all the ultra-alpha packed for me. He should have let me pack for myself. Those skimpy bathing suits aren't appropriate for a family vacation, Sadik."

I kissed her again. "You'll be fine."

"Because I managed to get my cover ups in the suitcase," she argued.

"Uncle Deek!" Iesha called out.

"Ms. Bilan!" Ivy was right behind her.

Iesha came flying toward me, sandwiching herself between Bilan and me. Ivy was more hospitable. She hugged Bilan right away.

"How's my little cousin in there?' Ivy asked in *her* baby voice while rubbing Bilan's belly.

Bilan laughed. "Dancing on my bladder. Can you show me where the bathroom is?"

"Sure," Ivana took Bilan by the hand and pulled her down the gallery. "I can show you to your cabin, too. Nana told us!"

Bilan managed to hand me her things before she went.

I glanced down at Iesha. "How's my princess? You going right to sleep after we take off?"

She shook her head. "I'm not sleepy. I'm mad."

That gave me pause. "Why, baby?"

"Because Daddy's not coming. He's gonna spend Thanksgiving with that baby." Her words were delivered devoid of emotion, just matter-of-fact.

I fell to my haunches, seeing Monica with the new baby not too far down the gallery. "Did he tell you that?"

Iesha shook her head. "No. But he's not here." She pointed toward her mother and brand new sister. "And the newer baby is here."

I pulled her in my arms. "I'm sorry, baby girl. I know there's been a lot of changes happening around you that you don't understand. But I'm your dad's brother, and I know him pretty well. I know he loves you, Ivana, Mommy, and baby Irene so much. Okay?"

She nodded, emotionless. That broke my damn heart.

I stood and grabbed our bags to continue down the jet. Iesha led the way, then sat next to her mother.

"How's my niece doing?" I asked as Monica put little socks on.

"Ugh! You missed the massive poop she laid on me—literally!" I tittered. Baby Irene looked so innocent, sleeping like a log. "You're laughing now, but your countdown has begun already, buddy." That made me laugh even more. "I'll have to shower once we're in the air!"

"Awwww..." I calmed myself to reach down for a kiss on baby Irene's soft hand. "She smells like Iesha used to as a baby." My eyes jumped to Iesha. She tried hiding her smile. "Remember that?" I asked her mother.

"Yup." Monica agreed. "You were crazy about that little girl."

I couldn't help my cheap ass grin. "I was crazy about both my girls." I winked at Iesha. Then I softly wiggled baby Irene's foot. "Just like I'm crazy over you, NeNe."

As I walked off, Monica asked, "Oh, is that the nickname we're going with?"

I laughed. "Let me try it out for a few days and see if it sticks."

As I traveled down the gallery, I spoke to a few of my mother's kitchen staff. My smaller jet could have carried the Ellis family proper; however, there were more attendees to account for. So Double E Bags had to fuel up the big dog *Global 7500*. We traveled with staff for the house, nannies for the children, and security. I typically only took Rory on trips like this, but my father brought more than one, as he had to consider protection for his entire family.

"Hey, Queen," I acknowledged my mother when she stepped into the aisle with Kema.

"Hi, baby!" She stalked my way. "I just saw Ivana take Bilan to the master bed back there. I told Monica she could have that second bed with the baby if she needed," she managed before planting a kiss on my cheek.

"That's cool. Everybody here?"

"For the most part. Taaliba's back there with Bilan. I think she got her heart broken for the first time, or something. She's been moping since coming back from West Bengal. I think she's back there talking to Bilan about it." She shook her head. "At least she's talking to somebody. To answer your question, we're just waiting on a couple of staff and security. We still have a few minutes."

"Where's the old man?"

She used her forehead to point. "You passed him. He's up in that small lounge cabin, closed in alone."

"Alone?"

"I think he felt some kind of way when you requested...family only," she hesitated when Ivana came skipping down the aisle.

After tossing my mother a wink, I followed Ivana back to the front of the aircraft to go check in on the old man.

He was sitting in a small, private cabin closed off by a sliding door. With his reading glasses on, he read the newspaper. He always looked cranky when reading, lips pointed downward. There was a small stack of them on the floor, and on the table attached to his chair was a tablet.

Earl Ellis was ready for flight. My father still read newspapers, particularly local ones. He needed to know what was being reported on his business relations: arrests, investigations, murders, etc. I told him years ago, the news business was leaving print and going digital. Even bought the tablet he uses, now that Nena has a dummy IG account for him.

"So, it's true?" I finally spoke.

He glanced up at me, eyes looked to be in a fishbowl behind the spectacles. "What?"

"You being salty. You damn sure look it with them geriatric ass glasses."

He pulled them off. "Man, fuck you." He chuckled. "Yo ass gone age, too. Them exotic colored eyes and dirty blond ass hair won't keep you from getting old, man."

I laughed. "And you would know."

"Yup. 'Cause I gave them shits to you. You gone need these to use 'em." He dangled his reading glasses in the air.

"Nah. Seriously. Thanks for making this one just about the family and not lovers. I'm not the one to encroach on your personal life, it's just that I'm trying to make this family more appealing so I can get a damn wife."

He shook his head, frowning. "No problem at all! I can dig it. I want her happy, too. We all good here."

I didn't exactly believe him. "Where're the girls?"

He sighed. "Shit... I sent Nena's ass back to Chicago. And Diane spending Thanksgiving with her stepfather's family."

"Shit." I exhaled.

"Yeah. She fuckin' heated, but..." He shrugged.

That sounded lonely as hell. I would have asked about her biological family, but never inquired about my parents' lovers.

"That's why you poutin'?"

My father sighed again, rubbing his face down with his hands. "Hell no. I'm just...I guess feeling a lil' anxious about this week-end. You know how much I done kicked out so far to get this house up out there, furniture, workers, special imports, and other shit?"

"Hit me."

"Six big ones." His eyes were wide as hell.

Six million dollars.

I scoffed, leaning into the doorway. "Boss status. You're chasing your dreams, even at your age. That's what these kids refer to as goals."

"Yeah. But the whole project ain't done."

"No?"

He shook his head, facing the blackened television panel ahead of him. "My wife wants some shit for the kids and y'all out there. That's gone take some diggin'. Once that's all said and done, it'll be another two million."

"You'll recoup it." Probably already had.

"Any update on Lopez?"

I shook my head. "Laying low before the pounce." He nodded. "Where's Iban spending the holiday?"

My father looked away, a hint of a groan leaving his chest. "Who the hell knows. I'll hit him up later today."

It was my turn to nod. "I need to go turn down Bilan. See you in four hours on the Caribbean Sea."

After a salute to him, I slid the door closed and trekked back down the gallery. When I opened the door to the bedroom, I heard the last of their conversation.

Bilan lay stretched out on her side while facing Taaliba, who was curled in the chair across from her.

"I think you should hear him out," Bilan advised. "Life's too short, and you two have been at this for too long."

"Hear who out?" I asked, carrying the bags inside.

Taaliba turned in her seat. There was a pause before she chirped. "Y'all cute in matching sweat suits with the hoodies pulled over your heads." She began to dance in her seat, snapping her fingers. "Boo goals!"

"Hear who out?" I asked again, standing over the two of them.

Bilan's expressive regard was on Taaliba.

"None of your damn business. This is girl talk. You a girl?"

"If I need to be."

"Then it still wouldn't be your business." She was partially serious. Defensive.

"Then get the hell out."

"Sadik!" Bilan was alarmed by my shit talk to my sassy ass sister.

Taaliba jumped to her feet, performed a twirl as she watched me through narrowed eyes. "I've got better places to be." She blew me an air kiss and sashayed out of the room, closing the door behind her.

I peeled off my hoodie, tossing it on the chair before sitting on the bed next to Bilan's feet.

"That was mean," she argued.

I picked up her feet, tossing off her sneakers. "That was us joking around."

"You told her to get the hell out."

"You're tired," I explained. "I'm tired."

She swallowed back a yawn. "I'm fine."

I grabbed the folded blanket at the foot of the bed, took it as I crawled up next to her, and opened it over us. Bilan unzipped her hoodie, pulling it off to lay under me. I loved the way her body curled around mine. And after all the shifting she did to find that perfect space of comfort, when Bilan sighed with contentment, I was made to believe I had some level of control in the world.

As she released herself to slumber, I thought. The sun had yet to come up when Captain Willie announced takeoff. It was still asleep when we ascended into the clouds. My brain continued to go, measuring actions against consequences, scenarios against caution.

My father met with Lopez and was given demands of taking over Rizzo's territories. This was a strange request considering how, unlike any of the other five *Commission* members, Rizzo had no primary business. He moved shit for those who had product coming in. In doing so, he'd move modest amounts of powder and pills, sell arms bartered to him in a deal, sell stolen cars, and even stashed human traffic coming into the port. He made a great living from controlling the traffic as the superintendent of the port. But he had no prime real estate as my father, Lopez, and Damien did.

Unless, he knew something my father didn't. Perhaps Lopez had a plan of merging with someone in *The Commission*. I couldn't see who that would be, considering the cultural prides and divides. The Italians would never replace Rizzo with a Dominican.

One thing was for sure: Lopez wasn't the person cooperating with the *FEDs*. He'd been too busy trying to take out the largest army in the state.

Bilan's vibrating phone snapped me out of my thoughts. My eyes blinked from peering out of the window. I rubbed my tight face, feeling sleep creeping up on me. I reached inside the pockets of her sweats to silence it. Before my finger found the sleep button, his name lit on the screen raised my fucking hackles.

Jason: *have you left yet? i wanna know what type of jet they have. i bet it's a BBJ or maybe a larger airliner. i'm dying to see. take a few pix for me.*

It vibrated in my hand.

Jason: *and don't go getting private on me again!*

And then a third new message pinged.

Jason: *and your belly. i need to see it. can't imagine you preggo. you said you were big. let me see!*

I felt lightheaded suddenly. My eyes closed to help with the spinning. Deep breaths managed the fucking nausea.

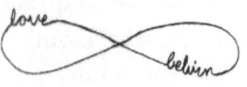

"You're doing so good in the water, NeNe," I cooed, wiggling her little legs in the clear turquoise water. I could see straight to the sugary white sanded ocean floor. Just too beautiful not to bring her in with me. The water reached just above my ankles as I squatted low. "Isn't the sand soft?"

"Say 'cheese,' baby girl!" Monica coaxed, circling around us in the water, snapping pictures with her phone.

"Mommy!" Ivy shouted from the shore. "Look at my sandcastle!"

I couldn't look, needing to keep my attention focused on little Irene. I wouldn't keep her out here too long. She had awakened from another nap and was fed and changed. Before she dozed back off, I wanted to bring her out. Monica gave me her blessing and I went for it.

Monica got her pictures, and I decided it was time to take her back in.

"Shit! That ass was the best view from here!" Taaliba whistled.

"Taaliba!" Monica admonished her. "The girls!"

Taaliba flashed her teeth in shame. "My bad! Y'all ain't hear that," she told the girls, who were good at ignoring profane language.

Sadik's baby sister was on her fifth drink at two in the afternoon. Last night after Thanksgiving dinner, she excused herself for a call. On my trip to the bathroom, I heard her arguing with Danny. She told me two days ago, on the plane before we left New Jersey, how some girl posted pictures in his arms at a bar on *Instagram*. That didn't bode too well with her. He'd been trying to apologize, and Taaliba had shut him down at every turn. Although she hadn't mentioned speaking to him today, I could see she was medicating her hurt feelings with alcohol. It started with mimosas at breakfast.

"Takes one to know one, Taali," I returned her gesture of flattery.

It was the truth. Taaliba had the body of an athlete. Like her brother, she was fit. Earl's body was impressive for his age, too. I couldn't believe we celebrated his seventieth birthday earlier this month. Admittedly, I could see Irene's draw to him. It couldn't have been much different than mine to their son. Earl still had the drip. He was flirtatious with his wife and romantic. After dinner last night, to thank her for putting together the family's Thanksgiving meal in the new Ellis home, he presented her with a diamond necklace in a silver salver with a dome. Irene was completely surprised as we cheered them on. I was becoming convinced of his unique commitment to her.

I handed baby Irene over to Monica. Appreciative of the view, I strode back into the water, gazing at the scenery. Thanksgiving with the Ellises was an experience. This family's incongruity knew no bounds. In every sense, it was a traditional meal. A massive table topped with countless serving dishes filled with all types of foods, authentic china to eat from, expensive wine and brandy, and loving energy. Eating was preceded by prayer from the patriarch. Earl weaved together words of gratitude, pride, and purpose as it related to his family. Laughter filled the air, as did lighthearted conversations amongst all.

An act I considered corny had been the highlight of the event. Each person had to recite what they were grateful for. All of the Ellises proper named my bundle of joy as one source of their gratitude. I fought the pending emotions, not wanting to express that side in front of them. It was senseless seeing Iban wasn't here, eliminating my usual discomfort. The sweetest thing was Earl and Irene going around to rooms, to say goodnight and actually thanking their children, grandchildren, and daughter-in-law for spending the holiday with them.

Picture that!

Earl had this elaborate beach home built on a Caribbean island he purchased, flew us out, and then thanked us for coming. Sadik said it was a tradition since they became adults and were able to decide against the holidays with their family.

Taking a deep breath, I was finally getting it. I could see how this family remained cohesive. I'd been witnessing their "glue." I walked over to the Ivana and Iesha, dropping to my haunches as they worked.

"Iesha, this is next level architecture," I complimented their dedicated work using various shaped sand buckets to create towers.

Iesha shrugged, not uttering a word. Her cold wall was still up between us. I didn't like it and couldn't figure out what I'd done. We'd been so cool. She was the first to make me feel welcomed in this family...other than her uncle.

"Ms. Bilan, come look at mine," Ivy invited. "It's a princess tower!"

I shuffled closer to her. "And it's amazing! I bet no bad guys can reach her!"

"Nope. Uncle Deek said no thugs can touch the princess. That mean you, too, Auntie B."

"Ms. Bilan!" Iesha corrected so loudly and unexpected, my frame twisted too fast to face her and I fell on my butt.

"Iesha!" Monica chided.

"Eshy!" Taaliba shouted at the same time. "Listen, Uncle Deek wouldn't like that."

"Iesha," Ivana followed up with, shooting to her feet and curling her miniature fists. "Uncle Deek may be your favorite guy, but he need a wife like Daddy and PaPa. He need babies like them, too. Be nice!"

Iesha leaped from her bottom even faster. "That's not true, Ivana!" She began to wail. "You don't know what you're talking about!" She ran off to her mother, just as Monica was handing baby Irene over to Stacy, the kids' nanny and Sadik's mother's executive assistant for the compound and family.

Monica's mouth was open, face folded as she glared over to her oldest daughter, but no words left her mouth. It was telling of just how overwhelmed she'd been. She was here with two school-aged girls and a newborn without her husband. Yes; from my observation, having a nanny was a huge help. But it assisted none with her emotional needs. Monica had been stretched, and I had no clue how to address it. And, of course, that gave way to my doubts of having a child by an Ellis man with a demanding lifestyle.

I watched Iesha sob into her mother's neck. Ivana threw her shovel to the sand and dropped down herself, sulking toward the water. I felt my heart rend at the discord it seemed I participated in. These Ellis girls were exceptional; articulate and loving. I didn't want on their bad side, neither did I want to be the root of their conflict.

"Rory's little South Park Shawtie looking ass," Taaliba grounded out, gazing into the distance.

"Taaliba!" Monica reproved. "You're not helping."

Taaliba dropped her face into her palm. "I'm stressed out, Monica!"

A sharp whistle had me glancing around. Taaliba's comment wasn't random. Rory was boppin' down the beach, trying to get our attention.

"I think that's for you, Bilan." Monica suggested. "Sadik's back."

My heart opened in my chest at that announcement, and I began my trek down the white sand. We'd been not too far from the house.

The house...

It was immaculate. A two-story structure with beautiful ocean views. According to Earl the morning we arrived, it was more than five thousand square feet with seven bedrooms. Complete with a full kitchen, living room, den, dining room, and six bathrooms, it was no *Elliswoods Palace*, but certainly an Ellis-worthy property.

I met Rory on the beach, almost in front of the house.

"S.Q.E. want you," she informed, pointing behind her to the pier. "I'm 'bout to shower this fish shit off and lay up till dinner."

She trekked off to the small cottage Earl had for security. Sadik explained they didn't want to be in the house with their employer, needing privacy themselves. Oddly, Rory was the only female in there, and completely comfortable.

I continued toward the pier, seeing two boats there, both pulling in. I knew he was on one. Sadik left a couple of hours ago to go fishing. Irene suggested we have more seafood on the menu for dinner tonight. That's all she had to say for her son to make it happen. Sadik found one of the grounds people and they took a boat out on the water.

As I approached the pier, I broke my steps. The sight of Sadik swinging a rope to anchor the boat made my uterus flip. A gush of arousal flooded the bottoms of my bikini. My eyes shot around guiltily. My response to the sight so visceral, it was shameful. His cut arms were rocky and strident. Shoulders carved better than the Farnese Hercules statue. His abdomen a bubbled surface of perfect symmetry. The waist of his shorts hung low on his hips as the *Ase Garb* scarf he'd been wearing outdoors was wrapped around his bald head to protect against the sun. Sadik was a complete work of art.

I waited for him to finish and notice me. When he did, I didn't get as much of a reaction as I'd had to him.

However, he did ask, "Wanna go out on the water?" He pointed to the other boat coming in. "I got a cabin cruiser if you want to eat out there."

How could I say no?

Soft kisses beneath my belly button had me stirring from my sleep. My eyes opened to bright primary colors, various prints wrapped into a sloppy, yet secure knot about his head. Then the scarf lifted and a dark brown perimeter enclosing a hue of green, then yellow, and an impossible orange before a speck of black at the mecca appeared in the form of irises.

Pulling in a deep breath, I stretched my arms over my head. I couldn't believe I'd dozed off. Then I could. The guy Sadik rented the boat from took us to a restaurant a few miles from the house. We ate—or he fed me—beans and rice and rock lobster. We walked a flea market, enjoying the culture, then got back on the boat, docking in the middle of the water. That's when I'd dozed off.

My head jerked down when I felt something cool on my skin. Sadik was polishing me with sunscreen. A faint smile awakened the muscles in my face.

"Are you happy?" Sadik's chords were thick, telling me he'd fallen asleep, too.

I was curious about the time, but not too much. In the moment, time didn't matter.

"I don't know." I considered it a little and smiled. "You throwing me one of my questions?"

"You gonna answer my question?"

I lay my head back on the pad of the bow of the boat, humming as I thought. "I don't know. I used to ask that question because you seemed to have it all: money, family, influence, power. Now, like you,

I have my needs met. I used to worry about shelter and losing my family's home. But now you've bought it for me. I used to dream of having nice clothes like Randi. Now, I have a closet flooded with them—good, designer ones. Randi asks me to borrow them. Food had never been an issue because I'd always had food around me. I used to worry about being alone. Being alone was a big deal for me, but now, it's not; at every turn, I have an Ellis around." I chuckled, returning the inquiry as he gently rubbed the lotion onto my belly. "Are you happy?"

Sadik's hands moved to my chest and neck. I'd taken my cover-up off at some point before dozing off. The black bikini with the cut-out panels over my breasts would leave an interesting tan.

"I think I'll be happy once my life's complete."

"How does that happen?" I asked with one brow hiked.

"Once you're my wife and my child is delivered, I'll be a complete man."

I snickered. "Are you asking me to marry you, Sadik?"

With placidity, his busy hands went to my arms with the sunscreen. "I've already asked and now I'm waiting for you to do it."

This time, I laughed. "Look at me! I'm pregnant."

Sadik didn't exactly share in the humor. "And I would marry you if your face was green. That's not a factor for me. I want you with me."

I hummed again, sitting up so he could get my back. "*Bilan Ellis.* That sounds...heady."

"I know," he mumbled. "I've been dealing with it all my life."

"And how have you survived it?"

"By just knowing the obvious."

"What's that?"

"Specifically, no one can be trusted. You have to filter the allies from the snakes. People will try to infiltrate the family, whether it's to harm my father, mother...brother or sister. I always have to look out for the wolves. The wolves are always there. Even people once considered friends create conflict with another member of the family, and you can find yourself giving them the tools."

My head jerked back to look at him. There was something

causing the black in the mecca of his irises to pulse. This wasn't random. There was a deeper meaning to this chat than the ultra-alpha pushing my hand in marriage.

"Do you think I'd betray you?"

There was a delay in his answer. "Not intentionally, I don't."

Silence bounced between us for a spell. Something about me troubled the usually implacable Sadik.

"I would rather you be in love with me as my wife," he shared. "but I'll take whatever you give me just to have the opportunity to be at your side."

My eyes welled immediately. Something *was* off. That was such a soft, vulnerable statement coming from him, and Sadik couldn't look at me.

"Sadik, I've never even been in love. I don't even know the first of it. Look at you. You're thirty-eight years old; you have me by leaps and bounds on the experience." I swiped my wet cheeks. "I don't even know my left from my right most days, and you're talking about being in love. That's a lot for someone like me."

"It doesn't have to be," he uttered, gaze caught in the moving waters as we headed back to the private island. "People fall in love every day."

That angered me.

"What is being in love to you?"

He finally met my eyes. "Looking in a person's eyes, and feeling something so deeply tied to her, that when her emotions are flared —whether she smiles or gets angry—there's a pull inside your gut. There's a constant need to make her happy. There's a constant need to pursue her wellbeing. You can look at *any*thing beautiful and see resemblance of her. Those are the things I feel and see about you."

A wrench resonated in my chest. I was utterly speechless. Completely. Sadik must have run out of words himself, because we motored all the way back to the island in silence. The guy dropped us off on the opposite end from where we left. It was the back of the house where there was a small lot of tropical trees. When we pulled up to the pier, Sadik carried a rope he purchased at the market. It wasn't his usual type; this one was a white nylon from what I saw on the sign hanging over the box he picked it from.

As we hiked through the faux forest, the sound of a motor caught both our attention, relatively at the same time. Sadik stopped first then spun around. From the short distance, we could see a man step out of the boat, carrying a duffle bag. The sun setting compromised our view.

"Who is that?" I murmured.

Sadik didn't answer. As the man began into the tropical forest, Sadik's gaze whipped all around. He held up his index finger, telling me to be quiet. He walked me over to a tree and motioned for me to wait. My anxiety kicked in right away. I struggled with managing it. This was not the time to allow it to get ahead of me.

These damn Ellises...

There was always drama with them!

But this was Sadik. He wouldn't let a breath of harm come to me. I'd have to trust him. I'd get past this—we'd get past this.

I took deep breaths, trying to calm myself as the strange man neared me. Sadik had disappeared, I was sure to make himself a surprise presence sooner or later. A few steps farther, the man noticed me and his steps sped up. I tried keeping my eyes on him rather than looking for Sadik, something my panic wanted to give into.

"Excuse me!" the stranger shouted to me, watching his steps.

I balled my fists, nails cutting into my skin, pulse racing, and skin perspiring.

He was closer now and I could make out his features. He had light skin with a base of melanin. His hair was thick, not course. Eyes dark, lips full, yet not thick. He lowered the duffle bag he carried, hiked over his shoulders, to his knees. It was a black *Louis Vuitton Damier* print *KeepAll*. Sadik had two of the same duffle in different colors and finishes. He wore expensive looking sunglasses over his head, a small gold hoop in his right ear. His black tee stretched over his chest and his shorts fit his thighs similarly close. His boat shoes looked expensive and...soaked.

"Hey!" He finally approached me. "This is the Ellis—"

His words were cut when Sadik dropped from the air behind the man, wrapping his arm around his neck. The guy's bag dropped when accosted and his body followed seconds later when Sadik took him down.

Rope...

It appeared out of nowhere. The white nylon rope was around his wrists as he lay face down in the sanded dirt, where Sadik squatted over him. Next were his feet to be tied as he tried kicking. It was too late. Sadik moved faster than my brain could process. My sex throbbed, and nipples stung.

"Hold the fuck up, man!" the guy shouted. "Let me explain!"

"Shut the fuck up! Sadik barked before turning to me. "Nalib, go to his bag and grab the gun!"

It took seconds, it seemed, for my body to move.

"Bilan!" Sadik yelped again, connecting my brain with my body.

I went near the two for the duffle bag. My hands swinging rashly for metal. Nothing.

"Baby!"

"I don't feel anything!" I replied in an out of body experience.

"You sure? Check again," Sadik demanded.

"There's nothing in there!" the guy shrilled.

"Who're you with?" Sadik asked.

"Nobody! If you let me explain, bro!" The man wiggled beneath Sadik.

"Honey!"

"Sadik!" I chirped nervously, annoyed. So I dumped the bag, allowing its contents to hit the ground for him to see.

"Sadik!" The guy seemed to sigh. I wasn't sure if it was of relief or defeat. "It's me. Danny—"

"I know exactly who you are, muthafucka! What I need to know is why are you here and where are the rest, Danny Lopez?"

Danny... Danny...

That name rang familiar.

"I came for Taaliba!"

Sadik echoed, "Taaliba?" He yanked the rope, causing the man to cry out in pain. "You fuckin' with me now. Bilan," He tossed his head. "get to the house and get Rory or one of the other security.

"Just get Taaliba," Danny begged, voice strained from the pain. "Please!"

That's when it clicked.

"*No, no, no, no, no, no,*" rumbled from my lungs in quick succession. I rushed toward Sadik. "Baby, he's Taaliba's friend!" My nerves were so bad, I assumed the role of a woman I didn't know. I, too, was now begging for Sadik's mercy.

"Taaliba?" Sadik barked again. "Bullshit! Taaliba wouldn't fuck with a Lopez and not say shit!" I didn't recognize the evil in his eyes.

"Yes, Taaliba!" Danny shouted.

I nodded, my eyes closing as nausea began to threaten. I swallowed hard. "Yes, Sadik. Taaliba and Danny have been friends since kids. She's crazy about this guy—in love and don't even know it!"

He didn't believe me. There was betrayal in his eyes. I knew a piece of information from his dark world that he didn't. I hated it. The tears fell. I couldn't witness another murder.

I took a chance at placing a soft touch on his hard, bare shoulder, peering him straight in his feline irises. "I'm the ally, not the snake, Sadik. Just give him a chance to prove it."

"*Bila—*"

"Sadik!" I screamed with squeezed eyes. "I'm about to be sick thinking about how I'm about to witness death again, so unnecessarily."

He stared at me hard and long for an eternity.

Sadik jumped to his feet, releasing Danny's ankles, but not his arms. "Get the fuck up! Let's go!"

∞22∞

"Taaliba!" I shouted, out of breath as I went from room to room. My muscles vibrating beneath my clammy skin. "Where are you?"

The staff in the kitchen looked at me like I was crazy, and I was. Another death almost occurred in front of me. I had every right to my current anxious state.

"She's in the bathroom down the hall," Terri, one of the cooks, informed.

I shot back into the hallway, calling her. My bare sanded feet slapped against the hardwood floor.

"What?" I heard faintly, increasing my steps.

"Taaliba! Where are—"

A door opened and she craned her neck into the hallway.

"What the hell, Bilan?" Her face was tight.

"Come here!" I waved her on. "Now! Let's go!"

"What?" She stepped into the hall, her stumble not missed by me.

I met her halfway, snatching her by the arm. Taaliba protested when I began to jog.

"The fuck, B?"

The door to the back porch couldn't appear fast enough. When the oceanic outdoors came into view, Danny being patted down by Earl's beefy security was the first thing I saw. Sadik observed with his arms folded over his bubbled, inked chest and legs a mile apart as he grimaced.

"Danny?" Taaliba screeched. It was the most feminine pitch I'd ever heard of her. At first, she stopped running. "Danny!" She took off, bolting down the stairs. "Danny!"

Taaliba lunged, grabbing his wide frame into her thin arms. Her force so unexpected, Danny barely saw her coming, making him lose his balance. They fell onto the sand.

"The hell are you doing here?" It sounded as a cry.

But what was certain was when she pulled him at the sides of his face and kissed him with tongue and lips. Danny's hand instinctively went to her butt as he returned her reception to his presence.

"That's enough!" Sadik barked, moving toward the contrary pair.

Earl was right behind him in approach.

This is soooo inappropriate...

The naïve side of me wanted to perceive this as a romance story unfolding in front of me. The more rational side recognized this wasn't healthy, and I was just as sick as these people around me. It was clear to me as my clitoris continued to throb and breasts felt heavier in the skimpy bikini top as I observed Sadik's aggression with another man.

The nylon rope hung from the back pocket of his trunks.

Sadik

"Look..." Danny's palms lifted in the air. "I won't lie and say I don't know what's going on, but I ain't gonna cop to something I ain't with."

"You're a fuckin' Lopez, son." My father lit his cigar.

"I am. Till I die, but I'm not my father."

Palmer and my father's security, Bobby, flexed over Danny seated at a table in the washroom near the back of the house. They didn't believe him, and I didn't understand him.

"Explain, Danny," I requested.

Danny exhaled, sitting up in his chair. His clothes still sanded, hair standing in every direction on his head.

His eyes returned to me. "Why does this feel like a life or death type of deal?"

"Son, you're sitting amongst the Ellises as the son of a man who tried taking the life of my prized possession and unborn legacy," my father answered.

I amended, deathly seriously, "You better be lucky we brought you in our home to decide if your life is worth the boat you came in on instead of gutting your ass out on the beach and feeding you to the sharks at sea."

Danny blinked hard and sat back this time. He used both his hands to brush frustration from his face. "I don't fuck with Luis Lopez."

"He's ya father," Palmer challenged him.

"And an egotistical maniac, obsessed with power!" He shot back at Palmer standing over him, nose flared. "So sick and twisted in the head, he can't even enjoy the shit he afforded himself, hustling all these years. He can't even enjoy the family he created. He destroyed us before we could even make good on him."

"Luis is still with Maria," my father half inquired, half stated.

Danny snorted. "On paper. When she isn't drunk off her ass,

she's crying about how unwanted she is. He fucked her life up. Had two kids with her, beat her ass and all of ours for years. I was lucky. My mother shipped me back home to DR every summer and break I got in school. My father wouldn't let her do the same with my sister."

I recalled Lopez having a son and daughter, but because they were so much younger than me, the news of her death came and went when I learned of it years ago. I knew what was coming next.

"He wanted her there so he could fuck with her," Danny continued, eyes falling. No one in the room reacted. We were trained to be indifferent to pleas from a man begging for his life. While Danny wasn't exactly in that situation, he infiltrated our home. We needed answers. "She said he started molesting her when she was seven. I didn't see it, though. I only saw the beatings. Those were done with open doors. He kept her isolated. I didn't realize it back then, like he does his house of whores now. But the summer I was back home with my grandmother, he was fucked up on coke when he fucked with her and ended up killing her. She was twelve, just a little girl."

"Your sister went to one of my wife's schools," my father verified.

"We both did," Danny corrected. "But he knew where to hit and where to bruise. I was fifteen when my sister died. The shit was hard. Who would I tell that would believe me?" Danny's eyes reached my father. "Taaliba was the only person I could talk to about it. She was the only person I could admit wanting to kill to."

"You want to kill Lopez?" I asked in disbelief.

"I will." His tone was a matter of fact.

For seconds, there was a notable chill in the room and no one spoke. It gave me a moment to consider his story, body language, and what I'd known of Lopez. He'd been in business with Popov, who sold more than guns. Popov sold human livestock in the northeast.

My father's eyes caught mine for my verdict. I believed Danny. I'd have to look into his story more, and I damn sure couldn't relate to his venom for his father. But I believed him. I gave my father a soft nod.

"House of whores?" I questioned.

"Popov." Danny confirmed my suspicion.

"What do you plan to do after you kill Lopez?"

"Take over. Restore integrity. My father has built a formidable organization, but it's only as strong as he is. His ego makes him weak. For him to think he could have Luiz run up in *Pulse* to kill you was foolish. He doesn't think; only dreams. He wants your head, Double E Bags, because you have the most territory, drug-wise. You run the state. When I take over—and I will—I'd like to work with you. Find a way to make money without violence. Layout territories and abide by them."

"So what you saying? You want a alliance with the Ellises now," Palmer scoffed, rocking on his heels with folded arms as he stood over Danny.

"No." Danny shook his head. "I know who I am. I'm a proud Dominicano." He peered my father in the eyes. "I've watched you. I've seen how you move. How you raised your sons with a pride...an oath to the Ellis name. That's what I want to pass down to my men. It's the honor I want the men working with me to have. Dominican pride. What I want is your permission to be with Taaliba. I'm gonna pursue her regardless. I'd just like to do it without your pushback."

"And you think you gone fuck my only daughter, give her Black babies, and give them that Dominican pride?" My father's brows met. "*Shiiiiit*... You ever met Irene Sharon Ellis, that lil' girl's momma?"

"Taaliba..." Danny shook his head, his eyes falling for the second time in this interrogation. The first was his family's debauchery. "Babies aren't on the horizon with her. Getting her to trust me is the current battle. Sex would be after, and babies..." He shook his head. "Let's put it this way. Men like us have a line of women throwing fucking uteruses at us. Taaliba's has sage and other shit to keep me away."

"My fuckin' baby girl!" My father smacked the plastic table proudly.

Danny scoffed, sitting back. Strangely, I could sense his frustration. It wasn't until recently my Ellis ego had been killed and buried when it came to women. Bilan may have been carrying my baby, but it wasn't by choice, rather by force, determination, and manipulation by me.

"You're right to speak of my father's reign, describing his organization as a great leviathan of power and influence," I explained. "It's been proven in over forty years of leadership. Your desire of an alliance with him will be decided by him. Your...thing with Taaliba will be at his discretion, too. However, your plan for your father would need a timeline. Lopez's infractions on your family are serious, but so was his attempt on my life and my fiancée's. Your desire to kill him may be met with familial disinclination. Mine is immediate."

For years, I'd been working to dry the blood on the Ellis name. So many had been killed by our hands because of my father's line of work. It was why I took so long to address Damien's transgressions. I implored my father's trust to use patience as a tool of revenge instead of acting on his usual violent manner. My plan failed, partly because of my obsession with Ab's sister. Pursuing her compromised my father's vengeance. Yes, Damien and all his accomplices were dead. Yet it was a guilt I still carried. Maybe I proved my theory of not having to be the actual gun with Rizzo's decimation. But not even that could explain what I'd do to Lopez for putting the lives of my Nalib and son at risk.

Danny's head shook as he peered me directly in the eye. "I won't share the details of my plan. But I'll lose my father before you become one."

I reached across the table, offering my hand. Danny reciprocated without a moment of dithering.

"Alright!" my father shouted, clapping his hands as he laughed. It pleased me to see him happy. "I 'on't know about you and that Taaliba. We can talk more over brandy." He stood from the table. "What do you say?"

Slowly, Danny rose to his feet. He chuckled. "Shit. Can a brother get a shower...wash this sand off me?"

The guys in the room laughed, the atmosphere light again.

"Yeah, man." My father took Danny at the shoulder and led him out of the room. "I'll have them find you a bathroom."

The moment I glanced up through the doorway, I saw Bilan. I felt my eyes widen from shock and concern. I knew I frightened her earlier. Her face was open; eyes rather wide, lips parted. But she didn't speak or move. Then a curvy figure eclipsed her.

My head reared when I recognized Tiffany.

No wonder Bilan's expression. Tiff must have come while we were speaking to Danny. It appeared the island had a welcome sign for uninvited guests. But Tiff wasn't exactly a guest. She damn sure wasn't expected.

"I thought you were with your girls," I began my inquiry.

Her birthday was yesterday.

"I was." She stepped into the room and closed the door. "I decided to come out here. I missed my family."

Without a moment of hesitation, I moved toward the door and opened it. That quickly was too late. Bilan was gone.

"How did you get out here?"

"The flight crew. They flew in tonight to make you guys' flight in the morning." She was right. We were due to leave tomorrow at eleven AM. "Them bitches got old real quick." She swiped her hand in the air. "I was bored as shit. When Iban told me the jet was leaving to pick y'all up, I decided to get flewed out."

I chuckled. "A four-hour flight. Okay."

"You asked for information. I printed it out before I left my office this afternoon." She reached into a tote and handed me a folder.

I thumbed through the pages of Ricky's guest list. There were notes on RSVP's and those who actually attended.

"You could have emailed this," I advised, still scanning.

"What would have been the point if I was coming." She walked toward the door. "Oh," her chirp had my attention lifting from the papers. "My assistant printed out texts from Ricky, too."

"What texts?"

"He kept asking me to confirm your attendance." She shrugged. "Clout chasing ass."

Tiffany left as I considered that. This shit with Ricky and Lopez was perplexing.

"King." Peering up from the list of names, I found my mother, craning her neck into the room. "We're starting dinner. I can't find Bilan right now. You guys should head into the dining room."

"You can have Marjorie bring our food up to the room."

"Really?"

I'd been planning a night alone with her since the first day we'd arrived. She was awakened with an orgasm yesterday, but I hadn't fucked Bilan since we landed. After what happened earlier, I knew she needed the regulation, especially after Tiffany's popup visit.

"Okay," her voice brought my attention back from the folder I'd found myself back into. "I'll have her bring it up. Should I find Bilan to say goodnight now?"

I nodded without looking at my queen. She knew what time it was.

The moment I opened the door, I saw her pull clothes from a drawer, marching them to one of the suitcases on the bed, and toss them in. I knew then, she was on one, and predictably so. Bilan was still adjusting to my life.

I stepped in and closed the door behind me. Bilan sensed me and her eyes brushed over quickly, not breaking her step. I cocked my head to the side, considering my next move. She continued to ignore me.

"You're mad at me."

"Just getting ready for this flight in the morning," she murmured while in motion. "Oh, and I'm tired. Not up for dinner."

"Why not?"

"I just said I'm tired."

I calmly suggested, "You still need to eat."

"I'm still full from lunch." Her eyes wouldn't meet mine.

"Tiffany's an extended member of the family." It was fucked up for her to pop up the way she did, but it didn't surprise me.

One thing Bilan and Tiffany had in common was their lack of

family. Tiffany wanted to fit in with the Ellises. Bilan was hesitating on her invitation to become one.

"She's also a former fuck buddy of yours."

"I have them, you know." When her head swung to face me, I amended. "Former lovers."

Bilan froze. "Good for you. Another advantage you have over me. Even though there's nothing I can do to change what you two did together or had at one point, it's still unfair to ask me to be immune to her presence around here. You'd never be able to handle a man who wants me around, much less one who had me."

My abs constricted as though hit with a blow. She was angry.

"Don't suppose shit like that. It turns my stomach."

"Turns your stomach and makes you murderous. You think I've forgotten about Derrick?"

The last look in his eyes when he realized he was about to die was still a crisp memory. My indifference to his fear concerned me. My inspiration for killing him thwarted my regret.

"Do you want me to apologize for that?" My delivery still soft.

"Would an apology change your dark capabilities?" She turned to continue inside the suitcase, making work of just a few days' worth of clothing. "Just sick! It's all so sick!"

I pulled the rope from the back pocket of my shorts and lifted it in the air.

"This makes me sick, Nalib?" My tone unintentionally husky.

Bilan glanced up with wide eyes at the rope dusted with sand. I could perceive the dilation of her pupils. Her nipples pushed through the triangle covering. Her lips parted slowly.

"Does this make you sick, too? Because if it does, I don't mind being ill with you, Nalib."

Her head twitched, then she blinked several times before shaking her head. I moved toward her, eyes roving over her expectant frame.

"Admittedly," I whispered honestly, feeling my dick grow against my thigh. "I've never roped a pregnant woman, but from that first night you slept beautifully naked against me in Costa Rica, I've had fantasies."

"Sadi—"

I grabbed her hands and pulled them over her head. Together, we walked to the tufted bench in front of the bed.

"Sadik," she cried, eyes now heavy.

"Shhhhh... This is a simple double column tie. It's basic...quick to get you bound," I produced huskily, so turned the fuck on. "Did you know I can perform forty-one rope and ties? This one is the Frogtie." I explained while working the rope around her arms. Bilan's breaths were coming fast and hard. "I want your pussy exposed." I kissed the back of her neck.

When I moved to her legs, my hands reached to her swollen belly. I pressed my lips into her warm flesh.

"Listen here, son. I need you to close your eyes and ears because I'm about to violate your incubator in the most carnal way. Remember, she was my home first. I implanted you in my space."

I let go of a soft chuckle when lifting my regard to Bilan. Her head fell back in lustful defeat. I loved her. So fucking much; I loved everything about the mother of my child.

Naïve.

Vulnerable.

Bound.

Fucking intoxicating. My eyes went between winding the rope around her thigh and leg as they were pushed together. I moved on to the next one, smelling the aroma of her pussy. When I was done, I stood to my feet to observe my work. Bilan lay on her elbows with her arms crossed behind her back. Her legs bent to her chest and spread eagle. Her chest heaved, eyes could hardly stay open.

I moved to release the ties of her bikini top, then the bottom. We didn't have much time. And I didn't have much patience, viewing her like this. I took to my knees on the side of the bench, between her open thighs.

"Watch me, Nalib." I croaked, intoxicated by the scent of her.

The moment my tongue connected with her flesh in a stroke, she made sounds of sizzle. A tortured breath pushed from her gritted teeth.

Under sieged.

I couldn't keep my eyes open. Those determined irises as he watched me closely held me entranced. His hands cupped my butt beneath me, pulling my core to his mouth. The dark brown perimeter enclosing a hue of green, then yellow, and an impossible orange before a speck of black at the mecca took on new patterns as his mouth opened wide and his tongue smeared each inch of my sex.

When he squeezed my cheeks, my lids fell too low. His tongue flapped wide and he wanted me to see its lashings. They started off slow then sped up, zeroing in on my clitoris. My breasts heaved, nipples two tingling peaks. Rope, my flesh, the smoothness of his stubbled head, kaleidoscopic eyes, overgrown goatee, and flapping tongue. The optics erotic, which made it hard not to watch. But the pleasure in my groin built. The more I watched, the more I felt the message of supplication and desire from his expression and actions, the less control I had.

And that's what I loved about being intimate with Sadik. I could relinquish all control to him and know he'd catch me. He'd provide. He'd been making efforts to be a friend...had been my lover, and even now, protected me from my own fears and insecurity.

"Mmmhhhnnn..." I whimpered at the first wave of my orgasm.

My hips bucked into his face, creating a pull on my constrained thighs and shoulders. The rope constricted me. It forced me to endure bliss in the same fashion.

God, I was sick. Just like him.

Who enjoyed dark ecstasy like this? The rope he used to subdue what he believed to be an intruder was the very same he did to evoke arousal and orgasms from me. Grains of sand pushed into my skin as it vibrated from my explosion.

I watched as Sadik stood to remove his trunks; his cock jutted out veiny and thick. He moved me, on top of the bench, away from the bed and straddled it. The sight of his agility had me lose control of the muscles of my neck and my head dropped back.

"Look at us, baby," he purred thickly.

I lifted my head, forcing my eyes open at the most beautiful sight of the head of his erection meeting my sex. For the first time, I watched it disappear inside me. Each inch on its way inside made my spine curl. The sight of his golden legs parted as he thrusted into me made me delirious. I could feel myself lubricating even more.

Heavy...

His appendage pushed inside with force and lagged on the way out. Sadik moved too slow. I needed friction. He was so thick inside me, I could feel him throbbing. I tried lifting my hips to meet him.

"Greedy pussy," he declared tautly.

I was. My desire for this man was unlike any petty crush I'd ever had for a guy. My imagination for eroticism had never reached the lengths of what Sadik had introduced to me in these six months.

"I'm going to speed this along." The muscles around his eyes were loose as he leaned over me, shifting the pressure in my core. His mouth reached mine. "Keep quiet."

His flesh began to slap into mine. The hairs on his thighs teased the bottom of my feet and the sides of my hips. Those of his chest stimulated my nipples, though he didn't put his full weight on me. I needed the mobility of my hands to hold him. The movement of my legs to control the pressure. But I had none of that. All I had was the wild verve of an ultra-alpha plunging into me until a cry ripped from my throat.

Sadik quieted my wild abandon with his mouth. His tongue moved just as disturbingly as his cock inside, spurring my release. My entire frame quaked recklessly. Eruption so potent, my cries turned into shrills through my nostrils. The sounds just as primal as Danny's when he realized he'd had a murderer on his back.

Sadik released my mouth.

"Fuck..." he breathed before he reared out of me than bucked continually, emptying himself inside my womb.

His breathing was harsh as he rode out his orgasm, hips slowed. My brain was fried. Completely. It had retreated, it seemed. My emotions were so flared, it dazed me. My entire frame throbbed and felt heavy. I was no help when he lifted me to untie the rope. I sat still the entire time. Spent.

There was a knock at the door.

"Yeah?" Sadik barked, still gaining his breath, freeing me.

I heard a muzzled, "Dinner's here."

"You can leave it there, Marjorie. Thanks."

When done, Sadik lifted my weakened frame into his arms and whisked into the small bathroom for a shower. He helped me wash and conditioned my hair before he cleaned himself. I rested in the corner of the intimate space, drained.

Sadik finished rinsing, turning toward me as he moved from under the faucet, wiping down his face. "I believe the worst lie perpetuated in our society is the one about love being blemish-free. As kids, we somehow believe each union consists of harmony so rich, no adversity can cut through it. It's false and a danger to humanity." He moved a lock of wet hair from my forehead. "We're all the sum of our experiences, many of them from our childhood. Being unable to join lives with a person because of the flaws in their childhood is grossly unfair. Sometimes, those flaws are their handicap. It can be no different from discrimination. I love you. All of you, even the parts I don't understand."

His eyes fastened into me. "You don't have to like to love, but you do have to love to commit. Having you only like facets of me isn't enough. Your love is required to gain the commitment of a lifetime I need."

His words moved me, sounding more like a heeding rather than a shared revelation.

"What do you want from me?" I gritted.

It was seconds long before he returned, "For you to let me be your lover without the guilt of accepting who the hell I am. If you're sick, then dammit, we're fuckin' sick together. We're together. At the end of the day, nothing more matters."

After a piercing gape into the recesses of me, he turned to shut off the water. Then Sadik left the shower.

We dumped our heavy coats in empty chairs and sat down at the small table set up in the center of the dining room. It was the second week in January and, once again, Earl Ellis surprised me outside of the *Ellis Academy* administration building with buying out the restaurant to have lunch with me.

"I'm going to have to change my schedule," I threatened, teasingly.

Earl shrugged, warm smile playing at his lips. "Then I'd have to call somebody in that building for your new one."

"And what if I start working from home?"

"You think Sadik'll stop me from pulling up to have lunch with the mother of my first grandson?" he challenged. When I nodded, Earl's smile broadened. "Yeah. You probably right."

We both laughed at that.

"Sadik can be..." I searched for the right word.

"A fuckin' beast with his rock head ass," he sputtered a laugh.

My head bobbed up and down. "Yup!" I laughed along with him. "I've never seen anything like him."

"That's because you ain't meet me before running into that joker. He's definitely my son."

"So I've been told."

"Oh, yes!" He motioned to the buffet tables lining the walls. "Shall we?"

This had been the fourth time Earl surprised me with lunch. Oddly, eating with him became easier each time. He allowed me to go first, as usual, picking salad and a half sandwich. I made it back to the table not too long before Earl.

When he took his seat, I asked, "How did Irene deal with your... ultra-alpha when you met?"

Earl chuckled. "That's the fancy phrase we going with?"

I enjoyed his loose vernacular. Earl's roots were from Paterson and so were his mannerisms. But his presentation was that of a businessman. He typically wore suits, as did his sons, and his face, hair, and nails were impeccably groomed. He had the drip.

"Absolutely!" I ate a forkful of salad.

"Well, she had no choice but to deal with it. Plus, she couldn't resist it no way."

"She was sixteen. Right?" I recalled Sadik telling about their ten-year age gap.

Now that I'd been around them, and especially having seen them gather their family, I'd never guess that. They seemed the same age, if Earl didn't appear younger from his lean frame.

Earl nodded, chewing his food. "Yup. The smartest woman I met at the time. Still is. She was never a girl, not even at sixteen. Irene made me a man."

"Because of having Iban?"

"No. Because she made me see how fucked—" He nodded respectfully. "How messed up I was. She always told me the truth."

"What do you mean?"

Earl fed himself and chewed before answering. "She was the one that told me I was a dummy for having a half a million dollars stashed around the city with no bank account." He snorted, "I'll never forget. She called me a gorilla ass dummy."

I covered my mouth, cracking up. "That sounds like Irene."

He shook his head. "No. I ain't tell you I was ass naked, and ain't tell you what we just finish doing when the topic came up."

Sex...

"Ewwwww, Earl!" I pushed my tongue out as though gagging. "Don't need any visuals."

"And you ain't gone get none. I'm just saying." He wiped his mouth. "That next day, we went down to the bank and opened up a couple accounts. She said she needed security for her baby, Iban, and I wasn't it. But my money could be if I played my cards right."

My brows met. "That was mean."

"That was smart. I was all heart, no brains back then like my daddy. I ain't fear nothing. Until Irene." He shrugged. "My first fear was disappointing her. I started to get obsessed with that shit... proving I could be a man in her eyes. She was a good girl. Scholarly. You can be a savior and archfiend any day of the week in my line of work. She was pure. So I needed to prove I could be, too, *as much as my work allowed me to.*"

I considered that while continuing to eat.

"But you have another lover...two." That came out easier than the decision to speak it.

At first, Earl wouldn't look at me. He just forked the food in his plate.

Then he sat up. "But I only have one love." He pushed the fork speared with food into his mouth.

"So you don't love Nena and Diane?"

Unlike Thanksgiving, the lovers were allowed to attend Christmas in Colorado with the family. Tom, however, didn't attend. It was pointless, in my opinion, because we saw very little of Diane and Nena. They stayed in the in-law suite just off the house while Earl shared a bed with Irene each night. That bizarre fact, along with Iban's absence, had still been confounding to me.

"I care for them deeply."

"In love with them?"

Earl put his fork down and issued me a radiant gaze with those honeyed irises. "Sweetheart, I'm too old to be giving my heart away to anyone at my age." He resumed his fork, his attention to his plate. "Besides, it belongs to Irene Ellis anyway. It's safe there where no bad can come to it," his tone dejected.

"So what do you share with your...girlfriends?"

I waited again for Earl to eat, then answer.

"I 'on't know what I share with them. I know what I like in them. Nena's sassy. Fashionable and don't take no shit. My lil' D... She just as fiery. Spit some Black power shit on that ass." He nodded, gaze across the room. "She believe in family. They both know the Word. You know... Nena's a PK." He chuckled, much to himself. Earl shook his head again, going back to his plate. "Sadik said I like grooming women because I never got a chance to do that with his mother. She groomed me."

That was strange. It also led to a revelation of my own.

"You think that's his attraction to me? He's ten years older than me, too."

A guttural chortle spilled from Earl's lungs. "Young lady, you don't know much about my son then. When it comes to women, Sadik and I are different birds."

That statement made my heart skip a beat. It made my mind flash back to just this morning, when his face was buried between my cheeks from behind. The way my heart cried out to him as he held me after my explosion.

"Maybe you should explain the man you created." I dropped my fork, clasping my hands together.

"Why you keep your hair so short?" Ivana asked, combing through it.

I sighed, flipping through "New Releases" on the *Girl, Have You Read?* website. One Christina C. Jones' non-fiction book led to a Christina C. Jones' fiction book, then another and another. I trolled her and her beautiful family on social media, wanting her "normal" pace of a lifestyle. I couldn't find what her husband did, but he seemed..."normal." I soooo craved that in these last weeks of my pregnancy. Inhaling her reading catalogue, had me curious about more Black authors.

"Ummmm..." I hummed, clicking on a name I'd heard mentioned with Jones' in passing. "Because when I was a little girl like you two, my mother worked from sun up to sun down and my hair got neglected a lot. It was so bad, I got teased."

"Awwww! That's so not cool!" Ivana protested. "That would never happen in my school. We have a no tolerance rule."

"Zero tolerance, Ivana," Iesha corrected, rolling her eyes then returning to her sketch book on the floor.

She'd still been cold to me, and once again, she was taking it out on her big sister.

I tried rolling over it. "Yeah. I know, now that I work for *E.A.* But back then, anti-bullying policies weren't as tough as they are now. So when I was a kid, I told myself I would cut my hair bald the minute I became an adult."

"Bald?" Ivana's hand in my head stilled.

I nodded, enjoying the scent of the new candle Kimmy lit in here. It contributed to the cozy vibe of the all ivory and ebony wood themed room.

"But you're not bald," Iesha murmured toward her pad, not speaking to me directly.

"I changed my mind when I got into high school. I started seeing hairstyles with short hair I liked and went that route."

This story was easy to recite because it was one of many I'd been reminiscing over a lot lately. Memories of my family and childhood had been popping up throughout the day, and even in my sleep. I read online being pregnant with your first child can produce repressed memories of your own childhood. They weren't all bad. I had plenty of loving times to recount. But it all ultimately reminded me, I was without my family.

It had taken lots of reiterations to my psyche that I was not alone or lonely, because I hadn't been. Sadik had made sure of it. Even now, the Ellis family was experiencing a crisis of sorts. Monica was three months postpartum, but struggling with depression. Irene believed it was hormonal. Monica said it was Iban. He hadn't been around since the last days of summer when we announced my pregnancy to the family. According to Monica, Iban had been spending increasing amounts of time with Lia and their baby. This was hard, considering she'd just had baby Irene. Either way, Monica needed a break. Sadik and I agreed to take the big girls for the week...the week he'd be gone.

On top of that, I'd been dealing with the news of Ricky hitting Randi. They got into a fight a couple of nights ago and he knocked her out cold. Randi had the mind to go to the emergency room, thanks to the girl with her at a bar where the fight happened. She had a concussion and abrasions on her face and upper body. I visited her at Tasche's place on my lunch, and her bruises still haunted me. It was something I wanted to talk to someone about. Tasche had enough on her hands with having Randi at her place again.

"When's Uncle Deek coming back again?" Ivana asked over me.

I was stretched out over the sofa in the television room with the girls. We had another afternoon of adventure, ending the school week. After school, I picked the girls up and headed over to the library to do their homework. When we got back to the apartment, Kimmy was finishing up on dinner and had all the ingredients out for us to bake fresh double chocolate chip cookies. We washed up and made the dough, then baked the cookies while eating dinner. I learned from the first time the Ellis girls stayed with us in October while their mother delivered, they enjoyed being in the kitchen. If there was anything I could teach them, it was to bake. So we'd done a lot of that this week.

Sadik being away for over a week had been hard on me. It was strange. I'd missed him. Missed him in a needy manner. Sadik had, in no time, become a tower of strength. He was a barometer to my emotions, reading them well. But since I'd been back from *Macen Beach*, he also regulated them. If he was calm and collected, so was I. He addressed my needs. So the last thing I wanted to do was alert him to these blues of nostalgia I'd been feeling.

"Tomorrow night," I answered Ivy.

That prompted me to reach for my phone to check in with him. Maybe I should send him pictures we took earlier. I debated that. It felt needy. I was a big girl. Although Iesha was still giving me her funk, I had no problem enduring it if it meant time for Iban and Monica to sort out their marriage.

"I wish it was tonight," Iesha sighed. "It's boring when he's not here."

My lips pouted and eyes ballooned. "I'm sorry you've been bored, Iesha."

Ivana sucked her teeth, dropping from my head to beside me on the oversized, plush sofa. "You say that about Daddy now that he ain't home."

"Not-uhn!" Iesha shrieked. "Uncle Deek is way more fun than Daddy!"

"You say that now," Ivana grounded out as she lifted her device to her face. "I'm having fun. Just mad we have to go back home tomorrow."

I caressed her little leg. "We still have tomorrow. We go for our manicures and pedicures in the afternoon," I reminded Ivana. Then I addressed Iesha on the floor. "And don't forget about our trip to the *American Girl* store right after that."

"Oh, yeah!" Ivana's smile was a mile long.

Iesha didn't react at all. That's when I decided to reach out to Sadik. While I wouldn't cry about his niece's rudeness, doing this without him increased my longing for their uncle. He was so good with them, and the girls adored him.

"How many months are you, Auntie B?" Ivana asked while into her tablet.

I took a deep breath. "Whew!" I let it out as I considered it. "I'm in my thirty-sixth week, which puts me in my third trimester. You know what that means?" She shook her head, eyes still below. "It means I'm almost done. We're at the end."

As my eyes roamed my swollen feet, I felt grateful. They tended to swell at the end of a long day now. Overall, I had a wonderful pregnancy: no excessive weight gain, no illness after the first trimester's morning sickness, and my sexual appetite was still normal. I read some women experience an increase in sex drive the first few months of pregnancy, thanks to hormonal influx, and a decrease midway as their bodies expanded. But I'd been just as horny as I'd been those weeks leading into my sexual relationship with the man who frustrated me almost as much as he intrigued me.

I texted Sadik a few pictures I took of the girls and me today, then sent a second, more personal one.

Me: I miss your lips.

"Bilan," Kimmy, calling me from the doorway, disrupted my thoughts.

I turned to find her wrapped inside her coat and scarf.

"You're out?"

"Yes. I'm done for the day. Night, princesses."

"Night, Ms. Kimmy!" Iesha bade.

"Night!" Ivana followed with.

"Oh!" Kimmy chirped. "And Ms. Tiffany's on her way up. The security called a minute ago for clearance." The V between her brows didn't go unnoticed by me.

It was bizarre for Tiffany to come here. I stood from the sofa, tightening my robe.

"Auntie Tiff?" Iesha squealed, taking off for the hall.

Ivana seemed just as pleasantly surprised, only muted. I glanced curiously at Kimmy, whose expression was just as animated.

"This is quite unusual," she admitted as we took off for the hall.

The girls arrived at the door before we did and opened it. Tiffany stood there, a new beach blonde wig fell across her shoulders and the winter white wool trench coat made her appear like an hourglass. The metal stiletto heels assisted with her seductive posture.

"Auntie!" Iesha cried. "You came!" She jumped into her arms.

Ivana jumped on her toes, holding the door open. "How you know we were here?"

Tiffany laughed, trying to balance Iesha's little frame on her hip. "So many questions!"

I sidled behind Ivana. "And yet so much time to answer it." My forehead stretched, brows hiked.

I didn't like Tiffany. I decided that long ago. Whether it was for petty jealousy reasons or good ol' female intuition, I needed to keep an eye on the woman who rubbed her familial ties with Sadik in my face. I couldn't forget they had a sexual history. I'll never forget her reaction to the announcement of my pregnancy. It was one of a betrayed lover, not a relative.

"Goodnight." Kimmy slipped past our cypher, leaving for the day.

"Well, for one, Iesha texted me, telling me to come through," Tiffany explained, then tickled Iesha. "Secondly," she sang. "I left *Chanel* earrings on Sadik's jet. I want to ask him about them."

"On his jet when?"

Tiffany made a show at thinking about that. "Back in August when we flew to Rome together."

I hated the spike in adrenaline I experienced in just seconds.

"Come in!" Iesha insisted. "I wanna show you my new sketch!"

I was too angry to respond. Tiffany's snake eyes were on me, deciding.

She placed Iesha down. "I would love to," her pitch so unnatural.

The girls ran down hall, past the foyer with excitement. My wary glare remained on Tiffany. I wasn't aware of her being very close to the girls outside of family gatherings. Monica confided in me how she never had the inclination to get close to Tiffany, though Tiffany had made attempts over the years.

She scoffed, rolling her eyes while grinning. "I heard about Monica and Iban. When I called Irene, she told me the girls were with you and Sadik and gave me their iPod contacts. I texted them to check in and Iesha hit me back, saying she wanted me to come through."

That stung. Iesha was successful in finally hurting my feelings. Yet there was nothing I could do. She was a child and had no clue of the type of relationship her uncle once had with Tiffany. When Tiffany stepped inside, anger surged in my veins. I slid in front of her, my distended belly being the barrier.

"You've got fifteen minutes to make up an excuse to leave or I'll give you one."

I slammed the door closed.

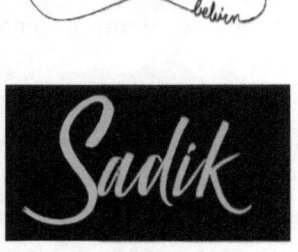

Her Lover: *I miss your lips.*

The last text from her, eight hours ago, nearly knocked me off task. It reminded me of my fatigue from having been awake for close to thirty-six hours. What I'd give to be wrapped over her, face buried in her bosom. I'd been away nine days. The first stop was a three-day trip up to Montreal to meet with a tech team we'd taken on for better breathalyzer sensors built inside of vehicles. I knew little on the subject, so the company built a curriculum lasting two days to catch me up to speed. After Canada was Silicon Valley, where the actual warehouses were for testing and production. It was there where I had meetings set up with associates who knew more about the industry and my investee's competition. Two were from the *US National Highway Traffic Safety Administration*. I needed to weigh all factors, considering this was a multimillion dollar venture I'd committed to. Then I had to check on my dispensary in Los Angeles and spend a few days there, making my presence known.

Days before all of the travel, I received the call from Monica, needing help distracting the girls. Bilan agreed we couldn't decline her request and volunteered to keep the girls, although I'd be away. I had a feeling the task would be a lot on Bilan and involve lots of changes to her daily routine. I brought Rory with me for these stops, leaving Johnson with Bilan. She just began her ninth month of pregnancy. The last thing I needed was Bilan overwhelmed, and not because she was fragile, but because my life was.

This pregnancy journey was a beautiful one. I'd lost the first three and a half months of it, but was right on time for seeing her belly grow. I'd been obsessed with it, taking pictures and videos anytime I could. There were even two of her in bondage I found myself staring at when alone this week. I talked to my son, kissed him where he kicked, and had upped my foot massage game. It was tricky with a pregnant woman, but ironically aroused mine greatly. Her nose spread, areolae darkened...coming up with creative positions to satisfy her sexually, and even working out with her had all delighted me. Still, having only five months of these beautiful changes, I felt cheated. I was owed more.

As I gazed at the pictures with her and Ivana—*Iesha conspicuously missing in some*—guilt washed over me. She was bloated and beautiful. And I'd been neglecting her needs. I could feel Bilan taking increased trips into her head before I left. She hadn't mentioned anything about it or complained since I'd been away, but it was one of those things I could sense; her patterns.

A tap on my shoulders popped the affectionate bubble I found myself in that quickly from a simple text. Rory nodded toward the monitor we'd been watching inside a room of my father's warehouse. I broke my vow to never step foot inside of here again. This late night—or early morning—I'd invited myself. There was a matter I could no longer delay.

I watched my father engage Danny Lopez and Haitian Ricky at a conference table in another room as I'd instructed. Rory, Jamil, and I'd been observing the progress.

"Fuck that nigga," my father declared.

"Fuck Popov?" Ricky asked in disbelief, a spark of humor in his eyes.

"Yeah. He ain't never fit in with us no way. Now that we got new blood here," He gestured toward Danny. "we can do something new."

"New." Ricky scoffed.

Danny sat back with one arm on the table and nodded in agreement with my father.

"A new alliance. The one Rizzo had was fuckin' flawed. Fuck *The Commission*! Anybody over forty years old know he took that shit from the mafia anyway. With what I got in mind, we can share distributors. You can expand your bread to dope and pills at a reasonable wholesale price, and Lopez can increase his guns inventory."

Danny had made good on his promise to me. Three days after Christmas, Luis Lopez was found dead with a bullet in his face, chest, and groin in an Atlantic City parking lot. His five-man security were casualties the officials were chalking up to victims of a robbery.

"Without Popov?"

"Fuck him."

"But he's your connect." Ricky's French accent rearing was an indicator that he'd bought into it.

My father shook his head. "If we do this, we share connects. We go with yours."

Ricky always had his own connect, someone he never shared. His primary trade was guns. He could move them fast on the streets, sales exceeding my father's because it was Ricky's specialty. Sharing it cut Popov out, which was now paramount.

The room grew quiet, waiting on an answer. Ricky made a show of pulling out a cigarette, and lighting it. He pulled several times to have the flame catch, which meant he was stalling. Patience was key here.

"How much you talking on powder and pills?" Ricky asked, blowing smoke into the air.

"I'll give you fifteen percent over what I give my distros," my father offered.

"Me? Fifteen percent?" Ricky doubted the offer.

My father shrugged. "Nigga, you forget I'm a wealthy man? Bringing you in levies the income I'll gain from your distributor."

Ricky took a few more puffs on his cigarette to think more. "I want a connect fee." He pointed to my father and Danny. "From both you niggas."

"How much're you talking?" Danny asked.

Ricky considered it. "A quarter." He narrowed his gaze, challenging him.

"Hell, no!" Danny shook his head.

"A quarter of a million?" My father asked, testing out the theory.

"From both y'all." Ricky pulled from his cigarette again, appearing to be feeling himself.

My father snorted. "Muthafucka, if I'm paying a quarter, I need to hear from your connect we good on this."

Ricky's eyes slid over to Danny for his answer.

"Look," Danny's eyes blinked hard several times. "You asking for that type of bread, there better be some guarantees. Get that muthafucka on the phone now."

Ricky's face folded. "C'mon, my niggas. It's almost four in the goddamn morning."

"Man, listen..." My father scratched the back of his head. "I been in this game longer than both you niggas been alive. If it's one thing I know, there's only two reasons to be woken out of ya sleep: pussy and money."

"Damn." Danny laughed. "Not even death?"

"Not even death should interrupt that muthafucka. What the fuck you gone do? The person's gone, my nigga!" My father's arms shot into the air, shrugging.

He meant those words. It was one of many rules he'd passed on to Iban and me.

Danny and Ricky chuckled at my old man's adamancy.

"Look, man," Danny addressed Ricky. "What're you gonna do?"

Ricky let go of a sigh, mirth still playing at his lips. "Fuck it," he breathed out. He reached for his phone and began typing in it.

Minutes had passed before my father asked, "Fuck's going on?"

"I sent your numbers to his people." Ricky's phone ringing interrupted his next words. "Yo?" he answered, putting the call on speaker mode.

"Are they there?" a familiar voice inquired.

"Yup," Ricky replied.

"Mr. Lopez, my condolences," the man on the other line offered. "Mr. Ellis, your reputation precedes you. It's an honor." Ringing from devices could be heard as he finished his last sentence. "Those should be confirmation texts coming from my camp. It's your assigned number, along with figures I hope you agree to. When you're ready to 'shop', you reply with your assigned number to that text and my men will take it from there. Any questions?"

"Yeah," my father answered. "Can I get a damn name?"

"You, sir, must be the senior Ellis." He chuckled. "I go by the name Bartek. Bartek Kolwaski. And this has been my pleasure." The line disconnected.

I couldn't control the smile opening on my face.

"Okay," Ricky took a final pull from his cigarette before putting it out on the table. "There you have it. Now, run me that bread."

My father nodded, seemingly in deep thought. He turned and motioned for his security, Big John. That was my cue.

"I'll have the cash counted and brought to you," was all I heard before gaiting out of the room.

Less than a minute later, I was entering the room, seeing the two men Ricky had with him being escorted inside with their hands and legs tied up, mouths gagged. Their frames wobbling side to side from limited motion of their legs. I joined the gentlemen. Ricky's expression resembled someone who'd just seen a fucking ghost.

"Surprised to see me?" I asked in jest. That's when I saw it. The realization of a near ending of life washing over a man's face. Ricky's eyes bounced between Rory and me.

"The fuck going on here?" Ricky barked.

When he tried to stand, Danny pointed a gun to his temple. "Sit the fuck down."

"No need to rush out of here, Mr. Pierro. We need a little tête-à-tête before you go," I advised.

"Man," he groaned. "Don't tell me this shit about fuckin' Randi?"

I lifted a brow. "Randi?"

"She fucked up again...like she did with you. This time, I slapped her ass around a little. That ain't got shit to do with you or her friend."

I nodded, chuckling quietly. "I've told you once, I couldn't give a shit about Randi. But funny you mention my lady. It was fucked up that you let Lopez's men come into your party and almost shoot her. I mean, I get you not giving a fuck about Lopez sending his pups to murk me at your party." My face tightened. "Then again, I don't get that either. What beef do you have with me that you'd let Lopez convince your hermit ass to have a party, risking your freedom?"

"Look, man!" Ricky squirmed in his seat. "I ain't have shit to do with that. That was all Lopez." His eyes swung over to Danny.

"You wanna tell that bold face lie to a Lopez, Rick?" I chuckled. "Don't be silly."

"You can't prove I had shit to do with that."

"Actually, I can and did," I replied honestly. "You and Lopez wanted to eradicate my father from the business. You forget that

Danny here inheriting his father's business comes with his men, too. We're aware of the meetings you two took to plot this. You thought by killing me, you'd bring Double E Bags to his knees. All the calls you made to Tiffany about my RSVP were to make sure I'd be there. You probably had Randi's dumb ass pressuring Bilan for reasons Randi didn't know."

"Did that nigga pay you a quarter for your services?" my father posed, hands in his pockets, legs stretched apart. "I should put a bullet directly up your ass to prove how much of a hole you are."

"Man, y'all acting like this ain't the game," Ricky declared. "Just like you took Damien and Rizzo out, y'all got these side beefs happen all the fuckin' time. Lopez had a dope ass plan to make money. He tossed me a few dollars to make it happen; ain't nothing personal in this shit!"

My father's head shook. "Damien fucked me over, but Rizzo wasn't me."

Danny's gaze on my father was academic. He didn't know if he believed him. There had been several stories floating in the streets about Rizzo's death. One I'd created, and others that involved my father because of Lia and Iban. None impressed the police; I couldn't give a shit about anybody else.

"Yeah, just like your pretty boy son here ain't fuck my lady!" Ricky shouted, tweaking now.

My head reared and eyes shot wide. "You still holding on to that shit, bruh? I told you then, if I put my dick in your girl, I would cop to it then apologize. I don't lie on my dick, Rick. Wish you would believe me. Randi ain't exactly prize material. The mileage on that pussy supersedes what I allow on my fuckin' *May*—"

My instincts had me jump back when Ricky lunged from his chair, swinging a blade my way, knocking over the table. Before John could leap for him, I had Ricky's lanky ass kissing my *Ase Garbs*.

My heavy body vibrated on the elevator. I closed my burning eyes for half a second and we were stopping on the second floor.

"Rest up, big boy. You put in that work today," Rory rumbled, slapping my shoulder.

I was able to open my eyes just enough to see her wheel her suitcase off the elevator. The doors closed and I willed my body to stay upright. I couldn't remember the last time I was this drained. Having been up for over two days with mere junk food had my body breaking down.

When the elevator tolled, I drug myself and my luggage out. From the hallway, I could hear music playing. I tapped the keypad to open the door and heard the music even crisper. My brain was so fried, the volume didn't alarm me.

I left the suitcase in the foyer and hauled my vibrating frame down the hall. En route, a miniature figure appeared.

"Uncle Deek!" Iesha lunged at me, clasping her little arms around my sweatpants. "You're home!"

"Uncle Deek!" I heard Ivana cry from the kitchen. On autopilot, I turned to go to her. Both girls were set up at the island bar, eating cereal. Ivana still had food in her bowl. Iesha's across from her was empty. Ivana's lips were puckered. "Can you put two braids in my hair? Auntie B said we can't go to the indoor pool downstairs because my hair is out." A tear slipped. "She got swimming caps, but my hair like this can't fit it."

"Where's Bilan?" I rasped.

"She trying on clothes with that white lady," Iesha answered, putting her bowl away. "That's why this music's so loud."

"*JAGMisha Boutique*'s here. And Ms. Kimmy just went down on the service elevator to get the grocery delivery. She's been doing laundry and it's taking too long."

I could barely process the reservation I made for the boutique to come and have Bilan sized and suited for a surprise I had for her tomorrow was happening now. I didn't recall asking for the comb Ivana pushed into my hand. Wearily, I moved to stand behind her stool and began parting her hair. I learned how to braid when Taaliba was just as small as these girls. She had a tender-head and would give my mother and the staff hell, crying the whole time her hair was being done. One day, I braved taking over for the nanny. I had no idea what I was doing and had to be coached. Learning how to detangle hair to put into symmetric ponytails turned into me learning how to braid on a doll baby. Iban wrung my ass out over it for years. *Until he had daughters.* I taught him how to detangle and put ponytails in. Braiding was beyond his learning curve.

Kimmy sauntered in with bags of groceries as I managed the first symmetric French braid. The girls began chatting. I got the low down on the things that had taken place since they arrived. Iesha had been fresh to my Nalib, but I'd been too drained to address it. Tiffany's name came up in my haze. That had to be when they were at my mother's dinner. Tiff wouldn't come to my place. She knew Bilan lived here. Again, I didn't spend much time tossing that over; I had no capacity for rationale. My braid wasn't even the tightest, yet my swollen fingers trembled. I was able to finish the task and, without a word, I trudged out of the kitchen.

"You okay, Uncle Deek? You look like a bum."

"Yeah! Your beard is wild!"

The girls laughed.

"C'mon, girls," Kimmy tried quieting them. "Let me finish putting these away and I'll take you to the pool until Bilan's ready."

It felt like an eternity before I made it to the bathroom in the master suite. I peeled off my clothes with great labor. My arms worked slow in the shower, and eyes couldn't stay focused while brushing my teeth in the mirror. The music still rang loudly in the air, not rousing me a bit. I did, however, have the good judgment to force myself into the closet for boxers before approaching the bed. The comforter and sheets were still turned down on Bilan's side, which I was grateful for. I barely made it before collapsing.

A soul ballad broke my sleep. A soft, rhythmic and breathy falsetto. *Sabrina Claudio*... *"Frozen."*

It felt like I'd just left a dream about being on the set of *"The Fast and Furious."* That was until I felt steady tugs near my ass, then thighs. Sleep. I needed to get back there. I shifted, turning on my back to ease the pinching of my skin. Then I felt soft hands on my thighs, moving them apart. My eyes couldn't open. I didn't want them to. Back to the set, I wanted to go.

When a soft, wet gyration hit my cock, I thought I'd transcended spiritual planes. I'd never felt this disconnected from my body. My dick felt everything, my brain struggled to keep up. But when it did, my hips thrusted into the pleasure. My head rolled to the side, giving in to the compelling sensation.

Her hands were on my cheeks, breath in my face. "You're so hard." She was on my lips, soft and breathy. "Your beard is thick." I could perceive Bilan's voice. Then I felt what was indisputably her pussy at the apex of my cock...her hands, too. "You're tired, I know," she whispered close to my ear. I could feel the stiffness of her belly pressing into my abdomen when she kissed me with her tongue. "I'm so glad you're home."

She lifted from my chest, pushing back down to fit me all in. When my eyes strained to open, that dark line running from her navel to her black soft hairs appeared. That's when I knew where I was and what was happening. Bilan was fucking me. She was forcing her walls to open as she did. I felt the moment she was into her groove, her thighs pressing into the side of my abdomen, her weight distributed evenly, and her moans crooning in between the notes of the music.

Goddamn...

She was a beautiful, erotic image. Her full breasts plopped into the air, swollen lips slightly dry but damn enthralling. It was painful to keep my eyes open, but no way I could leave this erotic vision. Her splayed hands grabbed her belly, then pushed up to her engorged tits. They reached her neck, making me think she enjoyed her own touch. Her nails raked through the short hairs of her head before she threaded them on top, all the while grinding over me. Her lips parted, eyes closed, rolling behind their lids. Bilan moved in the same fashion of the song. Sultry and purposefully.

She increased her speed, arms dropping, fingers now on me. She grasped my pecs, using them as an anchor as she rocked hard. Through low lids, I observed the biting of her bottom lip while her eyes were half-mast. Then her walls spasmed around me. When her dives lost rhythm, my head rolled to the side. My Nalib was coming. Her pussy creamed, walls quaked, and cries shot from her mouth. Those cries didn't get lost in the loud music. I couldn't escape the perfect melody of them.

When she stopped, dropping down to my chest, I kissed her with all the passion I could muster. I loved her femininity. She'd just learned how to fuck months ago, yet worked herself to a climax without assistance from me. That reached something deeper than my loins. Bilan pricked my heart; penetrated it with her fearlessness.

Mine.

She was mine. Those were the last thoughts I could process when she lifted off my cock, her pelvis rocking, thighs straining.

"Baby, you didn't cum..."

∞**24**∞

I gaited down the hall, still a little groggy, but rested. Even having brushed my teeth and washed my face, I still didn't feel one hundred percent. The smell of food cooking awakened my stomach. I couldn't believe I slept an entire day away. Yesterday, after I rolled over from taking care of Bilan, she woke me later to eat. I dozed off in the middle of that as she told me the girls had been dropped off to Monica. Since then, I'd only awakened to take a leak and went back to bed.

When I stepped into the kitchen, the most enticing sight entranced me. Bilan stood over the stove wearing boy shorts, a sports bra, and an apron as she stirred a pot of grits.

"Does it come with eggs, because I see the damn biscuit," I chuckled, balls pulsated.

As I stretched my arms out over my head, Bilan peered over her shoulder at me for half a second before going back to her task.

"I was just about to wake you up," her tone total aplomb. "Have a seat."

I gazed over to the table and saw it was set for two.

"I should have called my mother to let her know we wouldn't be able to make church today."

"I told her last night when she called to check in," she answered with her back to me. "Your father must have told her you were back. Did you call him on your way in?"

I blinked, considering that. "Maybe Rory's spoken to him."

Telling her I'd been with my father the morning I returned to her bed, killing Ricky wasn't an option.

Bilan brought a plate of turkey bacon and eggs over to me, along with a bowl of grits. It was the perfect breakfast. She'd been doing better with the grits. They weren't exactly Irene's, but definitely a resemblance of hers. And she put them in a bowl, which meant she wanted me to fill my belly after not having eaten much yesterday.

When she brought her own food over, I was pleased to see she was making a show of eating. It had still been a concern of mine, though she says she'd gotten better for the baby. Bilan sat across from me and respectfully waited to eat. She didn't commit to saying "Grace," but would allow me time to before she ate. When I was done, we both began to eat.

"So, a successful trip overall?" she asked with her eyes in her plate, forking food.

"Depends on how you view the purpose of it."

"The company's methods are competitive to what's currently out now? What did your Silicon Valley insiders have to say about them?"

I swallowed my food before answering, "*Tomorrow's Innovations* seems to be cutting edge with this new breathalyzer method, but I still question their timetable for production." I shrugged, stirring creamy grits. "It's honestly not my job to be concerned about that. They know what they promised and what the deliverables are." I began on my grits. "These are good, by the way."

"Thanks," she murmured with food in her mouth. "How was your flight in?"

I shrugged. "A flight, not particularly eventful. Just happy I could cut my time away short, even if just for a few hours. Sorry I missed the girls."

I felt it. She was stewing on something. Bilan found more interest in her plate than on my face. That was fucking unusual.

"It's okay. You didn't miss any new developments. Iesha still hates me."

"No, she doesn't." I leaned away from the table, face contorting. "She loved you from first sight, and you know that. It's the baby."

"No." Her eyes rolled into her plate as she chewed. "It's you."

"Me?"

"Those girls don't have their dad like they used to and they're feeling it. When they don't have him, apparently, you're the next staple they look to. So, it's you and your brother. I hear their private conversations during bath time...and playtime. You mean so much to them. Lia's baby, to them, is a distractor from them. The baby takes their dad's attention from them, in their little heads. So..."

I finished her theory, "Uncle Deek having a baby will complete the ruin of their family."

She nodded. "Of their 'normal.' Uncle Deek is a huge part of their normal."

I took a minute to think about that. "Kids adjust. The girls are no different."

"Yeah, but they're little girls. They don't get Iban's absence isn't indicative of his love for them."

My eyes fell unexpectedly and I scratched my head. "I've never told you this, but Ib's on meds."

"For what?"

It was hard to share. Our family had been protective of him since learning it. "It's called Brief Psychotic Disorder."

"What's that?"

I took a deep breath. It was one of several mental disorders my brother had been diagnosed with. "It's hard to explain because there are several symptoms for it that he doesn't present, but according to two clinicians, Iban displays. It's when one has short, sudden episodes of psychotic behavior in response to a stressful situation. The episode lasts less than a month."

"So, that's why he's been missing lately? No dinners when we're there, no Thanksgiving or Christmas?"

I cut out a piece of scrambled eggs to fork. The most difficult part of being in a relationship, for men like me, was deciding when to lie and when to omit. It's not that I didn't trust Bilan. I wasn't convinced she could handle the unsavory facts, especially because on those few days when Bilan went into a dark hole, I feared she, too, struggled from mental illness. I'd been pretty convinced of it, yet unsure of what exactly. I didn't want her seeing a therapist or on medication while expecting her first child, so I hadn't pushed for her to seek help. It was selfish of me, I knew. I only wanted the best for her, and now, our son.

"I can't say for sure, but possibly," I answered.

Bilan sat back, sighing. The last thing I needed was her pitying Iban. He didn't adhere to his treatment schedules to better manage his shit. He was bullheaded, and I wouldn't have him projecting that bullshit onto Bilan.

She shook her head. "If it ain't one thing, it's another."

"What do you mean?" I continued to eat.

"I guess you didn't hear when rolling over to check your phones yesterday."

I shook my head, not wanting to even think about the work awaiting me. "I don't even know where they are. Probably somewhere in my clothes."

"Ricky's dead."

My hand froze midway to my mouth. I lay the spoon down in the bowl. "Ricky?"

With hiked brows, Bilan bobbed her head. "Ricky. Randi's Ricky. The Ricky whose party we went to last September. The Ricky in your father's organization," she whispered the last one.

Bilan's eyes were pink. She was upset.

I took a deep breath, not wanting her wild speculations to be greater than what she'd just exposed. "Ricky has never been a part of my father's organization. They've never had transactions in business. That's not what *The Commission* was."

"Was?"

"Yes. They've disbanded."

"When?" shot from her lips. "Why?"

I shook my head. "Baby, that's not my line of work. I know the little I know because of my relationship with my family, but none of it affects our world."

"As long as it's your father's world, it will affect yours. And what affects you, affects my baby and me. It's happened to my friend, Sadik. Ricky's gone. They weren't married, so she has no legal ties to anything. She has no money and no place to go."

She didn't cry. Bilan was upset, but not helplessly emotional. And for that, I was relieved.

I reached across the table for her hand. "I'm sorry to hear this."

"And I feel so helpless. I have nothing to offer her. She's been staying at Tasche's because Ricky had the nerve to hit her a few days ago. But she can't stay with Tasche forever. They're more associates than friends. If I'd still been at my parents', she would have been with me."

"But you're not, Bilan."

And she damn sure ain't coming here...

"I know, but I just wish there was something I could do, like rent out my parents' place to her, or something."

Hell no.

"Where does she work?"

Sighing, Bilan pinched the bridge of her nose. "She doesn't. Jason made the same argument."

I steeled in my chair, the remnants of food in my mouth suddenly sour and distasteful.

Bilan's eyes widened with revelation. "Sadi—"

"What did you discuss with him that you couldn't with me?"

Her mouth opened with only a sound croaking from it. Bilan licked her lips. "I was just venting with him last night. You were sleep."

"I am here for you, Bilan!" I barked, losing my cool. Then I thought to close my eyes, counting to ten to calm myself. "I'm awake now, Nalib. What did you tell Jason?"

Here was yet another reason I couldn't disclose everything to my love. She could tell the smallest detail that could prove damning for my family to a so-called friend, who had been in touch with the *FBI* regarding me. Similar to the other night with my father and his associates, I couldn't compromise my intel, Jefferson, putting him at risk.

Bilan shrugged. "He just texted to check in. I called him back, needing to talk to someone after the conversation I'd just had with Randi. She tries to play tough, but the girl was shaken. And I felt helpless."

"What did you say to him, Bilan?" I asked, voice firm.

"I told him what I told you, how I wish I could rent her one of your properties."

"And?"

"And he said it was a bad idea because she didn't have income."

"Did you tell him about your parents' home?"

"That would be dumb, Sadik. You told me you couldn't have purchased it as my fiancé."

Internally, I sighed. She'd been listening. She understood.

"Please don't speak to him again." I looked her dead in the eyes. "In my home, in my cars, or on any of the devices I've bought."

Bilan's neck snapped, bringing her head back. "Excuse me?"

"I didn't stutter, neither did I misuse my words. I don't want you speaking to him, Bilan. He tried to fuck you in our home. He's always wanted to fuck you."

"I don't want you speaking to *Mrs. Buttersworth*. And guess what? You've actually fucked her. Again and again and again."

My reaction was similar to hers a few seconds ago, just internally.

"Tiffany?"

"Yes!"

"What does she have to do with anything?"

"She's a physical manifestation of your past. I have to see her across dinner tables, away at holiday destinations, and even my door —excuse me—*your* door, now that we're itemizing your things."

The girls did *mention Tiffany...*

"Tiffany was here?"

"Yes."

"For what?"

"Yeah. This is my favorite part: to see about the personal items she left in your jet last August when you two visited Rome."

"Is that all she said?"

Her head swung again. "Isn't that enough? It was for me. Now, it makes sense why you were at the governor's ball together."

I took a deep breath. "Did she tell you what she did there?"

"No. I figured I'd wait for you to share with me what you did *together*."

"I went on business. She asked to use the jet to get a gown done by a designer there. I figured I'd kill two birds with one stone and agreed to let her jump on the flight. "

"And that's it," she stated doubtfully.

"We didn't even share the same hotel."

"But I'm supposed to be okay knowing you were globetrotting without a care in the world while I was running for my life?"

"Bilan, while I was taking care of business to settle my life, I knew my fiancée was stowed away safely in our beach home, a place she found peaceful. If you think for a minute I was happy, restful, or worry-free, you've lost your damn mind."

"You tied her up?" With a tight grimace, Bilan tossed her chin toward me.

Shit...

"Where the fuck did that come from?"

What the hell did Tiff say?

"Where's my answer?"

"No." I wanted to.

"I don't believe you. You like it too much."

I scratched my chin. "Bilan, the shit I do with you hasn't all been done with women before."

"We're not talking about other women. I'm asking about Tiffany. I want to know if she knows what it feels like relinquishing all control to you when wrapped in one of your ropes."

My dick twitched at the mention of Bilan purring as I roped her.

"Nalib," I sighed. "My sexual history and that of my general dynamic with Tiffany was a unique one. For years, I'd known she maintained a crush on me—"

Bilan scoffed. "Apparently, applying and getting into *Blakewood* to be with you."

I forgot she knew about that. "Yes. But believe it or not, I have a tested level of self-control. I don't indulge every woman who seems interested. Tiffany is my father's goddaughter. Her father was like an uncle to me. I didn't fuck her until she was thirty, giving her the opportunity to find something real or have her share of experiences at casual relationships."

"You expect me to believe you didn't sleep with her until she was thirty? I'm twenty-eight, Sadik."

"And I'm Sadik fucking Qadir Ellis. You think Tiffany was the only woman in my face before I met you? I wasn't desperate when I'd finally decided. And even then, I was strategic in managing her expectations."

"How?"

I raked my hands over my head, groaning. Talking about women had never been a thing of mine. "By not fuckin' at our places. She's never stayed here, and I can count on one hand how many times I stayed at hers. Tiffany was fragile, so I had to be smart."

"You consider her a friend?"

"Do you, Jason?"

She hesitated. "I do, but not a confidant. You don't have to worry about me telling him anything about you."

"Do you tell him about our homes...our travel?"

"The traveling has come up when he'd asked what I'm doing for the holidays. But I've never detailed anything. I don't send him pictures, even though he's nosy and has asked."

My brows shot up, remembering his text to her. "What pictures?"

"Sadik, you have to trust me. I know how delicate your life—our life together—is. If you want me to fall back from Jason, I'll do it. But know, peace of mind goes both ways. I don't like Tiffany. She may try appearing mature by speaking to me, but her reaction to you expecting your first child confirmed so much for me."

"Like what?"

"Like you can't just be friends with a guy like you after having a sexual affair."

I nodded, pushing my food away. It was now cold. "Is that my insurance for your forever?"

Bilan rolled her eyes. "You didn't answer my question about Tiffany being your friend."

"Tiffany's family. It makes it complicated. Do I trust her?" I shrugged. "I guess as much as I would a relative."

"Even with the Ellis' secrets?"

I shook my head. "There are some she knows, some she never will. The same goes for my mother, sister, and Monica."

I watched as her lips parted. She knew. She got the message. There were just some things Bilan would have to be okay with not knowing. Like why I was in Rome with Tiffany.

Bilan's eyes rolled to the corner of the room. "Well, you need to return all her things from the jet. She'll never step foot on *The Ellis II* again. I hope we're clear on that."

"Crystal."

"Neither will she visit here. I don't want her in my face or my child's, posing as a relative. She may be your god-sister, but she's nothing to my son. Nothing."

"No objections." I tossed my napkin in my plate and stood from the table to leave.

"Where are you going?"

"To find my phones and catch up with work before six. We have a date tonight with that gown you were sized for by the boutique."

"What are we doing?"

I turned to her. "Pursuing our happily ever after. I've been working for over a week. I'm still not Mr. Bilan yet. I've got work to do."

"I'm not done with you, Sadik," she warned.

"I would hope not."

I left the kitchen.

The car stopped in front of a building with wooden veneer. A larger barn style door in front of us.

Sadik turned to me. "You ready?"

This was odd. I knew he wanted to go out tonight, but never said where.

"I guess."

He opened his door, leaving the car. At the same time, my door opened, Rory holding it for me. Sadik arrived and assisted me out. My heels needed settling in the gravel road. He held me, helping me onto the cemented walkway leading toward the barn door.

"You good?" he asked.

"Yeah." Mishka suggested a larger shoe size for tonight.

The idea worked because I was able to glide next to Sadik. I just didn't know how long the job would be effortless. I'd never in my life carried so much weight or had my body transform into something so unrecognizable. Some changes gradual, others seemed to develop overnight. That was the case with my feet. But I wouldn't change it. I was one of those crazy women who loved being pregnant.

"Are you going to hold up in those shoes until tonight when I fuck you in them?" Sadik murmured so crisply, causing an expected giggle to shoot from my belly.

"Yeah, right. Maybe in my *Uggs*."

"Dammit!" he playfully grunted like a child, tickling me even more.

We were just two steps away when the door slid open on a track. A burning glow of light burst from the inside, illuminating the way. Loose, pearl hued balloons covered the floor. And immediately, music could be heard. A soft, jazzy tune. Yellow and white light bulbs were everywhere: on the tall wooden walls, hanging from wires dropping from the ceiling. It was breathtakingly magical.

"Step over here," Sadik ordered the moment we crossed the threshold.

Behind us, I could see the man who opened the door operating a panel to close it. Sadik dropped to his knees and I felt him at my feet. When I glanced down, I saw a pair of flat, chic slippers. They were all white, like my dress.

I stepped out of the heels, allowing Sadik to exchange them for the slippers. As he stood, the gentleman was at my back, asking for my cape. Sadik removed his coat, handing it off, too. I couldn't keep my eyes off the details of the room, white and off-white.

On the adjacent walls were the words love, joy, peace, and my name assembled by balloons. It was simple, yet elegant and wholly intimate. I saw no one else in the massive room. The man disappeared with our coats.

"This is beautiful," I noted out loud as Sadik walked me to the center of the room.

"Not as beautiful as you are," he replied, sweeping me into his arms.

I didn't know about that. The details in the balloons, the glow of the room... It was a vibe. That's when something hit me.

"Why is your name missing from the balloons?"

"Because tonight's all about you." He kissed the center of my forehead gently. "I can't repay you for each day, hour, or second you endured, carrying my child. There's no reimbursement on the pain you've experienced while joining lives with me. You deserve to be celebrated. Just you."

"You did all this for me?"

I swayed against him to the tempo of the song. My belly couldn't get me as close as I would have liked, but the alluring scent of his cologne and heat of his body were an experience all unto themselves.

"I did," he admitted with a deep nod, his felines cast out into the room. "With the help of a dozen or so people."

I giggled at his honesty, admiring the spacing of the balloons and the details of the lighting.

"Why did you ask me to wear white?"

His feather light finger traced my temple adoringly. Then his eyes appeared on me. "Because you're pure, Nalib. You're my first, and I am yours."

"First what?" I laughed.

"You're my first love. I'm your first everything."

I whispered silkily, "You weren't my first, Deek."

His eyes narrowed, lips twisted with disbelief. "Knock it the fuck off, Nalib. You know I was your first in so many ways, especially sexually." He kissed the tip of my nose. "Your pretty pussy only knows me. Only acknowledges me. Should I prove it?" His lips were on my ears.

My eyes fluttered, lips ajar with heavy breaths pushing through. "You didn't come yesterday."

Sadik skipped a beat before returning, "I didn't need to. You did, and that's what I needed."

When he waxed selfless poetic in my ears, it chased fears of letting it all go with him. He leaned into my head as we swayed in a sea of balloons, humming the lyrics to the jazzy tune.

"*Maybe we're better misunderstood...*"

"Who is this?" I asked about the song. "It's beautiful."

"Lucky Daye." He reached down to get closer to me. "A kid out of New Orleans. Dope talent."

I smiled, eyes closed as we moved rhythmically. "It's really nice."

"We've got specifics to discuss," he advised.

"Like what?"

"Provisions for the baby. You're due in a few short weeks."

"Again, like what?" My smile was permanent.

"Like childcare. Short term and long term. Assistance. Who's going to help with caring for the baby? When are you going back to work? What will happen then?"

"That's a lot."

"It is."

"I thought you'd help with the baby," I made clear.

"It's my baby, my responsibility. Of course, I'll be there with him. But I work erratic hours. We need to think long term."

"I don't understand."

"We have nannies to help with our babies. My parents have employed them since Taaliba was born. The primary nanny is Stacy at *Elliswoods Palace*, but she lives there."

My smile dimmed. "You want to move into *Elliswoods Palace*?"

"If you want to, but it isn't necessary. We can find our own."

"Or I can do what millions of mothers survive and do without one."

He shook his head. "You're not an average woman, at least not your circumstances. You want to work and you're a fulltime student. I run three businesses, primarily, with more coming. *I'm* a fulltime obligation to you. That won't ever change. I don't need you overwhelmed, Nalib. I need you strong, confident, and with a sound mind. There's nothing wrong with help."

I was stumped. A nanny was such a foreign concept. However, Sadik was right. I'd been struggling to keep up this last semester with school. Fatigue was a different bird this trimester. All I'd been wanting had been Sadik's body and a pillow.

"I'll have to think about that," I murmured, so unsure.

"We don't have long. Talk to Monica and my mom. They can share their experiences."

I nodded. "Okay."

"And what about his name?" Sadik asked. I paused, pulling my head back to look at him. "I know you had a strong affection for your father. I would be okay if you wanted to name him Asad."

My heart melted in my chest. The gleam in his irises so sweet and sincere. I wondered when I'd ever see the last inch of his heart. Sadik never failed to amaze me with his generosity and forethought.

I shook my head. "He's an Ellis."

He snorted, "Of course, he is. That won't change."

Sadik didn't get it. "He's the first son and child of Sadik Ellis."

Sadik nodded, a humble smirk ghosting on his handsome face. "This is true."

"Then it's only fitting to name him after his chief and pops. Only Sadik Qadir Ellis would be a suitable name for my first son."

A harsh breath left his nostrils and his cheeks stretched wide, eyes narrowing with contentment. He brushed his soft lips against mine, the tips of his goatee tickling my face had butterflies sprouting in my stuffed belly.

"I'm honored, Bilan. Really, I am."

I chuckled. "I don't see where the options were. Just be responsible with him, Sadik. The Earl Ellis way isn't the only to raise a sound, law-abiding child."

His response to my bold admonishing was pulling me into his arms, one hand at the back of my neck, the other at the center of my butt. He held me possessively, determined for me to experience his happiness.

When he pulled back, Sadik asked, "What about the wedding?"

"I have to have the baby first, Sadik!" I squealed. "You're going to make me go into premature labor with all these details and demands."

"The summer too soon?"

"I'll have an infant!" I gasped.

"And you'll have me."

My eyes watered at the pledge. "That makes me happy to hear, Sadik," I croaked, looking silly.

He kissed my lips again. "Let's get you off your feet." He led me over to an adjacent wooden door on a sliding track similar to the one we entered the building using. This one was smaller. "Thanks for this quiet moment between us. That period before no babies, bottles, dirty diapers, pots clanging on the floor, lost pacifiers, funky preteens, and nagging teens." He tapped a button, and the door began to slide. "And let's not forget, doting friends and family."

The further the door slid, the clearer music could be heard. A familiar tune I distinctively tied to a memory shared with Sadik. The name of it didn't come because I was startled by the boisterous shouts of, "Surprise!"

My grasp on Sadik's hand tightened as I processed what was happening. Dozens of familiar faces—family, friends, pseudo-family, and his staff—glowed with elation. Rory was to the right blowing a noise-maker and tossing confetti over her head with a blank expression.

Irene beaming while beneath the arm of her husband, the senior Ellis. Earl's chest was out, a twinkle of joy in his eyes. My Aunt Franzel clapped with enthusiasm not much different than my cousin, Mimi, and other aunt, Astur. Coworkers I'd just became acquainted with at *Ellis Academy* cheered. Monica was without the baby, it seemed, but Ivana and Iesha were front line and center. Tears threatened at the sight of Carina Ricci, co-owner of *Michelle's Diner*, as well as Marta, a polish waitress I was cool with. I recognized Julius Richards and his wife, Keisha. So many people...too many for my brain to process.

Ivana ran to me with Tasche on her heels.

"You look pretty, Auntie B!" Ivana greeted.

I bent as much as I could to hug her. "And so do you, baby girl!"

"Like royalty, yo!" Tasche declared, looking like a chocolate vixen in her solid blue bodycon mini and silver heels. Her jet black tresses, long waves down her spine. "I'm feeling this slayage with your makeup. You ain't gain nothing but a stomach. Fuckin' royalty, yo!"

I was so overwhelmed by her presence, I pulled her into me for a hug, possibly the first of an emotional embrace I'd ever pulled from her. We stepped farther into the room, the guests opening a path for me to enter. That's when the song was clear. Vesta Williams' "*Sweet Sweet Love*" provided a maturing, loving celebratory ambiance. But that wasn't half the romantic discovery. There was a cover band, singing and playing it live on a stage across the room. And what an enormous room it was. This space was vastly larger than the one we'd just left and resembled a barn.

Tables with orange and ivory bulbs and candles were arranged in the center of what was clearly a ballroom. The light and balloon theme continued in here. All white draperies and a screen on one projecting pictures of Sadik as a baby and...me.

I turned to him in sheer shock. "Where did those come from?"

He smiled. "You forget I have the other key to the room where we house your parents' storage? Before I left, I went there and searched the boxes." He kissed my cheek. "You made it easy on me with your labels." He pointed ahead. "Look."

I turned in time to see images of me at various stages of my pregnancy since October rotating on in carousel fashion. Those annoying pictures Sadik had to have of me were displayed in the most loving manner. All except for me in manila and nylon ropes, thankfully. Then there were several from just outside of here, when Sadik and I exited his *Maybach* and walked toward the door. One was of me laughing when he requested sex in heels tonight.

"How did you do that?" I breathed, in complete awe.

Sadik winked. "I'd bring the moon and the stars to you if it meant the utter amazement you're displaying now. I hope you enjoy your baby shower, Nalib."

He pointed again, this time, in a different area of the room where a beautiful pearl, tiered cake with "*Sir Ellis*" in blue frosting running down a staircase was on a cloth table appearing regal.

I turned to Sadik. "*Michelle's?*" Had to be.

"Nicky," he qualified.

My heart blossomed.

"You look lovely!" I heard cried behind me. It was Aunt Franzel, and my family was in tow. "This place is amazing!" I returned her hug, noticing Sadik stepping off.

"I'm so happy his family includes us. It's important we stay connected." That odd and bold statement came from Aunt Astur, who was next to hug me.

"Well, thanks for coming. I'm so overwhelmed." I laughed, still coming out of a daze from all of this. "I had no clue. One minute, I'm being told to get a dress, the next I'm told to put it on and I'm here." My arms shot in the air.

They laughed along with me.

"That's sounds so sweet!" Mimi gushed.

"What I wanna know," Joslyn broke between my aunt and cousin with pinched brows. "is why did the invitation say adult only, making me leave my baby at home, but I see two little girls here."

My eyes ballooned and I pulled in a breath, stunned.

Mimi shooed her complaint with a wave of the hand. "She ain't got nothing to do with that, girl. You heard her just say she was surprised. She ain't even know this was happening."

My aunts seemed to agree with Mimi, side-eyeing Joslyn.

Tasche appeared out of nowhere. "They said they 'bout to get started, yo."

My family heard that and began to retreat to the tables.

Joslyn rolled her eyes following them, but not before I caught, "Well, I can go and take that twenty-five-dollar gift certificate out of the card I bought. Nobody knew about that either. Or my baby's old clothes I'm giving in those bags over there. I can take those back without nobody..." She was too far for me to hear the rest.

But Tasche caught on. "That bitch brought a fuckin' twenty-five dollar gift card and shitty ass hand-me-downs to a goddamn Ellis baby shower, and she think she stuntin'?"

I rolled my eyes, blowing Jos' statement off. There was a more important topic I needed to venture to. "No Randi, huhn?"

Tasche rolled her eyes, face crestfallen. "She fucked up, yo. Drunk as fuck in my living room."

"I can only imagine what losing Ricky means to her."

"It was before then. She been getting fucked up since the night she left the hospital, and shit. She got this dark ass energy in my crib, yo. I'm tryna help, but I 'on't know how much longer."

I grabbed her hand, holding it to my chest. "I'm going to figure out a way to help. I've been thinking already. I'll figure out something."

"Good evening, ladies and gentlemen," a gruffy alto spoke into the microphone. It was Earl Ellis. "I want to kick off the evening by thanking each and every one of you for coming out to celebrate the coming of the first male grandchild for me and my wife." The room exploded in applause. Monica and Taaliba stood in front of the stage, waving me over. Tasche and I went. I found Sadik leaning over the bar, watching from the side of the room. Earl waved his unlit cigar in the air for emphasis. "Now, you may already know I got a few favorite girls. One is my first and only born daughter. The apple of Daddy's eye, Taaliba." He left room for the small crowd's response. "I have a beautiful daughter-in-law, who bore the first of my grands, Monica." I smiled Monica's way, mirroring her response.

"And now I have a new favorite girl. She came in and knocked the damn door to my heart down. She's giving me my first grandson, a male heir to my legacy. Her name is Bilan." He gestured toward me. "Tonight, honey, we celebrate you at the end of this journey. I've found you to be a special, smart young lady, nothing less than I expected from the man of my own heart." His hand rested at the heart of his chest. The room applauded again.

That statement made me realize Iban wasn't in the room. It was strange, yet again relieving. This night had been magical from the moment we pulled up. It continued with kind words from Irene, then a sit-down dinner where Sadik annoyingly fed me while I tried talking to my cousins and friends. He was such a domineering alpha, unbothered by how it may have had us appear to my guests. And they looked. I caught a few elbow jabs and people pointing. But not even that could ruin the night.

The gifts were all beautiful and overwhelming at the same time. Taaliba and Monica hosted games and gave away prizes like hundred-dollar gift cards to *Urban Grind* and five hundred-dollar ones to *JAGMisha Boutique*. Aunt Astur won a dinner for two at *DiFillippo's*. And Marta, from the diner, won a pair of *Ase Garb* slippers. Those things were valued at three hundred-fifty dollars!

The cake cutting was an event. Sadik had to have his piece first and smeared a bit of frosting on my nose, then kissed it off. Of course, the women in the room swooned over that maneuver. After sitting for so long, I felt antsy. So when folks began chatting after the cake, I decided to hit the dancefloor.

The band began Patrice Rushen's *"Forget Me Nots"* and I took to the dance floor, swinging my hips with my hands in the air. People cheered me on, some joined me, and several watched. But when a set of familiar palms clasped my hips from behind, my gyrating was encouraged. Sadik's hands roving over my belly thrilled our guests and roused me.

Joy, peace, and love...just as those balloons declared. I felt all three and more in that moment. Finally, I felt the safety of love and commitment I'd been wishful and envious of when seeing it in other couples. This was an instance when peace had settled upon me. No violence, angst, weapons, or my insecurities. No loneliness or blues from being alone.

I was in the moment. My moment. With my lover.

Her skin was dewy. The balcony door of the master suite was open with the arctic March air of the Atlantic East Coast blasting through the door. The ceiling fan rotated above her on the bed, too. All of this, and she was still misted all over. I rubbed her back as she lay out on her side, breathing deeply. She wore just a sports bra and small boy shorts. Her hair spiked in every direction, and I'd never seen her more sexy.

Bilan groaned deeply. It was now four in the morning. I'd been up since eleven last night, monitoring her. A single candle was lit on the coffee table, creating a gentle light in the suite. A soft flow of "*Setembro*," the Ragee and Take 6 rendition, played on repeat. It was my attempt at creating a peaceful environment during this rough time for her.

I could sense another round of contractions coming on by the way her upper body cowered and fists balled to prepare. Taking a deep breath, I got ready, too. I removed my hand from her lower back, not touching her at all. I reached behind her, where I had three phones laid out on the bed: my two cells and the cordless house phone. I hit one of the cell phones to start the stopwatch. My eyes closed, and I said another prayer. It was the same I'd recited in my head for the past few hours.

Bilan's first contraction was yesterday at four, but they hadn't been regular until last night. When her body seemed to have loosened, I peered over at the time. It read one minute and three seconds. The house phone rang.

"Yeah…" My voice was throaty due to the hour.

"Where are we now?" Sheila, one of Dr. Clifford's nurses on duty, asked.

She'd been checking in for hours. He'd even called a couple of times.

"Just finished one a few seconds ago. One minute and three seconds."

"And the one before was how long ago?"

"Five minutes and twenty seconds."

"Okay. Let's go. Sir Ellis seems to be making his way to her cervix. I'll call Dr. Clifford now. We'll meet you at the hospital. Please feel free to grab a bite to eat on the way, Bilan. It may be quite a period before you eat again."

Bilan didn't move to respond.

"Thanks, Sheila. We'll see you soon."

"Oh!" she chirped. "Please call me right away if her water breaks while you're on the way."

Shit…

"Will do."

I disconnected the call, ignoring the waves in my belly. There was no damn way I'd give into fear. I couldn't even focus on the elation of meeting my boy soon. I had to remain calm for her. This was about my Nalib's comfort and safety.

"C'mon, baby." I rubbed Bilan's ass, feeling it was the safest area. "Let's go."

I grabbed one of my cells and texted Rory, who had been on

standby. Next, I gathered clothes for her to slip into. We were at the door, where I scooped up her bags, five minutes later.

After a knock on the door, Rory craned her neck inside, her big ass eyes red and bouncing around.

"You good, B?"

With her eyes closed, Bilan nodded.

"You sleep?"

Bilan shook her head.

"A'ight." Rory closed the door.

My mother giggled from across the room, holding her tablet. She looked over her reading glasses at Rory's display of nervousness once again.

"She more nervous than you," Tasche noted, sitting next to my mother.

I shook my head, standing at the window next to Bilan's bed. It had been four hours since we arrived, and after her getting an epidural and having constant cervical checks, the baby had still not come. Her contractions hadn't stopped and her water had broken. Her cervix dilated a couple of inches since we arrived, but not enough. They were now monitoring the baby and Bilan. Dr. Clifford expressed not being happy with the progress of labor.

My father walked back into the room, returning from his update to Stacy so she could pass it on to Monica and Taaliba. "I think we should call ya peoples, sweetheart," he advised Bilan.

He was referring to her family.

Bilan shook her head faintly. My baby was tired: this labor had wracked her body. She wet her lips. "I'll call them after."

"After what?" my father asked, sitting down.

"After she's gotten through her labor. After her baby boy has arrived safely," my mother answered for her.

She knew what time it was with Bilan's family. Bilan had told her.

We'd been inclusive with them, but respected Bilan's lead on how much we'd reach out to them.

"Irene's going to call once I deliver," Bilan murmured, eyes closed.

The door opened and Dr. Clifford swept into the room. "Okay, Ellises!" He slapped his hands together. "Good news is we're about to meet young Sadik. The bad news is, it won't be via vaginal delivery."

"What?" Tasche and my mother gasped at the same time.

"Yup." He nodded at Bilan, whose eyes were now open, though narrowly. "Your labor's stalling and his oxygen supply has been disrupted by a prolapsed cord. It's okay. No need to panic. This is a common wrong we can address through caesarean section." The door opened again with nurses coming through. "The girls are going to get you suited up to deliver him safely. I'll meet you in the operating room. And Sadik..." He peered over to me. "You need to get suited, too. They'll tell you when and where." He pointed to the door with both index fingers in the air. "And I'm out."

I went over to Bilan, leaning over the bed to whisper into her ear. "You okay?"

She nodded, a single tear leaving her eye.

"Yes, you are. And I'm going to be here for you every step of the way. Our family's here, too. You're not alone."

She nodded again, and I'd never felt so fucking helpless in my life. A damn C-section? How quickly things can change. Surgery.

Fucking surgery!

I kissed her sweet lips before they wheeled her bed out of the room.

"Everything's going to be okay," my mother stated firmly. My goddamn head was spinning. This was moving too fast in the wrong direction. "Let's pray before you go." She stood from her chair, reaching for my hands, a warrior's mask etched into her face.

I sat in a small room wearing scrubs, waiting to be invited in. My head leaned back against the wall, the mask lowered at my neck. Being at her side right now was paramount. I could fucking strangle Dr. Clifford for having us separated for so long.

The door opened, and Rory stepped in handing me a phone. Just as I grabbed it, I realized it was Bilan's with a text across the screen.

Jason: *you haven't checked in in weeks. today's your due date. i told you i've been back in jersey. i want to see you and if your baby's here, it'll be perfect. PLEASE CALL ME. i'm worried out of my mind here.*

I handed her back the phone. "I want a copy of his obituary."

Rory scoffed. "Nah. Bilan'll kick ya ass!"

I rolled my head over to look her dead ass in the face.

"I know what you saying, big dawg. I swear. But now ain't the time. B don't give a fuck about this dude. He just a piece of her old world. Something she see as safe. Fuck that nigga, man."

I could give a shit about her logic. Right now wasn't the time for it. She knew this as I gaped at her.

"We'll talk about it later. Okay?" Rory's approach was delicate.

The door opened on the other side. "Mr. Ellis?" Sheila called with a smile. "We're ready."

My fucking heart dropped from my chest.

"And here he is!" Dr. Clifford announced to the room. "Come here, Dad!"

I stood from the stool at Bilan's upper torso to peek. Sadik was being pulled out with amazed onlookers *ooh*'ing and *ahh*'ing. He was staunch white with debris covering his skin, including blood. I couldn't avoid the sight of Bilan's abdomen being gutted, skewered back by some metal implement. The shit was unreal.

Gory...

"Oh, my!" Sheila cried. "He has blond hair."

He did. A sheet of gold lay slicked over his head. Dr. Clifford walked him over from behind the sheet apparatus they used to separate her torso for the surgery to Bilan's face so she could see him.

"Hey, S.Q. II," she greeted, voice uneven from shivering. Bilan glanced over to me, smiling. "He wanted his mom to see his eyes."

They were mottled, a possible genetic telling. The photographer my mother hired snapped away over our heads. Sadik remained muted, until he was placed on a table to be cleaned and evaluated. The sound of my son's lungs raised goosebumps all over my body. He roared like a cub, unhappy with the intrusion. His little arms and legs kicked, marking his presence in the world.

Damn...

This is what it felt like to have an extension of you...your loins alive and breathing. As I gazed at him, lost to a sensation of accomplishment, something felt off. That's when I turned to his mother. Bilan's watering gape was on me. Her body shivered, lips dry.

I damn near lost consciousness when she mouthed, "Thank you. I love you so much."

Being a father had been the most unpredictable venture. It began with Sadik having to stay in the hospital an extra two days due to jaundice. They treated him under a lamp incubator he hated. Then he had to be taken to a pediatric urologist for his snipping. Dr. Clifford recommended it for some technical term I didn't understand. Seeing my son circumcised was a horrific event. I almost fucking vomited, couldn't even watch as they violated the Ellis jewels a week after his birth. Bilan was a trooper, helping me to the car as she wheeled a sleeping Sadik in his stroller.

After the baby shower, Bilan and I decided to stay at *Elliswoods Palace* during her six weeks of postpartum. It made sense for her to have around the clock care for herself and Sadik. There she could rest, had food prepared and served, have emotional support, and, now, wound nursing care. The decision thrilled my mother. She had the sitting area in my room at the house made into a nursery. Stacy, her executive assistant at the house, was also a licensed nurse practitioner. My parents employed another staff member who was a nurse as well.

So for weeks, we had the support Bilan and Sadik needed through a transitional period. The commute from *Elliswoods Palace* to my office at *Ellis International* was an adjustment. However, it was minor when I considered the benefits. I'd work out of my mother's office when deciding to not leave Sadik.

Bilan worked out with my mother's trainer, Jackie. She was able to assist her in stretching and light exercises a couple of days a week. Being at my parents' helped Bilan continue virtually seamlessly with her courses, which was one of my selling points to her before we decided. She didn't have to be inundated with the responsibility of cooking or laundry if she didn't choose to. When she needed to nap, there was someone, often times me, available to take Sadik.

Taaliba slowed her travel to be home to assist, too. She loved Sadik, as did Ivana. It was clear Iesha needed more time. Monica was able to give Bilan pointers on healing and caring for herself postpartum. Bilan's family was notified of Sadik's birth from the hospital. They didn't come around to see him until after her and the baby were released. Their trip to *Elliswoods Palace* was a comical experience to me, but annoyed Bilan. She felt her aunts and cousins, specifically Joslyn, was more pretentious when around my family. She said it was almost as though they enjoyed acting above their class. I didn't mind; neither did my parents, so long as Bilan was supported.

My parents enjoyed having us, I could tell. My mother's photographer visited regularly, taking pictures of a sleeping Sadik all throughout the house. It was something we were all accustomed to. She did it with all her grands, even Lia's baby when she visited. It was important for my mother to capture their development over the first year, according to her. My father, however, was more present for Sadik's photoshoots, more than I'd seen of any of the other grands. None of us had the heart to call him out on it. Earl Ellis was in his glory, having his grandson under his roof.

Bilan and I had our time with him, too. I enjoyed napping with him on my chest. Bathing him after his umbilical cord fell off and circumcision healed. I read him poems and would sit and listen to classical music with him while his mother washed his bottles or napped. He grew to be a friend in no time.

Bilan talked to Sadik a lot. She referenced her parents a lot, nothing inappropriate. She would sing songs they sang and stories they shared with her as a child. She'd often say Sadik had her father's grin. She'd watched him while he slept, something I found myself doing, too. It had been amazing bonding with our son.

We celebrated our birthdays together. The first part was spent at the gun range on the compound. Bilan needed to learn to shoot a gun. She was eager to learn and unafraid. After I sent her off to the spa for a few hours with Tasche, Taaliba, and Monica, she rejoined me for dinner at DiFillippo's. That's where I presented her a five-carat diamond tennis bracelet, a check for just over four-hundred thousand dollars from the sale of her parents' home to do with as she wished, and the listings for three lots available for sale in two different counties in the state. She could decide which land she'd like for us to purchase and build our third home on.

She gifted me a beaded bracelet with a handmade charm of Sadik's newborn face. On the back was inscribed: *to my love, my gift giver*. That shit tightened my chest. I still hadn't been used to Bilan proclaiming her love for me, but I was desperate for it. We joked on the way back to *Elliswoods Palace* about how expensive a month March would now be for the both of us seeing our birthdays and Sadik's were just weeks apart.

March eventfully blended into April, and soon, Easter would be upon us. Bilan didn't protest when my parents requested Sadik visiting church for the first time at six weeks. She was, however, ready to return to the apartment. She made it clear in the most unexpected, erotic way.

It was two in the morning, and I'd just fed, burped, and rocked Sadik back to sleep. I laid him in his bassinet and sauntered back to bed. Tired as fuck, I was dozing almost as soon as my head hit the pillow. Warm lips brushed against my ear, then teeth gently pulled at my lobe. When I felt the wetness of her tongue tracing the rim, the haze of sleep dissipated.

Next was her hand at the waist of my boxers, pushing south. Her nails scraped against my thigh as she attempted to wrap her palm around me. She began stroking me from root to tip, my dick growing against her skin. We'd just hit the five-week mark of postpartum. And I'd just stopped seeing images of circumcision in my head each time I thought about her pussy. But Bilan hadn't been cleared for sex yet.

"Sadik," she whispered from behind me. "I want you."

My eyes opened slowly. Bilan rolled me onto my back. Her mouth reached mine, and our tongues danced. Immediately, I was entranced. Her hand job and mouth at this point in the game was lethal. It had seemed like forever since I'd had her.

"It's time to go home," she whispered in my mouth. "I miss the ropes. I need you to myself."

That had my erection go from hard to stone. I could feel her smear my precum around my head.

"Nalib, it hasn't been six weeks."

"Shhhhh. I'm healed down...there."

She kissed me once more before sliding gingerly down the mattress and yanking my boxers until I lifted to help her pull them off. Then she arranged herself on top of me 69 fashion. Her face in my crotch, her pussy inches away from my mouth.

"Bilan..." I groaned, loving the scent of her musk.

I didn't trust myself to be as gentle as she needed handling.

"It's not broken, Deek," she moaned over my dick.

Deek.

She used that term when being charming or expressing sarcasm. Either way, I was too damn horny to care. Her mouth covered the head of my dick, her tongue swirling around it, those soft palms gripping me as her mouth took me deeper inside. When Bilan flopped her ass over my face, I lost it. I reached up, pushing my tongue to the nucleus of her pussy. Fuck. She was wet already. Her ass swirled over me already. I flapped my tongue between her lips, tasting from her clit to her ass. She knew I loved tasting her ass. I quickly decided to save that for another time.

The sounds of Bilan sucking me off were downright explicit. She gagged and spit on me. Her saliva coursing down my throbbing balls had my head fucking spinning. My long licks on her pussy turned into sucking on her clit. I felt it swell against my tongue as she danced on my face. My pelvis knocked into her hand and mouth coordination. Bilan's heavy breathing rolled into whimpers. Her gyration turned into hard grinds into my head. My Nalib was about to come. Damn, I missed this. When I felt her chords trickle as she moaned, my balls contracted and I bucked, coming inside her mouth while tasting her explosion at the same time. We lay shivering and groaning the echoes of our orgasms, mine feeling like the very first time.

With Bilan making a case for our privacy like that, how could I say no? I made a note to talk with Stacy about finding a nanny for the apartment.

A few days later, as I took a conference call from my mother's office, I gazed out of the window, finding two bodies taking a stroll in the garden. It was my father and Bilan. They enjoyed the spring breeze as the baby was harnessed to my father's chest. They were engaged in a conversation Bilan apparently found humorous. Her head snapped back and she laughed heartily. Hair undone, pressed straight to her head, face free of makeup, high cheekbones pronounced, and freckles shimmering, I was sure. She wore leggings, sneakers, and leather motorcycle jacket, appearing carefree. She'd just finished working out with Jackie.

They'd done this several times over the past six weeks. My father would call up to our wing of the house, and request time with Sadik and his mother. For some reason, they often walked the garden, but had occasional strolls down to the coffee shop on the compound. Bilan was likely breaking the news of our leaving to him. My father wouldn't take it well. He'd been in his glory having Sadik—father and son—at *Elliswoods Palace* day in and day out.

But Bilan had made her wishes known. The day after Easter, packed up with Sadik in his car seat, we left *Elliswoods Palace* for our private home. When we unpacked once arriving at our place, I was grateful for the peace that had surrounded us. Bilan deserved peace. The lawsuit Rachel filed against my company had been defeated. The investigations into my life, thanks to Jason's ongoing calls to the *FBI*, hadn't yielded anything as of yet. The snitch in the scattered *Commission*, who I was convinced was Popov, had been silent. There'd been little word from Popov regarding cutting him out as a weapons distributor. Ricky had been long shipped to Haiti to be buried. The local police didn't put any effort into investigating his murder, happy to have him apprehended, dead or alive.

Bigger than all of those developments was one with greater importance.

I'm a fucking father...

The sounds of his mouth laving over my sensitive, distended nipple made me delirious. My head collapsed backward. The feel of his erection brushing over my engorged clitoris was more than my incision should have endured. But I was desperate for him. Sadik was desperate for me, too.

We'd been back home with our son for just two nights and counted down until the nanny, Camille, one of Stacy's trusted subordinates at *Elliswoods Palace*, put the baby down for the night. I begged him via text message to use a rope. His simple response was *not yet*. Disappointment settled upon me until the doors to the master suite shut and he lunged my way, stripping off my clothes. No candles, no music, no wine or romantic rose petals. Just two souls, magnetically drawn to each other, and our raw passions combusting at first touch.

"You okay?" he whispered in my ear.

I nodded, readjusting myself on his hard thighs, straddling him. When he leaned over to lay me on my back, I protested, tensing all around him.

"No!" I panted. "I want to be on top."

"You ready for that?"

"I've been ready for you." Sometimes, I had to remind myself I'd only been having sex for less than a year.

One of many things I learned about passion with Sadik was it taught you how to move, how much pressure to apply, and how to release yourself to it. It had been close to two months, and I was more than ready.

His lips grazed my neck as he directed himself into me, wetting his head all over again. My heavy panting made me lightheaded, so I closed my mouth so I could fully enjoy this. But when he entered me and I pushed down, sinking onto him, I felt something my mother didn't teach. My walls remembered him. Sex isn't necessary to love someone: Sadik's soul riveted me. But when you felt him growing even more inside of you...when you felt the recesses of yourself recognizing his body from memory, I knew this was something more than an unfortunate circumstance I'd found myself in.

His tongue swirled in my mouth, licking the roof. Unable to endure the teasing, I caught and sucked on it, grinding onto his thickness. Sadik was life. Proof of it was the baby we'd made within months of knowing each other. It was in the family he'd made himself to me. The resources he made me a beneficiary of that he'd earned independently. As I plunged down on him, I knew this was something different. No amount of money could buy this, no amount of influence could bring it about. I looked at Randi and Ricky, together for years, and never had I seen evidence of the love I shared with this man.

"Slow down, baby..." he croaked, fingertips digging into my flesh.

The deep, internal massage weakened me. His firm and protective hold strengthened me. Forever would I be changed because of his fixation on being my friend. For eternity, he'd be the savage lover, claiming me like no one before him. And if I were lucky, I'd hide under the protection of his love for me, completely sheltered from the coldness of the world.

"I love you so much," I crooned, lost to this web of lust coated by love.

That emotional reveal spurred my orgasm, I felt myself loosening to him, hips propelled into motion. I rocked into him, feeling empowered by my truth, comforted by my admittance. Sadik clutched my shoulders, laying me onto my back. His glower set, his pecs contracted as he pounded into me. He was beautiful, erotic features and brute persona: my new favorite combination. My breasts bounced in the air, skin slapped by his. Lungs lost to harsh plunges, heart opened to the love of my life. I exploded, coming with a force I couldn't deny, welcoming his hot seeds jetting into me. I released with a fury and felt full at the same time.

"Fuck, Nalib!" he barked, pelting into me. He thrust three more times before suspending over me. I enjoyed his heavy breaths and flexed muscles as he ascended. "You doing that shit again gonna have me making another baby."

I welcomed him, feeling more than sex taking place. This was my lover. The man guarding over my heart.

Still throbbing around him, I panted in his ear, "One more. Let's do this...one more time."

Equally disheveled, he croaked, "Okay. Just give me a minute."

I laughed, taking my seat at the table with my food from the buffet. Earl sat across from me.

"What's so funny, young lady?"

"The fact that I haven't been off your compound a whole week and you're surprising me outside of work for lunch again."

Earl shrugged and bowed his head for prayer. I mimicked his

posture out of respect, but also whispering my own short "Grace." It had been a habit rubbing off from the Ellises.

"I'm not too prideful to say I've missed you three." He grabbed his fork to begin to eat. "Sadik stopped by last night to see Taaliba off for Antigua, so I got my fill of that cat."

"How long do you think Taaliba's going to be out there?" I joked.

Taaliba's attention deficit was a family joke I was now in on. I'd asked her to make me more teas two weeks ago and had still been waiting on them. She went to her father's private island to free her mind for painting. That's what she said her energy had been pulling toward lately.

"If I'm lucky, until the paint dries on her first damn project." He shook his head.

I laughed, chewing my food.

"How's my legacy?" Earl asked.

It no longer bothered me to hear claims of my son being made by Earl. After the support the Ellises showed me during the birth of my child, I had definitely been convinced of their commitment to family.

"He's good. Still not sleeping through the night, but doing so in longer stretches. He's starting to reach for things, and he's eating more."

"More?"

"Yeah. He's had an extra bottle for the last two days. Camille was blown away, too."

"Well, that's because he's—" Earl's frame jerked, and he punched his chest.

My eyes ballooned, startled. "You okay?"

"Yeah..." He belched. "Damn heartburn. What I was saying is, it's because he growing into his shoes. That's what my boys do."

I shook my head, laughing. Today, I tried the restaurant's eggplant parmesan. It wasn't too bad. Vinny's was better at the diner. That thought led to the congratulatory email I'd gotten from the gang at *Michelle's*. And that thought reminded me of the email I'd received from Irene's photographer.

"Those Easter pictures turned out beautifully. The kids looked amazing and were all behaved. Irene has them trained, I see. Little Sadik will have to fall in line."

"Yeah, he will. Just like the rest of them, he'll get comfortable in front of the camera. She don't play when it come down to none of them, including her kids."

I nodded, recounting how much of a force Irene had been over the past month and a half. She'd tended to all. Danny and Taaliba got into an argument over the phone that sent Taaliba over the edge emotionally. Earl sent Irene to her room to straighten her out. It had worked. She constantly checked in on Sadik after my surgery, outside of helping to care for me. She confided in me how spooked he was behind the experience. Baby Iliza had spent the night twice, sleeping in Irene's suite each time. She spent time with her alone off the compound, as well as with Ivana and Iesha. When Earl hadn't been feeling well one evening after dinner, she skipped dessert and took him up to their shared room and stayed with him that night. Irene was a true champion.

"That woman is a true matriarch. I've seen her tirelessly in action. She'd been busy the whole six weeks we were there. I'm sure she can use the downtime, get back to her normal schedule."

He scoffed. "She got a busy life."

My brows met. "What do you mean?"

"My Irene don't gather the kids and grands because she has no life. She do it because they are our lives. It's always sad to see Black families dispersed...all over the place. They leave the hood for prison or a better life and don't come back. Most times, they leave they parents, and brothers and sisters. 'Cause of my work, I couldn't bring my kids up in Paterson. I needed to be in the cut. But me and my wife wanted more. We wanted tradition, a pride, a community...we want them to know, not just where they going, but where they belong. I begged my kids not to leave the state. Once that happens, it's almost impossible to be regular on each other's developments. You know?"

"I never thought about it like that."

"Yeah. People need a root, especially a Black family. We been bastardized since they put us on them ships. We got scattered then, and we ain't no more together now with our families. Me and Irene wanna see our kids every week. We wanna be there when they fall and stumble. We wanna spank our grands. If you don't spank ya grands or chastise them, you don't know them."

I balled my mouth with suspicion. "When was the last time you raised your voice an angry octave at Ivana or Iesha?"

"That ain't the point. Them princesses know PaPa'll pop them little legs if they get outta line. My grands don't just embarrass their parents when they act out: they embarrass my wife and me, too. We put in time with them. Travel all over the world with them. Explore with them. Go to they schools. We just as much responsible as their parents, only we follow the parents' lead. All my family matter. Equally." He cleared his throat, visibly still recovering from that heartburn episode.

When he grabbed his water to drink, I murmured, "Not equally, Earl."

"Equally!" he argued adorably.

I shook my head, smiling. "I'm not the only person who finds Sadik Qadir Ellis I exceptional, and I don't simply mean great. I'm talking above the rest...unmatched, the brightest star in the sky." My eyes fell away shamefully as my belly fluttered.

I'd actually fallen head over heels in love with a man while denying it to myself and him.

"'Cause he *is* all that," Earl stated firmly. I noticed he hadn't touched his food again, only drank water. He seemed to still be out of breath a little, too. "He's all them things and more than I can find words for. Sadik is a leader. Good man. He come from good stock, but he gon' be better. Better for you. Better for that golden grandchild of mine."

Flattery wasn't always easy to experience, even if it was aimed at the two closest people to your heart.

"I love the way you guys dote on each other." My eyes rolled down to my plate. "You hold one another in such high regard."

"Because we're a unit...in my garden." He smiled. "And don't cry." He handed me his handkerchief. "Sadik'll think he can finally kick my ass if Rory told him."

"I'm not!" I whined, wiping the corners of my eyes before the tears fell.

Earl snickered, coughing in between. "Look...all I'm tryna say is —" He collapsed to the floor so hard, I screamed.

Chairs skidded and fell across the restaurant from us. Both of Earl's security guards and Rory, drew their weapons toward the windows, front door, and hall from the kitchen.

"He just collapsed!" I shouted, scared out of my mind as I leaped to the floor next to him. "Earl, can you hear me?" He was wet all over, struggling to breathe.

"Don't let them take me. Y'all stay with me till...hospital."

"Call 911!" I yelled at his swarming security.

"Nah, B." Rory tried grabbing me. "It's a hospital five minutes away. Let them get him there!"

"He could die on the way!" I was going into full panic attack.

"He could die waiting on them muthafuckas, B!" Her little arms were strong enough to pull me away, and I watched his security lift him from the floor and run him out the door.

"We have to follow them!"

"We is," Rory assured. "Grab his shit."

We left the restaurant, speeding behind Earl's *Mercedes*.

∞AND A BIT MORE∞

Startled, I jolted, awakening from my sleep. I checked the time.

10:04...

I'd slept a solid two hours in a blur. The past few nights had been horrible. The days had been just as grim. Glancing over to the other side of the bed, I saw no Sadik. That meant he was still at the hospital. He stayed overnight again. We'd all been there by Earl's side as he struggled to recover from a myocardial infarction. A heart attack. My head throbbed as I was reminded of what happened in that restaurant.

He hit the floor so hard!

Earl's security was able to get him to the hospital right away. Once he was stabilized, the family insisted he was transferred via helicopter to the same hospital Sadik had care for Abshir. For three days, the family had been turned topsy-turvy. We'd been at his side around the clock. Last night I came home, needing to be with little Sadik. I twisted and turned all night, checked on the baby every other hour. When he awakened to eat, I told Camille I'd handle it, grateful to have him to tend to as a distraction. Earl adored my son.

Just like now. My belly fluttered, and I had the urge to see my baby. Maybe I'd give him a bath and go for a walk around the park. I left the bed, my frame fatigued from a lack of sleep. Toeing to his nursery, I found the door ajar. I pushed inside, expecting to see Camille with him.

What I saw sent a chill down my spine.

I blinked several times, unable to speak. All I saw was my baby sniffling in his arm, preparing to cry.

"What are you doing here?" There was more air in my words than voice.

His hazel eyes roved from Sadik's wiggling frame to me. Emptiness in his eyes.

"I came to meet my nephew. Figured since I can't see my pops 'cause you wit' him, I could see the golden child."

My arms felt heavy as I lifted them. "Please hand him to me. He's about to cry, Iban."

The moment those words left my mouth, Sadik began to wail.

"You made him do that, opening ya fuckin' mouth. You shoulda left us alone." He turned to Sadik. "Right, nephew? We need our time to bond, too. Ya uncle ain't no damn animal. Rule number one: don't trust none of these muthafuckas," he advised softly. "They let bitches come in this family and kick you the fuck out when all you did was do what they told you to do." His eyes rolled over to me.

Sadik turned red, infuriated. "What did they tell you to do, Iban?"

My heart beat out my chest, body misted all over.

"You know what the fuck my pops said. He told me to take care of you and the Ab kid. Wasn't no way you shoulda stayed alive knowing I killed ya brother. Why the fuck you think I came to snuff you, too?"

A flashback of me balled beneath my window, blindly shooting behind a door made bile shoot from my belly. I caught it just in time, blinking away the wetness in my eyes from it.

I swallowed back. "That was you? *You* were shooting at me?"

He did try to kill me!

I never said a word to Sadik because I didn't believe it was Earl or Iban shooting rather than one of the men they employed or possibly an indiscriminate hitman they paid. They were heartless murderers! Earl, too! How could I have been so forgiving and reckless to slip back in bed with Sadik?

To fall in love with him?

He snorted. "It damn sure wasn't Deek. His soft ass left ya brother alive to go chase after you. Now look at what we got." He glanced down at my baby, sobbing louder than I'd ever heard.

"Are you hurting him?" I felt so helpless.

I didn't know what to do.

"Never! I don't hurt family!" he barked angrily. "That's the shit they do. They wanna change the rules outta nowhere! I try to get you in line, and my own brother tell me when and where I can come around *my* fuckin' family!"

My eyes shot open. "You weren't banished! You didn't show." I sobbed.

It dawned on me. Iban hadn't been at the house for Easter, or any of the time we'd stayed with the baby.

"You think I'm missing meals...holidays with my family? My fuckin' kids? Bitch, you the crazy one!"

Sadik wailed, arms and legs thrashing in the air.

"Please hand him over. I swear we can talk about it. I'll go to Sadik and you guys can work this out."

"This lil' nigga like two months old. Two months old, and this my first time seeing him!"

"I didn't know. I had no idea, Iban. I swear: no one told me. I thought you didn't want to come around because of me."

A tear fell from his eye. The look in them. It was blank, empty. Then metal flashed from below. He pulled out a gun.

My hands shot into the air!

"Kill *me*!" I demanded, undergoing another out of body experience. "I don't care about any of this. Shoot me. Just please let my baby live," I croaked, crossing the nursery.

The sounds of my baby crying mixed with the scent of Iban and the sight of a gun were a dangerous concoction. I continued to move. Then I was at the rocking chair, grabbing my baby. Iban tried to jerk him away. I punched him with the heel of my palm.

"Bitch!" he yelped.

"*IBAN!*" I heard a familiar bark, causing my head to swing over my shoulder, then I quickly grabbed my baby.

I leaped backward at the sight of an onrushing Sadik.

I bounded a one hundred-eighty-degree angle when I heard an explosive pop, then a crack. Blood splattered all over as I hit the floor with Sadik in my arms and his father over us.

———

TBC in

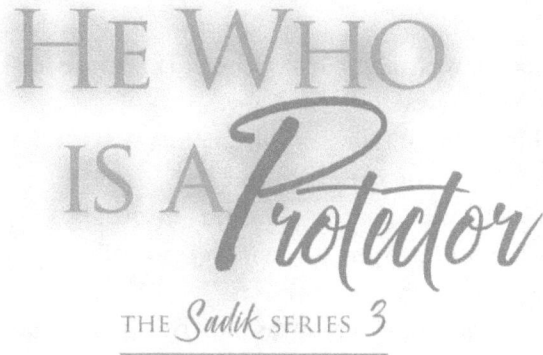

HE WHO IS A *Protector*

THE *Sadik* SERIES *3*

✍ #PenningWithoutParameters ✍
🤍 #ImGonnaMakeYouLoveMe 🤍

www.LoveBelvin.com

Available Now!

HE WHO IS A *Protector*

THE *Sadik* SERIES *3*

SADIK AND BILAN

See visuals from the series here on my website — https://www.lovebelvin.com/projects/sadik

~LOVE ACKNOWLEDGES

Visuals: 365 Photography – "Hello, Brooklyn!" Your talent is boundless. Thanks for taking a chance in literature. As you can tell, I'm ***still*** excited. Teehee! I look forward to more collaborations! **Fierce Faces** – Kaydene, I can't say thanks enough for brokering this deal. As we both learned, what's meant to be will gel seamlessly. Thanks for your artistry and patience (and not cussing me out as you threatened). KNGQ – Q. Williams & Brittney April, thanks so much for serving as visuals for our Sadik and Bilan. May this be another ideal step in the direction of your promising careers. My best to you in all your endeavors!

Researcher: Shumethia S. — I know you want to give me the boot. Too bad you can't. With this role, you can't quit no matter how far away you move! Thanks so much for always going the extra mile for me, even when it's inconvenient.

Beta Readers: Rocita & Christina, thanks for coming through in the eleventh hour! You both had strong opinions about this installment and I loved it all. Yorubia, *uggggg yoooooooooou* for harassing me then dropping me the moment you read the last sentence!

LBTR — Afi, Angela J.J., Artemysia, Ash, Ashleigh, Ashley, Ayanna, Ayo, Azaria, Bonita, Brittany, Courtney, Danielle, Dee,

Deidre, Denise, DeVona, Diane, Diva Dee, Doresha, Doris, Ericka M., Gail, Grace, Heather, Heidi, Hezie-Ann, Hyacinth, Jasmine, Jessica, Kamashia, Karmen, Katrina, Kendra, Kerry, Keyma, Kim, Kimmiko, Kita, Korei, LaLa, LaSonde, Linda R., Linda W., Lee, Malaika, Marshall, Michelle M., Michelle R.O., Michelle T., Mocha, Monique H., Monique N., Natoya, Nena, Nikki, Pamela, Rakia, Quan, Regina, Richell, Rose, Roslyn, Samona, Sharon L., Sharon F.W., Shaun, Sola, Stacey K., Erica B., Stacy M., Tamara, Tanisha, Tanya, Tara, Té, Teresa, Terri G., Tesha, Tia, Tiffany, Tineka, Tonya, Tralaina, Vivian, Wendi, Yolanda P., Yolanda U., Yorubia, and Yvette H., you each are individual gifts to me, wrapped in love. Thanks for being that core of support. *Jemeka* & *Rita*: For the first time, J is in love with our male visual, and Rita-Bita admitted to wanting help with 'smashing' on the fan page. What will the future bring for our union? ROTFL!!!! Love you two intensely.

Christina C. Jones aka CCJ — Your friendship grows more valuable by the day. Thanks so much for all you contribute to my life and brand. May God continue to increase everything you touch! *And Lord, heal her potty mouth!* Teehee!

Interior Artist: Cedeara Ardell McCollum — Thanks, baby girl, for the imagery you've designed for my books! Love you always!

Proof Reader: Tina V. Young — I'm so blessed to have you on my team. You went extra petty with this one. I needed so much. Thanks forever!

Editors:

Zakiya Walden of *I've Got Something to Say!* — I appreciate your hard work and dedication. This process reminds me of our L.I.P. days. LOL! May we have many more!

Santisha Taylor of *AccuProse Editing Services* — I was a pain. I know! Thanks for being a trooper and team player!

MDT: We're getting there, sire…

Master, my *Jireh*, my *Rohi*, 2 Corinthians 9:15 (AMP) "Now thanks be to God for His indescribable gift [which is precious beyond words]!" *My gift belongs to You.*

~OTHER BOOKS BY LOVE BELVIN

Love's Improbable Possibility series:

Love Lost, Love UnExpected, Love UnCharted & *Love Redeemed*

Waiting to Breathe series:

Love Delayed & Love Delivered

Love's Inconvenient Truth (Standalone)

***Love Unaccounted* series**:

In Covenant with Ezra, In Love with Ezra & Bonded with Ezra

***The Connecticut Kings* series:**

Love in the Red Zone, *Love on the Highlight Reel, *Determining Possession, End Zone Love, Love's Ineligible Receiver, *Pass Interference, Love's Encroachment, & *Offensive Formations (*by Christina C. Jones)

***Wayward Love* series:**

The Left of Love, The Low of Love & The Right of Love

Love in Rhythm & Blues series

The Rhythm of Blues & The Rhyme of Love

LOVE IN RHYTHM & BLUES series

The Sadik series

He Who Is a Friend, He Who Is a Lover & He Who Is a Protector

The Muted Hopelessness series:

My Muted Love, Our Muted Recklessness, & Our Reckless Hope

The Prism series:

Mercy, Grace, & The Promise

Low Love, Low Fidelity (Standalone)

~EXTRA

You can find Love Belvin at www.LoveBelvin.com
Facebook @ Author - Love Belvin
Twitter @LoveBelvin
Goodreads: Love Belvin
and on Instagram @LoveBelvin

Join the #TeamLove mailing list on my website to keep up with the happenings!

Click here (with WiFi) to join!